PLOWING THE DARK

Richard Powers is the author of seven novels, including *Galatea 2.2* and *The Gold Bug Variations*, both of which were nominated for the US National Book Critics Circle Award, *Gain*, and *Operation Wandering Soul*, were nominated for the US National Book Award for Fiction.

Richard Powers

PLOWING THE DARK

VINTAGE

Published by Vintage 2002

2 4 6 8 10 9 7 5 3 1

First published in Great Britain in 2001 by
William Heinemann

Vintage
Random House, 20 Vauxhall Bridge Road,
London SW1V 2SA

Random House Australia (Pty) Limited
20 Alfred Street, Milsons Point, Sydney
New South Wales 2061, Australia

Random House New Zealand Limited
18 Poland Road, Glenfield, Auckland 10,
New Zealand

Random House (Pty) Limited
Endulini, 5A Jubilee Road, Parktown 2193,
South Africa

The Random House Group Limited Reg. No. 954009
www.randomhouse.co.uk

A CIP catalogue record for this book
is available from the British Library

ISBN 0 09 928672 6

Printed and bound in Great Britain by
Cox & Wyman Limited, Reading, Berkshire

For poetry makes nothing happen: it survives
In the valley of its saying where executives
Would never want to tamper; it flows south . . .
—W. H. Auden, "In Memory of William Butler Yeats"

The first year of the war, Picasso and Eve, with whom he was living then, Gertrude Stein and myself, were walking down the boulevard Raspail a cold winter evening. There is nothing in the world colder than the Raspail on a cold winter evening, we used to call it the retreat from Moscow. All of a sudden down the street came some big cannon, the first any of us had seen painted, that is camouflaged. Pablo stopped, he was spell-bound. C'est nous qui avons fait ça, he said, it is we that have created that, he said. And he was right, he had. From Cézanne through him they had come to that. His foresight was justified.

—Gertrude Stein, *The Autobiography of Alice B. Toklas*

PLOWING THE DARK

"ROWING THE OVER"

This room is never anything o'clock.

Minutes slip through it like a thief in gloves. Hours fail even to raise the dust. Outside, deadlines expire. Buzzers erupt. Deals build to their frenzied conclusions. But in this chamber, now and forever combine.

This room lingers on the perpetual pitch of here. Its low local twilight outlasts the day's politics. It hangs fixed, between discovery and invention. It floats in pure potential, a strongbox in the inviolate vault.

Time does not keep to these parts, nor do these parts keep time. Time is too straight a line, too limiting. The comic tumbling act of causality never reaches this far. This room spreads under the stilled clock. Only when you step back into the corridor does now revive. Only escaped, beneath the failing sky.

Out in the template world, flowers still spill from the bud. Fruit runs from ripe to rot. Faces still recognize each other in surprise over a fire sale. Marriages go on reconciling and cracking up. Addicts swear never again. Children succumb in their beds after a long fever. But on this island, in this room: the faint rumble, the standing hum of a place that passes all understanding.

1

Years later, when she surfaced again, Adie Klarpol couldn't say just how she'd pictured the place. Couldn't even begin to draw what she'd imagined. Some subterranean confection of dripped stone, swarming with blind cave newts. A spelunker's scale model Carlsbad. Summer dacha of the Mountain King.

The Cavern, Stevie had called it. Stevie Spiegel, phoning her up out of nowhere, in the middle of the night, after years of their thinking one another dead, when they thought of each other at all. The Cavern. A name that formed every shape in her mind except its own.

She had not placed him on the phone. *It's Steve*, he said. And still, she was anywhere.

Adie fumbled with the handset in the dark. She struggled backward, upstream, toward a year when an a capella *Steve* might have meant something. Steve. You know: the twelfth most common name for American males between the ages of twenty-four and thirty-eight?

Steve Spiegel, he repeated, hurt by her confusion. *Madison? Your housemate and collaborator? Mahler Haus? Don't tell me: you've torched your entire past.*

A vision of herself at twenty-one congealed in front of her, like the Virgin come to taunt Slavic schoolchildren. Recollection swamped her carefully packed sandbags. Steve Spiegel. The three of them had planned to live the rest of their lives together, once. He, she, and the man who'd live long enough to become Adie's ex-husband.

Jesus! Stevie. Her voice skidded away from her, a gypsum imitation of pleasure's bronze. *Stevie. What on earth have you been doing with yourself?*

Doing . . . ? Adie, my love. You still make life sound like a summer camp craft project.

It isn't?

No, you decorative little dauber. It is not. Life is a double-blind, controlled placebo experiment. Has middle age taught you nothing?

Hah. I knew that at twenty. You were the one in denial.

Tag-team remembrance dissolved the years between them. OK, the gaps and rifts. OK, all the expended selves that would never again fit into the rag box of a single curriculum vitae.

Adie. Ade. You busy these days? I thought we might be able to hook up.

Outside her loft, the stink of singed oil and rotting vegetables settled. Car alarms clear down to the Battery sounded the predawn call to prayer. She cradled the phone under her chin, a fiddler between reels.

Steve, it's kind of late . . . She hoisted the guillotine window above her futon, its counterweights long ago lost at the bottom of the sash's well. She crawled out onto her fire hazard of a fire escape, adopting her favorite phone crouch, rocking on her haunches, her lumbar pressed to the rose brick.

Jesus Christ, he said. *I am so sorry. Entirely forgot the time difference. What is it out there: like after one?*

I mean, it's a little late for reunions, isn't it?

Missing the whole point, the sole purpose of reunions, their sad celebration of perpetual too-lateness, the basic one-step-behindhood of existence.

Oh, I don't want a reunion, Ade. I just want you.

She laughed him off and they pressed on. They made the obligatory exchange of hostages, each giving over the short versions of their overland passage across the intervening decade.

Seattle, he told her. *Can you believe it? Your doltish poet friend, the one who used to spout "Sunday Morning" until late Monday night. Supporting the computer industry's insidious plan for world domination.*

Still lower Manhattan, she replied. *Your washed-up watercolorist. Currently supporting the wall of my crumbling apartment building with the small of my back.*

Surprised? he asked.

About . . . ?

About where we've landed?

Nobody lands, she said. *So how is the world of software?*

It's the oddest thing, Ade. Ade: as if they still knew each other. *You know, I lied to get into this business in the first place. Told them I knew C^{++} when I didn't know it from B^{--}. But it turns out, I know this stuff in my sleep. Born to it. Code is everything I thought poetry was, back when we were in school. Clean, expressive, urgent, all-encompassing. Fourteen lines can open up to fill the available universe.*

Different kind of sonnet, though, right? Different rhyme scheme?

I don't know. Sometimes you gotta wonder.

Wonder, in fact, was why he'd called. He'd come to rest in a moist den of pine on a twisty black macadam road looking out over Puget Sound. He was coding for a start-up called the Realization Lab, the latest tendril of that runaway high-tech success story TeraSys. But the RL was still experimental, more of a tax write-off than a source of any near-term revenue.

TeraSys? You mean you work for that little Boy Billionaire?

Indirectly, he laughed. *And they're all boy billionaires out here.*

What does your building look like?

What do you mean? My building, building? What does that have to do with anything?

I'm trying to visualize where you are. You're calling from work, aren't you?

I . . . well, I guess I am.

William Butler Spiegel! The man who swore he'd never do anything more serious than wait on tables, so as not to compromise his muse. Still in his office in the middle of the night.

Middle . . . ? Out here, we're usually just getting started around 10 p.m.

Just tell me where you are. OK, look: I'll start. I'm squatting in my undershirt out on a black wrought-iron grille about twenty feet above the exhaust fan of the kitchen of a pasta dive . . .

He played along, the stakes high. *Khaki shorts and a green raglan T-shirt. Kicked back in a molded plastic office chair in the middle of a . . . well . . . redwood-and-cedar kind of thing. Lots of river stone. Local materials.*

Very tasteful, they declared in unison. Old shtick, recovered from a dozen lost lives ago.

Geez, I don't know. What does my building look like? I've never really thought about it, Adie.

Come on, poet. Look around you. Walk me through the front door.

Hmm. Let's see. Maybe 10,000 square feet of usable floor, all on a single story. Lots of brick and earth tones. A maze of little cubicles made out of those tan-fabric-lined divider things. There's a nice little sunken atrium and such. A ton of vegetation per cubic liter. Big panoramic expanse of passive-solar smart window looking out at Rainier, on the ventral side.

I see. Kind of a futuristic forest ranger's roost.

Sure. Why not? You'll love it.

Hang on. You? As in me . . . ?

He slowed and unfolded. *We're putting together a prototype immersion environment we're calling the Cavern. Computer-Assisted Virtual Environ— Look, Adie. I'm not going to describe this thing to you over the phone. You just have to come see it.*

Sure, Steve. I'll be out in an hour.

How about a week from next Tuesday? For a no-obligations site visit. All expenses paid.

Oh. Oh God. You told them I knew C⁺⁺?

Worse. I told them I knew the greatest illustrator since representational art self-destructed.

Illustrator, Stevie? How tasteful. Haven't lost your knack for words, I see.

Nothing had changed in him. He was still that kid of twenty, compelled to round up and protect everything he thought he loved. A mini-Moses, still shepherding around the dream of starting an artist's colony where he could gather all those who needed a hideout from the real world. His voice alone was proof, if Adie ever needed it: no one abandons his first survival kit. The most we ever do is upgrade the splints.

You're exactly what the project is looking for, Adie. We can make these incredible digital circus animals, and we can get them to jump through any hoop imaginable. We just need someone who can draw the hoops.

I don't get it, Stevie. Don't get it at all.

We're all coders and chrome monkeys. A bunch of logic monsters, trying to make walk-in, graphical worlds. We need someone who can see.

Know how I picture it out there? Open-toe sandals made out of silicon. Fuzzy-faced, bicycling Boeing executives. Tofu-eating knowledge engineers and multiply-pierced, purple-frosted meth heads waiting next to each other on the curb for the Walk light.

See? You know what the place looks like before you've even seen it. I told the team how you used to do those Draw-the-Pirate tests as a kid and fix all the original's errors. I showed them that ARTFORUM *sidebar. The reviews of your SoHo show in '79 . . .*

Oh God, Stevie. That's ancient history.

Oh, I went further back than that. I showed them my color slide of your huge acrylic group portrait of us. The one that won the university painting prize . . . ?

How dare you. I hate you.

I told them about the award controversy. How one of the judges thought you were using projection? How he refused to believe that you'd actually freehanded . . .

Steven. We were children then. You don't have to fly a stranger across the continent just to find someone who can draw. Courtroom portraitists are a dollar ninety-eight a square yard. Besides, I already have a life.

You're not a stranger, Ade. He sounded hurt. That's what's so perfect about this. You don't have to stop painting. Just come out here and do what you—

Steve. You have the wrong person. I don't do . . . I'm not painting anymore.

Silence pinged off the far coast, full duplex.

Did something happen? he asked.

Tons happened. Oh, all my parts are still intact, if that's what you mean. It's just that painting's over. No great loss, I assure you.

Loss? Adie! How can you say that? What . . . what are you doing, then?

About what? Oh. You mean for work? I freelance. Commercial stuff. Fliers and the like. Book jackets.

You'll do a book jacket but you won't . . . ?

Won't do original work. I have no problem with designing for a living. Copy and paste. All the pastel coffee mugs and cartoon cars that you want. But Art's done.

Adie. If you can still make . . . Do you see? This would be a chance to do something completely . . .

Sounds like you're looking for somebody else, Stevie. For the greatest illustrator since representation self-destructed.

Well, have it your way. Something in his voice said: You always did. *But do me a favor, Adie? Just make sure that you see this thing once before you die.*

The sentence jumped out at her, from a place she could not make out. The sound of the words, their roll, their order. See this thing once, before you die. The strange familiarity of the invitation caught her ear, if not yet her eyes.

Put it that way, she heard herself mouth, *I wouldn't mind.*

Sure, he said. He'd never asked for anything but the chance to save her. *Whenever you like. Preferably after 10 p.m.*

The hard rose building brick pressed up against the small of her back. From a flight and a half up above night's fire escape where she sat, she watched herself say, *How about a week from next Tuesday, then? On you.*

2

He gave her an address: a foothill road, twisting above the suburbs of that boomtown port built to service a forgotten gold rush. In her mind's eye, Adie pictured the Cavern, lying beached like art's ark, perched on a leeward Cascade slope greened by rains that forever returned yesterday's soaked breeze to the Pacific.

Spiegel expressed her the promotional brochures. In them, glossy images traced the Cavern back to the underground grottos of paint's nativity. In faded watermark beneath the tables of hardware specs, she could make out the faint traces of those Paleolithic herds, stained into stone thirty millennia before art even gave itself a name. Spectral digits, stenciled to the rock—outlines of the same phantom fingers that applied the rouge—waved at her from out of the world's original apse. And across the folds of the glossy brochure, from three hundred centuries on, 3-D, multiplanar, true-color, walk-around holograms waved back.

Adie arrived that first evening, after six hours trapped in the sealed hold of a 737. Stevie was there at the airport to Virgil her back to the Realization Lab. A dozen years. More. They hugged briefly at the arrival gate, laughed, started to falter over the baggage carousel, and drove straight out to his lair in the silence of small talk.

The RL baffled her. It resembled Stevie's description even less than he resembled the Wisconsin boy she'd gone to college with. It smelled faintly of ammonia and fake chemical lemon, the spoor of the late-night cleaning crew. She lingered in the central atrium, rubbing her hands along the redwood walls, trying to bring her image of the place into line with its real layout. She wanted to see the office he'd been sitting in when he'd called her. Steve gave her an impatient tour of the facility, under the compact fluorescent lights. Then he hurried her down the maze of runways, back into a room that opened onto a stalagmite-strewn pitch-blackness.

She knew black. Her friends in the downtown demimonde never deserted it, save for the sporadic bout of unavoidable nakedness. She did well around black. She understood it: one of the big two, not a true color, yet fraternizing with the deepest maroons, hoping to smuggle itself back over hue's closely guarded border.

But this ebony spooked her: the black of elaborate plans.

Gloom unfolded to her adjusting eyes. Stray, chaotic caches of chrome appeared on all sides of her, evil little Duchamp originals. Banks of lights blinked out of the pitch, like the beady red eyes of robotic rats. Connectors and controllers littered the floor, the metallic droppings of those circuit creatures.

She bobbed in a sea of digital serpents. VCRs on steroids, microwaves pumped up on growth hormone murmured at her. She wanted to hack at the silicon swarms—Michael driving off the fallen angels. Who had let these devices into the world? Who could possibly hope to track their various agendas? Adie, whose eidetic eye once re-created the putti, garlands, and cornucopias of a garish Baroque communion rail from memory, could not have sketched these consoles, even as they hissed at her.

If this was the fabled Cavern, then no. Absolutely not. She couldn't work here. Not in this room. No matter what these people hoped to make. No matter what they needed from her.

This is it? she said. *This is it?*

Stevie chuckled. *Almost there.* He pointed toward a luminous opening, a glowing white shoebox, shining like a lit stage set in the general dark.

That? The Cavern? No room ever less resembled its name.

A hardware guy, Spider Lim, ran the tour for them that first night. *The room's been crashing a lot for the last several days,* Lim apologized. *Remember, it's just a prototype.*

Yeah. Steve smirked at her in the glow of the projectors. *You'll have to use your imagination. You know how to do that, don't you, Ade?*

The two men led her through the mess of electronic umbilical cords. Spiegel touched her arm in the darkness. Adie flinched, despite herself, despite years of unlearning. But he only meant to steer her through the nested clutter on to the Cavern's mouth.

They stepped together through the missing rear wall, into the glowing room. Just like that: the audience, walking through an invisible proscenium, onto a floor-level stage. Adie found herself standing in an empty space, six by eight by ten feet, made from five large rectangles of white sandpaper. Even the floor and ceiling were movie screens.

This? You're joking. This is nothing but a glorified walk-in closet.

Put these on, Spider Lim answered. Plastic glasses: lightweight, tinted, wraparound. A high Hollywood fashion statement teetering between fabulously futuristic and ridiculously retro.

But they have wires coming out of them. She tweezed them at arm's length, between thumb and pinky.

Spider's face crimped. *So?* Years later, she would sketch him like that: the young Rembrandt scrunching up, incredulous, in the light of the mirror's report.

So I don't want wires anywhere near my head.

You're kidding me. Spider laughed. *Get out of my life.*

Doesn't . . . don't wires make a magnetic field or something?

Stevie reasoned with her. *You've used a Walkman, haven't you?*

I've never let my head anywhere near a Walkman. I don't even like saying the word.

Spider answered with a marvelous sound: a rapid click of the tongue against hard palate. The sound the neighborhood boys' baseball cards made once, rubber-banded to bicycle spokes. The noise of the industrious world engine, impatient for its next run.

She put the glasses on and waited for the view, like a Louisville deb holding tight after her first hit of acid, her virgin sight about to be forever despoiled. Her eyes looked through the tinted lenses, not knowing what to expect. And they saw nothing at all.

Hold it. Hang on. Spider stood between her and Spiegel, sporting his own set of glasses. He swayed, waving and clicking a thing that looked like a TV remote. *We're snagged on something.*

The trio stood staring at a blank wall. Spider Lim made the ratchet noise. Adie had to keep from slugging him with pleasure. *Do that again!*

What? Do what? Nothing's started yet.

That thing with your tongue.

Spider, lost to the problem, ignored her. His life's work: already to be someplace else by the time anyone else got there.

He temporized. *We've gone over to a new configuration. Just this week. A separate graphics engine for each wall. It's causing us some sync problems.*

The white is pretty, Adie offered.

Here we are. Here goes.

They gaped at the blank walls. Then the expanse of emptiness cleared. Up from a hidden seam in the whiteness, a stone slab emerged: a chunk of burnished marble chiseled with text, something Herod would have slapped up on an imperial stele to appall the natives, as deep into rebellious Judaea as he could get away with. The plaque twirled about in space before settling back down in midair, to be read.

That spinning stone even cast real shadows. No sooner did Spider land the first slab than he hooked another. The second plaque flopped out of the wall and pirouetted in space in front of Adie. She fought the urge to reach out and pinch it.

More stone tablets materialized from on high. They fell into formation alongside one another, forming the beveled buttons of a menu. A floating finger moved upon this list, a disembodied digit that tracked the waves of Spider's wand.

From the several choices, he selected a slab labeled Crayon World. *Here we go*, he said. *Hold on now*. He clicked, and the floating finger riffled. The marble button receded, as if really pressed. The menu beeped and dissolved. For a moment, the walls went dark. When they lit again, they were no longer walls.

A hailstorm of aquamarines filled Adie's vision, a shower of silver-blue shards, as if the air had just shattered. Then the shards condensed, reassembling into a blue ceiling. The three of them stood in their own bodies, under a blazing sky. Yet they floated above the scene they looked at, canted at an impossible angle. Adie's knees buckled. She pitched forward, compensating for this snub to gravity. When she righted herself, so did the Crayon World below.

Another cloudburst of topazes and Adie began to make out the place where they'd landed. Her gaze zoomed and panned, as dazed as an infant's eyes sifting their first light. No sooner did she right herself than nausea upended her again. She felt as she always had, on those five-thousand-mile childhood flights around the world to yet another new home, airsick for days at a pop. But this was the very opposite of motion sickness: still-illness, frozen in a yawing landscape that bobbed all around her.

Adie, now a cartoon of herself, stood treading on an invisible magic carpet. She, Steve, and Spider walked the plank above a seething grass sea. Only there was no plank, and the grass was no more than scribbles of crayon.

She looked up. The teal tent above them now billowed with cloud. She looked down at her shoes. They skimmed over the tops of trees, trees rooted well beneath the floor that projected them. Each crayon image slid seamlessly over the room's corners, erasing all sense of the cubicle that they inhabited. A few trillion bits of math, to fool a few billion years of ocular evolution: after a few seconds, Adie stopped noticing the conjuring act and began to believe.

Here, Spider said. *You drive.* And he thrust the wand into her hands.

Where's the clutch on this thing? She never could drive a stick. Adie bobbled the wand, jabbing at the buttons with her thumbs. The world's RPMs raced, and a burp rippled through its crayon portrait. The stand of would-be blue spruce they threaded went masts down and keel to heaven. She swung the wand hard to the right. She and the men banked back in the opposite direction.

What's that? she whispered, afraid the thing might bolt. *That. There. It just moved.*

God only knows, Steve whined. *That's our problem. Millions of dollars of funding, and nobody around this dump can draw worth squat.*

His voice seemed to come from just to her left, though Adie would never again trust her sense of distance. As she turned to look at him, the Crayon World wrapped around her, tracking her head. Spiegel's grin leaked out from under his own pair of wraparound glasses. *Go on and follow it, if you like.*

Adie squeezed the wand and steered away. In three short bursts, she put half a moraine between herself and where Steve stood. Yet he stayed right next to her, meadow for meadow, bog for bog.

What are those things supposed to be: cattails? bulrushes? What in the world is that Douglas fir doing over there, all by itself?

Stevie threw back his head and snickered. *Some chassis-jockey must have drawn that one. They have all the visual intelligence of a myopic, right-hemisphere-damaged eight-year-old loose with his first sixty-four-color box.*

Spider Lim just smiled at the coder's taunt. *Like software knows how to draw any better?*

But it's fantastic, Adie demurred. *Change one . . . one mark on it and I'll kill you in your sleep.*

Pixel, Spider corrected. *Change one pixel. And you'll kill us.*

Voxel, Spiegel overtrumped him. *Keep current, will you, Lim? Voxel or boxel. A 3-D pixel.*

How come you didn't paint the backs of anything? I mean, look at this stump. A very funky mahogany, although I do like the Cubist growth rings. But if we go around to the other side? Nothing but white.

That's the paper, Spider apologized.

The paper?

The paper we drew them on.

Yeah. We were too bloody lazy to . . .

Hardware elbowed software in the floating rib. *This particular world is not really about painting the stump, you know. It's about getting the head-position tracking to work . . .*

With the Kalman filtering . . .

Not to mention the human head . . .

While doing these massive bit-blits from one graphics array area to another at sufficiently high speeds and resolutions to—

Look, look! A house. Did you know there was a little house out there? Don't you boys snort at me. Can we walk behind it? Does the world go back that far? Look! Flowers. What—? Tul—, no iri—

How many times we gotta tell you? You're not dealing with bloody Pick-ax-o here . . .

Oh God! Adie shouted. *Little bees. And they're buzzing!*

Crude black-and-golden scraps with loops of straightened paper-clip wings jittered about in organized confusion. Something turned over in her, as small, as social, as buzzing and robotic as the living original.

They like it around the flowers. Steve pointed off into a glade. *Try waving the wand over there.*

She did. The magic scraps of would-be bees swarmed after every trail of digital scent she laid down willy-nilly.

Adie soared and looped and rolled. Each time she cocked her head, the trailing wires that tracked her goggles pulled the whole landscape along in her sight's wake. She waved the magic wand through ever more elaborate wingovers and Immelmanns. She skimmed above the trees and plowed through furrows between the grass blades. She navigated out to the farthest walls of this confinement and jiggled the ground beneath her feet with her giggling.

You like it, then? Steve demanded. *You really like it?*

I never dreamed . . . I've never seen anything like it.

Outside the Cavern, beyond the enveloping lab, past the research park's camouflaging cedar shingles, out on the fringe of the coastal forest, the hurt of a screech owl skipped like a stone across the night's glassy surface. Long-haul commerce whipped its errand trucks up and down the evacuated coast road, hard as scythes. But inside this womb of cool engineering, ingenuity schooled its hatchlings by moonlight.

You'll come in with us, then? Steve asked Adie. *You want to play?*

Some part of her had never wanted anything else. Had never hoped for more than to play in such a place, or even in its ugly machine imposture.

The three of them strolled out of the paper meadows and walked back into real weather. They left the high-tech monastery, stepping out into the actual night. It seemed to be seedtime, early in the curve of the world's regeneration. Say it was raining. A wrap of mist condensed on their clothing, coating them in a fine glaze. A few scared birds clicked and whistled in the night, to find themselves out.

They stood together in the dark parking lot, next to the rental car that was to take Adie back to her tepee-shaped theme hotel down along the old state highway. Lim toyed with a geode key ring. Spiegel leaned on the rental, awaiting her answer. Klarpol, for her part, could not stop laughing, shaking her head side to side in disbelief at what she'd just seen. Images built and broke inside her. For the first time in as long as she cared to remember, the future held more pictures than the past.

Stevie, it's amazing. But I can't. I really can't.

What does that mean, exactly?

What, indeed? The very weather, that first night, interrogated her, dared her to say exactly what she had sworn off. And the wider box of evening—the scrim of midnight—mocked all her available replies.

It's not paint, he said. *No paint involved at all. No original expression required, Ade. It's all drawing by numbers, out here. Don't think of it as art. Think of it as a massive data structure. What SoHo doesn't know won't hurt it.*

She laid out all her objections, lined them up in a mental pulldown menu. None held water except the last: a general hatred for all things that the cabled world hoped to become. Yet something tugged at her. Something darting and striped and buzzing.

Those bees, she answered him. *How do they know how to find those flowers? How do you get them to fly like that?*

Something in those jittery black-and-golden scraps recalled her sight's desire. So it always went, with life and its paler imitations. The things that needed renouncing—our little acts of abdication, our desperate Lents—finally caved in. They slunk off, subdued by hair of the dog, their only cure. The abandoned palette returned to press its suit, sue for time, advocate.

All Adie had ever wanted was to people this place with gentian and tree rings and hidden houses folded from out of cardstock, to raise stalks under an animated sky, a sky calling out for glade-crazed, pollinating paper honeybees that followed every trail of scent that the wave of thought's wand laid down.

You bastards, she said. *You filthy bitheads.* She looked up, helpless, ready, her wet eyes seeing everything.

3

In the Crayon Room, all strokes are broad.

Wax goes on nubby. It clumps and gaps. Your main repertoire here is the happy smear. Leaving an edge is hard. Any two colors mix to make coffee. From faint to heavy, from dawn to dusk, the crayon sea and the crayon causeway stay chirpy, pert monotones.

The grain beneath the page seeps up to enter any scene you draw. Spread your newsprint on the sidewalk and make a fish; your fish comes into the Crayon World already fossilized. Rub a stick of brown lengthwise against a nude page; the plank behind the paper clones its own knots and whorls, returning the pulp to its woody matrix.

Every crayon furnishing is a flat façade. The sun's disk serves as its own nametag. Head-on, distant hills flatten to platters. From the visitor's floating crow's nest, scarecrows deployed in this ripening grain have no more width than the paper they're scrawled on.

Signs of human life abound. A bitten apple hides amid the pile rotting at the foot of a tree. An abandoned bucket, half full, slops its squiggles of water. A bent rag doll sits compliant on a bench. A kite tied to a picket fence floats ripe for unleashing.

But this world leaves no trace of its makers. No people populate the Crayon Room. It is a simple place, pristine, prelapsarian. Curls of smoke craze up from the crippled chimney of one little summer cottage, too cozy for habitation. Behind gapped, sashed windows, a crayon cat purrs, fixed on a goldfish that darts against its rough-hewn bowl.

The Crayon World is a proud mother's gallery, the first retrospective refrigerator-magnet show of a budding child genius. But nothing here looks much like what it stands for. Only the conventions of a house, the insanely pitched roof, the burnt sienna front door lolling on its hinge. The code for cat and apple and bucket and tree and abandoned doll.

Visitors here face down their own ghostliness. The casual walker collides against nothing. Try to climb a hill, and you pass right through it. Hedgerows serve as mere suggestions. Approached, their bushes swell in detail, swimming toward the eye until they fill it. Then, with an optical pop, they vanish, freeing the scrawled grazing lands beyond them.

Now and then, an eagle shrills, invisible. Otherwise, silence, save for the gurgle of a hidden stream and, down in the gardens, the drone of the loosened hive. Circlets of scissored medallions buzz freely, in skittish digital trajectories, each striped with the icon for honeybee. Their randomly cycled rasp, the sound of fidget flight, stands in for the beating of insect wings.

A wheelbarrow in scarlet wax sits tilted on a path somewhere down a projected dell. The pasture is plain and the woods a welcoming cartoon. This mad perspective, drifting between dimensions, is perfect for getting lost in.

The Crayon World feels bigger than it is. Its space is curved. It wraps back onto itself. Hikers strike out to the southwest, into a weald of clumsy flowering horse chestnuts. The stroll unrolls, always a new copse in front of you. The hike moseys on, furlong stretching into mile, mile into league, for crayon measures conform to the lost imperial units of bedtime enchantment.

Sky blue drops to Prussian, then to a darker cobalt. And still, ever more southwest stretches out in front of you. More than when you started. Your walk in the woods threatens to turn into a panicked sprint. Then the crayon receptors at the edge of your retina say *wait*: that tree is wrong. That tree shouldn't be here. And in that mental crossing where scribbles synapse against words, you wonder: *Where have I seen that thing before?*

Sure enough, in a ridiculously few steps, the tree returns. It looms up from the same speck on the same compass point, without your shifting tack. It zooms to the same height as you draw close. It bares the same rift down the middle of its data. Even before you can wonder how you missed it, the trail loops and the whole scene recycles.

The wand you use to wend through this wilderness has a knob for leaving breadcrumbs. But as in all such worlds, the crumbs attract a murder of crayon crows that devour your trail markers the moment you lay them down. All your wax signs will not guide you for more than a virtual minute. The path is past preserving, and the crayon adventure knows no goal except itself. The Crayon World is just a broad-stroked test. The test of how to enter it, and walk back out intact.

4

When rage reprised itself, when you fell back again on the old bitter tit for tat, when the need to escape finally left you throwing darts at the world map, at last it hit you. Simple choice: replay the old routine, the self-triggering cycle of accusations, the verbal razor cuts daubed in love's alcohol. Traipse down the path of tender sadomasochism yet one more soul-shredding time. Or turn around and walk. Escape down the path that must still lie somewhere to the south, the way you walked in.

One more tearful reconciliation would only further demean you both. The place you pushed for—the tumbledown house in the country, your dream of intimacy that always made her bite in fear—vanishes now into fantasy. It gives way to that darker late-night venue, where hisses of desire shade off into abuse, abuse feeding back into desire.

You've been each other's shared addiction, slinking back repeatedly to the nightmare rush that you've both fought to be rid of. You've come back from the dead a dozen times, only to spin out again, worse, for whole weeks at a time. You've suffered the delirium of total withdrawal: one month, two, without so much as a word. Then, clean, virginal, at peace, calling again, just to see if you can. Just to see who's in charge. Just a quick little needle slipped into one another's waiting veins.

All that changes forever, this Friday. You're off to a place where you can't ask her to hurt you again, where neither of you can backslide into care. Where you can no longer reach one another, however much mutual tenderness revives. It rocks you, just to imagine.

Among your friends, the plan produces only stunned hilarity. "You're going *where*? Don't they shoot people in the street there, without even asking whose side they're on?"

"No," you shit them back. "You're thinking of D.C."

At last they realize, these friends who've witnessed your worst whiplash for years now. You mean it, and it blows them away.

You rush to assure everyone. The school you'll teach for is a virtual armed compound. Tensions are nowhere near what they were this time last year. The civil war is ending; all sides are talking compromise. The foreign armies have left. Their president has finally taken the reins. All that old insanity is a thing of the past.

And it's only for two terms, anyway. Eight months. Safer than a daily commute on the Edens Expressway.

You sleep well on the long flight, crushed up against the window with one of those squares of cotton gauze the stewardesses pass off as pillows. In your sleep, you already speak fluent Arabic. Even your dream marionette is struck by the strangeness: these guttural rapid bursts issuing from you, part nonsense, part gift of tongues.

Over the cabin speakers, the pilot warns that he must take the standard evasive maneuvers upon approach. Passengers are not to panic. The plane will simply lose a few thousand feet in a matter of seconds. Many on board seem used to the procedure.

You Stuka to a landing, safe, even exhilarated. The guard at the baggage claim totes a machine gun resembling an haute couture coat hanger. The school bursar is waiting in the terminal to meet you.

The metropolis lies dark and quiet. You cock your ears toward the south suburbs, but can hear nothing except traffic. The chauffeur from the school laughs: What did you expect? Grenade-toting crazies lurking behind every street vendor?

In the morning, you tour the compound. The school buildings are mostly intact. They sit up on a bluff, with a view down to the Corniche and the sea beyond. Your office balcony looks out on precarious pyramids of rubble being bulldozed into the water. You search for the Green Line, the vegetation growing up through the cracked concrete that divides the city. You see only a stand of high-rises, their pockmarks blending into this day's dappled shadows.

It's better than you imagined. All white and marine and accepting. A recovering place. A good place to recover. The resinous air, the olive mountains. Arid, azure, clear. Your sinuses haven't been this open since childhood. This city is returning. You can live here.

And as with all key conclusions you've reached in your thirty-three years, you're wrong.

5

She could not leave that room as easily as she entered. The Little Italy that Adie Klarpol flew back to now seemed a nostalgic, second-rate Bellows or Marsh. One visit to that high-tech wonderland and her old urban cityscape collapsed into back projection. Her friends shrank to animated sprites; her daily obligations, items to be clicked through with the wave of a wand.

The third night after her return, she dreamed of a shoebox-sized bungalow on an island in the Sound just off Seattle. In the morning, she flipped through the atlas, searching for possible culprit spots. The house that she'd dreamed of had dripped with gingerbread and its yard had sprouted bushels of cartoon beans. The island had sat in a ravishment of surrounding water, a private moat between her and the manufactured world. She could find nothing in the atlas that remotely resembled the spot.

That afternoon, while carrying two gallons of fake Maine springwater home from the corner grocery, she bumped into a groper. That is, he raked her, each hand cupping one of her defenseless breasts. The creep ran off before she could drop the gallon manacles and slug him. Four days later, a mugger on Houston grabbed her loose shoulder bag, and like an idiot, she pulled back. He slammed her into a street sign, cracked her on the cheek, and ran off screaming, *You fucking crazed bitch. What do you think you're doing?*

Panhandlers began to hiss at her with impunity. Clerks of both sexes handed over her purchases, wrapped in ambiguous offers. Something had gotten away from her. Some instinct, some cadence of survival. After a dozen years, New York turned on her, expelled her like an amateur. One more accosting, this one by a pack of grade-school thrashers in Chelsea using her as a crash-test dummy, and Adie realized what was happening. She'd started to make eye contact. Fallen back into that old, bad habit of looking up at people. And to look, in this place, was to beg for erasure.

She called Spiegel and asked him to send out some rental listings. And there it was, on page 4 of the second Rentals column: Cozy Island Home, with garden. The gingerbread cottage she'd seen in her sleep.

She called Steve right away, unable to wait a decent interval. *Is the offer still good?*

The cackle at the other end of the line seemed to be a yes.

She rented the house over the phone, sight unseen. She took possession on one of those rare Pacific crystalline afternoons, thick with the scent of white pine resin, when the Earth felt as freshly scrubbed as on the day it sat for its first formal portrait. The place was all she'd dreamed, and then some. She settled in on the Sound, forty minutes by ferry from town. Within a week of her moving into the cottage, she stopped dreaming of the city she'd abandoned.

She sat on her porch those first nights, wrapped in the brackish tidal air. The future's breeze split across her face and joined up again behind her. She felt herself a spinster whose sudden new suitor must be either sadistic, blind, or a confused fortune hunter. She'd read all the cautionary fairy tales and knew the one inevitable outcome. Still, she consented to this courtship, and even decided to court it back.

Seattle exceeded all expectation. She painted her gingerbreading a lovingly researched rainbow of maroons. She bought a chocolate

Labrador and named him Pinkham, the trusting companion that a New York apartment had always denied her. She put in a dozen mail-order rosebushes, each one tagged with a tin octagon embossed with the warning "Asexual reproduction of this plant without license is prohibited by the Plant Patent Act." She found that she could live on wild blueberries, honey, and crabs from the crab pot she sank off the neighborhood slip.

The sole catch was the corporate sponsor across the Sound, the one she had to report to, the one that footed the bill for this midlife summer bungalow. She rode over on the ferry, steeping herself in the blasted fifths of its foghorn. She freighted her secondhand, banged-up banana-colored Volvo across the Sound faster than it used to take her to get past the first pylon of the Verrazano Narrows.

A perky personnel officer took Adie on the formal TeraSys welcoming rounds. They toured the expensive new glass and polished sandstone headquarters that coiled itself like so much self-replicating luxury mall, five miles down the road's clear-cut from the Realization Lab. Preoccupied specialists of all stripes paused in mid-coffee-room brainstorming to give her hand distracted shakes. Workstation designers, systems-software adepts: scores of names she promptly forgot and faces she couldn't keep from remembering.

After a few hundred handshakes, Adie began to understand the hyena highlights in that phone cackle Spiegel had given her, when she asked if the offer was still good. Like the worst of number-dumb paint-box dabblers, she'd failed to guess the weight of this latest silicon thyroid case. Failed to gauge the size of the master hive, or just how many jobs it needed to fill.

She'd once freelanced for a software vendor, the makers of a time management product whose marketers commissioned from her a hideously cheery pastel mouse and keyboard, each made to look as if it were stitched out of taffeta. Now, on an office wall plastered with sales brochures, she saw her faux-folksy logo among those of a dozen other subsidiaries buried in the TeraSys tree structure. An adjacent brochure described the test bed of the hour, the Realization Lab, with its prototype Cavern: "a second-generation, experimental, total-immersion environment modeler."

TeraSys seemed to be seeking all manner of nightstands upon which to empty its deep-pocket change. These people could fund Adie's midlife crisis and keep her on fellowships for years without feeling the least pinch. They offered her an unlimited fantasy sandbox, perfect for a girl to get lost in.

She made her way back up the mountain, to the Realization Lab and its magic room in question. The look of the low-slung, clean-lined building nagged at her for several days, until she pegged it: an upscale group dental practice in, say, Westchester County. Inside the RL, the redwood and river rock gave way to long olive corridors and linen-lined cubicle partitions that teemed with the same jittery bee-loud buzz that had seduced her out here in the first place.

For the first two weeks, the look of her co-workers reduced her to giggles. Their sun-starved skin, their sparse but luxurious facial hair, their corduroy slacks and untucked flannel lumberjack shirts, their sandals over socks, their joyous, cause-filled eyes behind the silver-rimmed John Lennon glasses reduced them to so many industrious gnome battalions. It took her a month to learn to tell the hardware engineers from the hackers, the orcs from the elves.

These shaggy dungeon creatures had managed to turn their airy park ranger's roost into a subterranean wonderland. Hallway walls were everywhere taped over with flowcharts, logic listings, parodies of user documentation manuals, and autographed publicity photos of Yoda, Mr. Spock, and Steve Jobs. The earth-toned moldings reeked of cedar, fresh latex, and tennis shoes worn too long in a damp climate. Even the copious indoor plantings could not entirely soften the feel of chrome, steel circuit-card cages, and CRT screens. Here and there, squares of acoustical ceiling tile fell jimmied open, spilling out the snakes' nest of cabling they hid. Hardest of all on her, the place *whirred.* A perpetual low-grade hum hung in the air, the spin of disk drives, the clack of keys, the high-pitched metal ping of blocks of data being manipulated.

What made all this? Who supplied the hand-eye coordination? Who brought this team together and told each person what to do? How did the machines turn electrons into steerable pictures? Adie could not see herself painting the walls of this Cavern until she saw—if only in shadow—how the mechanism worked.

Spiegel assigned her a prodigy to call her own. A boy called Jack-daw—Jack Acquerelli. Jackdaw came fresh from California's largest computer science factory, although he looked barely old enough to mail in his own software registration forms. He was just her height, one of the reasons he'd taken up with computers in the first place. He might have been attractive, except for the steady diet of Doritos and the inability to abide much direct human contact without flinching. Adie took to him at once, if only for his mocking last name. Each time she met him she unbuttoned the top button of his habitual plaid flannel shirt, until she trained him to do so, all by himself.

Jack, she badgered him. *Why do those bees buzz? What holds that house up?* Could one make the grass grow under a visitor's feet? Conjure up some kid to come mow it for a silver-gray two bits? She grew worse than a five-year-old who'd just learned that every question bred another.

Jackdaw struggled mightily to address the barrage. But he could not parse her. Their interface was makeshift, the cable between them noisy, and their throughput limited to the intermittent burst.

Think of it all as a kind of trick, he said. He could not both look at her and address her at the same time. He wasn't comfortable talking to living things. Living female things. Their firmware algorithm eluded him.

I knew it. I knew it had to be a trick. But, but, but: how does the trick work?

We do it all with liquid crystal back projection. One Electrolamp Luminox projector throwing alternating double-buffered images onto each of the five walls. We cast the floor onto a refracting mirror, through a hole in the ceiling.

Liquid? Adie whimpered. *Crystal?*

It's the only way. Trust me. The alternatives are all too crude.

Her laughter battered him. She tried to squelch it. *Sorry, Jackie. That does not compute.*

Sure it does, he said. *So LCD streaks a little. It ghosts. So we don't get the brightness that we'd get out of a goosed-up electron beam. And the response speeds still aren't what you'd hope for. But don't forget: you can eliminate fade by simultaneous, multirow addressing . . .*

Sure. Of course! Adie smacked herself on the forehead. *What was I thinking? But tell me, Jackdaw. How do you get the pretty flowers to come off the wall like that? They just . . . float a few feet out into the room.*

The question stopped the boy short in mid-ratchet. He seized up, unable to pop all the way back off his internal stack. His conversation hung on that old scheduling puzzle beloved of multitasking programmers: the five dining philosophers who share four spoons. Some part of him forgot to put some other part's spoon down between courses, and the whole meal crashed to a halt.

Jackdaw fell back, slack-jawed at what stood flushed out into the open. Adie saw herself through his eyes: a totally alien life-form. A frilly, intuitive blur. Some non-carbon-based, vegetative intelligence. She read the proof in the boy's face. They shared no mother tongue, nor any father either.

Even at this point of derailment, Jackdaw refused eye contact. She spooked him, her loose, twill gaze worse than a Gorgon's. The boy quit his fiddling and stared off into the lab's black. He stroked the hood of a modular connector with thumb and forefinger. She watched a quorum of clear-thinking chip architects convene in his mind, debating what her question could possibly mean. How much they knew, these new children. How concentrated their knowledge of every mechanism, except for life.

Jackdaw slogged back into the breach. *You mean the stereoscopic effect?*

Maybe. She felt herself a brat in braids, prevailed upon to show her prize puree.

The stereoscopic effect comes from the glasses. Shuttered lenses. We've settled on a hundred-and-twenty-hertz oscillation. Alternate left-eye and right-eye views, each flashing sixty times a second. We sync the projected images to the shutter rate. Your eyes put the two back together. That's where you get the sense of depth. The stereo 3-D.

Oh God. You mean, like a big View-Master? That's what you're saying? I'm going to live the next several years of my life inside a giant View-Master?

That depends. What exactly is a View-Master?

She yelped. *You're kidding me. You never had . . . ? You never saw . . . ? Those round white paddle-wheel disks with the paired squares of Kodachrome at opposite ends? Old Faithful and Half Dome? Inside the Vatican Library? Goofy and Mickey on Holiday?*

A look stole across Jackdaw's face. The 3-D representation for Scared Shitless. This woman was infected. Something viral. Something contagious.

Forgive me, she explained. *I'm being silly.*

Huh. I see. His head jerked back, resetting the input stream. *Whatever. Anyway, our rendering rates don't come near to sixty frames a second yet. But as it turns out, the eye only needs about a dozen frames a second to trick it into fusing discrete images into continuous motion. Film is only twenty-four. So anything over thirty is more than adequate.* His eyebrows went up. *For now.*

Can you explain something else to me? What exactly is the difference between you and that Spider?

Which spider? Jackdaw clicked away at his keyboard, as if transcribing the whole conversation. *Oh. You mean Lim? He's mostly hardware. I'm mostly software.*

That's a difference?

He's like, Korean. I'm what you call Italian?

You're his baby brother, aren't you? You suck out his soul and use it in your own body when he's not around, don't you?

She shocked him into looking almost at her. He shook his head gravely: huh-uh. Honest injun.

You're all clones of the same experimental genetic material. Admit it.

At last Jackdaw smiled. But she still couldn't tell if he smiled at her inanity or at something on his monitor that his typing had produced.

She saw in the smile some spark of software loyalty. This boy would always do things for her. Small, stray errands and favors, whatever happened in the lab between them. And the seed of his devotion made her feel safe, here in this precarious new world. Safe, knowing that she would never ask anything from him but the smallest of favors.

Jackdaw, she said. *Jackie.* He flinched at the familiarity on her lips. *You still haven't answered my question. What makes the pictures?*

What makes the pictures? His face labored at the cipher. It squeezed itself through every real-time translation algorithm that he possessed. *What makes the pictures?*

Yeah.

Uh, we do? Not even hoping that he'd guessed right.

No! Not that! She pictured herself stamping on the floor, the spade-footed kick of a dwarf whose secret name has just slipped out. *You know what I mean.*

You mean, what hardware do we use to generate the graphics? What computers?

Yes. Probably.

Jackdaw took her back for her first look at the monsters. The Cavern's graphics engines filled a room at the far end of the RL's long central artery. Jackdaw and Adie threaded down this hall, past knots of flannel and corduroy that stood around volubly sharing their latest discoveries in a language entirely foreign to her. Those who noticed them waved, taking Adie in as if she'd been among them for years, laboring away on her few square inches of the common canvas.

Some unseen whole was taking shape here: a gargantuan corpse, hauled in chunks along this animated ant trail. Each worker they passed carried an integral piece of the spoils many times his own body weight, part of a prize orders of magnitude larger than all of them combined. *Hey,* her new colleagues called to her. *Hey.* The quick facial dip of acknowledgment: you're creating, I'm creating. We're at the peak of our assembled powers, joined together, about to set in place civilization's crowning capstone. Each distracted knowledge engineer exuded a happy preoccupation, needing no words. The whole picture scared the daylights out of her.

Jackdaw led her to the end of the corridor, and let her into a windowless back room. Between its dropped ceiling and raised floor, the space felt almost as cramped as the Cavern. Inside the sanctum, a woman in her mid-twenties, her hair the color of a Fabergé egg, paced between the machine furrows, chattering back at the murmuring chrome.

Hey, Jackdaw said. *Sue Loque. What's a software type doing down among the nuts and bolts?*

The woman's ambiguous splay of signals—biker leather trimmed with ratty lace—would have intimidated Adie, even back in blasé New York. Out here, in this flood of new rules, they left her feeling shamefully normative.

Sue Loque threw up her hands, the icon for distress. *If the hardware types would keep these things tweaked, we software types wouldn't have to get our hands dirty. Why do you think I went into coding in the first place? So that I wouldn't have to touch any printed circuits.*

What's the problem? Adie asked.

They're ugly and septic.

No, I mean with the machines.

Oh. Well, they're none too pretty either. And they just stopped polling.

Jackdaw shook his head. *What do you mean, they stopped polling?*

I mean they stopped polling.

Whatever it meant, Adie stopped polling, too. Or at least she stopped existing for the two professionals, who set out to backtrace their way into the heart of logic's arctic crystal. The Loque woman and Jackdaw called in Spider Lim, and all three of them disappeared into the printed-circuit thicket.

Adie glanced around the room. Its likeness had never once been painted. It glowed, an eerie, mechanical hatchery, replete with all the secret trip levers of an ingenious Max Ernst frottage. But all this complexity felt stunningly sterile: as still and smooth and sinister as a turquoise Hockney swimming pool.

Shame and amazement did a two-step inside her. This room was this present's wildest accomplishment, its printing press, its carrack and caravel, its haywain, hanging gardens, and basilica. These demure, humming boxes contained the densest working out, the highest tide of everything that collective ingenuity had yet learned how to pull off. It housed the race's deepest taboo dream, the thing humanity was trying to turn itself into. Yet for all that Adie had seen, art had fled headlong from it, in full retreat, toward some safe aesthetic den of denial, where it could lick its wounds in defeat.

She tried to picture the Arcadian landscapes hiding inside these boxes. But she could form no clearer picture than streams of signals,

waves and troughs rushing down narrow silicon sluices, each one setting off another massive cascade of signals. Somehow these signals all
lined up, countless dots in a cosmic halftone process, the hammers of a
trillion player pianos, the programmed nubs on the drum of a galaxy-
sized music box. The voltages performed their megabit marching-band
ballets, lining up to stand for anything in creation: a bank balance, an
airline ticket, a photo, a song, a letter from a friend, all fully portable,
all convertible, one into the other.

Several clock cycles later, hardware and software emerged triumphant, the offending bug squashed between them.

Got it? Adie polled them.

We always get it, eventually, Lim said. And he disappeared into the
next time-share emergency.

Who was that masked man? Sue asked.

Jackdaw grinned at some safe face in the air between the two
women. *Sorry for the interruption. Here they are, anyway. The brains
behind the operation.*

The Cavern's cavern, Sue added.

*You mean, all the pictures come from . . . here? You're trying to tell me
that the entire Crayon World is inside these five machines, somewhere?*

Sue snorted.

Don't snort at me, Adie warned.

Sue traced a wave in the air, half apologetic, half dismissive. She
squeezed Adie's shoulder, a reassurance that came off like somebody
pumping Windex onto a bathroom mirror. Adie fought the urge to
punch this woman, for if it came to blows, this woman could pummel
her and Jackdaw put together.

*They're all in there, sweetie. Every picture in existence. Every last
image ever imagined or imaginable. We just have to figure out how to get
them out.*

What are they called? These machines?

Jackdaw saw his chance. *They're all proprietary TeraSys graphics
boxes, of course. They start out life as 3-D accelerated Power Agate
servers, running one reality engine for each —*

I mean, what are their names?

Their . . . names?

Adie shook her head: all the commonsense groundwork left undone. *OK, how's about we call this one Da Vinci? He was pretty technological, huh? Inventing submarines, writing backwards, and all that. This one can be Claude. After all, we're going to be cranking out landscape by the gross hectare. Then here's Hsieh Ho, giver of the Six Principles . . .*

Jackdaw cleared his throat. *Is that anything like the six degrees of freedom?*

And we'll need a Rembrandt. For a lifetime devoted to the play of light against dark. And the last one ought to be Picasso, because—

Because he fucked everything that moved for the better part of a century? Sue suggested.

Jackdaw jerked at the profanity. He lurched for the door, and safety. *Uh, maybe we'd better vacate. Gotta get back to that Z-order filter . . .*

Sue fell in behind him. *Let's just hope that Rembrandt here doesn't decide to wig out again before the recompile, tomorrow.*

You see? Adie said. *It's useful to know their names, isn't it?*

Sue made her noise again, the one Adie warned her not to. Deeper in her sinuses, this time. *I love you art school chicks. I really do. You give the whole female race a little—how to say?—éclat.*

They might join forces, this female race. A woman who knew how to extract any one of imagination's images from these boxes. And another who knew just which images to extract.

Sue, Adie petitioned her fuchsia-haired colleague. *Can you show me how to make these suckers draw?*

Adie Klarpol and Sue Loque stood shoulder to shoulder, facing the front wall of the Cavern. Each sported a pair of those ridiculous shuttered glasses. A loud sprig of rhinestones studded the corners of Adie's, a giddy display brought on by the usual overexertion. Sue wore the head-tracking glasses, the ones with the cable conduit that recorded exactly what her eyes were doing at all times.

On the front wall, a wreath of laurel materialized out of an expanse of bridal white. It hung there, blowing in an invisible breeze. On the left wall, menus cascaded out of one another. The other cave walls darkened to a contrasting black, the soot of countless digital campfires.

The wreath in front of them had grown from a seed in Adie Klarpol's mental window box. The Crayon World had thawed the sap of images inside her. It left her needing to see a new bud germinate from scratch. To that end, she and her design colleagues had assembled for a series of tutorials, to learn the ways that virtual leaves might be made.

Grow me a rubber tree, she'd asked Spiegel. *Give me a philodendron tendril.* She had in mind a surface as rich and convoluted as the solar surf that shaped it. But anything more than a jagged crayon smear would have satisfied her.

Here, she told her fallen poet Stevie. *Something like these.* And she held out to the softwarewolf a picture in a book.

The color plate she held out was a supremely clumsy representation. Leaves everywhere: a veritable jungle of them. But no leaf that grew on any tree in any country Spiegel or Adie had ever lived in. A rash of stems, fruits, and flowers—all native to the republic of invention. And among the blooms, a naked white woman sprawled upon a jungle-violating sofa, listening to the tune of an ebony flute player from deep in the undergrowth.

Spiegel stared at this hemophiliac sunbather—lenticular, wrong—in a trance of memory. At last he looked away, breaking the picture's spell. He glanced up at his circle of apprentices and said, as if no one were naked: *We can make a leaf in several different ways. The simplest of all is to use basic trig.*

Spiegel hacked several quick expressions into a terminal. The points of a curve percolated up from out of the algebraic shorthand. He sliced off a conic section and roughed up its edges. He wrote out a well-behaved polynomial to describe the range and rise and run. The X of the thing, the willing Y, the demure Z.

Frame buffers then threw his results upon a screen for the design group to witness. Artists and engineers drifted through the room as Steve's shapes spun in space. Each time his right pinkie hit the Enter key, the screen turned into a luscious spirograph, pouring forth a petaled profusion.

Lunettes, Michael Vulgamott, the architect, called. *Spandrels. Tracery.* Adie heard, in the man's voice, a fellow displaced Gothamite. Vulgamott's manic, twitching fingers ticked off the terms as if he were stepping into a crowded midtown intersection to hail a thesaurus.

The words he used made the mathematician Ari Kaladjian's bushy eyebrows balkanize. *They're properly called cardioids and tricuspids and folia. Limaçon of Pascal. Plane algebraic geometry has been making these curves for at least two hundred years.* Kaladjian had fled the globe's chaos for the safety of mathematics, and he did not care to surrender his sanctuary to fuzzy-mindedness.

Spiegel quit his keyboard jabbing long enough to shrug. *Call them what you want. They're graphics primitives. All art is Euclid's baby.*

I can think of at least a couple of dubious paternity suits, Adie said.

I love my wife, Sue Loque stage-whispered. *But oh, Euclid!*

What's the point of starting with equations? Vulgamott wanted to know. *What do we gain?*

Kaladjian grunted. *Everything starts with equations.*

Spiegel spoke with the distraction of the engrossed encoder. *Plane curves are the fastest, easiest artifacts in the world to implement. And you can make trillions of them with just a few iterated expressions.*

Streams in the desert? Adie mocked. *Orchards from out of the arid places?*

Something like that. Yes. Spiegel smiled at her, immune to her aggression. Knowing it, of old.

She frowned at his geometric petals. *But where's the leaf? I see nothing that even faintly resembles the Rousseau I showed you. At best, they look like victims of a hit-and-run Calder mobile.*

That's what you lose when you generate leaves by algorithm. Everything's a trade-off. In this case, you trade off natural complexity for something that's easier and faster . . . and much too geometrical. Much too perfect.

Too perfect! Kaladjian shouted. *You cannot get too perfect.*

Where are the shadows and gradations? Adie sounded betrayed.

We'd have to add them. Spiegel demonstrated. A few calls to a shading routine produced a rough, pencil-sketched idea of surface.

Huh, Adie said, as the cardioid went crosshatched. *Huh. That puts us about three baby steps toward a Miró. Wait! Go back a little bit. There. Try the feathered edges with the Bonnard orange.*

Numbers and art both fell silent at how quickly Spiegel pulled a crepe carnation out of code's silk hat.

A pout stole over Adie's face. She extended her arm to slow things down, one palm out to break her fall.

You're trying to tell me that . . . math . . . is enough to get fake leaves to look real?

Math, Kaladjian snarled, *is enough to get real leaves to look real.*

Spiegel defended her. *I don't think that's what she means.*

What the hell does she mean, then? Kaladjian flicked one hand through the air, a disgusted scythe.

Spiegel turned to Adie. *Well, she? What the hell do you mean?*

God only knows. I was hoping someone here could tell me. I mean: are these equations—these cosine things—inside real plants?

Kaladjian's *Of course* rammed in midair into Spiegel's *Not really.*

The younger man, from the younger discipline, demurred. *Well. That all depends on what you mean by "inside."* Something in Spiegel's tone implied that no massively parallel array of processors short of the planet itself could hope to extract the perfect equation from out of imperfection's green.

Let's see some veins, Karl Ebesen said. He scrutinized the test leaves from the graphic designer's eye view. *How about a few burns and insect bites?* The ragged scars that silk imitations never bother to imitate.

Spiegel pressed on, coating the synthetic surface with ever-finer nubs and nuances. Boosting realism required forgoing simple polynomials and embracing a runaway explosion of polygons. *Here,* he told his charges, pointing at the color plate of the original jungle. *Here:* trying to keep his finger a safe distance from that woman's chalk-white breasts. *Here, this cluster of . . .*

Figs, Adie offered. *Figs, I think.*

That's supposed to be a fig tree? That? OK. Let's say fig. We turn this cluster of fig leaves into a thousand little trapezoids We manufacture every one of its kinks and blips out of tiny triangles, tilted to lie in every plane that interests us.

What they call a wire frame? Vulgamott, in his former life as an architect, had worked with endless screen-based blueprints—pale Pei imitation monoliths exploded into more tiny CAD corbels than a person could shake a French curve at.

Wire frame. Skeleton. Whatever. Groups of graph primitives: triangles, polygons. Hidden-line removal creates the sense of three-space. Lots more verisimilitude. But tons slower. Tons harder to draw.

Adie cleared her throat. *Drawing shouldn't be a problem. I thought that's why we clueless Bohemians are on the payroll.*

Oh, not harder for you. I meant harder for the graphics boxes. For . . . Rembrandt and Claude and Hsieh Ho. Ten video channels, in real time. We're talking real rendering overhead. Every object that we want to paint is an entire community. A whole ecosystem of polygons for each light-face. The better you want it, the smaller your polygons have to get, until your complex object is nothing but vertices. Hundreds of thousands of vertices, smack up against what the hard-cores call your polygon budget.

Couldn't we just go out and shoot 360 degrees of film around some actual leaf?

Could. But you'd still want to translate the picture back into data points. And you'd have to do that by hand, or something like it.

Why? Adie asked. *Why turn a continuous image of the real thing back into jagged little chunks?*

Because, Spiegel began, running the logic through his own internal simulation, like sunlight through foliage. *Because we'll want to give your leaf real qualities. Behaviors. We'll want to run operations against it. To subject it to gravity, fire, wind. A photo of a leaf won't ooze when cut. We want a clone that will do everything the original does. Catch rain or shrivel up in heat. Turn gold in a cold snap.*

The Cavern would settle for nothing less. Every community of polygons needed its catalogue of affordances: pliant, pulpy, wet, burnable, breakable, taut . . . And that behavioral catalogue itself decided how the described object glinted in twilight, how it aged and altered, how it floated on the sea of wider rules all around it.

Every fully modeled object became a machine. And every change in an object's catalogue altered the way that machine ran. Leaves programmed the light that fell on them. And every scar of light that leaves accumulated along their way fed back into the living inventory. A branch in the air modeled the wind that waved it, and wind bent that bough through the arc of its own prediction. For there was no real difference, finally, between property and behavior, data and command.

How smart an image was — how much it embodied. Whole volumes of words could not contain the information locked up in one road map. The art and design people knew this instinctively, from a lifetime of looking. The heft and feel of a thing, its list of nicks and bruises, the deed of its actions and of all the actions upon it: in the long lens, these rays met at a single focus, the Maker's outline. But art knew these facts only by other names, other procedures, methods lost in translation . . .

Spiegel came clean. *There's another way we can make you a leaf. The oldest process going, even though we're still pretty new to it. We can build the leaf's description the way a real leaf gets built. We can grow it.*

Over the course of more makeshift sessions, he showed them how. He drew up genetic algorithms: fractal, recursive code that crept forward from out of its own embryo. He worried over their sapling, a RAM-cached Johnny Appleseed. He spread the best iterative fertilizer on the shaded texture until it flung itself outward into a living branch. His commands no longer called for products but processes. They ceased to stipulate the stipule. The leaf grew itself, from the self-organizing rules arising along its lengthening blade.

Physical law alone laid down this palisade layer. The push of petiole, the stomata's maw, the closest-cubic packing of chloroplast and cuticle and conducting tube: the whole serrated sprig sprung its surprise from out of hidden inevitabilities.

The ad hoc committee of artists and technicians tested their successive grafts in the Cavern greenhouse. The blackness that these graphics primitives floated in was not yet the air. The planes of the confining flower box did not yet compose a volume. The Cavern walls were not even empty. They were whatever came before empty. But in that flat void, just below the front screen's midline, a leaf hung twirling.

And there Klarpol and Loque stood, shoulder to shoulder in the simulator, where their sprig of laurel turned on the mute breeze. Adie stared at the spinning wreath while Sue navigated through a menu waterfall with a tilt of her head, selecting from commands with a blink of her laser-tracked eye.

Loque blinked twice, choosing "Brightness" from a menu labeled "Chroma Tuning." A beveled representation of a knob sprung into existence, out of nothing. It acted exactly like the knob it represented, except that it slid back and forth in its track simply as Loque shook her head.

She slid the knob all the way to the left. In a literal eye blink, the laurel went dark. Each wrinkle and vein deepened into shadow. Dusk swept across the face of the plant. With another head wag Sue swung the slider to its opposite pole, bathing the branch in the overhead glare of midday.

How's that for turning over a whole new leaf?

Crikey, Adie answered. *I can't take it. What do all the numbers mean? How much is minus 170? What's a plus 190?*

They're arbitrary. The scale runs from zero to 255.

Two hundred and fifty-five? You people are truly occult.

It's a binary thing, babe. Give me this one on faith.

Sue shook her fuchsia head and twitched her ruby-studded eyebrow, dragging the knobs through their paces. She called up sliders for contrast, saturation, and hue. The laurel wreath metamorphosed into supersaturated narcissi and hyacinths. It hardened to a turn-of-the-century black-and-white lithograph. It ignited in a lurid laundry soap commercial.

We can tweak each color channel separately. Or we can nudge around points on a histogram or an active compensation curve.

Adie looked on her colleague in awe. Loque's own aggressive Papagena plumage began to make sense. *That's OK. I trust you.*

Big mistake. Here. Watch this. From out of a menu labeled "Transforms" came a choice called "Vortex." Sue blinked, and the laurel sprig descended into a Cartesian maelstrom. It wrung itself out like a topologist's spent dishrag. And still it twirled in the mythic blackness.

Wait. God. What have you done? You've wrecked it. It looks horrible.

Easy, sweetie. Haven't you heard? What's done can always be undone.
With a single click, Sue returned the spinning branch to mint condition. *There you are. Unblemished. Untouched by human tinkering.*

The idea grazed Adie, like a pile of bricks falling off a scaffold and killing the pedestrian in front of her. She saw why the mind raced to convert to digital. Why it needed this place where ingenuity could always hit the Undo button.

Sue Loque warped and bulged and folded the innocent sprig until it was no longer fit to grace a wilted salad. Laurel twisted into oak into maple. Each derangement offered its own custom parameters, permutations too numerous to investigate.

Adie watched her expert pilot steer them into "Shadows and Edges." On the Cavern wall, the leaves fell away to a penciled outline. The mottled surface of a thousand greens vanished into mere contour flapping in the invented breeze. Surface reduced to a ghostly mold, a pipe-cleaner sculpture that Adie reached out and poked her fingers through.

This isn't right. I can't cope . . .

Hang on. It gets worse.

We're not meant to be able to do all this. It's not good for us.

Loque turned her attention to the archaic creature. She fiddled with the chains dangling from her studded skirt. *I don't get it. You've never used a computer in your work?*

Adie shot her head back, horrified.

All those little pastel magic princess thingies of yours?

Thanks, Sue. By hand. Every one. You remember the human hand, don't you?

Do you? Sue asked, and reached out. Adie, despite herself, stepped back. Sue laughed, and snorted again at the color she brought to the artist woman's cheeks. *You've never seen* Monday Night Football? *Saturday cartoons? This stuff is all over every prime-time fifteen-second commercial spot that—*

Another horrified head shake. *I don't own a TV.*

Well. Aren't we precious? Wait until the baddies at TeraSys learn who they've hired.

Adie regrouped. *What they don't know can't hurt them.*

Oh, they know everything, finally. And nothing hurts them.

Sue popped backward through the Undo catalogue, the history of their voyage here. She retrieved the original plant from its pipe-cleaner outline. The thousand greens returned from their brief banishment to transparency, now deepening, by contrast, their mimicry of the living.

OK, doll. Pull up your virtual La-Z-Boy and kick back. Are you ready for this?

I severely doubt it.

You want a minute?

I want a lifetime.

Sue tsked. *Chill out, girl scout. Here goes. Let's start with "Watercolor."*

She blinked the word, and the fact followed. The result did not resemble a watercolor of a laurel sprig. It was one, down to the fibers in the moistened idea of rag paper. Down to the simulated color-bleeding, the dribbled imperfections of a gummed-up camel-hair brush, although the brush that painted it never existed outside this software library.

Everything was perfect: the palette, the semitransparent matte, the fuzzy borders, the splotchy jade inks running into each other like broken yolks in a crooked skillet. All the kinks and cutaneous leaf landmarks still laced this revamped image. Only now they appeared as manhandled, hand-mangled parodies of the original. The leaf bobbed on its stalk in front of Adie, a copy of a copy, a debasement of the debasement of the Forms.

Help me, Adie whimpered, appalled and euphoric at once. *I'm drowning.*

No prob. Heading for dry land here, boss. What'll it be? Chalks? Colored pencil? Dry point? Conté? Here's something a little offbeat: stained glass. At a blink, the laurel fractured into the leaded lozenges of a free-floating lancet, hued in cool Chartres blue.

They played like girls stumbling upon a rolltop desk in an attic, all the pigeonholes intact. Oil and Quilt; Paper Scrap and Tapestry; Putty Knife, Aluminum Foil, Fresco.

Agitated Cave Painting? What in creation . . . ?

As in Lascaux. I named that one. That's one of mine.

Yours? Hang on a minute. You wrote . . . ?

Sure. What'd you think? You think I'm just some Turbo Pascal farm-team stringer?

Math does all this, Adie chanted. *All some kind of— The greatest paint-by-numbers kit in the universe.*

Princess, I'm ready to love you, and all that. But you gotta pull it together a little, or we'll never manage to drag you over the finish line.

You mean there's more?

Always. "More" is what we do. "More" is this outfit's end product.

Always another level down, always another branch led off from the branch where they stood, until the spreading tree grew to fill all the available arbor. Submenu Art Effects. Submenu Filters. Submenu Artist Styles. Pointillism. Seurat. Their grafted leaves speckled into something from the Grande Jatte. The imitation was uncanny—an exact running average, stained on the mottled leaf, of every dot that the dead painter ever applied to canvas.

Oh Jesus. I can't believe this. God help me.

Sue dragged her stunned apprentice through a pantheon of styles. They tried on painters like teens trying on jeans at a factory outlet. Giotto bent the green into chalky sapphire chunks. The Caravaggio leaf darkened to *tenebrismo*. Van der Weyden glistened, hard-edged and luminous. Rothko bled a whole woodland of greens out of one monotone block. Artists who'd never dreamed of painting a leaf now did so in a perfect parody of their leafless life's work.

Adie stood still in the Cavern, straddling rapture and despair.

Who made all these things?

What do you mean who made them? We just did. Didn't you just see us?

No. I mean, who made the routines. Who made . . . Rothko? Cara-vaggio?

Oh. Yeah. That was us too.

Us?

Us. Me, Acquerelli, Rajasundaran, Spiegel . . .

Spiegel? My Spiegel? Does every one of you know more about paint-ing than I know about computers?

Watch this, Sue commanded. As if Adie could help but watch. Sue blinked onward, narrow and accurate. *We can take a Rubens palette and put it on top of Poussin shrubbery. Using Mary Cassatt's brushstrokes.*

Don't. Please. You realize that what makes these people great is . . . ?

That you can't reduce them to a statistical average? Yeah, yeah, we've looked into all that. But still, Sue wheedled. *I bet you know who this is.*

Adie did, at a glance. And the one after that was even more obvious. A little aura began to glow, just behind the globe of her left eye. The harbinger of an out-of-this-world migraine that would prostrate her for the next ten hours.

Gauguin, she called out. *I need to see Gauguin.*

Why? Guilty favorite or something? Was he so hot with foliage?

Adie didn't explain. Her need had nothing to do with the man's technique. She needed to see the colors behind that grimly named panorama, its name as long as the painting itself: *Where Do We Come From? What Are We? Where Are We Going?*

They did Gauguin, blessedly not all that convincing. *I've seen better Gauguin imitations on cruise-line brochures.*

Sue brayed. *Tell me about it. We wrote this great filter. But we didn't know who in the hell it looked like.*

Marc, Adie declared. *Franz Marc.*

You're the expert. Sue pulled up a C shell and jiggled the label of the offending menu. Gauguin became Marc, even more easily than he had in real life.

You want to write a decent Gauguin? We can start with this one and monkey with the parameters.

You mean to tell me I can be anyone? That every conceivable style . . . ? That everyone's hand in the history of Western . . . ?

Princess. Chill. Whatever we can describe, we can reproduce.

They played out the remainder of their reserved time slot, until Sybil Stance's climate modeling group came and kicked them out. By the time Klarpol and Loque left the Cavern, their laurel had become the spitting image of that bouquet just behind the sofa in Rousseau's *Dream.* A bouquet that never existed, until they plucked it and placed it there.

7

The staff at school exudes a nervous optimism that no one will jinx by speaking. They give you the guided tour prepared for all new hires. They leave the school driver to orient you, although all parties tastefully avoid that verb.

"I take you anywhere, Mr. Martin. You tell me, I drive."

He brings you down a newly broadened thoroughfare. On all sides of your closed car, life returns to trade. You pass the financial district and the open-air suqs, once more breathing with people. The anti-Ottoman statues in Martyrs' Square seem almost crater-free, from a distance. You hook around the Corniche along the Riviera, avoiding the checkpoints.

Here and there, steel girders tear loose from the sides of blasted buildings, dragging along sprays of concrete veil. Balconies crumble off high-rises like so many dried wasp nests. Freshly scrubbed laundry hangs from those that remain, blinding white flags flapping in the Levant sun.

Here is the Paris of the East, the once-chic orchid of the eastern Med. You speed along the shredded Rue des Banques to a palm-lined plaza, down by the turquoise bay. Fifteen minutes after setting out, the chauffeur spreads his hands in the air, palms up, disarmed. You see? Things are calming down. Returning to livable.

"Where does that street lead? No, this one here."

"Ha. Don't worry, Mr. Martin. Very boring. Very nothing."

"Can we head down this way? I'd just like a quick peek."

"Later, maybe. *Inshallah.*" *God willing.* As if healing required hiding the wounds.

No matter; you see it already. The thing your friends back home saw, even before you left. The thing you've half wished away, half sought out. Just behind the ivory facing, just beneath the glinting amethyst, this world is still shelling itself down to rubble.

You can't help but hear it, rumbling off in the direction of the Metn foothills. A shell barrels overhead, close enough to break your guide's composure. This war is not over. This war will never end. Yet this rumble is no more than cartoon thunder. It growls like linen scraped over a plywood drum. The bursts come no closer to hurting you than scoreboard fireworks. They detonate impotently, softer than the explosions of your recent American bug-out.

In fact, living on a powder keg has much to recommend it, providing one's driver knows a safe way back to the impregnable compound. A city's self-inflicted scars offer the prospect of unlimited further diversions.

The following week treats you to your first real teeth-rattling blast. The panic passes, leaving you more alive than you've felt in months. An artillery plume rises on the horizon—an old movie's Indian smoke signals. Your life is not yet over, whatever the last two years have insisted. Thirty-three is still young. The future remains your dominant tense. You're alive, unhit. Anything can still happen.

Simply being here proves that. You couldn't have scripted such a trip. Six years in Chicago, explaining your inexplicable country to Japanese businessmen, riding the emotional Tilt-a-Whirl with a miserable woman, keeping body and soul together on a largely ceremonial salary. Now living like a sultan, on hazard pay, in a place even more desperate than that woman.

There is a harsh humor to it: nailing the job interview because of your Muslim mother. Because you don't currently drink, no matter the historical reason. Because they mistake you for one who understands the Faithful. Because tenacious Lebanese need the same English your Japanese businessmen did.

You like them, these violence-inured twenty-year-olds raised along the Green Line's furrow. They possess an intensity you've never seen in any classroom. Pitching one's tent under the mortar's arc does wonders for a student's motivation.

"Why do you want to improve your English?" you ask them, on the first day of your new tenure. The diagnostic icebreaker, cheap but to the point.

It helps with trade, Phoenicia's descendants inform you. It's the world's second tongue, say the refugees of Sidon and Tyre.

A smiling, bearded Nawaf in the front of the room summarizes. "America bosses the world around in English. We need English, just to tell America to go to hell."

The whole class laughs. When learning another language, comprehension always outstrips production. It's true, the class agrees. Americans speak nothing and own everything. The world needs to learn English, just to talk back to its owner.

Your very existence astonishes them. "How can an American have your first name?"

"How can you let yourself be coming from such a place?"

The ones you like best explain the delusions you've been living under. "Black people in your country are killed like sheep here for the end of Ramadan."

"Americans pay forty million dollars to one man for putting a ball in a ring. Instead they could buy hamburgers for forty million starving people."

They offer these earnest indictments of Sodom for your own good. But greater forces attract them to this evil. Their interest reveals itself in dribs and drabs over your first two weeks. "This Rocky, sir? You think he fights so good? He doesn't last five minutes against my cousin with mujahideen."

"This Terminator? He's not so great. Take away the big gun . . ."

"The Terminator is Austrian," you tell them. "He's not our fault."

"Mr. Martin? What means this? 'I am leaving the material world, and I am immaterial girl'?"

"We'll work on that one next term," you promise.

Ardent children of civil war still bathed in first innocence, they seem strangely unhardened, even by the odds against survival. They might sit basking in the afternoon, out by the marina under the St. George, if that neighborhood still existed. But they stay on, by choice or compulsion, after a million of their countrymen have thought better and bailed. Each of them is too long trained by collapse to continue hoping, yet too angry to give it up. All of them are hungry to learn the true size of the world beyond this city: a world of glossy fictions, stable, rich, progressing, theirs to glimpse only through the shadow boxes of bootlegged videotape.

You are their model, their messenger from the outside world. Your job: to chat them up for hours at a shot, training them to survive the force of their imaginations. You work to hold them to the rules of polite conversation, in a city trying to believe again in the existence of rules. It is, by any measure, the perfect job description—the ticket you've been trying to write yourself for years. A golden existence. All that's missing is someone a little brave, someone just a little kind to share it with.

"Tell me how you got here," you assign them, early on. The topic provides a high personal interest. Good practice with the tricky past tense. And it's easy to answer without straying too far outside core vocabulary.

"How did *you* got here, Mr. Martin?" Nawaf baits you.

The whole class becomes a sea of colluding head bobs. "Yes. Yes. We all want to know."

"Nothing to tell," you tell them. "I came here to make sure that your subjects and verbs all agree with each other."

"What job have you done before being our teacher?" Nawaf asks.

"What did I do before coming here to teach?"

"Yeah. You said it."

"A lot of things. Most recently, I trained Asian businessmen to survive Chicago."

The sly bastard persists. "Why did you change your jobs?"

"Now why in the world would that interest you?"

"It's very interesting, Mr. Martin," the very interesting Zarai chips in.

"Well, for a lot of reasons. But we're not going to get into that."

"It's a secret?" Nawaf taunts.

"That's right. Yes. It's a secret."

"Top secret?" Zarai smiles at you from beneath her head wrapping. You smile back at her. "Tip-top secret."

They say that you know more about this place on the day you first touch your foot to it than you will ever know about it again. And they're right. Each day that passes leaves you more confused about this stew, let alone the recipe that produced it. You understand Shiite versus Sunni, Maronite versus Orthodox, Druze, Palestinian, Phalangist,

AMAL, the radical Party of God and their fanatical cell the Holy Warriors. But the fourteen other religions and splinter factions plunge you into the same despair that your students feel when confronting irregular English verbs.

This al-Jumhuriyah al-Lubnaniyah: even the name is a maze. The country's politics, like some unmappable Grand Bazaar out of Ali Baba, cannot be survived except by chance. Here civilization's ground rules disperse into the mists of fantasy. Standing agreements, tenuous at best, collapse back into the law of armed camps, each local militia staking out a few shelled blocks. No one is allowed to cross from zone to zone, not even the Red Crescent. Your students scrape by in a decaying landscape, one of those postapocalypse teen movies that so intrigue them.

But for all that, the streets still seem safer than Chicago's. Tomorrow feels more affirmed here, this city's pulse more surrendered to hope and devotion.

You learn a few words: *Na'am, shukran, merhadh, khubuz.* Yes, no, thank you, bathroom, bread. You begin to fantasize about meeting a woman, perhaps even a woman in head covering. About taking a crash course in the rules of her grammar.

Then the real woman calls you. Dead on schedule. Just as one of you recovers some semblance of health, some solidifying core of self-esteem, the other one calls to crash it. At least now, the two-dollar-a-minute taxi meter and the audible satellite lag protect you from extended conversation.

Or they would, if she weren't wild. Cost means nothing to her. Her words come through the phone like a violent cough. "Taimur. Tai. Thank God you're alive. You have to come back. Tonight. Now."

Too pathetic, even for retaliation. You can't even rouse yourself to decent brutality.

"I don't *think* so," you singsong into the receiver.

"I skipped my period."

You recover before the satellite link can click. "You skip every other month, Gwen. You're a high-strung, finger-pointing, street-brawling drama queen who never menstruates in the middle of a fight. Which is pretty much all the time."

Too many adjectives, and you've lost another round. Lost her. Lost yourself. Lost the person you were trying to become by coming here, one who refuses to return knee-jerk hurt for hurt.

She starts to sob, but softly, horribly. You hear her give up on the hope of consolation. And that, where nothing else could, makes you want to console her. Succor, once more, becomes your secret sickness. Your awful, tip-top secret.

"Gwen. Don't start. We can't do this again. We both promised."

"I need you, Tai. I can't do this by myself."

"Cut the theater, Gwen. You're fine. Give it another couple of weeks."

"I've given it *eight*."

It blossoms in you again, in the space of a second. Full-blown, the old, loving parasite you carry around inside, awaiting its chance to graze. A pillar of purity rises in your chest, so righteous it can't even be called anger. "Don't you think you ought to call the father, then?"

"You, Taimur. *You*. Don't you remember? Our long goodbye?" The weekend window when she seemed almost happy, knowing you were already gone. "Nobody before. Nobody since . . ."

The words are whiplash. And yet: they must be bluff. Florid, desperate, sadistic, even by the standards that the two of you have perfected.

"Gwen. As far as I remember from high-school biology, sperm must actually meet egg in order to—"

"Oh fuck. Oh fuck. I knew we shouldn't have . . . I told you that we shouldn't . . ."

"What you said was 'Sex with your ex is asking for trouble.' In a soft, slinky voice, if I remember correctly."

She starts shrieking, the performance over-the-top, incredible. "Come home, Tai. I can be better. You can."

The accusation maddens you. You: *better*. You, who she always punished, just for being you.

"I need you. I can't do this. Come home. Now."

The *now* is hideous; it gives the game away. You don't bother to tell her: you are home. Or as close as you're going to get, for the foreseeable future. You place the still-pleading stream of hysteria back into the cradle. And you don't pick up on the ringing phone again, for several days.

You leave the compound sometimes, between classes, for fried fava beans or a breath of air. A non-cigarette break. Escape from Butt Central. Staff doesn't like it, but no one can stay cooped up forever. You keep close, always doubling back after a few minutes.

Today, a knot of men a little younger than you mill around on the pavement outside school, examining a flat tire. Someone approaches for help. You walk toward him and he shows you something. And the something is metal, and a gun. And then he is not. Not asking for help.

"Please enter the car. Fast, fast."

Three of them persuade you of the idea. They're all shouting quietly, a Chinese fire drill. An improvised skit of confusion. One ties your hands behind you. Another shoves your head down to clear the car roof, just like in the cop shows. Too fast even for fear. A crazy mistake that'll have to wait to be straightened out. Wait until they remove the greasy rag they tie around your face. Wait until they settle down.

The engine starts. The car lurches forward. *There is no flat*, you realize, your thoughts even stupider than this crisis. The one sitting next to you pushes your head to the floor.

On your way down, he presses close to your ear. "Don't worry. Don't worry. This is just political." The comic diction comforts you. These men are amateurs.

On the floor of a dark car. Someone's foot rests on your temple, just for the thrill of disgracing you. They drive at least an hour. Maybe two. Time enough to catch up with your own pulse rate, with what's happening to you, your fatal stupidity. You give in to the heat of the floorboard, to the nail of the shoe on your skull, the sponge bath of terror. You start to quake. The rope around your wrists keeps your arms from banging together.

The car traces an enormous circle. They are playing some insane charade of distance, doubling back, trying to throw you off. You want to call out to them to get where they're going. You're long since lost. But every sound from you elicits a hiss and a heel crush.

They stop. They bang you out of the car. You cock back your head, to see beneath the oily blindfold. Someone chops you hard in the neck. They drag you, doubled over, inside.

They take your keys and the trinkets from your pockets. Your Swiss Army knife causes a buzz out of proportion to its two pinkie blades and nail clippers.

They confiscate your wallet, pulling it apart piece by piece. They demand an account of every scrap and wrapper. Your expired organ donor declarations. Your eyeglass prescription. Your student ID, ten years obsolete. Bank cards that you couldn't use anywhere within a thousand kilometers.

"What is this?" a venomous tenor shouts at you, sticking each enigma under your blindfold for inspection. "What these numbers mean?"

"Those . . . are phone numbers. Phone numbers of friends in America."

"Don't lie!" Another pair of hands slams you from the rear, more for the drama than for the pain.

"Codes," a neutral voice declares.

"Not codes. Phone numbers. Go ahead. Call them. Tell them I say hello."

The voice laughs without humor.

Another bodiless voice draws close to your face. "You American? Why you look like a Arab?"

You curse your failure to memorize the fourteen splinter groups. Who are these people? What do they need to hear? Answer wrong and you will never answer again. They'll kill you for your political ignorance.

"Why?" your interrogator shouts. "What kind of name is Taimur Martin?"

The question you grew up with. Your gut snaps tight. You roll the die and answer: "I am . . . half Iranian."

Rapid bursts of translation pass among several people. They argue, climbing up the pitches of virulent Arabic. You've never realized how much you need your eyes to converse.

"Where your passport?"

"I . . . didn't think I'd need it when I stepped out of the compound."

For a moment they soften, pat you on the shoulder. They shuffle around in the invisible room, collecting your things. They'll put you back in the car, return you to the school, drop you off, and fade back into whatever lunatic cabal of posturing boys put them up to this stunt.

Instead, they strip and search you. The hunt grows violent. Your body starts to convulse again. You will shit all over the floor. You will die here, and you won't even know why.

"Please, not the necklace," you beg. "That's a present. A gift from a—"

"Don't call us thieves." Spit sprays your cheek. And the necklace, Gwen's good-luck charm, disappears into the political.

They want names. Names of who? It's absurd. They can spot an American from ten kilometers, if they only look. What would they do with names? Saunter up and down the street, calling them out? Still they ask, but listlessly, a dry read-through of the barest minimum script.

"Tell us what we ask. We know how to use . . . electricity. You understand?"

You understand. You fake a weak composure. You tell them you'll do whatever they ask.

"What are you doing here?"

You cannot stop yourself. "You kidnapped me."

Something cracks you just above the left ear. Lights explode against the curtain of your blindfold. You bite into your tongue. You vomit, stinging and dry, in your mouth.

"What are you doing here?"

"I am a teacher." Slower and slower. "I give conversational English lessons at—"

"You are stupid. Big shit. You are American spy. You are CIA."

The first objecting syllable out of your throat whips your interrogator into fury. "You lie. You *lie*! We know why you come here. We know about your big secret."

Connections light you up at last. It comes back to you, the vanished lesson from your teacher-training days in Des Moines. The first rule of any classroom: Never resort to irony.

8

The first generation of imaginary landscapes began pouring from the simulator just as Adie settled in to her own new one. She took only a few weeks to see just what chambers the Cavern meant to mimic. She stood inside the room-sized box, watching a stream of images flicker across those living walls, the last, baffled Neanderthal standing by as *Homo sapiens* launched its breakout.

With her olive pullovers and her four-foot hank of hair falling like the stern line of a sponge boat in a braid down her back, she drew mixed reviews from the doughnut-packing hackers. Rajan Rajasundaran and the signal-processing team found her a mild abrasion. Ronan O'Reilly, the econometric modeler, plied her with polite indifference. Jackdaw Acquerelli responded to her like a spooled background process. Sue Loque slammed her New York provincialism at every opportunity. Spider Lim lavished her with almost ethnographic attention. Adie, for her part, clung to Stevie Spiegel. But the scent of an old friend only made the air of this new planet harder to breathe.

Jonathan Freese, the RL director, dragged her down the mountainside to a café. Over a healthy shot of triple mocha, he launched into a rambling monologue on Parmigianino, Tiepolo, and the baptistery doors at Pisa. Like asking your first black neighbor over to listen to your Duke Ellington.

A marvelous thing, the greatest pleasure we're allowed. Art.

It's OK, she assured him. *I'm not really all that into it.*

Freese, pushing fifty, was a good twenty years older than the lab's median age. He mimicked the general Birkenstock look. Yet he looked a shade less anarchical than the programmers who worked for him, crisper, more pigmented, as if he still got outside now and then.

Would you care for some bran muffin? he asked. *Good source of roughage, you know.*

Adie declined, sticking to her herbal tea and arrowroot biscuit. *Jonathan, I need to ask you something.*

Name it.

He might have sold encyclopedias, or utopian communities, or patriotic evidence to Senate investigations.

I'm not sure that I'm doing what's expected of me, she told him. *I want you to get your money's worth.*

Well, first of all, think of your first year as a learning fellowship. It's not really a question of our getting our money's worth. It's more of a question of you getting your time's worth.

Jonathan, be straight with me.

I am straight. The higher-ups are all impressed by your work.

What work? I haven't done any work.

Your portfolio. We just want to put you together with a bunch of other talented people and see what synergies come out.

What exactly is a synergy?

He laughed, without losing track of a single bran crumb. *That's what everyone's trying to figure out.*

She felt the force of this man's competence. He exuded an aura of the true administrator, the square-jawed command of those who understand how human organizations work. She saw why people of both sexes tried so hard to please him.

The Realization Lab is just a research facility at present. TeraSys doesn't have to get its money's worth out of us yet. Not directly, anyway. The Cavern is an experiment in assembling several advanced technologies. We simply want to see what the world is going to look like a few years down the rail cut.

But how do they pay for us?

Freese swallowed a careful packet of bran muffin and then laughed again. Something in that laugh nagged at Adie: the mirth of a man who belonged to a chain of being much larger than he was.

TeraSys has had a bit of a tax liability in the last few years, in case you've been living in Giverny and missed the annual reports. It can do no wrong, as far as windfall revenues go. R-and-D costs are the best write-offs available, and even those only make the problem worse, in the long run.

What exactly is this so-called research supposed to feel like?

Like any kind of exploration, I imagine. Like working up an altarpiece.

I can't possibly be contributing anything useful to this group. Any one of you knows more about art than I do. You have people who can make—

None of us knows what to do with this stuff. We need your hand. Your eye.

But I'm just thrashing around.

That's what learning is.

I need something specific to do.

Do? Do what you always do.

That would be making pretty designs to commercial specification.

The last of his muffin and mocha disappeared cleanly down the air lock. He smiled, the pan-and-scan smile of the career diplomat.

Look: Adie. I'll give you exact specifications. Make us the most beautiful Cavern room you can think of. Learn things. Enjoy yourself.

Learn. Enjoy. Make something beautiful. The man came from another galaxy. One that Adie had abandoned when she gave up art. One that art had abandoned around the turn of the century. Freese cupped her elbow in a friendly send-off. He stood to go, already striding back to his own corner of the RL in his seven-league, open-toed sandals.

She tried to get the real story from Jackdaw. The gentle Martian boy was as far from Freese's clipped competence as she could imagine. Between the two males, she hoped for something like a 3-D explanation. She found Acquerelli in his cubicle, in a network chat room. He scurried off-line, embarrassed, as she entered.

Jackdaw. Explain something to me. What are we doing here?

Doing? Eager, earnest, and utterly perplexed.

What's our business? What exactly is the end product?

He nodded his head encouragingly. Question: check. Parsed: check. Answer match: check. *Virtual Environments,* he said, still nodding.

No, I mean, how do you sell what we create? Who's buying? Why are we making these rooms?

Jackdaw thought a minute, flicking his eyes up and away, scanning some distant video scratch buffer. *Well. I guess, mostly what we do is demo?*

Good. Demo. Go on. Demos for . . . ?

For the Nametags.

She'd seen them. Groups of eager techies, under escort, touring the premises at odd hours. Earnest guys wearing TeraSys lapel pins who ducked and flinched in the Cavern during Jackdaw and Spiegel's simulated roller-coaster rides. No one had quite laid it out for her in so many words. The Realization Lab was a ruinously expensive classroom, a mental wind chamber. She had no problem with the arrangement, once she understood it. The knowledge sprung her. Freed her to labor over Rousseau's trousseau, to prune and water and fertilize her laurel sprig, to turn it into a teeming jungle.

Like an evening game of statue-maker drawing children out of the neighborhood's lit houses, Adie's creeping philodendrons brought all manner of players out of the redwood woodwork. They came by twilight to her cubicle, nocturnal creatures peeking through the undergrowth like Rousseau's monkeys and lions.

Each contributed some custom function or subroutine. Loque helped with the surface rendering. Even after she went home for the night, Sue would go on answering Adie's 911 calls. She steered the new girl around blind, over the phone, like ground control giving the stewardess a crash course in flying after the cockpit gets sideswiped by a Cessna. *Hon, hon. Don't panic. We got you. Now, how are you holding the mouse? Which way is the little wire tail pointing?*

Loque trained her in the high-level visual environment, its friendly paintbox metaphor protecting Adie from the intricacies underneath. Adie scorned the scanner, painting by hand into a slate that sensed the weight and bruise of her fingers' every movement. Charcoal, chalk, spray can: the paintbox mimicked every natural tool she'd ever used, as well as several unnatural ones. She could smudge and unsmudge, spatter, crisp, paint with potato or foil, even invent brushes of any shape or property, magic brushes that lifted or plumped or selectively edged some narrow band of crimson three shades toward gold, brushes that watermarked or cloned or cross-faded while still managing to undo the last dozen things that any other brush had done.

This was the way the angels in heaven painted: less with their hands than with their mind. She had never imagined that life would grant her such license. Some tasks were clumsier or more infuriating to perform than their oil or acrylic counterparts. Others were no less than miracles, closed loops between brain, eye, fingers, and screen that revolved within themselves, cosmic elaborations of light, visual excursions deep and dimensionless, color-chord progressions that admitted no beginning or end. But within two months, the miracles naturalized, and Adie habituated to them as she once had to her first set of colored pencils.

Spiegel taught her how to assemble a few shoots into massed, circumnavigable corsages. A single plant, by itself, was still just an image. But two plants next to each other in space, linked by data's rhizome, became the semblance of a live-in bower. From her workstation screen, Adie's hand-painted bouquets went out to an object script packager for transplanting to the virtual garden beds. All she lacked was dirt under her fingernails.

Vulgamott came by just to fuss, New Yorker to New Yorker. *Make sure you're leaving enough space between those plants. It's not the foliage that makes this painting so brilliant. It's all the space he somehow manages to cram in between.*

Don't worry, Michael. I'm good with air. Air is easy. There'll be plenty of air in the finished weed patch.

Once, she could have scrutinized the original *Dream*, whenever she wished. That canvas hung in her own personal attic, at MoMA, one flight up from the cafeteria where she had bussed tables and peddled coffee. Once she had lived almost close enough to hear the spillover from that flute player's tune. Now she had to scour around a little toy town of a port city for the best reproductions of the image she could lay her hands on, testing the defects of each against the print that still hung in her mind's clearing.

Most nights between ten-thirty and quarter to eleven, Karl Ebesen checked in to say good night. Or so Adie assumed, for on these visits, the senior visual designer mostly said nothing at all. He'd show up in a streaked trench coat, a prop out of some Mitchum film noir, his ratty portfolio of the day's digitizing under one arm. He'd heave himself into the corner across from Adie's workstation, capitulating to the gravity he'd fended off for five decades, wheezing through his mouth and scowling.

She'd ask him about the architectural fly-through that he and Vulgamott were assembling. Ebesen would answer snidely or just wave her off. Over the course of several evenings, Adie settled into returning the man's morose silences with the mirror of her own. The idiom had for Adie a comforting familiarity. The silent conversation of her childhood. The absence she was raised in.

Ebesen would sit mute for anywhere from five minutes to an hour, then shuffle off like one of those benign street people down by the ferry docks who accept all offered change without once asking for any. She came to think of Ebesen as her guardian bagman. Any sign of human drama caused him to slink off to whatever Presbyterian soup kitchen had coughed him up. When Karl was around, she could talk out loud without worrying about anyone answering. Drawing into a digital graphics tablet seemed less displacing, in the shadow of this odder interface.

Then one night, the derelict talked back. She was chattering, just making noise while her hand moved around the bits on her electronic palette, a little verbal dribbling, spinning through sentences the way some people spin through radio stations on the car dial, with no real intention of landing anywhere.

All these creatures, she said. *All these animal eyes. What are they all looking at? An elephant, a snake, two birds, two lions, two monkeys . . .*

How many monkeys? Ebesen sneered. A barking seal after the emergency tracheotomy.

Adie whipped around from her workstation. She stared at the man in the corner, the one she'd stopped looking up at half a dozen visits ago. He had his head down, circling ads in an old travel magazine with a red felt pen. She looked back at the twenty prints of the painting taped over every free corner of her cubicle. And saw the third monkey.

Bit by bit, bouquet by bouquet, she reconstructed the painted *Dream*. Every six days, she took her week's handiwork into the Cavern for a road test. Spiegel found her there one night, passing dismayed through a stand of Rousseau's head-high, alien anemones.

Stevie, help me. Nothing has depth. All the pieces are so planar. I want real furniture in my dollhouse. Not just cardboard flats.

He crafted her a solid lozenge, a blank batten upon which to paste her petals' surfaces. For each new blossom, now, she invented those sides hinted at but hidden in the plane of paint. Front folded seamlessly to back, and the flower stayed bulky from all points of the compass. Not much—and yet, dimension. All the axes that we're given to live in.

The vessel took form, piece by piece, each separate square of hull arc-welded onto the mold of the master scaffolding. Klarpol became a tourist in her own Eden. Her wand and glasses did more than bring the jungle to her eyes. They spied back on her, gathering the data streams released by her every glance. The lenses that tracked her head also logged her glances into saved tables, files of code detailing the angles her eyes subtended, the time she spent focusing on each leaf, the errors her glimpse made in selecting its target, the tries she took in moving through these blooms that, even here, in her infant clumsiness, had already commenced using her . . .

9

She would come from the Cavern recharged, in search of new techniques. Desire forced her out into the halls of the RL, that commonwealth beyond her cubicle, looking for new repertoire. In such a state, on a rainy spring evening, she found Spider Lim slumped over his workstation in a baby coma. He sat still, intent upon the screen, but dazed. Frothy, arrested, viscid, like someone in the first stages of hypoglycemia. His fingers no longer clacked at their keys. He'd gone off elsewhere, lost down the successive iterations of a nested loop.

Adie called him. Spider just sat there, holding the keyboard, subaudibly humming some catchy MIDI pop-synth arrangement. She bolted down the hall for the nearest live body. She found Steve and Rajan Rajasundaran, deep in conversation.

It's Spider, she said. *There's something wrong with him.*

The two men exchanged looks. Spiegel patted her. *It's OK, Ade. Sometimes when he's working at a screen? He forgets to breathe.*

The three trotted back to Spider's cubicle. Stevie and Raj stood above Lim and rubbed him gently. Their colleague sat numbed, a Seattle grunger dozing off for the afternoon in the entrance to the Space Needle.

Spider! Raj called. *Snap out of it, man. You're system-crashing again.*

Breathe in, Spider, Spiegel encouraged. *Come on, buddy.*

I'm breathing, Spider called back, irritated at the interruption. Still a little out of it, some tangled knot tying up his processor cycles. Some puzzle of fluid flow, of air convection wrapping its turbulence around a sculpted wing. Adie touched his forearm. His temperature had dropped, like a lizard caught in a shadow.

Spiegel harassed the returning patient. *What's with you, Spidey? This is some kind of meditation effect, isn't it? Something to do with your Qi?*

Spiegel, man, Rajasundaran warned. *Don't mess with the inscrutable East. Don't even try to scrute it. There are mysteries that the people of bologna and yellow mustard are not given to understand.*

I'm from Korea, Spider objected. He'd lived long enough in the States to speak with a slight Okie drawl. *We don't do Qi in Korea. That's a California thing.*

Keep breathing, Spidey. Spiegel urged him. *We need your expertise.*

Raj seconded. *Yes, man. Keep on working for Chairman Gatt. To get rich is glorious.*

Korea, Spider said. *Korea, you stupid Tamil.*

Asian transplants had no corner on weird physiological responses to the man-machine interface. All of this virtual country's immigrants tended to maze out on silicon's sub-micron boulevards, tranced over their keyboards, their carpal tunnels hollowed out for maximum brain-finger throughput. But Spider's body tracked the machine especially steeply. He could generally catch himself overheating, hyperventilating as he tested an overclocked processor or a heat-stressed IC. But a hang could snag him, pull him down under consciousness's event horizon.

We're going to find you crashed like that someday, Spiegel scolded. *Completely stalled. Like a token ring that's lost track of its packets. Like some student infinite do-loop. And we won't be able to spring your processes.*

Rajasundaran wagged his digit. *Not a team player. Does not work and play well with others.*

That's not true, Adie demurred. *He's more sociable than most of you crazies.*

Oh, right, Raj said. *As if you starving artistes get a clean bill of health in the social interaction department?*

Spider waved his hands for peace. *No biggie, guys. My Boolean-blood barrier is just a little weak.*

And that was the only possible diagnosis. Lim was like one of those sing-along car drivers whose speed halved whenever the tune on the radio slowed from boogie to ballad. He'd never done well in the Cavern for extended periods. Simulator sickness got him every time. When the simulation plunged from great heights, his ears popped. A simple projection of the winter constellations against the ceiling gave him hypothermia. He couldn't work on a circuit without simulating it in his own circulatory system. The same data traversing the chutes of gated arrays invariably ported over to that other platform, to bang around inside the test bed of Spider's cells.

The health scare subsiding, Adie exploited the gathered experts. *My jungle is a ghost. I pass right through every plant in it. I should bounce off the rubber trees. At least rustle the ivy.*

Spiegel nodded. *You need collision detection.*

Yeah, give me one of those. Are they expensive?

Collision had already cost the team a tidy sum of man-months. It wasn't enough for a garden-variety mushroom sprouting in the Cavern simply to look like one. Even a toadstool needed heft and weight and resistance. A simulated object had to bend or droop or bruise or any of several dozen other verbs that real things did when bumped up against in the grotto that the Cavern stood for.

Multiple coders had already implemented a reasonable fraction of collision's class library. They wrote out methods for a whole host of impacts. Each calculated aftermath got its own mongrel differential equations, trajectories mocking the ones that nature invented. Various variables toted up mass and speed and English, calculating the thresholds between bounce and break, between shatter and slide and spin.

Spiegel showed her how, from out of this catalogue of cases, to assign verbs for each set of possible contacts: hand on vine, vine on bird,

bird on monkey, monkey on tree limb, limb on hand. In the course of several weeks, Adie watched as software turned her jungle into a gym. The forest became a vast calculator, a gnarled orchard of countless parallel computations. Over the run of days, any pair of objects learned to calculate what to do when they met one another in space.

But calculation cost; the display code carried so much overhead that it ran too slowly to keep up with its events. Adie released a gingko ball in the air above her canopy. The seedy mace slid down the slope of its infinitesimal accelerations until it struck some surprise tendril or trunk. Contact produced a pop, then seized up. That wall's graphics buffer promptly dropped several frames while its reality engine did the myriad integrals needed to determine the respective obligations of striker and struck. The gingko pod hung in space, waiting for math to decide its fate.

Such a hiccup was not acceptable. Any jerk in the animation and the game was up. Material reality's supreme Cray never dropped frames. That's how you knew you were *in* the real world: all the flicker-free, smooth scrolling. The Cavern's goal—believability through total immersion—could not survive an image that sputtered.

Spiegel and Jackdaw worked up provisional fixes, clever step-saving approximations that shortcut the Cavern's calculations, cheats that would cover until Spider and the hardware boys could bring in more firepower. Continuous collision detection arrived after two triple-shift weeks during which, when Spider slept at all, he slept on a bed of fanfold paper spread two inches deep on the stockroom floor. He woke on that pallet one morning, the socket of his right eye richly black-and-blue, three shades deeper than his sepia skin.

O'Reilly, the Ulster economist, took one look and whistled. *Jays. Some shiner. I wasn't aware that you were currently involved with anyone.*

The glossy maroon smear entranced Sue Loque. *Ooh. That's a beauty. Can I touch it?*

No, of course you can't touch it. You're perverts. All of you.

Christ on a crutch, Spider, Sue said. *Don't be such a prude.*

Spider laughed, one of those single-syllable, apologize-for-existing laughs, still intact from his first few years of Korean existence.

When Adie saw the black eye, she lost it. *Oh no. God help us. Look what I've done.*

You? You haven't done anything. I've been sleeping on a hard mattress, is all.

You don't remember? Yesterday? Testing the back layers?

What are you talking about?

You don't remember running into that tree branch? She'd seen him wince.

Oh no, no, no. Don't be crazy.

A sympathetic fall in blood sugar lay within the realm of material possibility. But a virtual bruise . . . It fell too far outside his world model. Yet no real day's accident explained the shiner any better.

Maybe this Klarpol woman is right, Raj said. He milked the lilt of Hindu eschatology. *We've seen such things produced from out of your brain before.*

Spiegel piled on. *Why not? Impale the brain with something believable, and belief will leave its record in the skin.*

That's nuts, Lim insisted. *A black eye needs a real impact.*

Spoken with a true hardware bias.

I have to agree with Spiegel, Rajasundaran said. *True, the switches execute the code. But also true, the code still sets the switches.*

Loque fingered the wound, over Lim's objections. *You boys are making some real progress in veridicality.*

Spider Lim, Spiegel said. *The man who became his own collision algorithm.*

At these words, Lim's whole body blushed so deeply that his bruise vanished into the general background rose.

In the privacy of their own workstations, each player in the game mounted a run at that same threshold of belief. The heart of the Realization Lab beat to a single paradox. It hoped to mechanize any brute incident that existence offered. But imitation was itself just the first step in a greater program, the final escape from brute matter: the room that would replace the one where existence lay bound.

Spider's bruise prompted the Rousseau Room's first working demo. Artists and engineers alike turned out to see just how palpable Adie's mythic branches—the product of collective fiat—had in fact become. Color met number, fact chased invention through the shadows of an undergrowth past evolution's power to imagine.

All was yet still. The python hung slung in mid-slither. The birds held open their beaks to caw. The elephant readied to trumpet and the monkeys to scamper. The lions cocked their quizzical heads at this mass tourist intrusion. And spreading vegetation bent the white, oil-paint moonlight into as many greens as the viewing mind could grasp.

Spiegel presided, showing off the luscious prototype, their object lesson in objects. He took all parties on a walking tour as deep into the jungle as the jungle went. He pointed out the details of stalk and stamen, all spelled out in structured data—the crazy Frenchman's mother-in-law tongues turned tropical Egyptian. He popped the hood and revealed the diorama's underpinning gears. He laid out every effect they'd managed to produce. But he did not know what he was looking at until Adie told him.

We did this, the woman said. She clapped her hands together in what only Karl Ebesen recognized as a proof-perfect knockoff of St. Theresa's ecstasy. *We made this! It's so beautiful.*

The word lay beyond the rest of the team's list of formal descriptors. It seemed to have a real referent; the new woman apparently meant something when she used it. Beauty might even have had some physical reality, some selective advantage conferred over the last billion or so years. But what formal rules the quality adhered to, what behaviors it meant to elicit, not even Spider Lim's body could begin to guess.

Time for the people, Adie declared. *Are we ready to start populating this place?*

They went back to the color reproductions. They took the measure of the rain forest's two inhabitants: black and white, vertical and horizontal, male and female, player and listener . . . And the vegetative kingdom surrendered to its human sovereigns, those shapes that gave first green its order.

Then Spider's body began to specify, began to execute that undecidable function. However arbitrary, however recently contrived, beauty turned real inside him. It grew legible, a script as unambiguously phonetic as Korea's upstart Hangul.

For the woman began to invade him. Her inroads grew so wide they even upset his sleep. Not the living woman: he left Adie to the others, to the bit jockeys who ranked her overgenerously in the local hierarchy of desire purely on the basis of novelty. He left her to Spiegel, who saw in her some ghost of a lost shared life. He left the real woman to those who knew how to interact with such things. And he took up nightly with the imaginary one, the woman on the crested divan. The one who organized this profligate Eden and named it.

He watched art and science conspire to float that full, stuffed body among the foliage. Out of the electronic paintbox, she emerged, rising from the wedge of face, the coils draping her neck, extending through the crescent of almond opening just above her knees and down to those curious, stub toes.

Spider donned a pair of glasses and walked clear around the couch where she lay. She remained remote, aloof, still, exuding the hint of something he could not figure. *We did this. It's beautiful.*

Their first successful leaf, twirling in the Cavern darkness, had led to this—this pale, lentil body turning in his mind's dark. This scapular profile, these tow-line braids. Her hips fell somewhere on the limaçon of Pascal. The squares of her breasts' abscissas and ordinates summed to an integer. This was the math of women, a field he'd given up studying, female equations whose complexities had long ago surpassed his ability to differentiate. The flawless chestnut manikins, their grade-school desks fastened to the front of his, whose strands of brunette hair he'd once tried to number. The white film enigmas, beckoning to him to join them behind the projection screen. The cycles of magazine sirens, that March *Cosmopolitan* cover from his second year at Stanford, the anemic, skewed-thigh, dazed-eye vision he'd preserved for ongoing reference, the visible deed to this land of American license he'd somehow landed in.

He rebuilt her in detail at nights, on his drive home down the mountain, through the newly air-dropped communities where no one could tell him apart from any of the thousands of other thirty-year-old transpacific immigrant virgins with pronounced epicanthic folds wandering around the Greater Seattle area. Her crude constructedness tapped some secret in him, a figure beckoning at the entrance to the impenetrable undergrowth that fringed his life. A texture map that lay on a couch just past recall, prodding his body from its long forgetfulness.

Where does she come from? he asked Adie.

From the mind of a supremely bizarre customs official in a cold Paris atelier.

No. I mean . . . the way she looks. Where did he get her?

She showed him the river flowing through this figure. All the prone female flesh, up on one elbow, turned three-quarters to face the plane of paint. Those countless, recumbent, thinly veiled Renaissance mistresses, passed off as Venus. Titian's Urbino goddess, Madame Récamier, the naked Maja, ripe Olympia . . . She showed him the long genealogical tree, art's ancient bloodline: this fetishizing, fawning, degrading, loving, lurid intimacy played out in front of centuries of voyeurs, these canvases like mirrors on the ceiling of the race's collective motel room, rented, as always, this evening, by the hour.

As the spinning leaf programmed the light, so this strange almond algorithm programmed Spider Lim's body to take up some history too long to understand. The female nude wanted something from him, something commanded in a lost language, something Spider Lim hadn't the visual vocabulary to comprehend.

He took to avoiding the Cavern while the jungle group worked there. But his cure produced the symptoms it worked against. His policy of containment only multiplied the woman's nighttime visits. Soon, she came to him as regularly as a cross-sound ferry, demanding that he examine her every surface, gaze on her where she lay wrapped in a long, self-extending pageant, a *tableau vivant* he'd never dreamed himself capable of seeing . . .

Adie's peopled garden played to a full house. The virtual *Dream* was smaller, in square meters, than its Crayon World ancestor. It performed fewer interactive tricks. For the most part, the underbrush just sat there, fat, luminous, under its fixed beacon of moon.

But those who toured it at open house felt its leap in technique, its advances in surface modeling.

Seven or eight explorers pressed into the Cavern, taking turns wearing the master tracking glasses.

My word, Jonathan Freese admired. *It sure does feel robust.*

And responsive, O'Reilly added. *Not a whole lot of depth effect yet. But at least a body can recognize what's in front of it.*

Sue Loque just nodded her all-natural fright wig, like a teen keeping the beat under a pair of headphones.

Pretty flicker-free, Jackdaw said. *Nice ray tracing. Not too much latency as you walk around.*

The moon soaked them all in silence, from up in the highest branches. A handful of jungle visitors stood loose in their own overrun seedbed.

Steve Spiegel broke the spell. *Explain something to me, Ade? What exactly is the dame on the sofa doing in the middle of all this malaria action?*

Ha. Does that trouble your little bourgie norms? Adie jabbed her college chum in the ribs, her first attack on his underbelly in a dozen years. The underbelly had grown softer in the interim. So had the jab.

Sue jingled her tire-iron bracelets. *She's listening to the music, obviously. To the spooky ebony guy in the Day-Glo skirt.*

No, no, Spider said. *She lives there. She's some kind of jungle spirit. Like the other.*

Like him.

Yeah, right. On a Louis Philippe divan?

Uh, Rajan wavered. *You white people do happen to notice that she's buck naked?*

No one heard Karl Ebesen enter the room, until he snarled. *Idiots. The woman is not in the jungle. The jungle is in the woman's living room. It grows in through her window, while she dreams.*

10

The Jungle Room feels strangely familiar.

Your eye recognizes the place at once, although it has never been there. Or say your eye *has* been there, long ago. Back before childhood's childhood. Before your eye was even an eye. And say that you've toted this spurge around inside ever since, a keepsake of long-abandoned cover.

Origins converge in the Jungle Room. Choose your myth of preference: the garden banishment, the wayward chromosome. Either way, this green is a return engagement. Nostalgia sprawls from the overgrown nooks. Life leverages every cranny. Moonlit creepers spread a welcome mat. The pennant of mangrove branches announces Old Home Week.

Fronds appear with all the shocking clarity of fronds. Perhaps they began as metaphors. But now they grow into the species they once only represented. The Jungle Room creeps steadily toward arboretum: taxonomy without the formaldehyde, ripe fruit without the fall.

Something yearns to return to first vegetation, only this time at a cool remove. The body wants back in its abandoned nest, but now free to come and go, like a shameless tourist, without the fatal danger of travel, free to name the lush sprawl of this place from the safe vantage of a divan.

Here is the shape of reforestation, eons in germinating. Till this novel test patch, more flexible than the original starter bed. Speed the green revolution. Onto the teak's living trunk, graft a woody emblem. Fuse the fact of the branch to its depiction. Join stump and symbol into a single thing, a tree you can walk around, prune, replicate. The tree you came down from. The one you'd happily climb up again.

This is the aim of all bootstrapping: to lift the first curse and make dreams real. Here you can shed your wood skeleton and travel at will through groves of pure notion. Here you can gather up the pieces of something that shattered once, long ago, in childhood's childhood. Here you can reassemble all lost growth, and even back it up onto magnetic tape.

Through the Jungle Room, birds wing at liberty. Define a feather when condemned to the wind. Say how the shaft tapers, straining to be weightless. Describe what the vanes do on the air, how they luff and ruffle and flute, how the barbs somersault on the downward curve of their resisting ride. Specify the flight in full, and you have those jungle fliers. Fix the thing's rules, and you slough off the tyrannical thing. Mere birdness alone yields birds on demand. Whole flocks pepper the canopy, from out of description.

Ingenuity plays among these leaves. A snake slithers from the undergrowth, dappled by the moon that traces it. Mock ribs propel the python forward, muscles accurate down to a single strand. The pseudo-snakeskin glistens as you gaze, your sight renewed. But this time, the serpent takes no one in. You do not wholly buy this slithering bill of goods. This simulation cannot bruise your heel.

Still the Jungle Room swells, as awful as its template. For there may be no return, no quarter, no resting place behind these renderings. These leaves hide nothing but the signs of hunger. Even the myth of elemental loss somehow misses the point. It may not be in you, ever, to believe in a home of your own devising. The tree may not grow that can trick both heart and limbs.

11

Now that you've explained the mistake, they'll let you go. It may take a few hours for permission to filter down whatever chain of crazed command these hoodlums follow.

But you tell them: a schoolteacher. A teacher who used to have a decent job in industry before his private life fell apart.

Teacher. No spy. Joke. Bad joke. Very sorry.

You cost more to kidnap than they can hope to get for you. Not worth ten shekels a pound on the international terrorist spot market. Even these amateurs must see how ludicrous the whole mix-up is. What a story this will make, when it's all over. The greatest, most unbelievable letter back home ever.

They take your watch, along with everything else. They wedge you into some kind of root cellar, where you can't tell day from night.

Maybe two dozen hours have passed since they grabbed you. Surely not more than thirty. It might take a couple of days, even a week, to straighten everything out. You assume a courage you do not have, and settle in for however long you need.

The crib where they've dumped you is too dark to see. Inch by inch, your fingertips cover its surface. Good for passing a couple of hours, if nothing else. You're on a dirt floor, in a more or less rectangular room, maybe ten feet by six. The floor is little more than the flight of five steps they shoved you down. It stinks of soot and vegetables. Three of the walls are wooden; one is stone. The crumbling plaster ceiling is too low to stand up under. Your heart begins to race, despite your forced calm. You will perish here. Suffocate. You will never see light again.

Above the flight of steps lies a wooden trapdoor. You nudge at it. It doesn't move.

After some time, the trap opens. Through the flood of light comes a crisis of arms and legs. Someone barks three Arabic syllables. The trap closes, and the room fills with a putrid odor. You grope your way to the steps. On the top one a tin plate sits covered with a steaming mass they can't possibly expect you to eat.

It's some kind of evil game. See what the prisoner will put in his mouth, down there in the dark. The scent gags you. You remove your nose as far from the plate as the cramped quarters allow.

After the rush of danger passes, fatigue slams you. Fear has run you a marathon. Only now do hormones give up pointlessly dousing your muscles. You need to sleep as you've never needed to sleep in your life. But you can't. The room is too small and hard to stretch out in. The pain of your first handling pounds you. The stink of the refuse they've tried to pass off as food keeps you from losing consciousness. Sleep would strip you of whatever feeble protection your mind now gives. Sheer stupidity: you want to be awake when they come to release you. Above all, you fear what dreams sleep might bring.

The need to urinate grows unbearable. Banging on the trap and pee-ing in the corner seem equally humiliating, and you refuse to be humiliated. You try to ignore the swelling pressure on your bladder, to focus on making them open the trap. You'll make them break before you do.

Enough time must now have passed for the school to notice your absence. You try to figure how many classes you've missed. Your docile flock will have told administration that their teacher has failed to show up. Surely, in such a city, in such a climate, someone will know to expect the worst. Someone will sound the alarm, raise a search party . . .

Others have been taken before you. Others, with more powerful institutions lobbying for their release. Another thought to shove out of your mind. Still, your case is different. By now your kidnappers know they've made a mistake. You aren't what they thought you are. You're a schoolteacher. You have no secrets. None that would interest them, in any case. You'll be out in a matter of days, at the most.

You pee in the corner. You try to break up the ground beforehand, with your fingernails. So the liquid can soak down.

You fill the time by rehashing your abduction. You replay the car, the thugs, the questioning. You work up the details, make them more threatening or more comical in the recap. It's the most fantastic story that has ever happened, even without embroidering. But you'll wait awhile, after your release, before sending your mother even a sanitized account.

Soon you'll need to defecate. If your bowels revolt before anyone comes, you'll be in deep shit. Another thing not to think about. Thoughts to avoid begin to crowd the already cramped quarters.

Your mind mires and circles. Then a noise tears away the gauze. The ceiling above you explodes in banging. Someone shouts through the trap, "Cover you eyes. You no look. Cover eyes!"

You fall to the floor, searching. Somewhere you've shed the oily rag they used to blindfold you. Discarded the scrap, thinking you'd never suffer it again. Now you scramble in the dark, to find it and cover your eyes before the hole opens.

The rag slips on just in time for light to stream in under the folds. A voice you don't recognize commands you to climb up. "No talk," it adds. "No run."

You crack your head on a rafter, searching for the lip of the steps. False light, the flash of the blow rips across your closed eyes. You bite down hard, to keep from shouting. As you ascend, you trip on the plate of food, scattering it.

"Why you not eat?" the voice shouts. It holds a mania large enough to crush you.

"Terrible," you say. "Bad food. No good."

"No talk," he shouts, shoving you from behind.

You come from your suffocating cocoon. The upstairs feels warm, light, clear. You're good for another few hours. You will endure whatever face-saving show these men need to enact. Then you'll ask to use the bathroom. To pull yourself together a little, clean up for your release.

You flex, a gift from heaven. Behind you, you hear the puzzled crick of packing tape being ripped from its reel.

"You don't move," the voice tells you. "We tape you. For your safety."

You speak as softly as you can. You fall back on long practice, times trying to say two calming words to Gwen when just the sound of your voice lit her into frenzy.

"I am a schoolteacher. My student . . . misunderstood a joke of mine. I came to this city because—"

"Yes. We understand. Don't worry. We don't hurt you. We tape you. For safety. Short drive. Then you go home."

They wrap you like a mummy. They wind around and around you for half an hour. They tape right over your clothes, your hair, your ratty cotton blindfold. They leave just the crown of your head and a too-small sliver for your nose. With chops and shoves, they force you to kneel. But bound so tightly in this tape tourniquet, your knees can't bend.

They pummel you into a crate. The constriction bursts your arteries. You try to make some noise—the sound of refusal, of impossibility—through the tape. Nothing comes out but a muffled whimper. You can't fit in the box. You can't even tell them that you don't fit. Nothing but free fall into panic.

They put you in the crate and cover you. Your annihilation, your live burial. Several men try to lift the crate. The weight of a typical American in a box dismays them. You wish now that you had eaten the food, just to add injury to insult.

They trundle you down a flight of steps. Your skull caroms against the sides of the box. The foot of the crate crashes to the ground, splintering your ankles and knees. You hear the sounds of the street, snarling

7 1

mopeds, vendors hawking and haggling. If you called out? A voice seeping out of a sealed coffin, gagged, muffled, a single smeared phoneme: the stunt would only seal your fate.

A little patience, and you'll walk past this spot again, tomorrow, seeing, free.

From the sound and the smashing and what little light comes in through the cracks, you sense what is happening. They place you into a recessed well in the floor of a van. You must be hanging down in the undercarriage, given the sound of the engine.

The road is a single pothole from here to Kuala Lumpur. Every pit hammers your bound body. They've taped your face too tightly. Between the exhaust fumes, the closed crate, and the triangle of opening they leave your nose, you asphyxiate. First nausea and lightheadedness, your head and eyes, pressed through a grater. Then a black throb pushes forward against the inside of your face. Blind animal frenzy scrabbles at the base of your brain, a creature trapped under a sheet of resealing ice. If you pass out now, you'll never wake up.

You kick against the sides of your coffin, to make them pull over. But tape turns your kicks into a wad of socks tossed into a hamper. Every agitation now sends your lungs deeper into deficit. You try to slow your racing heart by force of will. Drop your pulse into a hibernation that will outlast this endless ride.

The crate heats up, from the engine, the sun, the dry sand whipped up from the road. You fight for air, for a slice of sanity. The engine slows. Covered voices trade a few words. You sense a barricade, a checkpoint. You shout. Death by gunfire would be a blessing. But the engine roars back to life before more than a dull moan can escape your mouth.

You force your taped knees against the lid of the box. With what strength remains, you manage to crack the seam. A gush of fresh air knifes into you. You shove your nose into the stream. It tastes like God in your nostrils.

The holy sliver of air keeps you alive until the van stops. A chorused confusion hauls you from the well. They tip you on end, and the shift crushes your legs under you. They hoist you to horizontal and pop the lid. Rough hands pull at your packaging. The tape tears your skin and hair as it rips off.

You fall to the ground, gasping. You lie still, sucking salvation into your lungs.

"You . . . animal-fucking bastards . . ."

"Not talk! No make noise!" Someone smashes you across the face. Black collapses inward, and you are nowhere.

You come to in a white room. Even this feeblest of lights overwhelms you. When your eyes adjust, you make out where you are. Nothing to make out. A squalid plaster box. The room is maybe ten feet wide and twelve feet long. You could stand up fully, if you could stand up.

Here and there, the otherwise featureless walls bear greasy black fingerpainted smudges. Near the corner of one long wall, a five-foot slab of boiler plate barricades the lone doorway. Light dusts the room, seeping around the edges of a wall-sized sheet of corrugated steel nailed over the remnants of French windows.

The planked floor hasn't been swept anytime during your adulthood. The room is devoid of finishing except for a balding mattress and a metal radiator bolted to the filthy floor. Attached to the radiator, a short steel chain. Attached to the chain, your left ankle.

"Hey," you call. Your voice is dry, broken. "Hello?" Louder.

The door rumbles and jerks outward. A young man, no more than twenty-five, stands in the frame. He is tawny, thin, medium height, black-eyed, black-haired, sleek-bearded, hang-nosed, white-shirted, blue-jeaned, and glaring. You've seen whole armies of him, waving small arms, hanging out of car windows patrolling both sides of the Green Line. He's young enough to be one of your English students. He looks, in the second that you are given to scan him, lamentably like your internal clip-art stereotype of an Arab terrorist.

"What are you doing?" he screams. "Cover your eyes! Don't look!"

You scramble on the floor near the mattress, searching for the blindfold that has chosen the wrong moment to go AWOL. Screaming, the guard rushes you and yanks down the rag that has been riding, this whole while, on your numbed head.

You fix it so that you are blind.

The boy does not retreat. He hovers by your head. His breath condenses on your neck. He presses something hard and cold and metal up into your ear.

"You hear me, you cover your eyes. You understand?"

You nod your head. Again. Harder.

"You look, you die."

12

The moment he glimpsed America's pet project, Ronan O'Reilly was addicted. He'd come to Ecotopia determined to loathe its insular, insulating Gore-Tex righteousness, and he ended up marrying it and moving in. One look at the Cavern and he knew he'd never work on any other project ever again.

He toured it first on a junket to the Northwest, a whirlwind dog-and-pony show up the Pacific Coast, peddling a set of economic modeling tools to American statistical package resellers. No vendor in the U.K. — leave off the Republic or the Continent — could go to market against the kind of distribution that the Ecotopians were just then ramping up. He hoped to make a few quick quid by licensing his algorithms before North American brute force rendered the whole idea quaintly obsolete. He planned to return with whatever modest profit a sale might net and use the proceeds to rescue the Queen's University's School of Social Sciences from hardware decrepitude. With a new generation of decent iron, O'Reilly might hand-roll a new generation of future-modeling tools. Remind his countrymen that there still was a future.

Ronan landed in Washington armed with a solid prediction package and an accent that the tone-deaf locals mistook for some Public Television Edwardian English monstrosity. He ran a tight slide show, with enough reheated Bernard Shaw cracks to keep the audiences entertained. American venture capitalists seemed ready to throw money at anything that ran on silicon. And the Erse slant on visual econometrics was just different enough to frighten his American competitors into interest. Only after he entered the glass palace of TeraSys, the Solution Builders, did O'Reilly get his first significant offer — a bid outstripping his most reckless projections. TeraSys had little interest in the goods he peddled. They were after the peddler himself.

It took just a glance to see that the Ecotopians were up to some kind of major madness. But O'Reilly failed to guess the extent of it—the source of that vibrant organic fascism, their sunny assumption of omnipotence. Only on entering the Cavern did he grasp the scale of the hubris. The Americans were launching an out-and-out frontal attack on electronic transcendence. Mankind's next migration.

Jesus Christ Made Seattle Under Protest: the guidebook's mnemonic for the downtown streets stayed with him after he returned home to his own flawed emerald. Under protest: apt dismissal of the entire Puget Sound. It was as if the Creator had spent eons developing the setting, then botched the city itself, under the project's deadline. The crabs, the salmon, Rainier, Olympus: all postcard perfect, when you could see it through the rain. Even the ice-cold beer wasn't bad, although the hapless microbreweries couldn't thicken a stout to save their souls. But the natives: gluts of aerospace secret-weapons contractors; technohippies with too much cash, clinging to the last stretch of Arcadia that Boeing hadn't yet denuded; philanthropic tele-solicitors who crucified themselves over the spotted owl while denying the massive subsistence economy that begged for a buck or grubbed for rotting lettuce heads down at Pike Place Market.

Odious, he reported back to his fellow Dismalists in University Square. *The whole Northwest coast. Hirsute, illiterate, and malodorously enthusiastic. Blinded by their birthright, which they stole in the first place from more tribes of Indians than even the inane guidebooks care to mention.* Adding: *I'm afraid I've agreed to join them.*

O'Reilly's fellow lecturers forgave him with contemptible haste. No excuses necessary. Part of the general exodus. We'd join you on the life raft, if we could.

He felt the self-defeating need to disabuse them. *Now don't go making me out to be just another evacuator.*

A nice side benefit, though, no? Not having to worry about getting gunned down for having a Republican name or a Unionist employer?

Oh for Christ's sake, he ranted at them. *Everything in creation does not boil down to the bloody Troubles. My decision has absolutely nothing political about it.*

Strictly a question of lucre, then?

Had his colleagues but known the figures involved. O'Reilly would never again need to muck about in the wilderness, piddling together bits of elastic and sticking plasters in heroic attempts to get his creations to run. Yet the cash per se wasn't the half of it.

How parochial home had grown, how imprisoning, in just his few weeks away. Belfast air choked him now, acrid and stifling. Bad for the lungs, and everything else that depended on them.

His beloved Maura refused even to consider a visit. *What am I supposed to do there, Ronan? Tell me that. It's not my country. I don't even understand the fuckin' language.*

You aren't suggesting that intelligibility is exactly our island's strong suit?

It's home, Ronan.

Well, woman, we'll bring the welcome mat.

How can you possibly want to live in such a place?

You don't understand, Mau. We're all paralyzed here. Rotting. Stagnant and cynical. Stuck in ancient history. Flogging a dead horse, for as long as anyone can remember, and it's never going to change, because nobody here even remotely believes that it can.

Oh, the Americans own belief now, do they?

Yes, they do. You have to see what they're doing. Those people are changing the rules of creation over there, month by month. They are bringing something absolutely new into existence.

New, sure. But you can't call anything on that continent existence.

They fought for weeks, at a pitch that made their previous five years of warfare seem a friendly match. Each had drawn a line down the Mid-Atlantic Ridge, and neither was budging.

Maura, listen to me. We have one another. What difference in hell does it make where we live?

If hell makes no difference to you, by all means go on and live there. I'll trim you up some pretty sulfur-colored curtains for your breakfast nook.

Damn your curtains. I can't believe you're going to insist on signing our death warrant.

You're the one who's doing the insisting, Ronan.

I need to join this thing, Mau. I need to know where the race is going. I want to see what happens next.

Stay here, Ronan. I'll tell you what happens next.

Christ help me, woman. I'm going to miss scrapping with you.

But the pace of American innovation left O'Reilly little time to miss anything older than six weeks. Even doing without televised club football hurt less than he anticipated. Work swallowed him, leaving no space for anything else. For months, he had to digest ten new ideas for every one he coughed up. In fact, he brought only a single fresh dish to the banquet, but one that multiplied faster than that original all-you-can-eat loaf-and-fish-fry. His idea was simple, but lay at the heart of practical prediction. He'd found a way to broker econometric modeling's compromise and arrive at that eternal oxymoron, the accurate approximation.

The problem was deep. The more parameters one added to a model, the more accurately the model predicted actual outcomes. But each variable multiplied the complexity of the solution. When would an eternally refined estimate become *real enough*? When would approximation suffice?

Economic theory stopped too soon, reducing the world's mad exchange to mere Supply, Demand, and Price. The result resembled the Budapest Quartet nobly sawing away at a transcription of Mahler's Eighth. But more practical modeling snagged on the opposite sin of profusion. In the real world, no set of simultaneous equations ever really worked out. The classical economist's answer to his functions' functional impotence consisted of adding an infinite series of ever-smaller local factors to the mix, calculated to ever-higher levels of ex post facto multidimensional exactitude. And still the experts couldn't put the dart inside the bull's-eye any more often than your average Thursday night side-slinger down at the local. Predictive economics crashed and burned with the frequency of a turn-of-the-century air show. The market? It will fluctuate.

Hilarious, really. Like one of those Weather Wizards standing up in front of his back-projection map of the New World: hot and humid over Panama, chillier throughout much of the Northwest Territories. Warming gradually toward August, and likely to cool off somewhat again as we head toward winter.

Now reality, at eye level, fell closer to sociology than it did to physics. A child stands in the back yard and hurls a ball. Where will the globe land? Newton trotted out mass and velocity, slow decelerations against gravity yielding a mirroring parabolic slip back down to ground. Close, but no Castro. Then out came all the elaborations: the coefficient of friction, the eddying wind, the spin of the ball off the wrist, the wobble of the Earth on its axis, the wobble of the child on his own pins . . .

Worse, the physicist conceded that the smallest change in the tyke's throwing posture could cascade out of control and land the projectile anywhere between here and Katmandu. This took the heirs of the infinitesimal calculus four centuries to come up with. Lower Kingdom Egyptian dads tossing around dried crocodile guts with their sons on Saturday afternoons down by the Nile had figured that one out six millennia ago.

The answer was awful. Let the child throw the ball two thousand times and make do with statistics. Chance perturbations canceled each other out, and the running average gave those who lived in the day's maelstrom their lone limited access to prediction. The compromise satisfied everyone except engineers, truth seekers, and the ball-chasing parent.

But when it came to predicting fishery yields five years down the causeway, no one was allowed two thousand throws. God wouldn't even spot you two. Extrapolating the graph worked for the first dash or two of the dotted line. But once one began extrapolating upon extrapolation, the whole bloody curve collapsed into fiction.

O'Reilly's idea lay in discarding the search for a set of predictive operators. The realm of real fact did not result from cranking through static functions, no matter how many variables those functions included. The world's events emerged as a resonance, the shifting states of mutually reshaping interactions, each fed back into the other in eternal circulation.

He convinced the Ecotopians with a simple propagation simulation, one that showed just how small the limiting case of complexity could be. He built an island world, sovereign inside its diminutive boundaries. Its entire populace consisted of just two kinds of agents that operated on only two entities, each existing as nothing more than two-dimensional arrays. Each entity came in four flavors and each of the two agents had four possible actions.

Such a market model seemed too brain-dead to generate real interest. But each change in a variable's state updated all the variables that prompted it. Entities influenced agents, and agents created or destroyed entities. Moreover, the application of these feedback loops over time altered the *way* that variables affected other variables. Not only did the elements of the simulation alter one another. So did the rules of alteration.

Out of this meager sea of ingredients, there issued amazingly lifelike phenomena. Segments of data spoke of saturation, conditioning, habituation, fads, cravings, lemming drop-offs, crash diets, lowest-common-denominationalism, prime time, rushes to the bottom, spontaneous altruism, unsponsored innovation, gratuitous novelty, brand loyalty, brand aging, arms races of acumen and finesse, co-optation, preemption, addiction, dumping . . . A few iterative, independent, self-modifying procedures created markets as complex as those run by the world at large.

Life was not algorithm. It was ongoing negotiation, a spreading series of overtones. But O'Reilly's cunning simulation presented a problem as large as its promise. Under its simple surface there flowed tide tables of deep intricacy, plumes of intelligence, surges of avarice and hunger that churned in turbulent eddies through the pool of data. How could even the simulation's designer see any one of them in real time? With his static-charting business graphics, O'Reilly could do no more than dredge his dipper into the vat and extract a few test ladles. He foundered on the problem of visualization, snarled at that old investigative impasse like a nineteenth-century neurologist stymied by how to study human thought without slicing into the living brain.

He needed a way to see into four- or six- or eight-dimensional space, even as those several simultaneous data streams unfolded. He needed color, texture, and motion laid on top of the traditional height, width, and depth. O'Reilly even sketched out a fantasy in which musical pitches and timbres let a user track the states of a dozen concurrent agents and actants.

And then he learned of the prototype's existence. Once he discovered the Cavern, no other spot on Mercator's botched projection would do. He needed the tool that only TeraSys could offer him. And the Cavern needed someone who saw what it might be used for. To be able to stand among the lights and sounds, inside the skeins of regenerating prediction too complex to take in any way but viscerally, in one surrounded glance: for such a chance, O'Reilly would give up most anything. And did.

He took the vow of cultural poverty gladly, throwing over his Neanderthal country without a backward glance. Even the vow of silence— the forfeiture of intelligent conversation—cost him little, in light of the potential payoff. Celibacy alone gave him pause. On nights of cold rain, O'Reilly cast about in the sphere of his sleep for the thermally generous Maura, and found only an empty half bed. He cursed her roundly and dug in, waiting for her to see what she was missing.

Meanwhile, his *son et lumière* show played across the walls of the Cavern as marvelous pure abstraction: a ravishing cityscape at night, seen from miles above, where the eye could pan and zoom through the concerted flares of halogen down to the smallest blush of a back-yard Japanese lantern. It took him weeks to learn how to read the gorgeous, motile tapestry. He forced himself to remember that each of these fantastic, fusing, fractal ice floes *meant* something—a transaction, an update, a changing variable in the world being modeled. Only when standing in this n-space flux, flanked on all sides by continuously updated data, reading the revelations with his body, thigh to math's thigh, neck-deep in simulation's Humboldt Current, only fully immersed could he begin to sense the cold, delineated meanings that coursed through these oceans of prediction.

This was the work O'Reilly was born for. Mankind's tenure here had come of age. All the Earth's land masses lay prostrate, mapped out to nauseatingly fine detail. We'd filled the map with knowledge. Now we had a tool with which to look *inside*. Now the real exploration could begin.

But to date, O'Reilly remained the lone living human who knew how to read this disco-stroboscopic lab report. Everyone else saw little more than an astonishing fireworks show. No matter; the real fireworks weren't yet ready. Much work remained before O'Reilly's pyrotechnic display could lift the veil and lay the future bare.

He'd made some attempt to initiate Rajan Rajasundaran: fellow member of the Decimated Neocolonial Island Club, Sri Lankan by way of Canada, coauthor of ORB, the simulation scripting language that O'Reilly employed to throw his arrays up against the walls of the Cavern. O'Reilly depended on Rajan, invaluable ally, to make the graphics code jump through ever-higher hoops. He kept Rajan on perpetual call for everything from emergency consults to simple sociological shit-shooting.

O'Reilly sought the man out at his favorite haunt, that poor excuse for a pub half a click down the mountain. The place whose inspiration peaked with its choice of name: The Office. As in, "Honey, I'm at The Office." The name worked, in a world that took names for the things they named.

He found Raj sitting in a corner booth, watching a talk show, partaking of the public arena's favorite therapy.

Thank God you've come, Ronan, man. Have a look at this exercise in dissociative schizophrenia, please. Women who tell their husbands, live on camera, that they have lesbian lovers, as brought to you by the Family Ties video salesmen of the Church of Jesus Christ of Latter-Day Saints. I'm afraid I must ask you: who invents all this?

Ah well, Rajan, my son. The Creator's ways are mysterious.

Please explain this phenomenon to me. You are the social scientist, after all.

Has it ever struck you that anyone with the word "scientist" in his job description probably isn't one?

We're all scientists, no? Rajasundaran waved his arms to encompass The Office at large. *I mean, every person running this little experiment in being alive?*

O'Reilly ordered a beer and a refill for the Sri Lankan. *An interesting formulation. But let's start with you. Do you count yourself an empiricist?*

Krishna destroy us. You don't really want to know.

I'm dead serious, man. What do you believe?

Rajasundaran held out his left hand. His index finger traced a clockwise circle in the air. Then another, quick, counterclockwise.

Now what's that supposed to mean? Some sort of mystic Ceylonese bit twiddling?

Rajan shrugged. *The breath in the mouth and the breath of the sun are both similarly hot.*

Translate, for Christ's sake.

The form seen in the eye is the same as the form seen in the sun. The joints of the one are the joints of the other.

Vulgamott appeared at their boothside.

Michael, O'Reilly greeted the architect. *Thank God for another Westerner. Have a seat, man. Would you say that you're a materialist at heart?*

Can this wait until I've gotten my blood-alcohol content to a respectable level?

O'Reilly ordered the American a Trappist Trippel. *Out with it now. What do you believe?*

Vulgamott looked around suspiciously. *I believe that God created the world one high-resolution frame at a time. And on the seventh frame, he rested.*

Rajan smiled. *And then he said, "You mean I'm supposed to do thirty of these things a second for the next ten billion years?"*

Thank you both, O'Reilly snapped. *I'll just tell you what you believe in, then.*

That'd be easier, Vulgamott agreed.

You both believe—as all good lab rats do—that reality is basically computational, whether or not we'll ever lay our hands on a good, clean copy of the computation. At the core of your deepest convictions about the universe lies a Monte Carlo simulation.

Sounds about right, Vulgamott said.

Even miracle-preaching evangelists, God love them, make their point statistically. Every modern mind is out there with a yardstick, a stopwatch, and a chi-square.

Hang on. You're not saying there's a hidden order behind all this? Vulgamott cast his eyes abroad. *Something bigger than statistics?*

O'Reilly smiled. *What do you mean, hidden order? That the universe is formalizable, but not from where we're standing? That it's unformalizable? Now there's a one-word contradiction in terms.*

Ronan, baba. Some of us believe in contradictions in terms.

O'Reilly faced down Rajasundaran. *Even mysticism is a non-Euclidean geometry. No, gentlemen. The world is a numbers racket, all the way down.*

Rajan drummed his hands on the booth top. *Come on, my friend. Don't quit now. This is even more entertaining than violent revelations of deep incestuous secrets as brought to you by the Mormons.*

But the Sponsor chose that moment to announce itself. Out of the depths of barroom broadcast, the TeraSys anthem unfurled. On a screen across the room, a commercial began. Its sound-track chorale of Renaissance recorders morphed—via the malleable magic of MIDI and sampled wave-table instrument definitions—in thirty seconds, over the entire spectrum of world music, cadencing on an ecstatic burst of Shona mbiras. Synched to the sound track with Balanchinean brilliance, a spinning globe mutated in dizzying succession into the rose window at Chartres, an exploding jigsaw puzzle, the condensing chains of a long polymer, inked ideograph characters on an unfurling scroll, tessellated Iznik tiles, solar cells on a space satellite, and finally, back to old Pangea doing its slow, stately breakup into Laurasia, Gondwanaland, and all the rest of the continental separatists, special interest groups, and irredentist movements.

Rajan beamed. *I'm afraid I contributed to that one. They used my interpolation routines for the pretty morphing sequence.*

What in the name of creation do they think they're doing, airing that spot on the Humiliating Public Disclosures Channel?

Big audience, Vulgamott said.

They're mad, you know.

Of course they're mad. Who's the "they" this time, O Ulsterman?

Americans. Every last soul in this national enterprise of yours.

Rajan raised his hand. *Excuse me. Exactly how long can a person live here before he is infected?*

None of them has a clue, you know, O'Reilly persisted. *Like children at Christmas, their whole bleeding lives. Every last mother's son of them.*

Be all you can be. Go for all the gusto you can get. Who says you can't have it all?

Well. Raj glanced at Vulgamott for confirmation. *There's their Internal Revenue Service, to start with.*

And this outfit that we work for? They're the worst instigators of all. "Realize your dreams." Clever foreigners really ought to pinch all their best ideas and smuggle them back over the border, into the lands of sanity.

Ach, sure. Vulgamott affected a frighteningly convincing brogue. *And tell me: what might a Belfast boy know about sanity?*

Precious little, you bastard. Yet I alone have held onto a fact that your obscenely inventive lot never seemed to have twigged.

And that would be . . . ?

There's a real world out there, underneath the elaborate slipcovers we're knitting for it.

Rajan rolled his eyes. *So you Caucasian materialists like to insist.*

Speaking of the real world . . . Vulgamott, the edgy quidnunc, had gone almost a full thirty minutes without a headline fix. *Any word on the Argentina situation today?*

As far as we know, Rajan said, *it's still down there, attached to the skinny part of South America.*

Belfast saluted Colombo. *You're blending in here splendidly, Raj.*

Listen. Vulgamott sounded desperate. *Would it upset your experiment in assimilation if we watched some news?*

Sure, no problem. Rajasundaran scanned through the channel selector, built into their booth. *How about this little thing called* Celebrity Police Blotter?

Some spin-off of CNN, O'Reilly guessed.

Or how about this so-called Channel 56? Sport Salary Update?

Vulgamott's agitation threatened to spill him out of the booth. *You two have no interest in learning what's going on?*

Absolutely, O'Reilly said. *That's why I vote for pulling the plug.*

Come on, man. We're living on the brink. The single most precarious moment in—

Rajan wagged his head. *This has all happened many times before, you know.*

This—?

All of this. The Tamil extended eight hands at once. *You and you and me. The celebrity police blotter. The Latter-Day Lesbian Saints. And it will continue to happen, endlessly, for as long as—*

Could we just . . . ? Vulgamott twitched, on the verge of full-scale DTs. *Just . . . for ten seconds? Would you . . . mind?*

Hey. It's your America. A self-described free country, in case you haven't heard.

The band of immigrants settled in for the closest thing to information this hemisphere offered. They sat in silence, listening to the front-line correspondents' patter. In quick cavalcade, the patchwork world morphed through a parade of protean shapes in front of their eyes, more fluid than any digital map could hope to mimic.

13

The room of economics runs to an open horizon.

Every compass heading stretches so far that even walking flat-out, for hours, scrolls you only the smallest fraction against the landscape. Your inlet reveals itself to be but a bight on a cove on a lagoon on a bay on a gulf opening onto a measureless ocean, the one continuous Panthalassa, its waters linking up, its surf cutting the complex curve of these shores.

Light and shadow play upon the deeps. The spills and splashes of geographic accident serve as this world's genes. Here woods work out the local exchange rates. Gorse trades its stored energies with geese. Tundra warehouses whole quantities of carbon. Bottoms, morasses, moors, plateaus, and rain basins bargain in a river pidgin that keeps the dimples of microclimate in nutrients all year.

Where is the nearest caravanserai? Who will swap salt for ocher? How goes the southern coffee bean harvest? Will the scares in Johannesburg tip the Frankfurt Börse?

Will the leading indicators level off? What of the anticipated export boom among the Asian tigers? When will collapse come? This room's tides will tell you.

Even its ceiling rises forever. High overhead, above the atmospheric tree line, past the edge where color thins out beyond blue, electronic kingfishers hover. Each beats its wings in blackness, fixed in place above its assigned coordinates. Stationary passenger pigeons, message-bearing corbies, each bird is but a bit in the widest imaginable linkup.

Perched in their geosynchronous orbits, the birds root out all data and beam it back down to the ground below. There, a trillion worker ants cull the factual wheat from its fallacious chaff, blind to the upshot of their tireless winnowing. The global economic simulator sieves out an answer in nanoseconds, in no time. This room can snare any fact you wish, faster than a gentled pointer can fetch your morning paper.

The cells of a continuous compound lens now cap the whole heavens above this ceiling. Near and far are as nothing. Scale is no issue. The Economics Room can zoom from the neighborhood fruit stand all the way up through the G7 annual deficits. Its simulation means to render mystery visible. To turn the market's enigmatic piano rolls into freewheeling rags. To throw open the global portfolios to public inspection, for close reading.

A crimson comet, at ten o'clock, just above the horizon, paints an upturn in third-quarter commodities. A rose of starbursts means stubborn unemployment. Hidden relations spill out, suddenly obvious, from a twist of the tabular data. Tendencies float like lanterns across the face of a summer's night.

In the Economics Room, you can freeze a frame or skip ten million. The press of a button throws a clean model eon into fast-forward or a hard reverse. The economics map requires only four colors, but can splinter into forty or four billion. Animated maps enact last season's cod haul off Georges Bank, this week's top box-office grossers, four centuries of Lycian olive pressing.

This room is deeper than its interface makes out. Bigger than will fit into the space that houses it. All the world's predictors, running flat out, fall back surprised by their own outcomes. Fresh winds mix, mistral on sirocco, chinook against levanter, khamsin with bise. Cusps touch off one another. Trends compound, too quick to name. Yugoslavian prices rise three thousand percent. Drought and war destroy East Africa.

Argentina heads into free fall. China comes alive, threatening to swamp the continental balance of trade. Sweeping liberalizations cascade. The median keeps to a holding pattern. Vested interests bitterly dig in.

Something is at work here, something momentous. You need only stand in mid-room and look. Once-in-a-lifetime headlines flower immodestly, poking up like shameless patches of crocus in the unmown spring. Yet no image can say what this sprouting means. Import remains oblique, geological, obscure. Interpretation is a sleight of hand, reversing itself with each new read. Streams of bits combine to produce a pocket score, astonishing, symphonic, but too small to read.

The data are here, in surfeit. In fact, this flood of noise and color never abates long enough to submit to a basin. Events transpire too fast to register before they go obsolete. Who can take their eyes off the ticker long enough to tabulate?

But here you can eavesdrop on the chaos of voices. When that ship-yard on the North Sea erupts again, you can examine the underlying inputs. Production as a function of hours. Hours as a function of volatility. Volatility as a function of morale. Morale as a function of expectation. Expectation as a function of income. Income as a function of production. This room combs out the Gordian tangle. Here you can watch the revolution unfold, at any speed, along any axis, at any magnification, testing each infinitesimal contingency's effect on every other.

The kingfisher satellites swoop down, hitting their minnowed marks. They snatch the silver data aloft, flapping in blackness, before dropping the catch back down to the globe's surface, where it repli-cates, shooting the rapids of broadband relays and repeaters, transmit-ter to transmitter, pooling ever more downstream, to school in the hatcheries of petabyte shoals.

In this room of open prediction, facts flash like a headland light. The search flares burst around you where you stand, lost in an informa-tional fantasia: tangled graphical dances of devaluation, industrial upheaval, protective tariffs, striking shipbuilders, the G7, Paraguay, Kabul. The sweep of the digital—now beyond its inventors' collective ability to index—falls back, cowed by the sprawl of the runaway analog.

Five billion parallel processors, each a world economy, update, revise, negate one another, capsize the simulation, pumping their dissatisfied gross national product beyond the reach of number.

This sea defeats all navigation. At best, the model can say only where in this, our flood, we will drown. Walk from this diorama on a May evening and feel the earth's persistent fact gust against your face. Sure as this disclosing spring breeze, it blows. Data survive all hope of learning. But hope must learn how to survive the data.

14

A woman, dead for a decade, steps out of a yellow Volvo. Walks back into a life that recalls her shape better than it remembers its own.

Of course she chose the worst imaginable moment to materialize. Returned to Karl Ebesen's life just to survey the maximum extent of the rubble. Came back to find him holed up in a decrepit trailer, on a lot that flooded from October to June, subsisting on microwave lasagna and apple chips, living only to get the work out, serving his daily penance with a precision that spooked even his most intense colleagues. Prepared to concede the final slide into bagmanhood.

Not exactly the state he cared to be found in. Not the ghost he cared to be found by, in any state. But that was how ghosts chose their moments. Disruption: the only gift that memory had to give.

Of course the ghost had no idea who she was. They never did. No sense of her death or untimely resurrection. The Volvo returned, day after day, obstinately yellow, to haunt its slot in the asphalt parking lot. Clearly the corpse came here to dog him. The only thing Ebesen couldn't figure out was the reason.

He made himself known to the woman. He paid evening visits to her cubicle, freely showing her the wreck of his present self. He spoke as little as possible, for her voice destroyed the illusion. He just sat in her presence, under the available cover, fussing with acetate stills or marking up old magazines with a greasy highlighter, trying not to stare at her. Hoping to dispel the ephemeral resemblance.

This living woman stayed a dead ringer, although the physical match was, in truth, but slight. Coloration similar, if the light was low enough. Height, build, and other such irrelevancies, close enough to pass. The eyes, cheeks, and jaw were only rough approximations, the best that God's plastic surgeons could restore them to. But the whole was Gail, as much as Gail had ever been.

Even now, Ebesen might have sketched the dead woman from memory and gotten more of her than any of the photographs that had graced her closed-casket wake. But he couldn't reconstruct this living woman's cheekbones from one night to the next. He, whose drafts- man's talents had always inclined toward that embarrassing anachro- nism, the human likeness; he, who might have made a brilliant portraitist, had he lived two centuries ago: he simply could not resolve this Adie's face into its gaunt primitives. His mind couldn't see her to draw her.

He'd felt the same doubt with the dead woman once, when she still lived. Every day that the two of them had spent together. The nagging suspicion that Gail was, in fact, her own succubus. He'd gaze on her illicitly in her sleep, when her musculature dropped its guard and returned to its preexistence, those terms before pain, before gravity, before the assault of sunlight, before the awful contortions that the pub- lic mirror induced in all faces.

He'd scrutinize her by lamplight, Eros hovering over his wife with the forbidden candle. He studied her features, unmasked by sleep, searching out what she looked like before she looked like this, looking for the face he recognized, from before he met her, the face that, like a rebus, an Arcimboldo, a hidden-picture game, spread itself out across the landscape of his synapses.

Her features held their own fossil record, her facial bones a skeleton key that picked with a click of recognition Ebesen's rusted lock. The face leapt out of his life's faded photo album, his brain's deepest Mari- anas, his infant pass-in-review, held on to long after it should have gone extinct. She killed his sense of safety, his feel for error, his certainty of light and dark. The haunted face had survived its own burial. The twitch of this Adie's cheek cut him. Her pits and shadows flirted with a familiarity they refused to settle into. He could not name it, this over-lap, or locate the crossover in any aspect of her appearance. Dead love and its living copy: two halves of a torn original.

He took to shaving more often, so as not to spook her. He hung his trousers over the bathroom door when he showered, to steam out the worst of the wrinkles. He worked dish soap on a worn toothbrush against the stains of his shirt collars, watching himself, wondering how far he might sink in the name of revived feeling.

Months after her arrival, the spell broke. Sight did nothing to disperse it. His eye was worthless, in the end. Three stray words delivered him: speech, the medium that Ebesen distrusted above all others. Of all the absurdities, something she *said*.

She was chattering. Something Ms. Klarpol did whenever he visited. Talking out loud, to anyone, to herself, to her chocolate Lab, the faithful Pinkham, who loved to accompany her to work. Chattering about the absurdly beautiful place she found herself living in.

An island cottage, Karl. Right out of a poem. Circling gulls wake me up in the morning. In New York, it was always sirens.

"New York" and "siren" fused, and Gail stood before him. Each plane of her face materialized, a frantic hologram. He looked up at this Adie, still amusing herself with a running account of her windfall. He stared at her, no longer caring if she caught him looking. The living woman resolved into her own parts, lost to all likeness. Nothing remained of the ghost story but his need to be near it.

He tried to stop visiting her. He started coming by again. She greeted him happily on his return, asking for no explanation. He contented himself with serving as her mascot of bitterness. He dispensed with any threat of recovered respectability. But as he carved mortise-and-tenon furnishings for Vulgamott's architectural fly-through or designed anvil thunderheads for Stance and Kaladjian's Weather Room, he felt the flinch of recollection, the awful willingness of arousal that he thought he'd put to death.

He taught her how to animate. *You only need to paint a few cels. Say, one at each two-second interval. Rajasundaran has written morphing software that will fill in all the midpoints.*

Then he sat back and watched her bring motion to the jungle's fixed planes. Already, bushes rustled and the moon strayed across the child sky. Soon her frozen birds would thaw into a flutter, the snake slink, the monkeys scamper, the flutist weave, and the lions crouch in the perfect impression of stalking.

He watched her paint dozens of frames, creatures in various postures. She painted each cross-sectioned creature as lovingly as the first, assembling them into time-lapse fragments that moved more surely than he did. *The Dream* awakened, channeling the dead painter's spirit through the hand of this living woman medium.

He heard her, when things got buggy, pleading with the terminal. *Please, nice Mr. Machine. Don't be mean to me. I haven't done anything wrong, aside from belonging to the organic life-forms. Karl, the little chips are acting up again. What should I do?*

Accept adversity, Ebesen said. *It's soul-strengthening.*

It's not my soul that needs work, she told him.

He watched her scratch at the drawing tablet. He stood behind her workstation screen while she willed her graphics pen through glad arcs. The lightness of her aping dazzled him. Her fingers played at the existing shapes, exhilarated by their constraint to copying. Something in that virtuosity did not want to be free.

You're good.

Thank you.

Watch out, he razzed her. *Not too original, now. They could get loose otherwise, your animals.*

She looked up at him. Doubtless she saw a stubble-faced fifty-five-year-old man with soap smears around his collar. She turned back to her cookie-cut time sequences and cooed at them.

That's right, my little beasties. You're getting loose someday, aren't you? That's exactly what you're going to do.

Something in her pet-coddling voice alerted her Labrador, until then curled up, on best behavior, in the corner. The dog padded over to his owner and nuzzled her.

Oh, you too, Pinkham. You too. Gonna cut loose someday? That your plan? Oh yes, you are, my sweetie.

Placated, Pinkham returned to his post and settled back in.

Ebesen, too, wandered back to his post. *Have you ever thought about work that didn't involve some violation of visual copyright?*

She scowled, the look one reserved for the drunken party pest. *I'm a good copyist, Karl. All God's creatures should do what they're best at.*

I know what you're best at. I saw your show.

Ah, yes! The latest Wild Kingdom. *Mr. Rousseau, version 2.0.* She held up a hand-drawn cel of an elephant rearing back to trumpet. She rocked the painted profile in the arc that animation planned for it.

I didn't mean Rousseau 2.0. I meant Klarpol 1.0.

Naw. You know the thing is a team effort. The guys wrote all the code. I plundered everybody, totally copycat. All I did was cut and paste Henri's Caesar salad onto lots of lollipop sticks. But wait until—

I mean your one-woman show. Your solo opener.

Her smile seized up, seeing the ambush. Gail's smile. Not in any curl or turn of the lip. Just its crumple of fear. Its carmine fight or flight.

What was the name of that shop again? God, I used to know them all by heart. Not to mention how much commission each of them scraped off the top. Near Broadway and Spring Street. Francis Hinger Gallery.

Francis Hinger, Adie echoed. The elephant stopped moving. She set it down.

How long ago was that, exactly?

Doesn't matter.

No, wait. I'll tell you exactly when it was. August of . . . What year is it now? August of 1979.

Opened in July, she said, through the side of her mouth. *But who's counting?*

Adie Klarpol. Only you were going by Adia back then.

My name.

What were you, all of seventeen?

Twenty-seven. Old enough to know better.

Oh, nobody's ever that. A well-received show, as these things go. Some kind of awful literary name . . .

"Halations." What's so awful about that?

What does it mean, anyway? It sounds like bad breath caused by asthma.

It's a technical term. Describing what I did.

Pastel penumbra halo stains. Lots of high-frequency colors. Not uninteresting. Inkblot tests on minor hallucinogens. Seemingly abstract, until you looked closely enough to make out the ghosted high realism. There was one called Infinite Coastline, *if I remember right. Kind of a hand-drawn Mandelbrot, a couple of years before everybody in the industrialized nations dosed out on Mandelbrots.*

I can't believe you remember that. I can't believe you even saw the show. I didn't think anyone saw that show. Except my mother, and she only came because I paid her airfare.

Come on. Nice little squib in ARTFORUM. *They built you up. The next hot commodity. All set to unfurl.*

Karl. Please.

Let me guess. You wanted to change the world. Right? Make a difference? Am I right?

Well, whatever I wanted . . . She laughed again. Her shoulders came down. She returned to her tablet. The ambush had passed. I didn't exactly produce the cure for cancer.

Were you any good, do you think?

Screw you, Karl. You saw the work. You're the voting public. You're supposed to tell me.

Now. If you really mean to give the last word to the voting public, the only mystery is how you lasted until twenty-seven. Ebesen picked at his fraying sleeve, at some crib-sheet answer inked there. *Beautiful was supposed to be back. Craft and exactitude and representation. That didn't even last the allotted fifteen minutes, now did it?*

She made herself a pillar of calm. Mary in the bower of roses, by Stefan Lochner. She returned to working at her creatures, under an impregnable halo. *Know what's funny? The only people who are willing to pay you a steady salary to paint? Businesspeople? They still kind of like those things.*

So that's what did it for you? That's what prompted you to quit the downtown scene and go straight?

Oh for heaven's sake. It doesn't matter.

I know it doesn't matter. The last person on earth to tell anyone that anything mattered. I'm just interested.

Leave me alone, Karl. You should talk. She flinched at her own words.

He stood still. *All right. I had no idea it was still a live topic.*

It's not a live topic.

I just wanted to know what made you . . .

She cocked forward on her stool, ready to spring. But some late-heard pressure on his "you" scattered the attack. She sat back and inhaled. *Art is . . . pretty sick now, isn't it?*

Life is sick. Art's just the recording nurse.

Either way. It's not something I needed to live with all day long.

He started to sing, in a tenor hinting at how it used to saunter, before the osteoporosis. *"I got troubles of my own."*

Exactly. Exactly! The first through tears, the second through a wet, cracked giggle. *What's it to ya, bub?*

She sat up, pulled her knees together, and folded her hands on them. Ebesen stood holding his greasy valise, ready to flee at anything that resembled intimacy.

Shit, she said. She wiped her face with the butt of her hands. *This is pathetic.* She consolidated her body, pulling and tucking. *OK. I'm OK. Here. Sit over there.* She stood and installed him at a vacant workstation. *At least make yourself useful, would you? Here's the palette and the set of brushes. Go on. Make the monkey jump.*

It was some proof for the God of the mathematicians that existence offered exactly as many penances as it afforded sins. The two artists worked away in silence. Her hands moved rapidly, like shorebirds, circling. His moved almost not at all, wavering as narrowly as a mantis's. He etched in short crosshatches, with brute, surgical fastidiousness. Each head bent down over its drawing, monks in a scriptorium furnishing a continent with gold leaf and cerulean.

Ebesen painted, satisfied to be Klarpol's apprentice, for as long as it took to pay off her distress. But not a heartbeat longer. An internal timer somewhere between his riddled heart and savaged liver told him the precise moment when it was safe to badger her again.

So what did it finally come down to? The bits of crockery glued to the canvas?

No. I kinda liked those. Wasn't crazy about the price tags . . .

Was it the prohibition against affirmation? As I remember, your stuff ranked pretty low in the doom-and-detritus department. More of the — how shall we say? — Glad Game persuasion.

She snorted at the caricature. *Let's just say that my talents . . . never really tended toward originality.*

Nu? That hasn't stopped half of the ARTFORUM *pantheon. The trick out there is exactly the same as it is in here. You just have to find a way of being uniquely derivative.*

Don't like it out there. Like it in here. Singsong pugilistic. *Safer in here.*

I don't get that at all. How can commercial art be safe, when it involves millions of viewers and trillions of dollars, and high art be dangerous when it sells for eight thousand bucks and sits in the foyer of some summer home in the Hamptons?

High art's a bit of a joke, wouldn't you say? The go-go frenzy. The lives chewed up and spit out for the sake of novelty and glam. Reputations manufactured and deflated, fortunes thrown at trash. Then the transaction written up as if it's the stock market. All that fuss about something that's not even real.

What is? Real, I mean.

She shrugged. She waved her hand around her to indicate her captors. *TeraSys. Exxon. GM. Things that make this world. Things people believe in. I'll tell you what's real. Microsoft is real. The gallery world is a wannabe dress-up game.*

Ebesen threw up his hands. For a moment he was the white-smocked firing-range victim in Goya's *Third of May. Then why stay with art at all? Why not ditch picture making altogether and go into a legitimate line of work? Something really real, like sales and marketing? I understand there are a few openings.*

Because making the elephant trumpet is not exactly what I'd call art. But it sure beats working.

Oh, I see. Pictures are fun, so long as they don't matter.

In his outburst's aftershock, Ebesen looked up. Adie was cringing again, crooked over her animations.

Don't ride me, Karl. I'm making a living, the same as you.

You had more talent than I did. He grunted at his screen.

Adie craned over, examining the work of his hands. The monkey lived. In three quickly executed slices, Rousseau's manic marmoset-macaque swung on his branch in a sweep that was pure simian.

She looked up at the bagman, the sorry statesman of all RL eccentricities. *Just how much talent did you have?*

Ebesen lifted his eyebrows and let them fall. He shuffled to his feet as if the bailiff had just proclaimed, "All rise." He scratched the dog Pinkham behind one ear and vanished from the room.

But he came back again, helpless, the following evening.

15

This new room still has no place to relieve yourself. The fact seems hopeful, although hope is fast going relative. They can't keep you here for long without leaving you somewhere to pee. Solid plank floors; plaster walls. The chain on your leg would restrict urination to a six-foot radius of where you sit. Surely even these zealots don't expect you to foul your own bed.

You wait. At least now you can wait in the half-light. Someone will come before the pressure to relieve yourself kills you. Come with food or word of your release. Or barring that, something to piss in.

You wait. The waiting becomes a game. Then the game becomes a contest. They mean to break your will. They find this cute. Some kind of victory for the world's downtrodden, to make mighty America wet its pants. So it turns into a State Department mission, to suppress your bladder until the enemy concedes respect.

The pain goes crippling. A stone forms in your urethra. The denied moisture begins to trickle out of your eyes. You've lost, lost against your body, against time, against your captors. You place the blindfold over your head and call out, as contritely as the pain allows.

Someone bangs once on your door and it opens. A voice from darkness's northeast calls out "Yes, please?"

Not your previous visitor, the one who fondled your ear with his gun. This one sounds shorter, rounder, slower on the uptake.

"I am sorry," you babble. "I need to pee very badly. Urinate. Toilet? You understand?"

You've learned the Arabic word, but in the press of need, the language tapes fail you. You stand and resort to body language, hips forward, hand to groin, the little Belgian boy, writing your name in the snow of some dream Low Country, universes away.

"Yes, please. OK. I know. You wait."

You burst out in a sharp laugh that splits your gut. The man leaves, raising an alarm like the home team's during the First Crusade. You must be the first person this band has ever chained up. That Americans have bladders has never occurred to them.

The little round voice scurries back. He holds something up to the vee of your pants. You peek under the lip of the blindfold, into the mouth of a sawn-off plastic bleach bottle. You unbutton yourself with your battered thumbs and roll down the waistband of your underwear. But it's hopeless. Desperation changes nothing. You never could piss in public.

"Please. I hold. You leave."

"OK." The man fumbles the container into your hands. "You take."

"Thank you. You go now. Goodbye." He walks off a few feet. But no door closes. It will have to do. Under the blindfold, by force of will, you imagine the room empty. Your boarded-up hole, bare but for the mattress and radiator. The floodgates open; coarse yarn pulls out of your urethra at high speed.

You collapse against the wall in relief. Your head falls back, slack against the plaster. "*Merhadh*." Toilet. "*Merhadh*," you sob, all fluids flowing out of you at once.

"Yes, yes," your captor laughs. "*Merhadh, merhadh*. I understand."

Not the word a native would have used. Pronunciation not even close. Failing to come until long after you needed it. Yet these two syllables, on his tongue, send him into delight.

"Good, good. I leave bottle here. You use . . . all the time. Make water only. No shit. Shit, mornings only. I come take you. Empty bottle. Good? Yes, please?"

"Listen. Can you bring me something to drink? Water. Another bottle for water. I am very dry . . ." You make obscure hand gestures meant to signify dehydration. Dust in the throat. "Not good. Not healthy. I must have water. A bottle to drink from." You will work on fluid for now. And put forward the concept of nourishment later.

"OK. No problem. I bring for you. Soon. *Inshallah.*"

God willing. You pray the tag line is just a formula.

The door closes upon silence. You lift your blindfold to the emptied room.

How long have they held you? You need some mileage markers. On the day of your capture, you refused to entertain any block of time longer than an hour. The crisis called for small steps, one in front of the other. Even figuring in days conceded defeat. To reckon in weeks already lay a week beyond survivable. Now survival depends upon the peace that only a calendar can give.

Taken on Tuesday, the eleventh of November. Armistice Day, it now hits you. After that, a long questioning, long enough to induce hallucination. Then a stretch in the Hole, where total darkness cut off the passage of time. Interminable transfer by van followed by a stint of unconsciousness. Now, around the edges of the sheet-metaled French windows, you see the last declarations of daylight, brackish, disappearing into darkness's salt sea.

But which day? You can't say, and it crazes you. You've lost count, by as much as two full days. Lost your link to the world that they've stolen you away from. Market day, school day, wash day, holiday, birthday: you fall into limbo. You can't live, without a date to live in.

You run the sum of hours every possible way, landing on different calendar squares each time. You walk in chained arcs around the radiator, trying to force up the real date as if it were a forgotten phone number. Here, in this empty cube, you choke like a child lost on a packed midnight train platform in some mass deportation. You'll call out. Yell for your captors. Trade a beating for today's date.

Then, through the muffling wall, a signal reaches you. The background hum of traffic modulates. The air erupts in a spectral cry, then its echo. The sound reverberates, a civil defense drill. Electronic muezzins pass the fugue, back and forth, like shoeless street kids passing around a soccer ball. The size of this call to prayer decides you. A smile floats up your throat to take dominion of your face. Friday. Holy day. Friday the fourteenth of November. 1986. You close your fingers around the prize and cling to it for sweet life.

Days go by. With each, so does the prospect of a quick release. You consider scratching each one into the soft wall plaster with your fingernails, stick men herded and tied diagonally into docile groups of seven, down the chute of time's slaughterhouse. But the gesture seems too cheaply cinematic, too much of a surrender. Instead, vague light and dark, a cycle of repugnant meals, the morning blindfold trip to that cesspool opposite your cell all keep time for you, sure and metronomic.

The days cross off more easily than the hours. You look inward for some diversion, a fidgety Iowa kid in the backseat of a Yellowstone-bound Rambler who exhausts the possibilities of license-plate bingo long before washing up on the lee shore of Nebraska. Your head is a gray-green, tidal emptiness. Your mind rebels against the smallest admission of your fate. Thought becomes a blur. Nothing there. No more than a reflection of the formless pit where they've pitched you.

Surely you knew something once, learned things, stored up diversions that might help pass the brutal infinity of an afternoon, the wall of minutes so monumental that your pulse can't even measure them? But your brain, ever vigilant, refuses to be caught exploring any other prospect than immediate release.

You talk to yourself, as to a stranger on a transatlantic flight. You study your résumé from above, hoping to remind yourself of some topic that interests you. Favorite sport. Musical instrument. No thread lasts for more than ten minutes. And you must slog through a hundred ten-minute intervals between any two bouts of blessed unconsciousness.

You sleep on the soggy mattress, a life-sized grease stain seeping along its length. The stench so gags you that, even lying on your back, you're afraid to slip off into unconsciousness. But with each new night, you habituate to the toxic fumes. You learn to doze intermittently, suppressing the reflex to retch.

Mornings they unchain you and march you through the latrine. You fix your blindfold to let you look down your cheekbones to your shuffling feet. You fake a blind stumble, so the guards don't catch on.

Then, for ten precious minutes, time returns, its sudden fast-forward mocking the previous twenty-four fossilized hours. You jump like a galvanized corpse, rinsing out your urine bottle and filling your canteen, fighting the giant roaches for a corner of the sink, shitting at the speed of sound, using any remaining seconds to scoop cold water over your head, armpits, and groin, a surreptitious shower that gets you no cleaner and costs you hours of mildewing chill. Yet it seems a guerrilla blow for decency, the smallest symbol of order keeping you alive.

Meals come capriciously, two or three times a day. They vary in quality, from inedible on downward. Breakfast usually consists of stewed okra scraps rimed with smashed chickpea. Lunch tends toward the chewed-over soup bone, what you pray are pickled tomatoes, and half a circle of *khobez*. Dinner arrives, at best some self-deluding parody of *baba ghanouj*.

Hostage: each passing day adds another letter to the hangman's word. It grows hourly harder to deny that you've become the next victim in a serial crime that you thought had exhausted itself in pointlessness. Just one more naïve Westerner picked off the streets for nothing, an uncashable token held to impress an enemy who doesn't grasp the first thing about the rules of exchange.

Independence Day passes on the twenty-second. At least it's the twenty-second by your private count. The street below your cell signals no celebration.

"Am I a hostage?" you ask the guard, the knife-voiced one, one morning, as he delivers your breakfast bowl of spotted cucumber rinds and curdled yogurt.

"I don't know," he replies. "You want I ask Chef."

"Yes, please. Please ask."

Your answer comes that evening, along with a plate of gristle rejected by its previous eater.

"Chef say you no hostage. America lets our brothers in Kuwait go free, you go free. Simple. Tomorrow. Tonight." You hear him shrug: *Now*, if we get the respect that Satan owes us. Or never. Makes no difference. Entirely up to your people.

He delivers his message and leaves. You fall on the clue as a devout falls upon his prayer mat. Kuwait. Incarcerated brothers. The men who slip your food into this box and lock the door behind it are Shiites. At last you have a label for them. Beyond that there is only your willed ignorance, your stupid refusal to have learned any more than the basics of the war you so blithely waltzed into. Something in you, even now, does not want to know this organization's name, the one-word credential stamped on their ransom notes. Something in your scrambling soul still denies that you've been taken by the only organization capable of doing so.

Not a hostage: just some collateral pawn, held for imaginary leverage in a game where no one can say just what constitutes winning. Word must be out by now, whatever the word is. The school knows that you're not playing hooky. And surely, in this city, they're left with only one conclusion.

By now you've made the world papers. "Yet another American," like the reports you used to read and file away, unimaginable. Chicago now knows the name of those who captured you, while you as yet do not.

Hand between your head and the infested mattress, your free leg slung across the manacled one, you force your two column inches of captivity to materialize on the crazed plaster ceiling. And along with it, you summon up the whole front section of today's *Tribune*—World's Greatest Newspaper—the first image of any resolution to grace your private screening room. The blue banner and the hedging headlines. The weather for Chicago and vicinity. Metroland meanderings, carping columnists, gridiron second-guessers: pages scroll across your field of view on microfiche of your own devising. And tucked away, make it page 12, safe where the news will spare Des Moines and hurt only those whom hurt will benefit, you put a black-and-white reduction of your college yearbook photo, a face so saddled with goofy impatience for the future that even you no longer recognize it.

Days pass without your marking them, days spent squinting at the accompanying text, at all the details of your mistaken capture, at reports of your captors' confident predictions that, all sides cooperating, you'll be home by Christmas. You read your life as only another would have told it. And you wonder, God help you, if your story has reached the one whom you vowed would never hear word of you again.

16

`You are standing at the end of a road before a`
`small brick building.`

Stark words flashed across the network's broadcast channel, like that
annual decree going out from Caesar Augustus. Like the first four measures or "Auld Lang Syne." Like the face of a friend bobbing out from a
crowd just clearing International Customs, lit in familiarity's halo.

Jackdaw Acquerelli, his day's work put to bed and his night's
fantasies brought up in a foreground window, laughed to himself at
the phantom text. Similar bursts of recognition must have passed
through everyone still logged in at this hour. The sender was good. The
message carried no header, no time stamp, no originating workstation
ID. Just a raw text stream, plopped down on a hundred screen status
lines, like a writ coming straight from God, Gates, or some other
upper-echelon SYSOP.

Jackdaw ran a quick check to see who was on. Eighty-six users, not
counting concurrent sessions. Folks at all six facilities, from the Sound
down along the coast, as far south as the Valley. Seven people right
here at the RL. Night and prototypes: something about 2 a.m. rendered
it the perfect hour for wire-wrapping.

Any dozen of these guys were good enough to have managed the
stunt. A few of them had written the damn operating system. There
were too many wizards for Jackdaw to trap the identity of the sender.
The words were best treated as a collective artifact.

Jackdaw killed the user check and popped back to the OS prompt.
In just those few seconds away, some fleet-fingered soul—a certain arj-
rao1, working on a TG Graphics box over at the mother ship—had
already managed to dispatch the follow-up any one of these late-night
acolytes could have supplied:

`Around you is a forest. A small stream flows`
`out of the building and down a gully.`

The words filled Jackdaw with a great sense of well-being. Happiness
flowed in its own small stream out of Jackdaw's chest and down into his
typing digits. It felt like a snatch of last year's plaintive progressive-rock
waif bleeding out of the radio of a car that tracked up a mountain road

in the dark. Like a drug, maybe, though Jackdaw had never partaken. Like first love. Like learning, word of mouth, that your first love loved you back.

His eyes took in the summons of the words. His hands on their keys felt the fingers of that seventh-grader still inside them. He stared at the sentences and saw his father, one Saturday morning in 1977 when young Jackie had been acting out, taking him to the office and parking him in front of a gleaming Televideo 910, hooked up to a remote mainframe through the magic of a Tymeshare 300-baud modem.

All a trick, Jackdaw saw in retrospect, an elaborate diversionary tactic to fool a boy into — of all things — reading. The screen had glowed at him then, each letter a phosphorescent worm made up of a couple of dozen discrete pinpricks of green light. You are standing at the end of a road. Before a small brick building.

"So?" eleven-year-old Jackdaw had pouted. "So what?" But half-enthralled already, half-guessing that this place might be vastly more interesting than the larger one that was good for so little except disappointment.

"So," his father mocked. "So type something."

"Type something? Type what?"

"Anything. You're standing in front of a building. What do you do?"

"Anything? You mean, like . . . anything?"

"For heaven's sake. Just try something and see what happens."

Belief, at eleven, was still wide. And those words were even wider. Boy Jackie read the sentences on the screen again. This time the road, and the small building, and the forest, and the stream flowing out of the building, and the gully it flowed into jumped out at him in all dimensions, cobbling up some temporary, extensible, magic scratch-pad valley expressly created for getting lost in.

The idea of walking through this valley lifted him out of that morning's misery and set him loose along that small stream. He found himself split over two locales: at the end of a road and in the middle of a chorus line of letters, through which he hunted, with escalating excitement, for the key *e*.

`Enter building`, Jackdaw typed into the broadcast dialog box and let it rip. The message echoed on his screen's status line, amid a hail of identical messages bouncing around the wide area network all over the North Coast.

His was not the only private raft out on this nostalgia cruise. Most of late-working TeraSys, apparently, remembered the archaic incantations, the geographies of pleasure buried in the mists of a dozen years back. Like calls to a radio contest, the responses flooded in. Exhortations to `Enter building` and `Go building` piled up along the bottom of his screen. Even a simple `Building` and a simpler `Enter`.

Get out of my life, Jackdaw howled. *You gotta be kidding me.*

Spider Lim, dozing on the cubicle couch, shot up, spilling the bag of Sun Chips balanced on his sternum. *What is it? What's happening? Something crash?*

Original Adventure?

Huh? What about it?

You could just type "Enter" to go into the building?

Oh yeah. Sure.

I played that thing for over twenty thousand minutes, and I still have all the logs and hand-drawn maps to prove it. Two years, on and off. And I never knew you could get into the building without typing "Building."

That's all right. I never got past the dragon sleeping on the carpet.

The dragon? You just kill it.

With your bare hands?

Yes.

Damn. Spider fell back prone on the couch, palm-butting his forehead. *Idiot! That never occurred to me.*

```
You are inside a building, a well house for a
large spring.


There are some keys on the ground here.
There is a shiny brass lamp nearby.
There is food here.
There is a bottle of water here.
```

Once in a lifetime, if lucky, a soul stumbles onto pure potential. Young Jackie, on the end of a road, felt himself transported in the blink of an electronic eye into this building, this well house for a large spring. Some patient genie in this molded box—circuits too complex to imagine—promised to act upon Jackie's every demand. You are inside a building. You are inside a book. Inside a story that knows you're in there, a tale ready to advance in any direction you send it.

Eleven years of existence had already wearied the child. The world was no more than a monotonous, predictable tease, a limited reward with unlimited restrictions. TV was a sadistic trick, one he'd seen through at the age of nine. He failed to grasp the appeal of cars, which only served to move human stupidity around a little faster. Sports were beyond him, girls incoherent, and food a bore.

But this: this was something he'd given up on ever seeing outside of his own, private theater. This was salvation. This was where he'd always hoped to live.

He stood at the base camp of pure possibility, his remote puppet free to roam the universe at will. He looked up at his father, helpless with deliverance. His father mistook his crumpled smile of bewildered arrival. "Try going west."

Too blissed out even to be irritated, the boy typed: `Go west`.

`It is now pitch-dark. If you proceed you will likely fall into a pit.`

Of course it was dark. Why else was a lamp sitting in the foyer? His father was senile, pitiful, a liability on this unprecedented journey. Without thinking, the boy doubled back, got the lamp, and lit it. Get lamp, light lamp: somehow, the machine *knew*. Objects existed, as did actions. Things had the qualities they embodied. He moved about in this terrain, changing it with everything he chose to do, leaving the land and its pilgrim sprite forever updated.

The light came on, revealing a debris-filled room. A low cobbled passage blocked up with mud.

"What's this called?" he pleaded with his father.

"Adventure."

"No," he said, panicked with impatience. Pointing at the screen. "What's *this* called?" This latitude. This venue. This concept.

"Oh. The place, you mean? Colossal Cave."

A simple Telnet session could now give Jackdaw the entire original classic, FTP'd from any of several hundred UNIX boxes where the solution, like some fire-breathing beast, now lay curled and dormant, guarding its ancient hoard. Five minutes would have brought up the full walk-through on his screen, scripture to be cut and pasted from the editor window into his tiled message buffer. But Jackdaw had no time to cheat. The real-time gauntlet had been thrown down.

Comments began to fly, faster than he could read them. Choruses of `Plugh you, too!` and `Fee, Fie, Foe, Foobar`, the inside jokes of pioneers queued up and blazed their brief transmission. One-meg-per-second whispers of `Wave wand` and `Go west`, the hushed remembrances of those who were there at the beginning, the first generation of celestial navigators ever to look upon this cosmology, ever to take the fabulous new orrery out for a test spin cast off into the unmapped depths all over again.

`You have crawled around in some little holes,` Jackdaw typed, `and wound up back in the main passage.`

He hit the Send key four times. Four copies of these words meandered out over night's mazed network. Thirty seconds later, someone down in San Jose echoed back:

`Thanks a brickload, ja-aqul. Like I really needed to be reminded of that part.`

It had been clear to little Jackie, from the first Return key, just what he was facing. This game was nothing less than the transcendental Lego set of the human soul, its pieces infinite in both number and variety. He scoured that room, the well house for a large spring. He got the keys, got the food, got the water bottle, and never looked back. He left the building. He wandered outside, into the virgin forest. He followed the gully downstream, where the water entered a little grate. He toyed tirelessly at the grate's slit, trying to pry away its stubborn secret.

"What on earth are you doing?" came his father's fatherly dismay.

"Nothing." Exploring. Sampling utter open-endedness, nibbling the full fruit of possibility down to the core.

"The cave's back in there. In the cobbled passage. You were right at the entrance, dum-dum."

But there were too many possibilities already overlooked. Too much to investigate before Jackie could allow himself the luxury of the cave entrance. He stood in the great outdoors, that raw expanse of valley, typing `Look trees, look leaves, look rock, look water`.

It took only an hour to discover just how small the adventure really was. What had seemed wider than the whole of California was, in fact, largely a cardboard prop. He could not, for instance, climb a tree in the forest and look out from its crest. He could not scoop soil up into his bottle and pour it down the little grate. He could not spread food pellets in the woods to coax out wild animals. If he walked too far in one direction, the newfound continent simply stopped. `You cannot go in that direction.`

The machine replied with a paralyzed `Huh??` more often than it acted upon his command. The machine, it turned out, was nearly as brain-dead as his father. Weight, containment, edge, resonance, extension, heft: one by one, the qualities that the cave's strewn treasures promised fell away into chicken wire and papier-mâché. Infinity shrunk with each primitive property that this universe shed.

Infinite, instead, were the things this machine would *not* let you do. Colossal Cave was just a come-on, a tricked-up fox-farmer-hen puzzle that dealt successfully only with the answers it already expected. But the place it mocked lay too close to the Northwest Territories deep in Jackie's head for the resemblance to be anything short of real. He didn't fault the idea of the game but only this particular work-up: this flawed, first-run parody of the land that this land really wanted to become.

A further hour of bumping up against the program's limits, and disillusionment turned to challenge. Another hour, and challenge became obsession. Jackie had at last found a place on this forsaken globe where he might live. He crawled around in the cobbled passages that computing threw open, the tunnels blasted through with a further update, another thousand lines of code, the next implementation.

For all that it lacked, Colossal Cave was still endless. However deterministic, however canned the script or pointed the narrative, it still promoted him from victim to collaborator. You are in a room, with passages leading off in all directions. The room itself was still an experiment, still a lab more richly stocked with prospects than any that the rest of waking San Jose had to offer.

Jackie begged his father to get a terminal at home. Thereafter, whole days passed, unmarked except for the ghostly pencil lines spreading across his expedition's graph-paper map. He spent days in a blocked gallery, dislodging himself in a rush, on an aha, a dream inspiration as exhilarating as anything life had to offer. Freed up for further caving.

And while he collected his crystal rods, his gems the size of a plover's egg, his journey pushed forward on another plane, down channels more wonderfully insidious. The quest for arrival, for the perfect score, left him tunneling through a maze of chambers with passages leading off in all directions, filaments no more than a fraction of a micron thick.

Know what? That program taught me how to type. The voice from behind Jackdaw shocked him out of the network relay chat. Spider, eyes closed, cheek to the cushions, playing ventriloquist in his own throat, exercised that Vulcan mind link he enjoyed with anyone stroking a keyboard within a twenty-meter radius.

Jackdaw nodded, his gesture invisible. *That program taught me how to hack the operating system.*

Huh?

Serious. I started by learning how to do a hex dump of the game file, peeking into its guts for any text strings that might give me a clue. Anything to nail down another twenty points. Then I taught myself assembly language so I could disassemble the entire program. Follow the logic. Finally see how to beat it.

Oh sure. I tried that too. Only I got sidetracked somewhere in the ALU. Hooked by exactly what was happening in those registers when they added the contents of two memory addresses. Somehow forgot all about the sleeping dragon and his damn Persian carpet.

But Jackdaw had not forgotten. Nor had any of these eighty-six users scattered around the eastern Pacific rim. A distributed horde of boys attacked the cave with a fierce single-mindedness that mathematicians reserve for intractable proofs. They exchanged clues by electronic bulletin board, by satellite uplink, posting their discoveries through their technocrat fathers' primitive e-mail accounts. They formed clubs, networks of the estranged and ludicrous, their memberships only waiting to inherit a future they knew to be solely theirs . . .

Anyone ever figure out the Hall of Mists?

Anybody else still have his back issues of *Spelunker Today*?

An incalculable expenditure of time. A colossal waste of his life's potential. And yet Jackie's life: the vapor trail of narrative left simply from playing the game. Time-sharing, pirating, paying out extortionate prices to secure each spin-off, each latest extension to the great underground empire, the next, hot upgrade of the ongoing adventure, each more tantalizingly realized than the last. Worlds with a two-thousand-word vocabulary, then four thousand, then eight. Interactive novels that grew to parse whole sentences. Places where glass bottles broke and food molded. Where trees could be cut down and formed into planks or paper, boats or battlements. Lands where your accumulated actions changed your own stamina and strength and wisdom, where these changing numbers altered the further paths allowed you. Lands that allowed actions and responded in ways that surprised their very programmers.

Inevitably, there arose graphics. At first the pictures were a rush, each panorama ever more glorious than the last. But the pretty picture adventures came, within a year or two, to sadden Jack past saying. He could not explain it, explanations only saddening him all the more. Some richness, some open-endedness had been crushed under the inescapable visible.

His father sympathized. "I felt the same way when TV killed off radio. Hearing about creatures from the eighth dimension beat having to look at them." His father's wisdom rating had somehow soared in the years since Jack was a kid.

Whatever else they spoiled, graphics threw open portals all their own. The visual interface launched habitations faster than anyone could click through them. Any eleven-year-old who'd ever touched a video game was way out in front of the scientists on that score. Scientific visualization was born in the first wave of Space Invaders.

They came in rapid succession, games neither adventure nor role-playing, creatures unique to this infant medium. The sandbox games, with their feedback growth and their open-ended tool chests. The God games, with no victory except survival, no goal but to steep yourself in ever more elaborate playing.

Adolescent Jack governed his own surging metropolises. He assembled whole utopian societies of shifting, conflicting needs. He hauled hops across the British Midlands, returning to London with trainloads of finished beer. He nursed branching ant colonies and interplanetary mining enterprises. He hired quarrymen and masons and carpenters to build him a castle that allowed him to cultivate the surrounding countryside, then tax it for every turnip he could squeeze out of it.

He sailed his sloops and pinnaces around the Caribbean, raiding Nevis and St. Kitts, buttressing the economy of Curaçao. He trained botanists and missionaries and game hunters and sent them up the Nile in makeshift canoes. He brought a peace-loving subcontinental Stone Age tribe up through the Renaissance, into the Industrial Revolution, and on into space. Then he repeated the journey in another neck of the random earth, spewing carnage and mayhem as he advanced.

He spent his teens alone, sealed in his bedroom, voyaging. All the while, he held on to that first hint, hoping to locate the fecundity that he'd wrongly thought already inhabited that first adventure. Each new release, each innovation in design, produced in him the sliver of recovery. But Closer only stoked the fire of Not Quite.

Life's turn-based game led Jack Acquerelli into programming, less to make ends meet than to bring about those playgrounds that did not yet exist. College provided him with the silicon sandbox of his dreams. He worked alone and in teams, the line between the two progressively blurring. He collaborated with coders he never met, people he wouldn't have known had he passed them on the street, guys who went by tags like SubClinical, TopX, and BotTot. He built his share of dungeon crawls, each populated with increasingly more anatomically correct homunculi. He helped write a primitive multiuser talk channel, code that allowed his fellow undergrad designers to collaborate at all hours and paved the way for multiplayer spaces.

His senior honors project was called Development, a resource management game with a twist. Randomly generated world maps laid down reserves of various resources—coal, iron, gems, and soil. The Hittites, Cretans, and Phoenicians of this archaic Earth set to the usual task of discovering, extracting, and refining the hidden treasure, then selling off the finished goods. The capital they amassed they plowed back into new technologies, new levels of goods created from out of the storehouse of further raw finds.

But then came Jack Acquerelli's special contribution to smart games. The available research paths—the papyrus you could press from your fibers, the metals you could smelt from your coal and ore—varied from game to game, depending upon the proficiency and research of the pursuing tribe. All skills expanded, contingent on their honing. No two races ever followed the same path. No two games of Development ever developed the same way. And of course—the holy grail of strategy gaming—no session of Development ever needed to end. It could spin itself out forever, unpredictably, to any of an infinitude of never-to-be-reached outcomes.

In the spirit of the digital age's gift economy, Acquerelli gave his masterpiece away, free for the downloading. The cheaper the game, the more players it gathered. And the more players that played, the more ingenious the strategies. Strategies proliferated, each one a complex program in its own right. And the more unanticipated strategies that poured into his game, the closer Jackdaw came to that sense of total liberty he hadn't felt since the age of eleven.

The game went cult, producing its own spin-offs. In his act of hacker's generosity, Jackdaw lost his chance to retire by the age of twenty-two. But the success did write him a ticket to any of the game-design outfits just then capitalizing on the housebroken PC. TeraSys discovered his work just as Jackdaw began sending around his résumé. In the summer of 1987, a rash of Development addiction at TeraSys brought in-house applications productivity to a standstill. The game had exactly that deep, replayable economics that all good simulation craved. TeraSys put in a bid for Jackdaw's services, one that, as always, preempted the competition.

From the instant that Jackdaw stood in the first prototype Cavern, no other bids existed. For the second time in one lifetime, he'd stumbled upon pure potential. Here was a story one could walk around in, only life-sized, this time for keeps. He would have signed on for half what they offered him. He would have given everything to be able to fly his father up to this mountain, stand him inside this play fort strung from blank white sheets. Would have given the world to tell him, *You're standing in front of the sky-blue future. Here's the wand. Do something. Anything. What do you want to do?*

But his father was through with doing. His father was six months beyond wanting anything. Adventure had taken him beyond the need for machines. His father had ported off somewhere where parsers weren't required, over a border where all the checkpoints of disembodied imagination stood flung wide open.

And Jackdaw had lost all chance of ever repaying the man. No way to thank him aside from submersion in the new project. Even among colleagues who slept and breathed the Cavern, Jackdaw stood out. Steve Spiegel joked about having the kid's mail forwarded here. Sue Loque suggested he go on a monthly pizza plan. Jon Freese rode him about stepping into the sunlight now and then, if only to refresh his personal hit points.

But the truth was, no outward life compelled Jackdaw half as much as the life inside. In a footrace against the hardware clock, every real-time hour counted. He endowed the Crayon World with depth. He scented its flowers as a labor of love, one that left him with more energy than he expended. He taught the paper bees their acts of floralocation, showing all the patience of a Trappist honey farmer. He worked with the biochemist Dale Bergen, tirelessly parking massive 3-D enzymatic molecules with all the skill of a veteran valet tearing down the corkscrew ramp of a multideck car park.

He lived to breathe life into the Cavern. The lamp, the food, the brass keys, all led him deeper into the labyrinth, from one state-of-the-art implementation to the next. Each line of his code inched toward that higher library of manipulable Forms. Each control structure and array assignment further eked out the shape of this new biome's indigenous life.

He felt himself out on the leading edge of the thing that humanity was assembling—this copious, ultimate answer to whatever, in fact, the question was. How much time had passed, how many Saturdays since the one when his father had led him here? No time at all. A day. Yet here was this wide-area token ring connecting scores of users up and down the coast, assembled from hardware that made the Televideo and Tymeshare look like the crudest flint. Here was this community of visionary cavers, hours past midnight, hacking away on whatever sequel to discovery that discovery allotted them, shooting off nostalgic messages into the broadband, their elegies for the end of adventure's opening chapter. He'd watched the leapfrogging machine design itself, every year more potent and incredible. He'd tuned his bootstrapping algorithms beyond the best debugger's ability to backtrace until at last he found himself here, in pitch-darkness, not at the end of that valley road but at its start, reading the semaphore sent by his circle of colleagues, few of whom he'd ever met face-to-face, typing out his own contribution to the group quest into the compliant keyboard—Go north, go north, go north— the joint goal receding Zenoesque in front of them, down vistas twisting in all directions.

Somewhere over the course of playing, the underground adventure had gone mainstream, had come aboveground, warlocks taking to the surface without a single, unsuspecting non-gamer quite knowing the shape of the new rules or the size of the global coup. Digital toys came alive, every living soul's life history and health and bank account now a comprehensive Save Game file. Moore's law—performance doubling every eighteen months—fell from being civilization's pace rabbit to a drag on the exploding system. Some days, the digital revolution seemed to poke along too slowly ever to bring Jackdaw into his inheritance. He and his people rode a geometric increase that outpaced all things except the appetite for more performance, the need to reach escape velocity.

Boys who came alive on a fantasy game had launched an entire planet-shattering industry. Boys solitary and communal, dispossessed and omnipotent: remote avatars in a wizard's romp of their own devising. Each month, the combined anarchy of invention made more brute headway on the final ascent than had all of history up until Hollerith. And still the revolution had not yet filled more than a thimble of its potential. The latest virtual engines were still nowhere near to delivering what the terrified, yearning boys' collective needed them to deliver.

Yet out of these walk-in caves had come a game as attentive, as robust, as responsive as life should have been. At long last, in this lucky lifetime, coders would succeed in constructing the place that the brain had first mistaken the world for: the deep, accountable, pliant, original adventure that Jackdaw, for his eager audience, now labored to complete.

He perched over the wan light of his terminal, as over the heat of a desert campfire. He tapped out his private contribution, as yet a secret kept from everyone else on the Cavern project. Across the wires, his remote, ghostly fellowship continued to recite its litany of lost landmarks:

`You are in the Hall of Mists . . .`

`You are in a complex junction . . .`

`You are on the edge of a breathtaking view . . .`

Lured out by the topic, the contributors perched over workstations as distant as six hundred miles and as near as just down the hall. But each participant might as well have been in another galaxy far, far away. Filled with commemorative desire, Jackdaw typed:

`Anybody ever make it through to the end?`

Silence flashed across the broadband. Silence turned into more silence, a coaxial glitch, a pileup in the packet traffic. Then the lag grew too long to be anything but these faceless agents, each deferring to the others to go first. Eighty-six boys—give or take the stray girl who'd stumbled in among them—each waited for someone to send back word of the ultimate solution.

Comic, then embarrassing, the silence lengthened into strangeness. Like one of those lulls in the party conversation that snaps all the diners into an embargoing self-consciousness. Like the silence of shipboard refugees, out on the top deck, looking up at the hollow stars. Your night is so great and our network so small, O Lord.

You kidding? someone typed, followed by a spurt of expletive-laced negatives. **A hundred points short. Fifty. Ten.** The confessions poured in, and the broadband conference drifted into static, releasing its system resources, relinquishing the moment of brief coalescence, dispersing all participants to chip away again at their various private galleries, their maze of tunnels spreading through the unmappable hive.

17

Summer approached across the mountain. Tendrils of warmth and light, accumulating news, linked up for a month or two to drive the rains back out to sea. Days lengthened under the sky's stained egg. Scrubbed clean, the coast air refreshed itself with each high tide. The whole Sound seemed a bee-loud glade.

The hive hummed, like so many scraps of animated paper. Lim and company quadrupled the pipelines and octupled the graphics-processing arrays that ran each wall. Da Vinci, Claude, Hsieh Ho, Rembrandt, and Picasso wordlessly endured their brain surgeries, returning from their trips to digital Italy with more painting ability in their spinal cords than they previously enjoyed in their entire cerebella. And so the project moved forward, recapitulating the quattrocento assault on plastic realism.

Kaladjian screwed down the calculation of Euler angles so tightly they began to scream. Loque tuned the hidden-line removal, speeding up the z-buffer algorithm. Da Vinci and friends, now faster in discarding all the points invisible to the eye, had that much more processing power to spare for the visible planes.

Rajan Rajasundaran worked on foveal concentration. Only the smallest fraction of the eye actually saw with any degree of resolution — say 5 percent of the full field of vision, with the rest shading off into soft focus. If the human eye could get away with that massive shortcut, why should the Cavern have to work any harder? Like everything else at the RL, head tracking doubled its performance every other month. Pupil tracking followed in its wake, suffering only from occasional bouts of the Midas touch, where everything that the user looked at triggered an unwanted mouse click. Minor kinks aside, the Cavern knew, at any instant, just what the user looked at. It even opened a comprehensive log file of the retina's itinerary. Monitoring the glance, the Cavern could concentrate its growing rendering power on the center of that slice, sliding around a high-resolution insert in front of the moving gaze. The trick grew impossible for multiuser expeditions. But Rajan felt alive only when pitting himself against what others discarded as impossible.

For a few weeks, the Cavern's capabilities outpaced the demands of its suite of chameleon rooms. Software struggled to keep pace. Reserving time in the grotto to prototype a new environment became tougher. Slots filled up weeks in advance, all hours spoken for by a queue of researcher squatters, giddy with the pace of forward motion.

The drabbest of new rooms hid the most awesome software drivers. Stance's and Kaladjian's microclimate test bed looked like a passel of stained Popsicle sticks poorly glued together. The user floated omnisciently above a stylized eastern Washington, zoomable from a hundred miles per yard down to about ten. The view could pitch and roll and yaw, peering straight down on the map or swooping tangent to the surface to expose a crude topographical relief that resembled piled-up pillbox hats.

But the map was just the placeholder for the real pizzazz. Under the hood lay all the region's nooks and crannies, the details of local soil albedo and solar radiation, air pressure and water current domesticated into mathematics. Alongside these, compacted into the same code, lay the full scope of physical law—thermal convection and conduction, hydrologic processes, turbulence. The simulation played on the chief insight of the Information Age: the interchangeability of data and command. The Cascades were a set of data points, elemental elevations, rules in their own right, programming the air where to split and rise. By the same token, the laws of adiabatic cooling produced their own data set in the shape of the Cascade Glacier.

A click of the left wand button colored the air in a temperature gradient from rose to cobalt. Each shaded band stood for an isobar. A click of the middle button toggled a hailstorm of vectors—pulsating Aeolian arrows whose curl and thickness, like so many coasting petrels, revealed the caprice of wind. The right button placed and removed centers of pressure, adjusted the sawtooth fronts, painted in cloud banks, and otherwise granted control over the palette of meteorological events. With time, patience, and a satellite weather map, Kaladjian and Stance could reproduce the prevailing conditions of the previous day. Then, like the best of Deist deities, they stood back and let their clockwork turn.

The whole round of the bruised horizon then went grandly processional. Over grim Olympus, across the straits of Juan de Fuca, the lanes of atmosphere released their own vital throes. Points of storm and sunburst smeared outward, spreading like time-lapse microbes. Local conditions reciprocally persuaded their neighbors, rippling outward along a weighted average. Temperatures flumed. Rains fell and rose again to fall. The weather map *became* the weather. From east to west, projectors spread a panorama wider than any glance could consume. The wand's thumbwheel fast-forwarded the live-in movie or slowed it to a frozen frame. Spun past zero, the film ran in reverse. Floods got sucked back up into whitening cumulus. Winds unsplit, reconstituted themselves, backing off the mountain's wedge.

As a predictor, the Weather Room was worthless. Noise crept in at the edges, for the simple reason that the would-be world *had* edges. They dropped off like the incognitas of old cartography, the blank spaces filled in with the guesswork variable: *Past this point, monsters.* Across the map's center, fronts spread well, feeding off the turbulence around them. But at the extremes of the compass, data ran out. Storms on the simulation's boundaries ran aground on the nothingness adjacent to them. Weather grew contaminated by its opposite, and flaws spread through the dataset until clouds and rains and winds and temperatures lapsed into pure fiction.

But as a test, the Weather Room passed with flying colors. Oceans of air could be mounted and hung, made to behave credibly in a display that beat any other attempt to visualize them. The maps would grow, expanding the length of time that these weather pockets preserved their real-world referent. The day would come when a Cavern navigator might reach the east by wanding off at a healthy clip to the west. Then this room, like the one it stood for, would wrap back onto itself and lose its contaminating boundaries.

Until then, the Weather Room remained a triumphant tease. Its sea breezes blew in, reeking of strong mathematics. Red skies at night: analytic geometer's delight. Despite the primitive block graphics, the panorama of heat and cold showed off the hardware to maximum advantage. And in its spiderweb algorithm — each point on the map calculating all the others — the Weather Room became a microcosm of the world machine at large.

Only O'Reilly's Economics Room rivaled it. But Ronan worked by himself, as yet unwilling to trot out his rough drafts in front of the critical public. His displays remained abstract shows of hue and contour, smashing as theater, but as thesis, illegible — a Labanotation readable only by the enlightened novitiate. His multiagent economies were like brilliant autistic children. They had answers, but could not speak them. It took some months for him to admit it, but for any coherent macroeconomic display, O'Reilly needed a simplified interface.

A guided tour of the Weather Room, from which he emerged shaken, inspired Ronan to write one. The choice all but made itself: a world globe, the whole geopolitical pizza pie, sliced down to subnational regions, the slightly pear-shaped sphere spinning on its canted axis, with its chance tilt of 23.5 degrees off the ecliptic sufficing to decide the entire human cycle of decline and renewal, the variations in latitudinal destiny that rendered one soul implacably Hindu and another an evangelical Protestant. But even a globe, projected by the Cavern, was no mere globe. Focused in space by five convergent projectors, this one came down off the front wall to float freely in space, in the volume of vacant air.

The first time he coaxed the spinning marble down into the room, even O'Reilly, its nominal author, could not keep from swiping at it. A little wrist action on the wand — something that those from less charged regions of said globe insisted on calling body English — and he learned how to bat the thing around the room like a glorified beach ball. While engaged in a private match of planetary jai alai, he failed to notice Adie Klarpol's Labrador nosing its way in through the Cavern door. Mistaking the ghostly orb for a moon gone violently wrong, Pinkham went off the doggy deep end, baying uncontrollably, until Adie dragged him away and chained him up.

Pinching from Stance and Kaladjian, O'Reilly assigned the wand's thumbwheel to a zoom function. A little scrolling and the Earth swelled to a medicine ball or imploded into an atom. With the rub of a thumb, Afghanistan, as it had lately in the world imagination, ballooned from an invisible speck to a billboard that filled the field of view.

When the globe grew large enough, O'Reilly simply stepped inside. The Cavern knew where his head was at all times, and rehung its coordinates accordingly. The crust of countries that the projectors served up looked even better from the underside than from the out. Inside, from the vantage of the earth's core, O'Reilly could inspect the whole theater at one glance, with no hidden hemisphere on the far side of a projection. The unbroken surface spread out above him in all directions, like the constellations of the night sky.

He set the wand's buttons to throw various layers over his planetarium display. The slices of tonal register tracked the range of a variable as it wrestled its way through the proving grounds. Armed with canned data, O'Reilly took the globe out for a test spin. Per capita GDP, in single-year time frames. As a function of energy consumption. As a function of consumer spending. All the classical formulae, for which he had only clinical patience, ran as ten-second, color-strobing short subjects before Our Feature Attraction.

To this clean, coherent display, Ronan fused his ten-dimensional recursive cellular automata. All the furious systems, the flex and tension of abductors and carpals clasped together in an invisible hand to rock a cradle now eminently observable. On the surface, sunsets and dawns illuminated the familiar jigsaw of the world's nations. Underneath, a seething snake's nest of cooperation and competition rippled through the global markets, deciding them.

O'Reilly plagiarized Stance and Kaladjian for one more essential component. Their backward-running breezes inspired him to flip the vector heads on time's arrow. The simplest possible test for any futures game consisted in finding out whether it could predict the past.

He created three dozen interdependent variables, each chained recursively to the others, a multivoiced conversation about per capita petrochemical consumption. He initialized his starting point to mimic the data for 1989. His seed numbers came straight out of definitive industry tables. He assigned the range of output values to the visible spectrum. North America read out as a hot red, Europe more magenta. China languished down in the aquamarines, but clearly coming on strong.

The touch of a button set the film in motion upon inexorable sprockets. He let the simulation run for a few years. From the still point of the turning world, O'Reilly watched the colors craze like maples in a Vermont October. The foliage exploded with all the glorious look and feel of fact. The passage of three real months seemed to vindicate his three-month trial runs. But did small errors of assumption—miscues in the continuous conversation—propagate through the system, breeding phantom spikes and dives, nonsensical artifacts, spurious squalls from out of the blank boundaries of forecast?

Ronan had no way to say with any certainty. Short-term success implied nothing at all about the long run. And just because a simulation worked once or twice or even a thousand times under divergent circumstances, that said nothing about the ever-irreducible *next time*. The future had this tenacious way of turning a pebble in the streambed into a continent-sculpting meander.

No amount of success proved that the gears in O'Reilly's box bore any relation to the great gears that he hoped to model. The world at large had no gears. Nothing in it knew how the futures market would work out. Regarding crude oil sales, the world at large knew only last year's numbers.

So be it: O'Reilly had last year's figures as well. Past would be his entrée into posterity. While not rigidly deterministic, his iterative democratic negotiations were still reversible. If modeling could spill the milk, modeling could just as easily unspill it. O'Reilly reset his simulated world to his own moment. He took up his viewing post at the planetary core and ran the history of petroleum consumption in reverse. He rewound in slow motion, eyeballing each region's patina of color as it eased back down the rainbow. After a year, he froze the frame and toggled to the numeric display. The values fell within acceptable thresholds of error.

He threaded back another three years. The transcript coughed up a bubble here or there, but nothing that seriously undermined data's likeness. The readout's colors hove remarkably tightly to the curve of actual shortage and glut. Session after session, Ronan laid into the rewind button. He lifted a decade off the world's life, then a dozen years, reversing the effects of global aging with his fast-acting wrinkle cream.

Then he arrived back at the middle 1970s, the great oil crisis. There he and history abruptly parted company. His numbers hit that geopolitical slick patch, and the loss of traction sent them skidding off into an alternate universe. From there on back, all resemblance between estimate and fact broke down.

For the span of a month, Ronan himself hit the skids. He reverted to a rate of alcohol consumption that matched the worst of his Belfast days. Work had come to nothing. How could math—even the innovative math of multiagent dialogs—ever hope to factor in such a wild card? It seemed that, in order for simulation to cope with the shocks of radical sheik, it would have to contain as many interdependent variables as the Arabian Peninsula had grains of sand.

Rajasundaran found him at The Office, defeated. *What's your problem today, Irishman?*

The bloody Arabs.

And what have they done this time? It's never-ending with those chaps, isn't it? You'd think that your Crusaders would have long ago taught them to mind their manners.

They've messed up the world of rational multivariable extrapolation, is what they've done.

Oh. I thought that was your Adam and Eve.

Desperate, O'Reilly took Rajan and Spiegel into the Cavern. To show them the extent of the leak and to enlist their help in bailing.

Rajan thrust his head into the spinning globe. *Oh my beautiful word. This is amazing. Pardon me, Ronan baba, but I'm never coming out of here.*

Spiegel whistled. *Nice stuff, Ronan. Freese is going to pop with pleasure.*

Yes, you apes. But it doesn't mean anything. It's a piece of pretty gibberish.

Hey, Spiegel said. *That's what the nineties will be looking for.*

My code couldn't reverse-calculate the last oil crisis. How in the hell is it going to predict the next one?

May I ask the possibly obvious question? Rajan said. *Why, in fact, do you want to know these things?*

The future? Why do I want to know the future? You must be kidding me. That's the grand prize, friend. The end of the tunnel. The great escape.

These people. These white people. They're truly dangerous.

I don't get it, Spiegel said. *What's with all this backward prediction stuff?*

It's just a calibration tool. A convenient way of seeing how reliable the simulation engine is. Since I can't very well test my numbers by peeking forward . . .

No. I mean, if you want to see if you can predict 1973, why don't you just start in 1968 and—

Oh bloody Christ. That's brilliant. Utterly brilliant. That never would have occurred to me in a million years.

Rajan cackled like a banshee. *Yours is a wilderness mind, Ulsterman. A true wilderness mind.*

O'Reilly returned to them a week later, even more dejected. *No luck. I queued up a simulation, setting all the starting variables to three years before the embargo. And the program blew right through the decade without so much as a hiccup. Oh, it managed a tiny spike, I suppose. But according to my little digital men, oil never rose more than a few dollars a barrel.*

Put me down for a Valdez's *worth,* Rajan ordered.

Well, Spiegel said. *Time to make a better model. What actually did cause the oil embargo?*

Rajan raised his hand. *I believe it had something to do with a little Arab boy sticking his finger in the—*

Shut up, Raj. I'm serious. Listen, Ronan. If your multiagent negotia-

tions can really model the processes behind macroeconomic events, then they ought to be able to do political events as well. Expand the dialog. Include the missing contingencies. It seems to me that if patterns of petroleum consumption depend upon oil price, and oil price depends upon Western-Arab relations, and Western-Arab . . .

O'Reilly wandered away in mid-clause, his wilderness mind already laying the groundwork for the vast expansion.

Midyear gave all coders ample study in expanding variables. From a dozen local epicenters, rashes of pure negotiation broke out. Inside the spinning hologram, the Realization Lab looked out on a planet intent on running its own model. Politics-at-large doubled faster than the most aggressive formulations of Moore's law could pace. April blanched at May's developments, and June made a mockery of May's wildest predictions.

Mad days spilled over into their madder sequels. The nightly news awoke from its filler sprigs of human interest into full-fledged epic, building toward some precarious denouement whose final shape even the anchormen refused to guess at. Event lumbered into sudden view, like some saurian kneecap swinging in front of a tenth-story window.

Lim cobbled together a TV receiver card and mounted it in a server chassis. Anyone in the lab could pop a window up on their terminal and run twenty-four-hour cable headlines as a background task. Even the most reality-challenged were converted overnight, swept up into detail mongering. Lunchroom conversations hung on the latest developments in a story too sprawling to track except in its component images.

Will you look at those Russians? Trapped into validating their own fabrication. Propping up the marionette, feeding and clothing it, until the damn democracy thing stands up and walks off on them.

I love it. The teen cashiers down at the Redi-Mart are throwing around the name Erich Honecker like he's one of their Saturday-night doper buddies.

We need a TelePrompTer here. Just tell me who to cue on this week. Still Poland?

Czechoslovakia. Poland's halfway to personal camcorders by now.

Something was under way, too wide to be astigmatism, too persistent to be the usual, fleeting, collective hallucination. Millennial developments began popping up in doses massive and frequent enough to string along any event addict.

Freese played spokesman for his hushed team. *Almost makes one believe in a Zeitgeist.*

It's all electronics, Spider said. *Those Chinese students? That couldn't happen without satellite dishes. Cell phones. Faxes and photocopy machines. Notebooks and laser printers.*

Machines, bringing to the earth's backwaters word of their dispossession, leaving them hungry to join the informational integration.

Not just an idea whose time has come. A time whose tech has come. Lim scanned the images of teeming students, as if looking for someone.

Adie took to patrolling the RL's central atrium, calling out idiotic Cory Aquino parodies to anyone she passed. *People Power! People Power!*

Spiegel laughed to see her, more gangly and unguarded than the girl she'd been at twenty-one. *People Power? Isn't that being a little anthropocentric?*

His old friend had come alive in this great awakening, more manic than he could have hoped for when he'd lured her out of her early retirement. The abdicated craftswoman, who'd sworn off any art beyond paint-by-numbers, who'd renounced all pleasures of the retina, now became the first to run down the halls, recidivist, proclaiming the world's latest Renaissance.

Nor could Spiegel say exactly what had tipped her back into the camp of the living. Something in the Cavern's proving grounds had prepped her for these global velvet uprisings. Some hybrid possibility, laid down in Rousseau's walk-in jungle, brought to life in each night's newscast of delirious Beijing students camped out under the Gates of Heavenly Peace. This miracle year, not yet halfway done, conspired to salve art's guilty conscience and free it for further indulgence.

The Adie that Spiegel had loved, the poised, potent undergrad who'd believed in the pencil's ability to redraw the world, was long dead the night he'd called to recruit her, a casualty of adulthood. He'd invited her out anyway, fantasizing that some lost fraction of her might revive at a glimpse of the prodigious world-redrawing pencil the RL was building. But for the world at large to choose this moment to collaborate in redrawing itself: he'd never been so mad as to count on that.

Maybe Lim was right. Maybe the spreading world machine was catalyzing this mass revolution. Maybe silicon seeds had planted in the human populace an image of its own potential. After ten thousand years of false starts, civilization was at last about to assemble the thing all history conspired toward: a place wide enough to house human restlessness. A device to defeat matter and turn dreams real. This was what those crowds of awakened students demanded: a room where people might finally live. Every displaced peasant would become a painter of the first rank. Every crippled life a restored landscape.

On Tuesdays and Thursdays, the extent of Spiegel's puerile, wishful thinking embarrassed him. Mondays, Wednesdays, and Fridays, he was ready to put money on it. But whatever the cause, whatever the outcome, collective life was undeniably igniting. And Spiegel had his private, world-blessing Adie back.

It's sad, though, Stevie. Wouldn't you say?

Sad, woman? How do you figure?

Suppose that . . . ah, it's crazy even to think it. But it is crazy, isn't it? Everything that's happening.

Adie gestured to her terminal, as if the gathering worldwide protest were occurring there, in a background window, through the cable of headline news.

Suppose that peaceful world pluralism really is breaking out. What happens next?

What do you mean, what happens next? Next, we live it.

Live peace? Live arrival?

Sure. Sounds pretty good to me.

I don't know. Maybe this is just perversity. But something about complete consensus would just . . . sadden me. Think of art, all the shockers and rule breakers. Masaccio, Hals, Turner, Manet, Duchamp. All the guys up on the barricades: Caravaggio, David, Rodchenko, Siqueiros, Rivera . . . All of them! All the good ones were either iconoclasts or revolutionaries. We need something to take up arms against. I'm not sure

I want to live in a time when all battles have already been fought and won.

I can't believe you're saying this. It's like something I would have come up with, back in our school days. Back at Mahler Haus.

Oh, probably.

First you say that art doesn't count for anything. Then you try to make it out to be the elitist conscience of the whole heedless race.

Silly me.

Make up your mind, hey?

OK. It doesn't count for anything.

That's better.

I feel strangely relieved. Here's to global peace and a common style.

To the age of wallpaper. Bottoms up!

But Adie Klarpol could not stand under the coaxial cable's shower-head, the spray of pixels pouring down from bobbing satellites, and keep from feeling that the race's picture-making was only now begin-ning. A quorum of scribbling children had gotten loose, taken their pastel chalks out onto the sidewalk, over the curb, into the street beyond. Images from this group show of *refusés* streamed in on the con-tinuous electron feed, images blunter and more impudent than the streetwalking *Demoiselles*. Images poured out in black-and-white into the next morning's print, then peeled off of four-color presses for the weekend highlights roundup.

Those pictures worked Adie's visual transference. Their portal swal-lowed her. They seized her by the neck hairs, held her gaze, and returned it. That crowd gathering in the world's largest public square — the student camp, the swelling hunger strike — touched off her sympa-thetic candlelight vigil in a chrome and molded-plastic corporate cafeteria perched on the American coast, ten thousand miles across a spreading seafloor.

Look at that, Adie told her hypnotized colleagues. *Beyond belief. The largest army in the world, brought to a complete standstill by a bunch of college kids.*

A lot of bunches of college kids, Spiegel said.

A lot of lot of bunches, Rajan added.

Kaladjian scowled, dismayed by this latest proof of human irrationality. But the math intrigued him. *Day after day. Spontaneous globular clustering.*

Freese could say nothing these days without shaking his head. *I'm sorry, Spider, but there's something more than cell phones causing all this.*

Spider scanned the nearest screen for evidence. *They do seem to have reached a critical mass.*

Incredible, Adie said. *The largest government on earth forced to back down. Nothing else to do. They waited too long.*

Hang on, hang on. Spiegel waved his arms at the television tableau of protesters. *Can everybody just relax and regroup for a few months? I can't do things at this speed. This is not my postwar world. Little boy from La Crosse learning how to hide under his school desk from the atom bombs.*

Even Ebesen stood and stared. *I can't believe I've lived long enough to witness this.*

Oh shit, Michael Vulgamott said. *Here I just bought an expensive new atlas.*

What a win. What an astonishing win. Adie looked about the gathered witnesses for confirmation. *It is a win, isn't it?*

Data brightened all the witnesses' faces. Only O'Reilly still wore the curled Cold War lip. *Bliss was it in that dawn to be alive.* He hunched up his pained shoulders. *But to be young was very heaven!*

Freese rose to the Irishman's quote-a-thon challenge. *Come, my friends, 'Tis not too late to seek a newer world.* The words urged his nominal employees back to their own complicit work. For deep in the bowels of the lab, inside the revolution's deepest recesses, an even newer world waited, eager to be made.

18

There in the land of spruce and cedar, fast Fourier transforms and the draftswoman's fine Italian hand unleashed a profusion of banana leaves, slit and droopy, indecent in their greens. Klarpol's magic gamboge grew, riddled through with movement. Banana leaves played like children in the undergrowth. Dreamlike bananas floated up to tickle the insouciant moon.

Adie grafted Rousseau's peculiar tangerines onto her proliferating trees. Orange Christmas ornaments decked her branches. She extended the given foliage, working like those golden age landscapists who painted whole woods from asparagus tips and broccoli. The rain forest retrieved its original boundaries. She sought more creatures to people her garden, working for a patron she almost failed to recognize. For the first time since she was twenty-one, Adie felt that pleasure might be not only blameless; it might even be a moral imperative.

She stepped into this *Dream*, recalling herself to things long forgotten, the way one remembered one's body after a sustained illness. The thicket parted before her wand. Copses split open, inviting her to lose herself down a new path in the tangle. Every fork worked the ploy of artificial nature, its burrs adhering to her pants cuffs, hitching a ride into the real.

Under the shelter of a spreading yucca, a diminutive Venus, no larger than a mouse deer, rose from a puddle of water on her surfboard scallop. She surged upward for a few seconds, then sank back beneath the waves, only to rise again a moment later, her flat, scanned bitmap set to perform an eternal do-loop.

Paths led on deeper into the forest, trails blazed by their own repeated use. Down one, the vegetation thinned into a clearing. In this open meadow, hemmed in by palms, there grazed another color Xerox: shepherds huddled around a rock tomb that bore a strange inscription, rustic archaeologists probing a vanished civilization whose technology dwarfed their own.

At another fork in the forest, a plowman tore into the stony soil. A convex mirror nailed to a nearby tree trunk bared its surprise reflection. Up in the highest limbs, a boy threatened to release a soap bubble that quivered forever on the end of his straw. A golden-haired girl stared at him from across a chasm of vines. Between the branches of a spreading banyan, a dark projectile hovered on nothing. Only from directly underneath could the viewer make out a lady's slipper, hung motionless in space.

Through the gaps in the jungle, off at the vanishing distance, there spread other woodlands, further rivers, seascapes, crags and cliffs floating dimensionless against the jungle night. On the far edge of the woods, where a road cut through midnight, a lone figure pumped gas. From a hewn trunk standing on a skull-strewn hill, furtive figures took down the body of an executed man and laid him in the lap of a grieving pyramid, female and blue.

So it went: trinkets scattered like prizes through the boscage, a scavenger hunt of visual quotations obeying neither history nor influence nor significance nor theme nor any other principle of inclusion aside from one woman's private affections. A solitary trail of loved things, digitized. A haphazard, walk-in Cornell box of essential scraps, larger than life: her life.

It baffled Jackdaw. *So what exactly is all this crap?*

These? The escape valve for surviving the pressure of culture, she told him.

She took Stevie on a tour. They slowed in front of a couple, knotted together under the vines. *Schiele's* Embrace, Spiegel said. *What do I win?*

You're lucky if I let you break even, she said.

Incredibly sexy. Two people melting into each other.

Really? I always thought they were writhing in agony.

They walked on, through the clipping gallery.

What do I get if I name the rest of them?

You get to live.

What? You mean no one has lived unless they know the classics?

No. I mean you name them and I won't kill you. Yet.

Lim came through early one evening, agitated from reading a new book on prehistoric art.

You have to read this. The author claims that the Upper Paleolithic caves were the first VR.

Sure. Spiegel twisted his palm in the air. *What else can you call them?*

No. Literally. Theater-sized, total-immersion staging chambers where they'd drag initiates by torchlight. The shock of the supernatural sound-

and-light show supposedly altered the viewer's consciousness. Lim stopped, mazed by the idea. *Can you imagine? Catching your first ever glimpse of images, flickering out of pitch-darkness. Like nothing you've ever seen. Your deepest mental illusions made real.*

Adie held up her hand to stop the stream, until she could improvise a bridge across it. *You're saying that cave art begets all this?* She waved to include the whole RL. *That Lascaux starts a chain reaction that leads to . . . ?*

I'm saying that art explodes at exactly the same moment as tool-based culture. That cave pictures prepared the leap, after a million and a half years of static existence. That pictures were the tool that enabled human liftoff, the Ur-tech that planted the idea of a separate symbolic existence in the mind of—

Oh Jesus.

You see? You see? If we can makes these . . . scratch lines come to life, then life is not just some outside thing that happens to us. It's something we come into and remake.

Spiegel sat stilled, in a small reflecting pool. *I read somewhere that Lascaux has become a simulation of itself? Tourism was killing the paintings. So the authorities built these complete underground replicas so that—*

Lim's impatience cut him dead. *You still don't get it. They were simulations to begin with. Consciousness holding itself up to its own light, for a look. An initiation ceremony for the new universe of symbolic thought.*

If that's right . . . I can't begin . . . I don't even want to think what technologies the Cavern is trying to shock us into.

Lim traced the lines of the widening hunt in the air in front of him. *The mind is the first virtual reality.* He groped for the concept, by smoky torchlight. *It gets to say what the world isn't yet. Its first speculations bootstrap all the others . . .*

It's true, Adie said. She gestured at their rhizome, proliferating into the distance. A chill seeped up her spine, spreading at the entrance to her brain. *Do you remember the night the two of you showed me the Crayon World? Now look!*

Oh Lord. Spiegel held his head. *What have we done? We've taken a decent, law-abiding hater of technology . . .*

Oh, I still hate technology. I'm just learning how to make it please me.

Adie's new pleasure drew Spider back with greater frequency. He checked up on the Jungle Room's smallest alterations, like a log house owner watching a neighbor put in a barbecue pit too close to the property line.

Go on, she encouraged him. *Just head down that way a little. That opening to the left of the divan.*

Nah. I kind of like it out here.

Even after a dozen solo trips, he refused to leave the comfortable foyer of Rousseau for the expanses of the greater mansion.

She . . . reminds you of someone?

Who? he bluffed.

Adie smiled at him. Pointed at the pointing woman, recumbent on her berth. Spider made no sign.

Someone from around here?

He turned to look at her. Through their two sets of 3-D glasses, she couldn't see his eyes. He looked away.

Depends on what you mean by "here."

Where were you born? she asked.

He shrugged.

You don't want to say?

He swung around, hard. *Not a question of wanting.*

How old were you when . . . you came over?

He turned away again. *Young.*

She waited a decent interval. *Adopted?*

You know the odd thing? He spoke to the woman on the sofa. *They say I have an older brother. Somewhere.*

She came and put her arm around him, where he stood in the foliage. He took off his glasses, but would not look at Adie.

I really wish you'd paint some clothes on her.

Ebesen paid a visit one day, when Adie had the Cavern. For the first time since their near-conversation, he reappeared, ready to talk. He checked up on her progress. She walked him through the moving animals, including the monkey he'd animated.

Were you aware that your innocent customs official–turned–naïve painter once did time in La Santé prison? Ebesen spoke as though the crime were hers.

No! Impossible.

Yes indeed. Aiding and abetting a forgery and embezzlement scheme.

I can't believe it. Did he know what he was doing?

Probably not. You folks rarely do.

You folks? Me folks?

A surfeit of wide-eyed artistic trust. At least that's what the authorities concluded. They let him out after a month.

She took Ebesen down the paths into the scanned anthology. They passed by the Botticelli without comment. They skirted the Poussin. Ebesen showed nothing more than a twitch of recognition around the lips. He took the controls, steering them down the jungle track as if in an ATV. Soon he refused even to slow down at the passing wayside attractions.

They reached the far end of the simulation, where the unbordered world dropped off into white. Ebesen removed his glasses and nodded. *Interesting.*

That's it? That's all the critique I get?

Well, unless I missed it down a hidden fork somewhere, you've left out something obvious. Something essential.

No Dr. Tulp, she said. *No Gross Clinic. I refuse to do anything where anyone's veins are outside their body.*

Hands. Red handprints. Elk. Bison. Magic arrows.

Oh! Yes, of course! A glow infused her eyes, the idea of perfection. *Can't have a Cavern exhibition without a little cave painting.*

Ebesen didn't register. The bagman was lost in disputation with himself. When he spoke again, it wasn't to her. *Huh. That's it. That's how you need to do this.*

He walked out of the Cavern. She watched him leave. The seat of his sagging khaki pants had worn through in two moth-eyed spots on either side of the inseam. It stabbed at her. The battle for existence shrunk to a decent pair of trousers — one meager gift that she'd never be able to give the man without humiliating him.

Against all indication, Ebesen came back. He dragged with him a massive quarto volume, its spine long ago broken, its loose pages in various degrees of prison break. A venerable book with the smell of mold and water damage to authenticate it. A text that had hectored generations of students when Janson's unfocused eyes still baffled themselves on that print of *The Peaceable Kingdom* pasted above his crib.

Here, Ebesen said, cracking open the tome. All the plates were black-and-white. Or had been black-and-white once. They'd since all mildewed to ashen and ivory. He held out his specimen for Adie's inspection: a wildly shadowed flamenco dancer. Adie kinked her brows and looked at him for explanation.

You don't know it? She shook her head. *You don't know it. I'm disappointed in you. El Jaleo? By Sargent? You do know Sargent, don't you?*

Karl. Be nice.

I am being nice. You haven't seen mean yet. Here. Look here. He pressed his thumb to where she was supposed to look, further smudging her chances of making out the data.

She stared, feeling her old loupes kick in. She scoured the wall behind the dancer, the play of macabre shadow, obscured in a cheap print, rubbed out through years of shameless use by hands that probably prayed more often than they washed. Seeing anything there was a hopeless prospect, except for his insistence that she see it.

And then she saw. Painted on the painting's painted plaster wall: a replica of the first-made images.

He's quoting Altamira, Karl said. *Just discovered by Sautuola and his little daughter. Written up the year before Sargent does the painting. A Spanish cave, you see. The painting's not really about the dancer. It's about the first-ever proof that we have to paint. Paint like we clap our hands. Took four more decades for the experts to accept the idea of Stone Age art. Nobody wanted to believe that these bison were the real thing. Except for painters, of course.*

She looked at him, taken apart by what she saw.

Scan Sargent and stick him in your nature walk, he said. *You'll get Altamira for free.* He stared back at the image inside the image, shaking his head a little sadly. *Think of it. All these centuries of greater realisms, more light, deeper psychological penetration, and the golem still never came alive. Paint: disowned by technology, discredited, until technology needed it again. And now,* he said, shrugging at the Cavern walls, *the water and the mud and the spark are finally coming together. Now we're at last threatening to pull it off . . .*

Karl. Karl. Who was this man? *Why aren't you an art history professor?*

His face flushed, as if her words had slapped him. A hard, red hand slap. Flamenco.

Fuck you, too, doll.

Ebesen bundled up his yellowing gift and removed it from the negotiating table. He turned his threadbare trousers on her—pallid mandrill on its deathbed—and made for the exit.

Karl. Stop. Stop right now! I meant that as a compliment.

He turned in the doorway. His face twisted up, as if he were a non-native speaker, trying to remember "compliment," the shifty homonym, the false friend.

Help me with this, she said, waving to include all that was now invisible. *It's the greatest game in the world. But it would be even more fun with someone who understood all the jokes.*

His face came forward a nanometer. *Jokes?*

Ah. Sorry. I mean "allusions."

Ebesen suppressed a lip twitch. He studied the Cavern walls, empty now, their projections shut down. Bled of all electrons, they looked as blank and white as heavyweight bond. *You'll help us out with the architectural fly-through, in return?*

Sure, sure. Although I warn you, I can't tell a corbel from a cornice.

And you'll let me litter your little theme park with my personal favorites?

Of course. That's the whole point. Only . . . ?

Go ahead. Say what you were going to say. Only?

She winced. *Only . . . we might want to work from some more recent prints.*

Ebesen held the grubby book to his chest for an awful moment. *You want me, you get my anthology.*

I'm sure we can find an out-of-the-way bush to stick you both under.

So Design's senior derelict led Adie down the overgrown path of Western art. Ebesen muttered to himself while he worked, reciting stray facts and vesper-captions that kept him to the task at hand. She listened as inconspicuously as she could, from across the cubicle, reacquainting herself with all his old, exhausted favorites from scratch. From another's eye.

The man pattered on everything from Paleolithic fertility figures to late-day silk-screened sex sirens. *On New Britain,* he told her, *people believed that humans came to life when the gods dribbled blood on drawings of them.*

Or: *Picasso thought he'd invented camouflage.* And by free association: *You know how the Dutch kept the* Night Watch *out of the hands of the Nazis? They hid it underground, in the Limburg marl grottos.*

He'd hold two prints up for her, side by side. Comic in their contrast: Watteau and El Greco. *Art has only two obsessions. Denial of death and preoccupation with it. Real achievement depends on either utter indifference or utter terror.*

Genuflecting in front of the Ghent Altarpiece, he'd say, *Do you know why Mary's hand towel is dirty? The angel took her by surprise, at her prayers. No time to tidy up for the guests. Know why the Annunciation script is upside down? God's dictating, from above . . .*

Karl, Karl. Where on earth do you come up with these things?

She asked his opinion about the eighties international superstars, the market where art now lived. Ebesen just shrugged. His knowledge ended abruptly in the year that Adie's SoHo show had opened.

It passed for friendship in the low fluorescent light, Ebesen's halting glosses, his overture of closeness. And Adie kept her end of the bargain. She cleared herself a workspace in the room that Ebesen shared with Michael Vulgamott. The bagman and the architect had already used their Cavern tool kit to simulate a skeletal bungalow. The viewer could wand through this interior, not just along predetermined paths, but in any direction she cared to explore. Their simulated rooms occupied real volume. Although little more than hasty polygon fills with a dash of surface texture, their interiors held together from any angle. Walls blocked access and doors allowed it. Light streamed through windows from a consistent source. Stairs led up and down. Opposite views supplied each other's complements.

Proof of concept, Vulgamott said. *Enough to show how the Cavern can bust open spatial visualization. But just a five-finger exercise. A mock-up for the real tool.*

Their idea was to assemble a chest of architectural primitives: three-dimensional icons, universal building blocks for creating countless further rooms. They imagined a visual catalogue of prefab parts, designed once, reused forever—the full Vitruvian library of any building component that imagination might require. Each solid piece had to be deformable along any axis. When Adie joined them, Ebesen had already been working on the Ionic capital for weeks.

We figured we'd start with your more high-demand items, he explained.

Doric was done. Abacus and echinus each bore resizable handles that one could click and drag to shrink or swell the capital. The moldings below adjusted accordingly, while the necking and flutes stretched to fit snugly onto any column underneath them. The Ionic model improved upon this basic unit, upping the number of flutes, changing the echinus to egg and dart, and adding adjustable volutes.

Ebesen worked the stone meticulously, testing on a flat-screen monitor. He carved, examined, jimmied, and carved again. The tedious scut work fell as far below design as design fell below the skills of the man who, Adie suspected, could freehand any object in creation.

Vulgamott fussed at a nearby screen, perfecting his own pier and shaft. *Nobody here is exactly looking forward to Corinthian. Adjustable acanthus leaves. It's going to be a bloody nightmare.*

The tool-kit language took ordinary architectural descriptions and parsed them into tiny aesthetic machines. Someday—with luck, before the hour that TeraSys set for a final Cavern rollout—a goggled architect would be able to stand inside this wraparound drafting table and, by clicking, cutting, and pasting in the empty air, produce a ghostly scale-model Parthenon, on the fly. The designer, immersed in a virtual design environment: Vulgamott christened the idea V-CAD. It had a certain recursive beauty, using a chamber of the Cavern itself to build more stately chambers . . .

So use me already, she told them. *Tell me what to work on.*

How would you like to be the greatest expert on triglyphs and metopes north of the Bay Area? Michael Vulgamott asked. *No experience necessary.*

He spoke with a perpetual mope, that burlesque of depression that could only be depression-induced. Even expressions of appreciation sounded like a dental complaint. She slaved over bits of frieze and pediment that she felt sure would please the man. But when he came and stood over her shoulder to monitor her monitor, he could manage no more than a whimper. He'd start to object, and then—objecting to his own objections—trip himself up before he could get back to his sentence's line of scrimmage.

What? she said. *Tell me. What'd I do wrong?*

It isn't you, doll. He'd turn his back and throw one operatic hand up in the air. *It's humanity at large. A persistent source of stress to me.*

Michael, Michael, Michael. It's like being back in the Union Square subway station, talking to you. Where'd you grow up, anyway?

Hattiesburg, Mississippi. Who wants to know?

Vulgamott nagged at Adie. She couldn't read him. *Is he being flip?* she finally had to ask Karl one night. *Or is he just permanently testy?* Adie wasn't sure she could always tell the difference in Karl himself.

Who, Vulgate? The man is holding on by his fingernails for the moment of worldwide redemption. He wants to make the Cavern into a giant ark. He's in a race against the clock to save everything of worth that has ever existed from the flood. It's a thankless business, and the odds are, shall we say, not in his favor.

It was, for Adie, the ideal apprenticeship: time-sharing between her jungle, strewn with its snippets from the West's crumbling museum, and this growing warehouse of Lego blocks, Michael Vulgamott's windbreak against the coming long night. She moved freely between the adjacent countries. Her knowledge of architecture had never extended beyond the obligatory chapter in the survey texts. Now, viewing the trade from the crypt up, she made the connection. Buildings were art's skin, the pictures we lived in. They were many-planed concoctions of color, line, and shape, paintings that had to stand up to the rain. The simplest self-supporting structure involved as many aesthetic decisions as a midsized Titian. A temple's texture and light changed with the season, the hour, the thousand-and-one viewing angles. Frozen music, yes. But also thawed paint: harmony and radiance made whole by an accountability to engineering.

She loved the idea: programming the programmable room to house its own model progeny. Even more perfect were those two models of male strangeness, her supervisors in architecture. For Michael's high-strung perfectionism, she felt increasing respect. Toward her surly bagman, she developed something like a maternal impulse. Proprietary zeal. Finder's pride. The curator's interest in the wrongly discarded.

The deposits into her word hoard alone more than paid for this exchange of labor. Architrave, entablature, stylobate, fillet, fret, torus, scotia, plinth, anta, oculus, entasis, brattishing, extrados, acroterion, spandrel, finial, bargeboard, tympanum, coving, diaper, mandorla, crocket, archivolt, salomónica, baldachin, reredos, rinceau, boss, bucranium, coffering, rustication, lancet, anthemion, swag, corbie step, dado, moucharaby, lunette, flèche, exedra, mullion, newel, oriel, quoin, shoin, stoa, loggia, joist, squinch, pendentive . . . A term for every feature that ever made for decorated shelter. The plainest ornament, the smallest piece of frozen function, bore its own label, however obscure, in the encyclopedia of available parts.

In her dreams, she ran through a fitness course of free-floating vaults and arches, each requiring some maneuver as she pushed through the reticulated air. And that sense of swimming freedom stayed with her when she awoke each morning. For the first time since Spiegel's and her failed college experiment in cooperative living, she felt a panic at sunset, at the racing clock cheating her out of her rightful hours.

Life was not long enough to finish all the projects it wanted from her. She could live with that. But the idea that any one of the projects now haunting her might take all the years she had left and still not reach fruition seemed cruel, even by creation's sadistic baseline. She would return home on a late ferry to her island cottage — her neglected berry bushes and weed-shot garden — reeling from all that she'd learned that day. Something hurt inside her. She'd forgotten the feel of it: that eager pain of bone growing faster than its own muscle.

Down the mountain from the lab, the world's wider growth continued to outstrip her. Her day's discoveries began showing up on the evening news. If she cleared a space on the edge of her forest for a Bruegel crowd, that same milling throng would show up on the cable feed later that night, bounced off a satellite from Wenceslas Square. When she spent an evening on the drapery of a resizable caryatid, the statue promptly materialized on all the breakfast cavalcades — a surreal Goddess of Democracy, a ten-meter imitation of Liberty coming to life on the numbered cobblestones in front of the Great Hall of the People. Art's impudence was nothing, held up to its source. Imitation fell back, astonished by the scale of the original.

Vulgamott needed the spigot of cabled images wide open at all times. Ebesen just as violently needed it off. They worked out a tacit deal between them. Michael sat at his workstation, the daily cataclysm pouring in, live, through a corner of his screen, its sound track turned down just loud enough for him to hear. Karl sat as far as possible across the room, hunched over his own graphics box, piping in a bit of annihilating trickle from an audio disk in the CD drive — Ockeghem's *Missa Prolationum* or Byrd's *Great Service*.

Holy shit, Vulgamott would exclaim at the image feed, a couple times a day. *I can't believe this is happening. You have to see this.*

Ebesen never flinched. *Let me guess. Shocking pictorial. Demi Moore fully clad.* And each would carry on living, in the face of the other.

The compromise satisfied both men, each content to live in that band of the event spectrum that he accredited. But Adie, sitting alongside them, trapped between both data channels, at the focal tip of their stereo cone, would get so agitated by the chill intersection of polyphony and politics that she'd have to go out and trot the half-mile loop around the lab parking lot just to calm down.

In the first few days of June, the rains giving way in the approach of summer, Adie sat in that cross fire. She sketched on her screen while the peaks and troughs of CNN and Renaissance counterpoint canceled each other out into a standing wave. The work she gave her hands seemed good, a sustainable development, something to tinker at indefinitely, to learn a little bit more from each day until the lesson was whole.

If we make six perfect frames in a row, do we get to rest?

You dream, Vulgamott answered, not looking up. *After six million, you can knock off for a fifteen-minute latte.* Then, in another voice altogether, he said, *No. Oh no.* He sounded like a mother, thick with disappointment, scolding a child who'd just spilled sauce down the front of his Sunday best. Then, *Jesus Christ. No. No!* And the game changed for good.

Michael? What is it? What's wrong?

Don't mind him, Ebesen said. *Some blip on the AP wire. Our friend thinks he's holding the world together by the force of personal concentration.*

But Vulgamott kept repeating his hypnotic mantra. *Please no. Not that.*

Adie crossed over to his desk. She leaned and looked at his screen, the source of distress. In a postage-stamp window, difficult to make out, a human crowd milled. It looked like the same continuous surge they'd been watching daily for the last several weeks. Only this crowd was panicking.

What is it? What's happening?

Vulgamott stared at the screen, fixed by occluded revelation.

Make it bigger, she said. He did. But when the picture reached viewable size, it pixilated. The blocky clip only fed her ignorance.

Some newsreader's voice in New York rambled on over the blurred film stock, something about Deng learning from his previous mistakes and sending in young Mongolians. *The number of casualties is still not known.*

Not known? Vulgamott yelled at the disembodied voice. *Not known? Can't you see?*

He stood and left the room. Adie, in an informational trance, followed behind. She moved as in some ancient school fire drill out of tornado season. Only when they reached the hall and began drifting like dust motes did it dawn on her. Vulgamott didn't know where he was going.

They ran into Spider. *Listen,* Michael asked. *Can you patch an analog signal into the Cavern?*

Sure. But Ronan's booked in there for another—

Thank God. Someone who knows what's going on. I'll deal with O'Reilly. You just give us the feed.

By the time Lim succeeded in piping the massacre into the Cavern, a small crowd had gathered. No glasses. No parallax. Just the standard mayhem of aerial film, trained on the walls of the theater box. Cadets shooting into crowds; kids thrashing each other through clouds of gas; a lone semaphore signaler, for a few electrifying minutes, holding up a column of tanks: the scenes the whole world would watch again and again, until broadcast made sure to inure all viewers.

A small, stunned congregation assembled in this smaller public square, surrounded on all sides by planes of video. Tiananmen filled the horizon, at eye level, all around them. Then, punishing them for their silence, video plunged the dozen viewers into another crowd. On no logic but the quick cut, they floated in an ocean of mad, mourning black. A different riot moved to the same nightmare surge. Now no soldiers, no Mongolian trainees offered up group death. Now just mass self-mutilation, grief over the lost Imam, returned from his state of exile to redeem the world.

Adie stood pinned in the group hysteria. The madness of crowds swept over her, even in this back projection. Only when the cameras cut for a commercial could she breathe. She turned and walked out through the Cavern's open wall. Up from the nightmare, no chains or checkpoints. She cast a look back from the outer doorway. And there she saw a scene that haunted her long after Tehran and Tiananmen faded to black: a dozen stunned lives, huddled in a picture-pitched tent, trapped in the rising information flood.

She moved back to the jungle full-time, away from the press of all facts, out of the reach of news. Off on a spur in the far corner of the Rousseau room, down a path unreachable from the jungle's entrance, she placed a detail from that most beautiful version of the *Massacre of the Innocents*. After that, she used nothing more troubled than Matisse, Chagall, and Corot. Trees feathering on Creation's breath. Goldfish floating ravished in the refracting ether.

Underground, she told Ebesen. *Deep in the marl grottos. Nobody will bother looking for them there.*

Her island cottage gave her refuge. That summer was the Sound's sunniest in recorded memory. She worked at her columbine and tea roses, bringing them back from weed. She pruned the blackberries and set the crab pots from the dock off her inlet, then sat back and waited for a peace that refused to come. Instead, the sight of those panicked crowds ambushed her, in the surreal hours flanking 2 a.m., when low blood sugar and abetting blackness combined to docent her around her own private Bosch.

Lost, her eye grew stronger. She would sit in the RL's atrium, looking out through its expanse of picture window, gazing down on the unbroken mountainside. She'd sit and squint, applying to this real scene all of Loque's anthology of software filters. She'd work it like the aged Renoir, a brush strapped to his wrists just above the worthless claws. She'd slide a mental adjustor knob from left to right, pulling the whole landscape through discrete, imagined steps from Patinir to Goyen to Ruisdael to Hobbema, on through Kensett and Cole and Bierstadt, then down to Millet, Sisley, or Signac, stopping only when the light started to fail.

This scenic outlook became her private outpost, a place where she could be among people yet not have to look at them. From a hundred yards away, she caught sight of a leaf fat with July's solar spoon-feeding, and saw in it the sprig that Stevie had grown for her, so long ago. She stared for hours out this picture window on the unearthly convolutions of nature's prototype, the only view large enough to erase the human.

One afternoon, on the downward slope of summer, she sat surveying that people-free Barbizon. Everywhere across the landscape's panel, life cast its filaments. She watched a northern flicker lift off a branch in mid-distance, its ventral gold splash flashing as it took flight. Drawn by her glance, the bird bore straight for the RL. Helpless, she stared as it slammed into the picture window, a feathered fist bouncing off the plate glass with a smack.

At the sickening pop, Adie's body ruptured. She screamed, but nothing came out. She ran pointlessly to the pane. The thing lay on the ground in a broken heap, striped, tawny, stilled.

A smear of grease on the glass marked the impact, like the chalk outline around a corpse. Adie fought the gasps coming out of her, an effort that only made her sound even more like a strangled animal. By luck, Spiegel came across her first. Stevie, she didn't care about. Steve had seen her a lot worse off.

Adie, what's happened? What's wrong?

She pointed to the crumpled sack of taxidermy. The bright crest of red in the grass.

Spiegel looked at the window smudge. *Aiy. A hard hit.* Innocence always hit hardest. He glanced behind them, into the expanse of room. *Confused by the atrium, probably. From out there, it must look like more of the same.*

My fault. My fault.

Your . . . ? Now, how in creation do you—?

I saw it coming. I . . . I drew it . . .

Adie. He put his arm around her. She neither let him nor refused.

They stared down at the dead thing, appealing the verdict. Absurdly, the bird chose that exact moment to come to life again. It flapped once or twice, thumping on the ground.

Then it found its gears, lifted up, and followed some remembered angle of incidence back to its delayed errand.

Oh Jesus, Spiegel laughed. *Would you look at that.*

Brute animal persistence. Adie followed the escape, incredulous. She gathered herself in. *It should have died.*

Spiegel broke off cackling and stared. He took his arm from her shoulder. *I'm sorry? It should have what?*

Better off dead than that. You saw how it flew off? More sky, as if nothing at all had changed.

Ade, it's a bird. A bird, for Christ's sake. A second ago, you were grieving for it.

She shook her head, insistent. There were worse things to be killed by than false distances. Worse things to die of than naïveté.

19

In imagination's room, all things work out.

This is the place's guiding rule. Nothing gets in that doesn't already fit. No twist of plot, except what is slated.

In this room, nothing bleeds. Nothing rots. Nothing breaks. There is pain here, but there is no suffering. Things do grow, but never past their prime. All local flesh has learned that lizard trick of regeneration. The cheetah takes no more than half the antelope's flank. Then the sacrifice grows back again.

Grizzlies stand in the rapids, swiping at stray salmon. But they fish more for sport than out of real need. Theirs is strictly a catch and release. The fish, too, understand the game, the pure run of it, there being no strong line between loss and win. They leap free, teasing, or go belly-up, surrender a pound like a tree sheds fruit, then drift back downstream to try their luck again tomorrow.

The politics of watering holes resolves itself through negotiation. Dogs still fight for their place in the pack's pyramid, but every Omega will have his day. Ant colonies still go to glorious war, although their fronts remain static. Soldiers give their lives to the cause, and the giving completes them.

Every accident has its repair. Nests crumble in the wind, just to gratify the oriole's need to rebuild. Unfledged chicks still blow to the ground, injured. But some benevolent biped ultimately returns them to their high, woven safety.

The people in this room grow up to become what they've always dreamed of being. The human economy teems with doctors and firemen. Oil bubbles up in the back yards of tar-paper shacks. Lost children find their parents again, after many harrowing adventures. Abused orphans wind up adopted by kind uncles and aunts.

Lovers quarrel, slam down the receiver, swear off each other, remember everything, and call each other back laughing in embarrassment. Widowers receive nightly visits from their mates' ghosts. Lonely souls, locked in their own timidity, finally write each other letters, three days before it would have been too late.

All countries move steadily toward democratic free markets. Poor nations catch spark, enjoying the advantages of the late starter. Growth is everywhere export-driven, yet all lands enjoy a favorable balance of trade. Disease yields new insights into how the body works. Someone invents the solar-powered car. Someone discovers how to extract energy from tepid water.

Zealots, on the road to some mass persecution, fall down blind and rise ecumenical. Hotbeds of factionalism succumb to improvements in communication.

Music here heads through the occasional passing dissonance. But always, by cadence, it finds its way back to Do. Revolutions in style still build upon the past. Art constantly refreshes itself, and the occasional harshness, after years of study, proves to be beauty by another name. Lost cantatas now and then come to light. The stolen panel of the Just Judges turns up in a Carthusian monastery.

Age-old mysteries at last get solved in court. Criminals come across life-changing novels in prison, bold-stroked tales that show what still lies ahead of them to accomplish. Each day ends in some illustrative sunset, shattering or subtle.

But this room can't brook any depth or width. Dimension is already too degraded to sustain. This room leaves no place to sit and absorb it. No spot where any outsider might just gaze. Even the weight of a solid glance would tip it, wreck this room's precarious equilibrium.

This is the room to which dying people retire. This is the room from which infants are taken to be born.

This is the soul's balanced window box, the domain of finished poems.

This is the heaven of last imagination. The paradise of detachment. The room of no consequence in the least. Of making no difference in the whole known world.

20

Yeki bood. Yeki nabood.

That is how the world's best storytellers always start: It was so. And it was not so. One of the few Persian phrases you can remember, from out of a whole childhood of your mother's Persian phrases that you never paid any attention to. They must be in there still, an attic of lost fables that wants only unlocking.

It's like this, and it's not like this. There was a time, and there was not a time. They are right to start that way. And they are not.

Like so: you find yourself in a small room. There is a mattress here. Before you is a radiator. On that radiator, a chain. The routine: crushingly familiar. Two and a half meals a day, ranging from the vaguely edible to the deeply disgusting. A ten-minute fire drill each morning in the Black Hole of Calcutta, where your stunned bowels must set land speed records if you wish to preserve what trappings of humanity your captors still allow.

And not like so: you are not here. Hope refuses even these temporary lodgings. You know the day only by running estimate. You know the hour only by the vague passage from dark to darker. A cell is nothing against this train of thought.

Your mind is clearer, now that clarity can do nothing for you. Freed from the state of emergency, you have some time to turn things over. To make sense of the senseless. They give their word that you will be out soon. But you now know to measure "soon" in more realistic units. You make the necessary conversions from Central Arab Time. But even your guards picture you out of here by New Year's, at the latest. And January 1, you insist. Not March 21.

You plan to spend New Year's Eve, 1987, in the middle of Daley Plaza, underneath the Picasso monstrosity, singing "The Star-Spangled Banner" at the top of your lungs.

Taken by surprise. Taken by accident. An insignificant foreign language teacher who never took sides in his life. Half Islamic, for God's sake. You mean nothing to your government. Nothing you can be swapped for. You're of no value to your captors whatsoever. In fact, you can only cost them, to imprison and feed you. Cost them in international prestige, to harm you in any way. All they can hope is to salvage some face-saving way to set you free.

With all the time in the world to think, it dawns on you. If they grabbed you by mistake, then the person they really want must still be out there, walking around at liberty. That CIA operative they jabbered on about during your first interrogation. If they can find him, you'll walk away from this nightmare with all your limbs intact.

You spend the whole of a waking day reconsidering everyone in the City of Wells you've ever met. Your life depends on finding the spy. On turning up the name that can save you. Only at nightfall does the full revulsion hit you. There is no such man. Yet you were ready to Kapo him off. Sell out a real life to the monsters of invention.

You wake up still horrified, unwilling to go near yourself. But by noon, you creep back again. You replay the mistake, reconsider the spy. It passes the time, at least. And time is more of an enemy than any other terrorist.

Deciding who turned you in is good for a brief twenty minutes every midafternoon. You still know the whole class roster from memory. The group must have harbored some closet Shiite, passing above his class, passing for a Sunni merchant learning the language of world trade. Or maybe one of the smiling Sunni elites sold you out, covering his tuition by making a few pounds on the side. Could have been any of them. All still washed in their first innocence.

These speculative minutes can last forever, without an outside tick to clock it. A single afternoon supplies all the endless time in the world to figure out who put you here. To figure out where you've put yourself. Just another slumming American, priding yourself on acing the interview, on marketing yourself with a bit of fast talk. How exhilarating it was, that sense that you'd gotten away with something. Now you see that the school would have taken anyone at all. Anyone who could speak English. Anyone not insane. And even that requirement, they went ahead and waived.

You've brought this all on yourself. Walked open-armed into a civil war. You've negotiated with it since childhood, this sick desire for event. You weigh every other explanation and come back to the only one possible. The happy, affable, well-adjusted guy with his whole life in front of him wanted to sample prison. But not even your old self-destruction could have imagined this.

Dinner saves you from more self-punishment. But your dinner guests turn out to be total duds. Conversation is sporadic and banal, and no one seems to have any sports scores fresher than three months old.

The smashed chickpeas do help to fortify. With something inside you, the crush lifts a little. So what if you were trying to kill yourself by coming here? Beating yourself up about it now won't help. Truth has less to recommend it at this point than survival. You must outlive whatever part of yourself that wants something else.

You double back on the healthier obsession of figuring out which innocent student turned you in. But that fondled theme fails to divert you all the way up to sleep. You graduate to trying to work out exactly which group you've been handed over to. Three million people. Sixteen officially recognized religions. You read once that twenty different militia groups can rule a single refugee camp. Two dozen autonomous armies have carved up this country, staked out their sovereign checkpoints. Two dozen independent nation-states, laws unto themselves, rove from the Bekáa to the coast, armed with anything that the Security Council countries will sell them, their assault rifle butts stenciled with everything from verses from the hadith to decals of the Virgin Mary. And you can name only five of these groups at most.

So much rides on figuring out who has taken you. And so much doesn't. The means for finding out are somewhat limited. You decide to ask them, point-blank. You've gotten pretty good with the blindfold. Putting it on, when anyone shows, so that a wide swatch of the world remains visible beneath. And your ears have attenuated, too, to the point where you can tell your guards apart by the way they rattle your cage.

There are at least three regulars. You assemble them from bits and pieces, in gauzy darkness. One of them, the Angry Parent, is short, with a belly potting if not already pot. He wears a khaki pseudo-uniform and must be in his fifties, although you've yet to make out his face.

The second you've gotten a hurried look at. He came into the room once without knocking, as you scrambled to fit the blindfold onto your head. The bare bulb of the hallway threw his outline into high relief. White hair, a medium build, alert but bemused features. The Shiite Walter Cronkite.

The third is the Crazy Child. The one who beat and threatened you with his gun. You keep your head bowed when he is in the room. You know him from his knees on down: pencil legs, always the same pair of blue jeans ending in, God help you, a spanking red-and-white pair of Adidas.

You sniff out each of their walks, easily telling them apart even before they open the door. But you want more chance to study their voices. The Shiite Cronkite brings you dinner one night. "*Salaam alaykum*," you try him.

After a pause, he replies with a polite "*Alaykum as-salaam*." The longest conversation with a real person that you've had for a week.

You try it out on the Crazy Child. "*Salaam alaykum*," you greet him, the next time he bangs on your door with his pistol butt.

"Heh? A! *Salaam, salaam!* How do you know? Where do you learn *salaam*, hey?" He giggles, a low, hick chuckle. "We talk my talk now?" He releases a high-speed stream of syllables that sounds like abuse in any lexicon.

"Who are you?" you try, without a hope in hell that he'll tell you anything.

"Who?" Another throaty giggle, but slower. Mountain kid in the big city. Trying to enjoy himself and make it back home without getting fleeced. "Me? I am Ali."

It's your turn to giggle. You run the risk of pistol-whipping, or worse. But you cannot help yourself. "Hold on. Let me guess. Ali . . . Smith?"

"Hnn?" You brace for the blow. "Ali Smith?" He laughs like a jackal. "Yes, good! I am Ali Smith."

"Who are your people? What is this group that has taken me?"

But Ali just clucks with his tongue: *What do you take me for?*

Days later, the next time the Angry Parent hustles you to your morning sprint through the latrine, you try your greeting on him.

"*Salaam alaykum. Salaam alaykum.*"

The Angry Parent makes no reply.

Your beard grows in. You play with the two bald spots on each side of your mouth, the spots that have always stopped you from growing a beard in real life. For the first time ever, you have the luxury of growing facial hair without any social consequences. You twist the longest chin strands into twin points, untwist them, repeat. It's good for what feels like hours at a shot.

You peel off a wafer of plaster from behind the radiator large enough to balance over the opening of your urine bottle. You keep the makeshift cap in place at all times. It reduces the room's stench. You find a way of lying along the radiator so that you can do sit-ups and push-ups without the chain chafing. You jump in place, run two-meter laps in a shrunken oval.

Ali hears your morning workout. He bangs on the door to break it up. "Hey? What you doing in there?"

"I need exercise. If I don't exercise, I will grow sick and weak."

"You stupid shit," he explains.

But no one intervenes when you start up again, quieter.

Knowledge of who is holding you arrives by the worst of couriers. The Angry Parent shakes your door late one evening, the signal to submit and cover your eyes. He enters your cell and places something on the floor in front of you. Then he circles around behind your back.

"Take off your cloth, please." His English, though thick, is surprisingly fluid.

You remove your blindfold. The sight on the floor in front of you turns your eyes hot and viscid. A pencil and a sheet of blank paper, your first since captivity.

"You must write a letter." He sounds forceful, but not violent.

"Oh yes. Oh, bless you. Thank God. *al-Hamdallah.*"

His hand on your head prevents you from turning around in joy.

"No, no," he corrects, patient as a first-grade teacher. "I tell you what you must write."

You must write: *To the people of the United States.*

I am alive and healthy. I am being kept by the soldiers of Sacred Conflict, a unit fighting for God's Partisans. They are not terrorists. They do this thing as the only way to win justice.

I am being treated and fed well. I will not be hurt in any way, as long as the United States and its leaders act honorably. I will be freed as soon as the demands of God's Partisans and of God's higher laws are met. If they are not, then the failure will be upon you. And the failure will be serious.

You spell several words wrong. The Angry Parent doesn't notice. This is your desperate code, the only word you can smuggle out to the outside, the lone assurance that you know the letter is nonsense. Your mother will tell them. The Chicago office, Gwen: anyone who knows you in the slightest. Nothing if not a perfect speller.

"Please sign the letter," the Angry Parent commands. "Now place your cloth back on your eyes." He gathers up the paper and pencil and walks to the door. "Thank you," he says, and closes you back in on nothing.

Worse than nothing. The sound of the clicking lock forces you under, into a despair like the closing of a metal crypt. It's Sacred Conflict. The group that brought down the American embassy like a stack of mah-jongg tiles. The ones who slammed a car bomb into a crowd of Lebanese scrambling to grab American visas. The group whose eager foot soldier, smiling as he ran his truck through an armed checkpoint, blew himself away with 2,000 pounds of TNT, taking 241 Marines along with him to the heaven of martyrs. The one group in this Babel of factions that you prayed it wouldn't be.

Sacred Conflict: their balance sheet is so huge, so mysterious, that you can't be anything higher than an expendable pawn. These men have the consortium of rational nations on the run, reeling from the power of their conviction. The terrorist group of the hour, just now enjoying their moment on the geopolitical stage, their suicidal, scene-stealing walk-on. Your letter gives them one more holy weapon to brandish at a cowering world.

The day after your exercise in dictation, you fall ill. Your body gives in to the infection it's been fighting since capture. A steel chill spreads from your extremities into your chest. You lie huddled on your mattress under the cheap acrylic blanket, shivering in the slip glaze of your own sweat. Sleep is a four-reel hallucination where radical factions take turns inscribing the details of your confession onto your abdomen with the point of an electric needle.

The next day's ten-minute sprint through the latrine does not last you through the morning. By the time the Shiite Cronkite brings you your pointless lunch, a demon—hot, yellow, and liquid—splays its claws against the wall of your intestines.

"Toilet," you croak. "*Merhadh.*"

"I ask Chef."

"No ask Chef. Tell Chef."

He disappears. You wait an eternity—150 seconds or more. Then you must defecate or die. No time even to scream for a can. You run as far from the bed as you can get, tear down your pants, and aim for the mouth of your urine bottle. Amazingly, almost half of the silty stream finds the bottle. You leave the putrefying rest and crawl back into bed, fetid, sticky, lower than an insect, a dung beetle. You fall into a raging fever.

You wake up, someone kicking you in the back, thumping you with an Adidas cross-trainer toe. Ali is shouting, "Hey. Hey! Why you shit all fucking over the floor?"

Your blindfold is on. He must have replaced it before commencing to kick you. You roll over and place your face in the path of his blows. He stops. You feel your power over him, power that comes from your total indifference.

"Sacred Conflict," you say. "Holy War."

"Hey," he bleats. "You gotta eat your food." The *gotta* learned dutifully from some Top 40 song.

Eating is death. Anything you eat now will pass right through the frictionless tube you have become. All you can do is squat it out, hope the virus dies of dehydration before you do.

"No eat," you say. "Hunger strike."

Your refusal enrages him. He shrieks deep in his throat. "Eat!" He kicks you again, in your mercifully emptied gut. He crouches down and inserts the cold tip of his pistol in your nostril. "Eat."

His growl sounds like a bad James Coburn. Even this wasted, you must laugh. He screams again, his rage ever more impotent. "What you want? What the hell you want?"

"Medicine. I need medicine."

"*Bukrah*," he says, shaken. "Tomorrow." Neither word means anything to you.

In your dream, Gwen reaches into your throat, deep in, deeper than you ever suspected a hand could go. She pulls up half-digested forms, eroded Cracker Jack prizes covered in decomposing clay, the hair and slime that accumulates in sink pipe traps. She holds out a handful, and the two of you lean in for a closer look. The crowns of your heads touch, the first kind touch you've suffered in months. You bend over the slime, examining. It crawls with tiny amphibians, pink cave newts no bigger than termites.

The medicine arrives by special delivery. Whether it is tomorrow or not, you cannot say. The room is anyway pitch-black. The medicine is a grayish powder. Ali, by flashlight, jabs a fistful into your hands, telling you to take it with water. The drink tastes like mine tailings. It gags you. But by now, so does the neutral air on your opened mouth.

"Is this poison? Are you trying to kill me?"

"We are not killing you," Ali counters. "America is killing you."

You sleep again. You wake as light seeps in under the cracks of the corrugated iron stapled over your French windows. You are hungry. At first you don't recognize the gnawing, so archaic is it, so unlikely. Even after several deep breaths, nothing hurts. You feel—well—*well*. You feel the reacquaintance that comes only after illness. Exhilarated, in spite of all cause.

You rise up on your stumps and walk, as far as the chain allows.

"Hello? Hey. Someone?"

Someone is there, opening the door. From the gentleness, you guess it to be the Shiite Walter.

"What you want?"

Blindfolded like justice, you point toward the smear of fecal accident in the corner. "Something to clean that up with." You pantomime rag, pantomime bucket.

"Yes. OK."

"Also . . . an orange juice, an Indonesian highland arabica, and a double order of eggs Benedict. Easy on the hollandaise."

Silence from your captor. Mute, threatening, ambiguous.

"Food, please."

"Yes. Sure. No problem."

21

The world machine bore on, in the face of the unbearable. Its overburdened angel engine failed to overheat. Not right away, in any event. Not all at once. It survived the latest massacre of hunger-striking students. It absorbed the intimate documentation, the grainy aerials and close-ups, the midrange establishing shots that saturated video's every free market. Knowledge returned, civilization's bad penny, even this late in the scheme of things. It played and replayed the rote vignette: armies firing on unarmed crowds. Only the scale, the mechanical efficiency, the presence of cameras made this round seem in any way unique.

History and its victims kept their hands to the plow, broken, exhausted, like an old married couple trapped for life in love's death lock, unable to break through to that sunlit upland. The future, under construction, leveraged to the hilt, could only press forward, hooked on its own possibility. Hope not only persisted; it made a schoolgirl spectacle of itself, skirt in the air, all shame on view.

Fall was well into its return engagement. The rains signaled an early and long winter. Adie Klarpol grieved for current events until she could no longer feel them. Then another shame gripped her, more private and local. She'd lived here for the better part of a year and had not yet learned the first thing about this town. It was as if she'd had room in her for only one exploration at a go. Now the days began to lose their length and weight, heading to winter. She vowed to get out a little, while there was still time.

She laid out a box around the downtown, one of those numbered grids that archaeologists use to inventory a virgin field. She rode to the top of the Space Needle, fixing a shorthand map of the streets' layout. From that bird's-eye view, she picked out sights to acquire over the next half-dozen Saturdays. She turned over every inch of the City Center. She got the Woodland Park Zoo out of the way early, racing past the various forms of captivity. She paid her overdue pilgrimage to the Asian Art Museum and the Frye, blasting through them with the same guilty squeamishness.

Jefferson, James, Cherry, Columbia, Marion, Madison, Spring, Seneca . . . She clicked the streets off, climbing and diving with the strangest sensation, feeling as if she were wanding through them. As she walked, the high-resolution, water-lapped horizon swelled and filled, without pixilating or dropping frames. She swung her head side to side, and life tracked her pan seamlessly. The piers, Alki Point, Pike Place Market: all appeared to her astonishingly solid, with fantastic color depth, and no trade-off between realism and responsiveness. When the sun chiseled its way through a chink in the stratocumulus and, for fifteen seconds, blazed the cityscape into highest contrast, Adie discovered the real use of binary. The greatest value of the clumsy, inexorable, accreting digitization of creation lay in showing, for the first time, how infinitely beyond formulation the analog would always run.

She prowled, one blustery Saturday, up and down the four floors of the Mindful Binding, that fantastic, expanding, used-book universe perfect for getting lost in. She headed first for Architecture, searching for scannable plans that might be of interest to Ebesen and Vulgamott, peace offerings for having abandoned them. Then—old bad habit— Art. The oversized color coffee-table books just sat there on the shelves, past hurting anyone. And there was no one at all to catch her looking.

She moved on to Travel, Victoriana, and Local History. Then, decorously delayed, she paid the obligatory visit to her first love, Juvenile Fiction. And there in that most unlikely place, she ran into Stevie Spiegel. The last person alive she would have figured on meeting under that heading.

He saw her, and his eyes darted quickly away to check if he might slip off unseen. But they were both caught. *Adia Klarpol! What brings you out into the light?*

She laughed. *Not a full-blooded vampire yet. Still just a novitiate, remember? Don't we get to venture abroad for short intervals during the first year?*

Sure, sure. Whatever gets you through the night.

Besides, I could ask you the same thing.

Me? I like the light. I make it a point to get out in it. Once every other month or so, whether I need to or not.

She gestured to the motley-colored bindings. *Kids' books, Stevie? You're not responsible for any illegitimate little charges that I don't know about, are you?*

He blushed. *Hope not. It's . . .* He wrestled with expediency. *It's just that I've been looking for this one story . . .*

Since you were nine?

Well, seven, if you must know.

Called?

Oh. Now. If I knew what the damn thing was called, I wouldn't still be looking for it after all this time, would I?

Author? Subject?

Gone. All gone. My daughter, my ducats.

Hang on a minute. You've been trying to locate a book for thirty years, and you can't remember what it's about?

Oh, it was a fabulous story, if that's what you mean. This boy has the ability to make the things he imagines come into existence, just by — and here I'm a little shaky on the exact mechanism —

Stevie. You're hopeless. Was this an older book? American? English? Translated?

It was about so big. Amazing illustrations, mostly sepia and magenta.

Oh. Why didn't you say so in the first place? That narrows it down considerably.

He hung his head. They scoured the shelves together, separately, in silence. Each looking for a secret buried treasure. Neither of them finding.

She capitulated first. *That's it. I'm taking off.*

You going somewhere? Or do you have a minute?

I have my whole life, she told him. *Until Monday.*

They wandered at random through the afternoon-soaked streets. The air thickened and expanded around them as they stirred it with their bodies. They talked shop, their only safe common denominator.

So how's Art's Greatest Hits going?

She shrugged. *It's still a jungle out there.*

They looked up: Pioneer Square. *Sit for a minute?* he asked. Expecting to be refused.

They found a vacant bench. Adie sat and exhaled. Unfolded. The sun ducked in and out through a scattering crowd of cloud.

God, she said. *Damn. I feel like the Mole-Woman. You know? The one they've buried in that hermetic sunken shelter? The woman who lives in that Ramada Inn lab at the bottom of a mine shaft, with the flock of video cameras and microphones pointed at her around the clock? What's her name again?*

Mmm . . . Doris . . . Singlegate?

Stevie. You never cease to amaze me. How long has she been underground?

Good question. It has to be at least a year.

And what's the point, again?

Study her physiology. Changes in biological clocks and such. In the absence of all outside cues.

You science types are all sickos.

He laughed, a little offended. *Since when do you lump your old fellow traveler with the science types?*

Ever since you wired up your iambs.

Look who's talking. But I'll admit to a certain sick fascination with the Mole-Woman. I hear she's gone sidereal. That her body's reset itself onto a twenty-five-hour cycle. Can you imagine? Every four weeks, she loses a whole day.

What do you mean, "imagine"? How long have I been working for you thugs, anyway? I'm ahead of schedule.

At least we let you come up for air now and then.

Spiegel produced a sack of slightly linted honey-coated peanuts from his jacket pocket. Adie ate the minimum that politeness dictated. Stevie swung his head east to west, a pivoting Minicam. Through his eyes, she saw the square unfold. A clump of people queued up for the next Seattle Underground tour. Knots of autonomous agents milled about the lost pergola, each holding to the hem of a private goal.

People school, Adie said. *They flock. Have you ever noticed?*

He nodded. *They're looking for places of power. But they can't find them, because none exists anymore.*

Places . . . ?

You know. Stone circles. Barrows. Temples, cathedrals, mosques, pagodas. Even town halls, I suppose, once upon a time.

Stevie. I thought you'd graduated from poetry. I thought you were sticking to subroutines these days.

He flashed his can't-hurt-me-with-that smile. *Not entirely incompatible, I've found.*

And these places of power of yours . . . ?

All dried up. Where's our Stonehenge these days?

What, they've moved it from Salisbury Plain? Those vandals.

Spiegel snickered. *No, it's still sitting there. Behind a chain-link fence. Salisbury Cathedral, down the road, is no better. Two pounds for a peek, and a little numbered walking booklet demystifying all the high points.*

Adie waved her hand outward. *I don't suppose you'd be willing to count a colorful totem pole and a tasteful bust of Chief Seathl as magic lenses?*

People don't even see those things. They blow right past them, on their way to the stores.

Well, the stores, then. The malls.

I'm talking about places where we can be subsumed by forces larger than ourselves.

You've obviously never run up a monolithic MasterCard tab at Bloomie's, have you?

Places where we can reconstruct ourselves and nature. Where people can share transforming experiences.

The Kingdome?

His lips tightened, without much mirth.

All right. Adie sobered. *Books, then.*

Who has time to read anymore?

Little magenta books from your childhood.

Lost. Broken.

Movies. Of course. Movies.

Too solipsistic. You sit there for an hour and a half, chained up in the dark. Immersed, sure, but eyes forward, on the screen. Your guts get turned inside out, completely manipulated, fine-tuned by the industry's latest big release. But two weeks later, you can't even paraphrase the plot.

Adie threw a few honeyed peanuts to the birds. Every pigeon in the Pacific Northwest went into an all-points feeding frenzy. *Why do I have this sneaking suspicion about where you're heading here?*

He nodded. *You got it. I mean, the car, the airplane, even printing. They only changed the speed with which humans can do existing tasks. But the computer . . .*

Ah ha! Adie said, slapping him on the thigh.

The computer changes the tasks. Other inventions alter the conditions of human existence. The computer alters the human. It's our complement, our partner, our vindication. The goal of all the previous stopgap inventions. It builds us an entirely new home.

Hey? What's wrong with the old home? I liked living in the old home.

Did you? He held her eye. She looked away first. *Well, however you feel about the new one, you have to admit, it's out of this world.*

Oh, that much I'm sure of.

You know what we're working on, don't you? Time travel, Ade. The matter transporter. Embodied art; a life-sized poem that we can live inside. It's the grail we've been after since the first campfire recital. The defeat of time and space. The final victory of the imagination.

Whoa there, cowboy. It's four bedsheets and some slide projectors.

Oh, you ain't seen nothin' yet. Forget the technology for a moment. I'm talking about the raw idea. The ability to make worlds—whole, dense, multisensory places that are both out there and in here at the same time. Invented worlds that respond to what we're doing, worlds where the interface disappears. Places we can meet in, across any distance. Places where we can change all the rules, one at a time, to see what happens. Fleshed-out mental labs to explore and extend. VR reinvents the terms of existence. It redefines what it means to be human. All those old dead-end ontological undergrad conundrums? They've now become questions of engineering.

Adie tilted her head, withholding and conceding at the same time. *What makes you think . . . ? Nothing else has ever worked. All the arts, all the technologies in the world have failed to placate people. Why should it be any different this time around?*

First, because we're assembling them all into a total—

Na, na. That's Wagner. That's Bayreuth. And you see all the good that did.

But the Cavern blows opera out of the box. We're not just passive recipients anymore. We'll become the characters in our own living drama.

She shook her head. *The problem isn't going to answer to technology, you know. The problem is inside us. In our bodies.*

The Cavern is the first art form to play directly to that body. We're on the verge of immediate, bodily knowledge.

It doesn't work that way, Stevie. We habituate. Something in us doesn't want to stay sublime for very long.

We can be refreshed. Revitalized, by the sheer density . . .

She took in Pioneer Square in one glance: this palpable place, the master foil to Stevie's crazy vision. All at once, the tap of sunlight opened. *Why not life, then?* she said. *Life itself, as our final art form. Our supreme high-tech invention. It's a lot more robust than anything else we've got going. Deeply interactive. And the resolution is outstanding.*

But we can't see life. He gestured to include the world's tourists, rushing through the miraculous density of day's data structure without so much as a second glance. *Not without some background to hold it up against. In order for the fish to know that it's swimming in an ocean—*

He has to jump into the frying pan?

Spiegel snorted. *Something like that. Something like that.*

Some cloud passed from off the face of the sun. The sky grew so briefly radiant that it forced Adie's face up. Something in the light felt so desperate for sharing that it stretched out the deficit in her heart and left it, for the length of that glint, fillable. Breezes were stronger than reason. They just didn't last as long.

Nothing, she said, *nothing we make will ever match sunlight. A beautiful day beats all the art in the world.*

He looked at her oddly. As if they were bound together. As if they had the luxury of the rest of their lives to come to terms with each other. *I wouldn't know. I live in Seattle.*

That reminds me, she said. *Car. Ferry. Island.* She stood and stretched. *Garden. Dinner. Sleep. Wake. Work.*

He stood with her. *Where are you parked? I'll walk you.*

They steered uphill, through the public sphere, avoiding by complex collision algorithm a throng of other autonomous agents loose on their own improvised routes. They pressed along Occidental, above the buried Underground warrens. A juggler to their left kept a small pastel solar system twirling in orbit. From the south floated the sound of a busker picking out "Will the Circle Be Unbroken?" Panhandlers of all races, colors, and creeds approached them with elaborate narratives — wives in vehicular distress, misunderstandings with employers involving salary moratoria, momentary misplacement of all worldly possessions — then retreated again, fifty cents richer, wishing them both the best of available afternoons.

They plotted a course through Occidental Park, midway between the totem pole and the knockoff pseudo-Greek plaster sculpture directly across the square from it. Adie threw repeated backward glances over her shoulder through the peopled fray.

It's bothering you, he caught her. *Isn't it?*

What is?

That statue. What's the matter? Can't name that tune?

Oh, I guess it's supposed to be an imitation of some kind of kouros. One of the Apollos, maybe? Hard to tell. It's not a very good copy, to say the least.

That's it? Don't look. What else?

She stopped and closed her eyes. *Well, the size, for one thing. Too big. And it has all its limbs. I don't think any real ones are that intact.*

That's all?

Can I peek again?

No.

The color's off. But I guess it's hard to make gypsum look like marble. And the face isn't right. More Roman than Archaic, I think.

And?

She shrugged.

Go ahead. Look.

Well, it bugs me that it's draped. I mean, really. Isn't the muzzling of the NEA bad enough? Next thing you know, the Met's going to be chipping off all the gonads with a chisel, like they did in the Middle Ages.

That's it?

She stamped in place. *You tell me, Stevie. I give.*

Come on. Let's go have a look.

They turned and doubled back. She stood in the prow of her step, watching the plaster statue swim into focus. Each step upped the resolution until she called out, *My God.*

Yep, Spiegel said. *You got it.*

She kept walking, as if additional evidence might overturn the obvious. They walked up to the threshold of the sculpture, its optimal viewing horizon. Close enough to see it blink, twitch, breathe.

Steve addressed the work. *She thinks it's a disgrace that you're draped.*

Adie dragged him away, trawling in her purse for some change to pitch into the inverted discus at the statue's feet.

She thinks that today's modern audience is mature enough to take their Classical antiquities without censorship . . .

She twisted his arm up behind his back, marching him. She cast another look over her shoulder, like Lot's wife. Like Orpheus. The statue refused to ripple so much as a crow's foot around its wet irises.

Across the square, she loosened her grip on his arm. *So your eye is better than mine. Is that what you're trying to tell me?*

He twisted free of her clamp. Their hands caught each other, holding on for a few awkward seconds.

Beginner's luck. Besides: I noticed him earlier, setting up.

Spiegel's futurist vision nagged at her for days afterward. He was mad, of course. But certain of his formulations made Adie wonder just what program she was, in fact, working on. For her, the electronic doll-house's sheer inconsequence had returned her to pleasure. And now pleasure — it shamed her to admit — intensified in the suggestion that it might be headed somewhere.

From the scorpion-tailed branch of one of her digital mango trees, she hung that fluid, flaming Munch painting of three northern women, hands behind their backs, midway between aesthetic transport and anxiety attack. And on the flip side of the bitmap, for anyone who walked around to the far side of the picture, she penciled a calligraphic quote from the painter: "Nature shows the images on the back side of the eye."

Jon Freese e-mailed her, asking for a jungle open house.

It's not ready yet, she cabled back.

He insisted. Just for the other in-house groups. So you can get some formal feedback.

The open house turned into a group show. Loque demoed a major new concept for writing paintbox filters. *Got the idea from working with the artsy chick.*

All hers, Adie objected. *Don't look at me.*

Instead of starting with bit-fiddling algorithms and trying to match them to artistic styles, we scan in a dozen examples of a given artist and make the edge-detection and signal-processing routines build up a catalog of stylistic tics.

Not tics, Adie said.

Pardonnez-moi. Mannerisms.

Love it, Spiegel said. *Sort of the opposite of paint-by-numbers?*

Ari Kaladjian stewed in place. *You mean that you are giving up on the idea of formulating those functions that—?*

We're not giving up on anything, Ari. We just thought we'd explore a new angle and see where it leads.

I ask you again: Does it do us any good to produce a cute little parroting routine, without learning how to formalize its behavior?

We're just letting the machine do the formalizing, Sue said.

Adie's turn came. Her colleagues kept together as a group down the twisting paths in the undergrowth, stumbling over each new visual quote as if by accident. They gasped at the nativities, oohed and aahed at the animated still lifes, and laughed at the illuminated monks embroidering their scrolls with vegetation that spilled off the vellum and grew into the jungle all around them.

On a path near the back edge of the forest, Kaladjian attacked. *Will someone please tell me the point of this whole peculiar exercise?*

Freese rose to Adie's defense. *Come on, Ari. It's a demo. No more than everyone else's.*

Yes. But what exactly does it demonstrate? It has no real three-dimensional modeling or ray tracing. The image field remains planar. There's no interaction to speak of. Aside from a few charming animal animations, the sprites are static. And the depicted data mean nothing at all. Hardly a state-of-the-art demonstration of what the environment might do.

The group fell silent, scuffing their collective feet on the forest floor. Spider Lim stood guard over his divan woman, as if the mathematician might attack her.

It struck Adie that the others were waiting for her to defend herself. *Well, I don't know. I thought it was kind of nice to look at.*

Only Rajan laughed.

Spiegel rushed into the gap, covering for his recruit. *Come on, Kaladjian. Who are you to tell potential clients how they should use a Cavern? It's just as interesting to build a room to visualize inspiration as it is to build one to visualize long hydrocarbon chains.*

This "inspiration." Can you tell me where, in all these—snippets— we are supposed to find it? Can you give me one little proof by induction, one simple rule for telling it from non-inspiration?

He's kind of right. Jackdaw looked away as he spoke. *I mean, sure, it's beautiful and all. But it doesn't do anything. It's basically a flat gallery. The user can't really . . . make anything happen.*

Adie's face shrank from him in a crooked smile. You. You child. What did I ever do to you? *What do you mean, "can't" . . . ?*

It's not really what I'd call interactive.

Of course it's interactive. You go down this path or you go down the other. You see something interesting, you go closer. What more interaction do you want?

Well, see, I mean: as far as the little artworks are concerned? They don't even know the user is there.

If a masterpiece bloomed in the forest, Rajan began, *and no one was there to appraise it, would it still be a—?*

And after the user leaves? Jackdaw said. *There's no trace in the database of anyone having ever been there. The jungle just keeps carrying on as if—*

Exactly, Adie interrupted. *And thank God.*

Spiegel tried to interface between the races. *What Jackie means, Ade, is that you need more collaboration between the humans and the data structures. More of the dance that is unique to this medium.*

I still don't get it. It's not like this place could exist anywhere else.

She's right. Freese stepped back in. *This is a legitimate virtual environment. And it's unlike any that I've seen anywhere else.*

Jackdaw shrugged. *Oh, it's fine as far as it goes. But it doesn't transform the ordinary.*

Sue Loque put her arm around the world's creator. *It's just not the future's transcendental art form yet. You can throw something like that together for us, can't you, babe?*

My God. Last month they were raving about it. Now they're bored.

Motionless, downwind, Kaladjian hit his sprint from out of the crouch. *I would just like to know what this teaches us? Either about the hardware, the software, or the exercise of European painting? I want to know what we learn here.*

That we couldn't learn in a good museum, Jackdaw said.

I'll go further, Kaladjian added. *What of any real consequence can we learn, even from the best of museums?*

The hook lodged deep in Adie's gills. *You obviously aren't in any danger of having to learn anything.*

Art is not capable of teaching. This is my point. It contains no formal knowledge about the world. No predictions. Nothing falsifiable. Nothing repeatable. It's not about anything except itself. Other art. And even about that, it's at best equivocal.

Adie took off her shuttered glasses and stared at him. *Mathematician, has anyone ever told you that you're a very unpleasant man?*

Well, the pleasure is mutual. But at least you say what you mean. Which is more than most artists bother to do.

I'm not an artist. I haven't made any art for more than—

Too late, Freese resorted to authority. *This is neither the time nor the place to air personality conflicts.*

This has nothing whatsoever to do with personality, Kaladjian shouted. *This is about certain, definitive—*

Can someone please give me one simple rule for telling personality from non-personality? Rajan said. And the gathering degenerated into a free-for-all. Art and math skulked away from the spitting match, both gangs compromised.

But out of the ugly exchange, the virulent parasite of Cavern innovation took up a new carrier. Inspiration passed through the tracts of its unwitting sponsors, using them and moving on. Now the virus lodged in Dale Bergen, the mousy University of Washington biochemist who lived by the iron precept of never attracting attention. Bergen's Large Molecule Docking Room threatened the next step in human mastery over matter. The user stood in microscopic space, among galaxies of enfolded polymers, zooming in on docking sites now large enough to walk inside and poke around. Shape and charge dictated this representation's behavior, just as they did in the physical world. The graphical atoms took up their available bonds, obeying the pull of electrostatics built into their data structures.

In the Cavern's viewing chamber, the giant molecules calculated their own obligatory behaviors on the fly. Classroom became laboratory. Bergen dreamed that his Tinkertoy docking simulator would one day drive the actual mechanisms it symbolized. In the cybernetics of enzymes, the mousy, invisible man saw the basic switching and feedback networks of natural selection. In these shape messages telegraphing among their senders he heard whole counterpointing choirs, choruses untestable in isolation.

Bergen stood in the Cavern, watching Ms. Klarpol's hallucinatory fronds brush up against the faces of this wayward safari. What if each of these static botanies could be made to grow, obeying internal curves like those that governed his graphic molecules? What if these plant genomes were allowed to compete with one another, egg each other on, converting the resources of simulated soil, air, water, and light into ever more convoluted conversations?

The Cavern as crucible for simulated evolution: it was just a thought. The implementation lay, for the moment, well beyond Bergen. But the idea tickled him. One learned to build the rooms one wanted to visit. And ecology was a room that wanted visiting.

He snagged Adie on her way out. *Could I borrow your rubber trees sometime?*

She blossomed at his words. *My flora and fauna are your flora and fauna. Just be sure to tell Dr. Calculus where you got them.*

She hunted down the traitor Jackdaw in his lair, where she rabbit-punched him in the sternum until he called out for mercy. *What's the big idea? You betrayed me.*

What are you talking about?

Total ambush. You turned me in to the authorities. Left me swinging in the breeze.

What? I didn't do anything.

Stale? Flat? Not very interactive?

His fingers cast about anxiously for a keyboard to stroke. *Well? You let people walk through the jungle. But you don't let them walk into it.*

What in the hell is that supposed to mean?

I can show you. Come on.

She followed Jackdaw into the Cavern, where he gave up the secret of his recent labors. She watched him from outside the open mouth of the cube, behind the fourth wall. He stood alone in the chamber, taped with body sensors. The room came to life in a gray penumbra. Jackdaw raised one palm. Off to the east rose a roseate sunrise. He shifted his weight to one leg, lifted an arm, and turned his head. The forward portion of the room slid down the rainbow into a band of violets.

He cycled through a suite of gyrations, wiggling like a traffic cop pegged to a busy intersection. His joints conducted the walls in a swirling Kandinsky, airbursts of color chords synched with an atonal MIDI accompaniment. He held up two fingers, and jagged lines lengthened across the horizon, thickening with the dove-flights of his hands.

He stopped just as suddenly. *You get the idea.* He took off the glasses and joined her outside the cave opening.

Adie stared into the gap between them. *I'm sure it's very interesting, from a technological standpoint.*

But?

Don't think I'm just trying to get back at you. It's . . . a little tedious to watch, after the first fifteen seconds? You say our jungle is flat? Unless I missed something, you don't create any depth here at all. Sure, it's neat that you can get the color washes to back your body movements. But they're still just color washes.

Try it. Here. Just try it for a minute.

She donned the tracking glasses, skeptical.

Keep your motions clean and distinct. Mark the starts and stops. Use your whole body, all the degrees of freedom.

She started small. Commas with her fingertips. At first she tried to register what each motion produced. But the Pollock feedback came so thick and furious, so hard upon any plan her heels hatched, that she stopped thinking of her movements as causing the explosions ripping all around her. Her body *was* the sound and light.

Nods became auroras. Angry lightning bolts loosed themselves with a shake of the head. She composed with her posture and drew by drawing breath. The uterine lining of color swallowed her—the breakthrough sensation she'd heretofore only read about. She passed into the walls, coming out on the far side, encrusted in light, her skin hovering huge around her.

She forgot herself. Or she remembered. Dancing inside her dance, she could not say which. She embarked on a spiritual aerobics, the leap that sex never quite freed itself from self-consciousness to make. She decamped into pigment, molded, molding.

She came out from behind the glasses and shuddered. She shook her head at the boy author, not wanting to talk about it. *Aiy.* She shook herself off, like her dog Pinkham, after a dousing. *That's like drugs. Like being out in a stormy night on a hit of Windowpane.*

I wouldn't know.

But it only works for the operator. The onlooker has no idea. You have to be at the steering wheel, even to imagine—

He nodded a little sadly. *One of its big problems. The other big one is that the graphics are . . . what do you call them? Abstract. Sooner or later, something recognizable needs to happen.* That, his voice hoped, was where she came in. *Then we'll have the start of a real, live-in adventure.*

She sat safe, outside the theater, staring back at the walls where her circulatory system's sonata had just debuted. *If this is just the primitive Marconi version . . . Television isn't even child's play. People are going to walk into these rooms, and they're never going to walk out again.* Even her laugh came out bewildered. *They'll starve in there. Like rats in those Skinner boxes, pressing their own pleasure buttons until they drop.*

Jackdaw perked up, pleased.

You sure we really want to go down this road? she asked. *Do we really want to hand something like this to an already addictive age? Aren't we in enough trouble the way things are?*

He squinted, not getting her. When had trouble ever been the issue?

She thought for a long minute. *I'm going to have to start all over again. From scratch.*

Sure, he said. *Start small. We've found that it's not how many plates you get in the air at the same time. It's how well the plates spin.*

Start . . . small?

Pick one thing. Your favorite place in existence. Something you connect to. Something you can go inside of.

She closed her eyes and made the old pilgrimage. *OK,* she said, opening them. *I have it.*

So what are we talking about, then?

A bed. A bed by the shore of the Mediterranean.

22

This is the room life lends you to sleep in.

Bedroom. *Slaapkamer. Chambre à coucher.* Simple accommodation, with all the basic fittings. Bed, washstand, chair, window, mirror: everything that you need to live. But closing your eyes, sleeping here may prove impossible. For this room fills with a relentless blaze. Clear sun pours in from all directions.

A canted floor meets the wall in a mock horizon: the joint of earth and sky, of wheat and azure. The life that sleeps here has scuffed permanent patches in the floor's varnish. The room's real inhabitant has just stepped out. He leaves his shirts draped on the shirt rack. Their short-sleeve billow remembers his body. A straw hat, his shield from this southern sun, waits on a peg for his bared head to reclaim it. He leaves his bottles, his brush, his book on the bed stand. His towel, scudded with dirty handprints, hangs on the hook by the bathroom door.

In the painted bedroom, the man's own paintings hang on view. The scenes his eyes have lived in cling listing to the drunken walls. They serve as this apartment's additions: tiny remodeled day rooms, cobbled onto this room of broadest day.

The tenant has bent this apartment with his breathing. He proves, before the scientists, that space is curved. The chairs, the bed, the tilted table: each stick of furniture passes its own law of gravity. Each would-be solid lays down its own perspective, its various vanishing points scattered like buckshot in the hinted distance. No two of these pauper's objects belong to the same cubic space. The foot of the bed juts mysteriously through the doorframe. The floor swells like the loose sea. Walls and ceiling amble together by the art of compromise. The shutters give up on accommodating their casement, by turns closing inward and throwing themselves open to the Provençal breeze.

Is he happy, living here? Does the work of his hands please him? Do his eyes read this light's simplicity, grateful for a chance to handle it? Or do the cracks in this pitcher, the tears in the chairs' caning spell some unlivable agony?

You know this fellow by his things. The shaving mirror above the water bowl holds his look, as surely as a photograph. His impression nestles in the wonky bed. The lay of this rented hideout explains him. There is a rhyme to how this bedroom works. It remembers the life it hides. This man's ways suffuse through his attic dormer. Sun assembles a life from these surrounding solids.

But entering this painted life overhauls it. Your eyes change the bedclothes just by settling on them. Looking leaves its fingerprints on his glass. His towels take on your hand smudges. His shirts start to memorize the creases of your body.

This will be your *kamer*, your *chambre*, for who can say how long. A place to enter and inhabit at will. A box whose every plank of wood furnishes your story. This life, now yours. These paintings, too, now belong to you. The bed, the chairs, the azure, the wheat, the window: everything this sleeping room speaks of will be yours, except—in such merciless light—for sleep.

23

Tell me, Jackdaw asked her. *Where?*

Arles, Adie answered.

Where is that, exactly?

In the South of France. You know France?

Don't abuse me. I may not get out very much. But I could find it on the Net.

Oh, sweetie, forgive me. I'm sure you could. It's an old Roman town, in Provence. When I was a girl, we used to play a game.

We?

My sister and I.

In the South of France?

No. In our bedroom. The running average of those nine bedrooms, swapped every two years, across the air bases of the Free World.

Did your sister have a name?

Elise. My mother's fault. She was looking to enliven a very banal life. Elise and I used to lie in bed, across from each other, after lights-out. Hold our eyes open with our fingers, until we could see in the dark. We'd chatter away, turning the cracks in the ceiling into the Shire, Moria, Mordor . . .

Been there. Made that map.

After a couple hours, Elise would fall asleep. Weak-fleshed girl, my sister. I'd lie underneath my covers, feeling abandoned. I became the last vigilant person on Earth. The whole, dark bedroom would tighten around me. I'd lie there like a stone effigy, feet to the east, toward Jerusalem. With enough time — and eleven-year-old insomniacs have forever — I could turn my coffin into a snug ship's cabin. A first-class berth on a transatlantic crossing.

Jackdaw nodded, replaying the trick in his own theater.

After a while, just by squinting into the dark, I could make out the nighttime ocean through the starboard portal. I worked out this detailed saga — my sister and I, recently orphaned, heading back to the Old World in the luxury befitting our recently recovered state.

Back? Recovered?

I've no idea where I got all that crap. One troubled little cookie, I guess. I'd lived in Germany, Turkey, Japan. But my fantasies always left me orphaned in New York. Anyway, in the dark, whatever Air Force barracks we were holed up in passed for a great stateroom. Walnut and brass. Tooled leather chairs. And I and my recently widowed sister —

Widowed? I thought you said orphaned?

Widowed, orphaned: depended on the night. You boys just don't get it, do you?

Go on. You and your widowed sister . . .

Me and my widowed thirteen-year-old sister furnished our cabin with a suite of priceless paintings that anyone who belonged to our same elevated station would instantly recognize.

Know that elevated station. I lived underneath it as a kid.

Oh, don't poor-mouth me, Acquerelli. You're as middle-class as they come. What was your father, a university professor?

Electrical engineer. Berg and Nordstrom.

There. So let a little girl indulge her harmless false consciousness, will you?

Go on. Your priceless painted masterpieces.

"Our art treasures," Elise always called them.

Hold it. I thought she was asleep?

I got her up now and then. Eventually, I taught her how to play in the day.

You could see them by daylight?

The pictures? Oh, the pictures were real.

You had priceless art on the walls of your bedroom?

Fake real. Not imaginary, I mean.

Ouch. My brain. Someone hit the Reset.

My mother used to buy us prints of famous paintings for our walls. Our Gallery of Visual Instruction. Cheap reproductions to remind the two of us of just how much our mother sacrificed to bring us into the world.

Sacrificed?

Her father sold insurance. Reasonably well-off. He warned her not to marry Air Force. She thought she was in love. She thought it'd be romantic, raising kids on air bases around the world. It wasn't. Raphael was supposed to compensate. The Hudson River School. She was indiscriminate, so long as the thing said "culture."

She told you all this?

In every way but words. It worked, I guess. We girls both bought in. Sometimes, in daylight, Elise and I would parade in front of the prints, saying, "Oh yes, we had to have them. Even though they cost us our millions."

Another planet. One of us is from another planet.

Would you be so kind as to tell me to whom you are referring?

Well, it sure the piss ain't me, sister.

Her laugh went up the wrong pipe. Choking on her spittle made her laugh all the harder. She flapped her arms. He would have patted her on the back, except that it involved touching.

She caught her breath. *I'd lie there in the dark, in that luxury stateroom, nursing this story in my head about bringing our millions back from exile in the form of the world's best bullion. The only truly priceless commodity: human genius. Things there would never be more than one of.*

Something harsh took over her face. Jackdaw looked harder away.

First there was that spoiled little blond Infanta, always bursting into our private stateroom as if she owned the joint. And then that sly, pretty girl at the half door. Our mother went to her grave insisting she was a Rembrandt, even after the Rembrandt scholars ruined her forever. For a long time, we had the world's most ethereal newlyweds, with their fantastic scrub brush of a dog. Their alcove seemed to open off our own cabin.

Show me, he told her.

Oh, I put them all in the jungle. Every painting that hung in any of the bedrooms I've ever lived in. You've seen little parodies of all of them. Except one.

That one being . . . ?

The Bedroom at Arles. The bed by the shores of the Mediterranean. She spoke in a trance, her eyes resting ten meters past the front wall of the Cavern, her voice addressing a thing long out of earshot. *The devastating one. All tilted and wrong. The bedroom of a man our mother made the mistake of telling us had gone mad.*

She looked at him: you know the man I mean? Jackdaw nodded. But he didn't know.

That room was my father's. My father was the madman. God, we saw so little of him, growing up. So absent, so enraged. Captain Klarpol, the silent warrior, gone for months at a stretch, flying those horrible machines ten times bigger than any house we lived in, dropping God knows what on God knows whom. And when he did come home, we three always paid for the latest round of missions. He . . . we . . . I thought: If I could just give him something. Find out what he needed . . .

A quiet room somewhere, by the other Mediterranean. The far shore, where they never got posted. A fictive, all-restoring summer home.

I'd peek out at this room, from under my down comforter. I'd gaze into that periscope, looking back into a miniature, blazing version of our room. Bed, chairs, washstand, shaving mirror, floor, shuttered window. Even the madman's own paintings, leaning out at crazy angles from the painted wall . . .

You could see all this? In the night. From across a dark room.

Well, see, that was the thing. I never could decide whether I actually saw them, or whether I just supplied all the brushstrokes from daylight viewings. And that got me thinking. Got me started playing the game.

Wait. I thought that was the game.

No, no. The real game. The game of free the shutters. Ocean crossings are never smooth, you know. You always hit some longitude, two nights out of wherever it is — Le Havre — when the sea rises up and bites you. The prevailing winds, the North Atlantic currents. Or maybe the captain just passes out on the ship's wheel at 3 a.m., after a bout with the aquavit.

She stared off at a bitter old friend. Images rose up around her — detailed, familiar still lifes she'd kept in deep storage for twenty years or longer, now back in vengeful retrospective.

I'm really sorry, he said. *But I have no idea what you're talking about.*

No, of course you don't, do you? The snarl surprised her. She recovered fast, waving off her lapse. *Ocean liners pitch. It's what you pay them to do. It's how you know they're ocean liners. And it was up to me, in my first-class berth, to preserve the laws of physics aboard ship by making the paintings shift when the cabin did.*

I'm not sure I want to hear about this.

Now, Jackie. You're the big advocate of interactivity. The first time it happened, it was an accident. I was looking without really seeing, and the bottom left of the Infanta frame, well, fluttered. I saw a ripple, something wrong in the corner of my eye. Like the shift in a branch that turns out to be a walking stick.

Trying to avoid the big mammal's notice.

Well, maybe this painting was doing just that. Because as soon as I whipped my head around for a good look, nothing.

Scared stiff.

That's what I figured. So I decided to lie in wait. Pretend I was busy noticing something else. I held my breath, as motionless as those pictures were pretending to be. And that's how I saw it again. I knew it was impossible, but I'd always suspected it. The frame around the Infanta shifted again.

Your ocean liner . . .

. . . listed toward port, and our gallery of visual instruction tipped with it. Don't you dare laugh. It really happened. And it scared me shitless.

I believe you. I'm not laughing. I . . . believe you.

Every slide of the pictures against the wall made the ocean swell beneath me. God. There's nothing more powerful than an eleven-year-old girl concentrating in the dark. Over several months, I trained myself to see the twitch, even when staring at the pictures dead on. First my body would yaw inside, then the frames would slip. After a while, I could rock the frames at will. No more than a few camel hairs' width. But visibly tilting, whenever I said so.

You're lucky you didn't drive yourself completely nuts, he said. Then caught himself.

Funny thing was, it felt like the most natural thing in the world. Something everyone should be able to do. I'm not saying it was effortless. It was exhausting. Sometimes it took hours. Clearing my mind of every thought except waiting. Concentrating on not concentrating. Waiting for the wave to hit my body. Wait without waiting. She shuddered at the description, panicked all over again. *I had to nudge at the paintings without trying. Tug at their corners with the side of my eye. They were stuck in amber, all the thickened time that had settled on them since they were painted. I had to glance past this crust to rock the picture underneath. The moment the idea of pushing came into my mind, I had to start all over. I didn't move them; I let them move. Then one day, I graduated to the game's next secret level. I let myself into that lopsided bedroom. You—you've really never seen it?*

Sorry. I've been busy.

Inside that painting there's another painted window, floating above the madman's bed. I could see it from my own crooked bunk, even with no light from my own window. The painted shutters are deeply wrong. They're way too big. Too much wood to close over the casement. There in the dark, I couldn't decide whether they floated in front of the window frame or behind it, folding into the bedroom or fanning outside. I had to find a way to close them, make them fit the frame. One night, without warning, I found I could wiggle them.

Time to wake the sister. Wake the sister. Please.

Not at all. Time to oil their hinges. Each night that I exercised the shutters, they got a little easier to open. Pretty soon, Elise had barely fallen asleep before I was stealing off to the painter's bedroom. And as soon as I got there, the breezes would start to blow. I loved it. My private little secret, which I had the good sense to hide from everyone. Making the wind blow. Making the ground move beneath my feet. All the things that pubescent girls eventually learn to do more prosaically.

Jackdaw turned away, hiding his rush of color.

I got . . . too good. Too skilled at animation. Each of the objects in that painted room wanted its turn. I made gusts of southern wind twist the towel and slap the cyan shaving mirror against the wall like a float slapping a dock. I got so I didn't even need breezes. I made the drawer in that crippled little bed table slide open unsponsored. I worried that the scraping would wake up Elise. But I couldn't stop. Couldn't keep from trying out new games . . . A night came when the room jumped, all by its lonesome. Started shaking before I gave it the mother-may-I. The chairs began to slide across the sloped floor. Horrible. I had to look away. But when I looked back, they'd start drifting all over again. Worse, the bed began creaking, from the weight of invisible bodies. It no longer had anything to do with gravity or wind or the ocean rolling. I wanted off the boat. I tried to steer our bedroom back to dry dock. I repeated the proof, over and over: the Earth was solid. The paint was fixed.

She pointed one finger up into the air. St. John of the Cross.

Then it was . . . like you said. The thing I should have had the sense to be afraid of all along. I walked past the room the next morning, in daylight. And saw the clack of a loose shutter. At last I figured what was happening. Hereditary. I'd go insane. As raving as the painter, whose private things I was stupid enough to play with while he was away.

You weren't about to lop off any body parts?

Don't. Even. Joke. I asked Elise if the paintings ever seemed . . . strange. "Our gallery of Visual Instruction?" She was a dozen games behind me. "Oh, perhaps to others. Never to us! Don't forget: we had the wisdom to pay millions for them . . ." I could have wrung her neck. I was frantic with imagination. I went back into the room and copied it, trying to make it stop. I fixed each furnishing at its exact distance from all its neighbors with a number-two pencil on blue-ruled paper. Then, to keep the colors from drifting, I went at it with my own paints. Once I got the folds of the towel down, it would stop flapping. When I found the exact *lip of the shutters with my brush, they'd never move again.* Her chin muscles twitched: *almost never. I thought that if I could paint this room . . . thought that if I could get the colors right . . .*

She stopped long enough for Jackdaw to hear them—the creakings downstairs, the middle-of-the-night shutter bangings, the armed father, family violences in some godforsaken Air Force barracks in yet another host country that did not want you there. When Adie resumed, her voice was perfect again.

Just a hysteric child's voyage, I guess. It passed with puberty. But all through my teens, I couldn't look at a painting without repainting it. You know how childhood nightmare goes. You roll it back, demon by demon. Twenty years later, all that's left is a colorful story.

That's how you learned to paint?

Adie smiled, the crisp crosshatch of a technical pen. *That's how I learned to copy. I never could make my hand do anything interesting without an original nearby, threatening me.*

But you're so good. You drew all those . . . things!

Her smile smeared outward into wet charcoal. *Lovely, reassuring trinkets that have sold everything from book jackets to fake Belgian chocolates. Never mind. Copying keeps fruit on the table. And it's landed me this job, on the bleeding edge of whatever we're on the edge of.*

You never told your sister? Elise?

Sort of. Years later. When we were out of school and both bussing tables at MoMA.

What did she say?

She said that I should get counseling. That Mom and Dad had fucked us over good, between the two of them. That going to a shrink was the best thing she'd ever done for herself. This was just before Elise moved uptown in the wake of the art bubble. Ah. Our millions!

Did you . . . ever . . . ?

Go to a shrink? No. I went downtown and tried to become a painter. It didn't work. But neither did Elise's therapy, in the long run. And hers was more expensive.

Did your mother ever . . . ?

Died, Adie interrupted. *At Langley Air Force Base, Virginia. A very unromantic death.*

Did your . . . father ever see . . . anything that you made?

That depends. She looked away, on a mythic place where gifts really reached their recipients. Nothing she'd ever made—offering, bribe, buyoff, retaliation—had ever come close to hitting its mark. *That depends on what you mean by "see."*

Jackdaw heard the current in her. He searched out the lab for a place to flee. But the chance for flight was over. *This painting. This bedroom of yours? You sure you want to . . . animate that one?*

No. I'm not sure. I've never been sure of anything in my life. Except that that place is beautiful.

Jackdaw nodded, ready to go there.

24

There was a song. A piece of music. A beautiful thing, you used to say, back when the word meant nothing. Back when existence let you listen. In another life, you loved that piece. Now every note is gone.

You lie in the constant dusk of this sealed carton, willing the tune to come back to you. You try all the possible opening intervals, checking off the permutations, like trying to remember someone's name by ticking off the letters of the alphabet. Chasing does nothing. A song like this returns only of its own volition. It will descend, or not, only by grace. All you can do is keep still and wait.

You lie waiting, without expectation. But the song does not come. Not one phrase. Only a shifting stumble of tones. You lie forever in the dark, inviting the melody. You spend days making yourself available, ready for any arrival. But all that comes to you is the piece's name: a convalescent's song of thanks to the Godhead.

You've heard the piece maybe all of three times in your life. Not really your music of choice. Not the stuff you ordinarily put on the player, except in those rare moments when something made you imagine that you understood it. Something like sudden sickness, sudden health. The music of a vanished past that you always thought you'd someday have time to learn.

Now there is time, more time than learning could hope to fill. But now there is no music. Now there is only a pitchless waiting.

Once, you tried to play the ancient thing for Gwen, a chant as much beyond you as listening was beyond her. A haunted few minutes that you needed to share with another living being. She failed to sit all the way through it. Could not, although you asked her. Could not, because you asked her. The ensuing three days of mutual escalation ended at the eternal, retaliatory impasse. *Why do you begrudge me ten minutes of shared pleasure with you?* To which: *Why do you have to control my life?*

Now your cell turns that anger laughable, horrible, murderous. How could you ever have felt anything but guilty amazement when you were still free? Felt anything but crazed, convalescent gratitude at being able to listen to any song at all?

Thanksgiving has long since passed, without observance. Couldn't bear celebrating a holiday that should have marked your release. Christmas, too, comes and goes, some time during your extended illness. If there was any sound of it, you didn't hear. If any celebrants marched *oud* and *doumbec* through the dusty streets—streets so near to Bethlehem, that source of the old intractable crisis, streets through which Christ himself dragged his own sorry and ultimately incarcerated ass, healing and wheedling—they did not pass beneath your barricaded shutters.

If believers walked out that night, taking their singing out under the angel-scattered skies . . . But no: Sacred Conflict would hardly be sheltering you anywhere near the Maronite districts, those neighborhoods across the impassable Green Line that even now, for Christmas, send and receive their selfless gifts of artillery, bright portents of comet tail rising stubbornly in the east, those daily repaying lobs whose parabola arcs remain blindly indifferent to the lives they offer up for sacrifice this holiday season.

New Year's Eve you do manage to celebrate, the only way possible. No way of saying for sure that you have the day right. The hour is pure speculation. No man will know it, as it says somewhere in what little you remember of Scripture. You declare the minute that Ali brings your dinner to be 8 p.m., and work forward from there.

Figuring your pulse at sixty beats a minute, your basic moderato, you map out the continent of ten minutes. You do two dozen of those, and on the last, you start your countdown. Across your ceiling, you tune in the mob in Times Square. The ball begins its stately descent. Only, nestled at the bottom of the globe's fall, absorbing the blow like the strength-testing lever at a vanished county fair, is not January 1, 1987, but January 1, 1988. And you are watching the mad cheer from ground zero on a television set, from a warm, womblike, walnut-appointed hotel room who knows where, holding on baby-possum-style to the amber underside of a woman whose comforts do not extend to a face that will resolve into features.

January will not defeat you: this is your New Year's resolution. All strength must go into preserving your strength. You chew your food until the puree passes osmotically through the membranes of your cheeks. You increase the reps of your sit-ups and push-ups, closing in on that asymptote that your meager diet can sustain. You resort to yoga. You meditate.

From the shards that you found when you arrived here, you reassemble your shattered concentration. Mental calisthenics tone up your mind's shapeless misery. You string together a few sentences of comfort to your mother. You store the letter in your head, grateful to find the whole composition intact and growing, every morning when you come looking for it.

Encouraged, you try a five-paragraph essay, the kind you used to make your students write. What brings you here? What are your plans following graduation? The essay grows into a magazine article that will go to the highest bidder upon your release.

Retention's daily exercises release deep captives. *I met a traveller from an antique land.* Mr. Cotrell, ninth grade. *Oh what is not a dream by day?* Mrs. Hamin, seventh. Over the course of five days, you stitch together 90 percent of Frost's "Oven Bird," a poem whose very existence you could not have sworn to half a year ago.

Shaken loose by storm, stray lines from triumphant roles in high-school plays flotsam up to the surface. Algy in *Earnest*. Biff Loman. Fragments of a teenager who thought he might want to act for a living.

Thou wall, O wall, you coax. *O sweet and lovely wall. Show me thy chink.* The plaster behind your head remains unmoved.

You stockpile all the arsenal of salvation that you can get away with. You sing the choruses of rock anthems until the Angry Parent breaks up the act. You teach Ali fake street jive, getting him to swagger back and forth in the dingy hall outside your cell, proclaiming, "I one shanky hamsta mushu."

You take to calling the Shiite Cronkite "Walter."

"Why you say me this? What this name means?"

"It means . . . Trustworthy Elder."

He snorts. His pleasure betrays itself. "Sure. No problem."

You call when you hear him scuffling outside the door, peering in through their observation crack. "Walter? Walter, is that you?"

"What you want? You need something?"

"Walter, I think I'll go for a little stroll this afternoon. Outside. Just a short one? Twenty minutes. I come right back."

Your two inverted fingers jog, yellow-pages-style. International sign language, for your surveillant's benefit. His silence kills the game. Brings you back to where no one is playing.

The next day, you repeat the announcement: "I'm just heading out for a little morning constitutional. Ten, twelve minutes, max. I'll be right out front."

You vary the declaration every day for about a week. You have an appointment with a dentist. You must meet a pretty woman down at the corner café. It becomes a little liturgy of survival. The guards stop reacting when you call out to them.

"Ali?" you call one morning. "Ali, is that you? I need to take the motorcycle in to get its cylinders cleaned."

As in some alternate universe where the laws of physics are all backward, the door jiggles and opens. You scramble for your blindfold, laughing. It's worked. Inconceivable. Persistence has won.

Ali advances on you, where you stumble to your feet. Your face swings blindly up into the downward arc of his pistol butt. Orange detonates across your field of vision. Something cracks, a jar filled with viscous sauce landing on the asphalt. He has broken your cheek. Can someone break a cheek? A fireball of radiant pain shuts down all thought.

Far away, someone is screaming. That someone is you. "Shut your fucking mouth," Ali screams, over you. No need. This student of American idiom shuts it for you.

Your head is split, but somehow there is no blood. You touch the second face growing from your face. It throbs like a creature trying to break loose. The swelling mashes shut your left eye. A trough cuts from your crushed upper lip to your temple. When your fascination wears off, the real pain sets in.

The Angry Parent comes to inspect you. He clicks his tongue, displeased but not distraught. At least he has the basic sense not to touch the wound. Finger to your chin, he steers your cubist head around, to catch the meager light. When he leaves, you hear shouts in the corridor—violence on both sides, venom that for a moment threatens to spill over. You rise to your tensed thighs, hoping for wider confusion, some rain of retribution that fails to fall.

The Parent calls a doctor. It opens your blindfolded eyes. This organization spreads deep enough to draw upon middle-class professionals. Sacred Conflict can rouse doctors in the night, bring them, blindfolded, to attend to their American captives, hidden under the nose of this ruptured city. The doctor spies in your mouth, up your nose, through your ear, every movement a blinding agony. Much Arabic scolding goes out in all directions. But he leaves no treatment, no medication, nothing to deaden the anguish.

Cling to nothing, you tell yourself. And that is what you cling to.

Ali disappears for a few weeks, bundled off to some Siberia in the Anti-Lebanon mountains, on the other side of the Bekáa. A change comes over your remaining guards, a horrified respect, the best measure of how gruesome the Technicolor highlights of your new face must be. They serve as your ghostly shaving mirror, these men whose cause must now look upon its own lustrous effect.

"What you want?" Walter asks. "You want something?"

You suppress the urge to ask for a quick trip to the 7-Eleven. "I want forty minutes." You try to make the terms sound self-evident, agreed upon in advance. You'll stop the foolishness. In exchange, they must take you off the chain for forty minutes a day. Forty minutes. Surely they're clever enough to keep an atrophied, blindfolded, unarmed, sheless, prison-garbed American locked up deep in the rat's nest of a hostile city secure for forty minutes a day?

They counter with a face-saving twenty. You shake on thirty minutes, an inconceivable figure. A treasure beyond the most bankrupt nation's debt. More than you bargained for in your maddest, most unguarded plans.

Half an hour's freedom saves you. It expands your known world, the overnight appearance of an American continent. You pace about, astonished. From the once-mythical far side of this cube, you look back across the ocean of air. Seeing your corner like this, from a distance — your mattress, radiator, chain; the grubby country that swallowed you entire — it looks bounded, known, livable.

Thirty minutes off the chain each day. Whole new universes open at your feet. As your head heals, your exploration picks up to a trot. The cell becomes an Olympic track, a loop of imaginary cinders that you circle around and around, training, whooping in your souped-up, pounding heart at this chance to move.

You calculate the coiled-up equivalent of a mile. You jog one. Then one-and-a-half. Then two.

You run for distance. Then for shorter sprints. Each footfall throbs in protest across your split face. But freedom makes the pain easy to run through. In fact, running is an analgesic, amphetamine, and tranquillizer by turns. You run through the hunger of this very exertion, the calorie deficit produced by these rationed, oval ecstasies.

Sometimes they unlock you in the mornings. Sometimes freedom fails to come until much later, the thrill of release stoked by a whole day of waiting. Some days they cheat you, curtailing the exercise after ten minutes. You have no proof, nor any court of appeals. But on other days they forget you, and you run until you drop. There is a drama to this variance, an unendurable tension to not knowing, every day waiting to write its script until the moment it's read aloud.

These runs are your slim exhilaration, their joy sharpened to a point by those annihilating days when something goes wrong and they fail to unchain you at all. On those days, you fall into the pit, a despair whose bottom you cannot feel. Your only weapon is to say nothing the next day, when the next day finally arrives. Give no hint of the power the enemy holds over your every feeling.

But for all the spikes on the graph, the unchecked swings between gloom and elation, your mind admits only one baseline. No mood, no insight, no exercise is large enough to fill the crushing size of a day. Hostage has but one place to return to, one owner, one prevailing emotion. All it knows is a thinly delineated, horizon-wide boredom.

Where the body is chained, the brain travels. In captivity, every inference is the freest flight. Nothing stops your associations or keeps them accountable. Your thoughts run through maniacal stunts, like radio-controlled drones at an air show. They blast through the countless embassies that offer limited asylum. Unchecked, your mind's maneuvers twist back on themselves in all directions, a nest of a million twigs that knits its own fixed prison in the static air.

You pass Gwen's birthday, the only other holiday capable of cutting through the morass of agitation and gloom. You wonder if it counts, your not sending her a card and all. Not quite the statement of indifference you'd planned—the long, pointed, unambiguous silence you had all mapped out as the answer to that last phone assault. Gwen's thirty-first: perhaps she finds it even more traumatic than her thirtieth. Once they were your allies, each extra year that thickened her. Accumulated age would remind her of the alternatives to a lasting truce. Once, you thought that all you needed was to sit back and let the years click off, until she chose you at last over permanent solitude.

By now, you're as good as dead to her. She's tucking into the birthday cake with someone simpler, someone less demanding. One of those men she always found under a rock with such surprise, so quickly, each time she fled your suffocation, so soon after deciding again that intimacy was beyond her. Some lost guy she smiled at, half a second too long, in the weight room at the gym.

You try to visualize the festivities, but can't. Can't imagine a cake, can't resolve a birthday present, make out a restaurant, or read the label on a bottle of wine. Can't imagine Gwen smiling or making a wish. If she's read about you, if the letter that Sacred Conflict dictated has made it into the American papers, then surely you must cross her mind as she blows out the candles, if only in some involuntary, reflex jaywalk. God keep you from her thoughts and let her save herself.

Winter slinks deep into Lebanon. The radiator does nothing, and the room temperature plummets. A damp cold: "dank" is the word that crawls up from the cellar of forgotten fiction. Moisture forms on the floor of the cell each night, drawn up through the capillaries in the mattress fiber to bathe you. Peat bog seeps through the cheap cotton clothes they give you. Your one thin blanket serves only to wrap your skin in moist acrylic.

Nothing dries out by day. You strip and wring your clothes out each morning during the bathroom ritual. "Heat," you beg Walter, searching for something to bargain with.

"I ask Chef," he says. "No problem. *Bukrah.*"

Needless to say, tomorrow never comes and heat is nowhere.

Outside—no consolation—must be colder and wetter. A colony of roaches moves in to share the shelter. Not your discreet, retiring, bourgeois North American species: monster Middle Eastern militiaforming creatures two inches and longer. They wake you from dreams where feathery hands incessantly strip-search you. There's no keeping them out of the mattress, off your prostrate body. Fearing disease, you launch a border war. You pinch one's head off and leave the decapitated carcass along their major thoroughfare, a lesson to the rest. But they're slow learners, one and all. In fact, the corpse draws ants.

You swat, smash, and sweep, first strategically, then more indiscriminately. But the cause starts to cost more than it repays. The great interspecies territorial war trickles out in an exhausted armistice, with victory going, as ever, to the bugs.

In the barren expanses stretching out in front of you, surely you have time to teach even the insect brain a trick or two. Prison narratives march through your mind, a pass in review, tales of all the desperate symbiotic relations struck up between inmates and other species. As far as you can remember reading, no one has ever laid claim to this virgin territory. It's yours for the taking: the Cockroach Man of Beirut.

Start modestly. Get them to walk in single file, keeping a rough group tempo. Parade them in simple formations—whatever twirling squares and stars you can remember from junior year playing clarinet in the Greater Des Moines Combined High Schools Marching Band. Then get them to form a few short words, strictly Anglo-Saxon monosyllables, lettered constellations of cockroach bodies, formations of synchronized scuttling, tricks for which they'll repay you with grateful companionship.

You read something once about how these creatures make high-frequency pitches by rubbing their rear legs together. Like bows across violin strings, or maybe that was crickets. You might start them on Suzuki-method arrangements of "Ninety-nine Bottles of Beer on the Wall," working up to barbershop quartets and four-part chorales pitched too high for any but the captive ear to hear.

You see yourself on your hands and knees, playing with your six-legged cellmates. Can you really need people that much? Each day widens your disbelief at the discovery. You wanted this solitary confinement. You made love to the idea. The whole reason you came to this country in the first place was to escape human connection. The endless birthday-present shopping. The interminable dinner parties. The relentless letters of recommendation. You came here hoping to reclaim your life, to sail over the edge of society into selfhood's new world.

But isolation warps you into someone you don't recognize. You feel the thing in all its nakedness: a need so great that you'd stupidly tried to shed it. Your invitation to the human party — the constant obligation, the stack on your desk you could never clear. The drain on your resources. The perpetual static in your ears that kept you from your own, coherent thoughts. That petty, niggling burden. Your trueing, your delight, your sanity, your only health. Others.

You've spent your whole life dining out, while bad-mouthing the meal. No better than a thief who helps himself to the movable goods, then slanders his victims' taste. Solitude proves how little of you is yours. Everything that you've ever thought, everything you've ever felt, you owe to that company you could never abide.

Somehow, you must boost the odds of surviving this suicide you've arranged. April is your month to start taking stock. Bare waiting has killed one hundred and fifty days, days of nothing, days you will never get back. You're through calculating how much longer they'll hold you. However long it takes, that will be your length. You'll walk out of here knowing what you did not know on walking in. You vow to study that dependent self you never looked at, to converse with it every day from dinner until bed.

You start by replaying every detail of your life you can remember. The years you've lost to evasion you must reclaim now, second by second. Surely some core must exist inside you, some essence that you haven't simply sponged from a world of others. Some green oasis of wherewithal that won't return to desert, now that its feeder springs are sealed off.

Some tune that Jihad unwittingly hums you. A hymn to the forgotten Source. A convalescent's song.

25

August gave birth to a human chain, large enough to be seen from outer space. It solidified in several hundred hamlets across a landscape of scrub and failing farmland, accreting like some fearsome, foretold northern serpent. It ran for five hundred kilometers across three national frontiers, from the coasts of the Gulf of Finland down beyond the shores of the Kaunas Sea. Link by link, it snaked across the Cartesian plane, person by person, hooking up digits.

Nothing, it seemed, had died under June's tread. Disaster in Asia, the resolve of power, had slowed the worldwide movement, but could not stop it. The largest empire ever assembled began to evaporate into fiction. Transcaucasia spun out of orbit. A handful of freed prisoners took control of Poland. And across the wastes of three nominal republics, a spontaneous human rope played Crack the Whip while the cable-ready world looked on, whiplashed.

Even impromptu, a chain the length of three nations needed wartime logistics. A division of vegetable trucks stood in for half tracks, bussing villagers to gaps in the line. All was ad hoc. A leviathan longer than any camera's ability to document arose from thousands of local committees messaging one another, as fluid and pointless as song.

Ari Kaladjian floated above the spectacle on a sky hook, watching the transcendental function roiling from out of a scattered set of points. *Don't any of these people have to work for a living?*

Jaysus, man! O'Reilly said, without taking his eyes off the screen. *Do you hear what you're saying?*

I'm saying that if these people had put this much effort into being economically competitive, they wouldn't be in this hole that they now have to climb out of so theatrically.

For love of the bleeding Mary. You're a traitor to your race.

What does my race have to do with the price of tea in Tallinn?

Where the hell do you come from? Don't you think Armenia is next up on this carousel?

Armenia, Georgia, Ukraine, Azerbaijan.

Didn't your family come to this country as refugees?

Not the same thing, Kaladjian snapped. *We're here because various powers have enjoyed killing us by the hundreds of thousands over the course of the century.*

And the Baltics . . . ?

The Baltics! My friend, what's happening there is not political. This is not about oppression. You're an economist. You of all people ought to know that.

Not political!

This is not about forms of government or appropriations of power or anything of the sort. This is about the globalization of markets, the apotheosis of consumerism. Your . . . human chain—Kaladjian spat both words—*is nothing more than a glorified product-promotional placement.*

Well I'm not going to stand around discussing the fall of Eastern Europe with this crypto-fascist.

Absolutely astonishing, Dale Bergen said, to no one. *It seems to be self-assembling.*

Michael Vulgamott snorted. *You mean the human chain, or the global socialist meltdown?*

I'm just a biologist, Bergen answered. *I couldn't tell you about the thing's politics. But from this distance, it looks an awful lot like a long polypeptide growing itself out of side chains.*

Adie broke in on the speculating circle. *This isn't happening,* she said. *Again? Didn't this dream die two months ago? I can't take any more developments. I'm overloading.*

You think you're overloading? Jackdaw gestured toward a screen, where news of the latest upheaval coursed through the system. *You ought to see what's happening to the network access points. Every time there's a new development, the whole Net grinds into gridlock.*

It's true, Spiegel said. *The Ethernet pipes can't keep up with all the excitement. The links are gummed to a standstill. Like southbound I-5 at late afternoon. Too much happening at once. We're generating more transcript than we can move.*

Lim grew defensive. *But we're doubling data capacity every—*

Don't flatter yourself, Kaladjian cut in. *Current events will always double faster.*

Adie stood spellbound by the five-hundred-kilometer game of Red Rover. Hands grasped one another, adhering like nerve cells into an embryonic spinal cord. *Someone? Please. What are we supposed to hope for here? How many times are we supposed to get burned?*

Loque laid her arm around Adie's shoulders. *You don't really want to know, do you, babe?*

I mean, is this the real thing, this time? Or just another bloody detour?

Kaladjian threw a hand up in the air. *It's all a detour. The Cold War is a detour. Yalta was a detour.*

You know what I'm asking. Are we supposed to believe, again?

What do you say, Ari, man? Rajan agitated. *History or mockery, doc? Signal-process this one for us.* He pointed to the sinuous line, its changing slope, its amorphous rise over run. *Differentiate that curve, mathematician.*

Kaladjian refused the bait. *Ask our friend from Belfast. He's the one who is building the electronic voodoo fortune-teller.*

Yeah, Ronan, baba. How come your time machine didn't predict this one?

O'Reilly stuck his chin out. *Quite simple. It happened too soon. Give me another year or two . . .*

If we have it, Vulgamott said, staring at the human chain.

The cameras hovered high in the air, scanning the Baltics in under two minutes. People were linking up. Whole countries of hand-holders shuttled about plugging the gaps, thrilled with the feel of a process larger than themselves. Their faces signaled one another, animated, weeping, hilarious. The vast act of logistics threatened to turn into a party.

It's beautiful, Spider Lim pronounced, in the flattest American diphthongs. *Whatever it is.*

What's that? Adie asked. *What did you just say?*

It's . . . beautiful?

Sorry. Syntax error. Command not recognized.

Lim smiled. *But it is. Look at it. A fractal tendril. You know that some flower is going to grow out of it. But you can't tell the shape or color.*

Spiegel came alongside him. *Too much distal stimuli, Spidey. Too exocentric. Better slow up a click or two. You're turning into a poet.* He made to take Lim's wrist, feel his pulse. Spider, mistaking the move, offered up his half of the smallest possible human chain. The weakest first link. He caught his error in mid-extension and retracted his embrace, embarrassed.

But it was. Was beautiful—a self-extending experiment, too massive for description. Event ran on an analog machine the size of the globe, a planetary computer that performed the necessary calculations and generated the required results. The world took its instructions from the shapes of its smallest parts, aggregate subroutines, reusable containers, object-oriented modules that forward-chained into ever-larger autonomous agents, extending the program even as it passed through its run-time interpreter. Trees from the branch, fruit from the tree, farms from the fruit, whole nation-states from the farms, until some sum of summer mass movements decided, on the basis of all this higher mathematics, the exact moment to send the drowsy empire to bed.

In September, Hungary opened its eroding border to Austria. East German vacationers trickled through the fissure into the West. Up in the RL studio, the Cavern illuminators fell into an unconscious footrace, to finish the plates in their book of hours before their calendar went obsolete.

One night in the Economics Room, Lim, Karpol, and O'Reilly took turns poking their heads into the floating globe. They watched from the fixed core, as the surface ran through its detailed rainbow. Economist turned to hardware engineer and asked, *How many MIPS can you deliver to me, two years from now?*

Lim thought for a while. He settled on a number that would have seemed outrageous, had human expectation still recognized the shape of outrage.

Why? Adie asked. *How many do you need?*

Ten times whatever you can give me at any moment. Desire, like file size, always overflowed the available capacity.

Adie nudged the Irishman. *Greedy little rasterbator, aren't you?*

O'Reilly nodded. *Life is greedy. It always requires an order of magnitude more juice than it has. How many millions of instructions per second do you think Hungary is executing, all told?* Adie just stared at him. Spider propagated the gesture. *Oh, I don't mean their computing capacity. I mean, how much processing power does the machine of Hungary involve? How much total storage?*

Hungary the country?

Yes, Hungary the country. As opposed to Hungary the condition of gastric distress.

Klarpol rolled her eyes. *All yours, Spidey.*

Lim closed his lids and read the paper tape of some invisible, emulated Turing machine floating in his wetware. *You mean, how many discrete pieces of data are involved in Hungary throwing over its old leaders?*

O'Reilly's nod narrowed to one bit. One single datum.

I couldn't begin to tell you, Lim said, *even to within a couple of exponents. I don't even know how to think about the problem. I don't even know how to start guessing.*

A big number, Adie suggested.

O'Reilly touched the tip of his nose and pointed at her. *A big number! Give the lady a Kewpie doll. How many millions of instructions per individual Hungarian?*

Adie giggled. *MIPS per IH. MIPSPIH. Not a sufficiently explored constant.*

Another big number, Lim conceded. *Bigger than any hardware is likely to deliver to you in the next few years.*

Exactly. Any problem of real interest explodes into polynomials. And there's no way around that explosion except icontics.

Stop. Lady wants to trade her Kewpie doll for a definition.

Ontic icons. Icons with real existence. Shorthand agents. Data structures that do for real-world behaviors what an icon does for visual appearance. If you want to convey the idea of Hungary, you don't need a multi-gigabyte geodetic map of the entire country. You can do it with a simple outline. By the same token, we should be able to implement a functional representation of—

Adie rocked her head from side to side, the icon of incredulity. *He really has you bugged, doesn't he?*

Who?

Kaladjian. He's got you by the axioms. That taunt about failing to predict the chain reaction in the Baltics?

A grin pulled at O'Reilly's top lip. *Perhaps. It is a well-defined problem, after all.*

I see. So you're totally insane, then? This is what you're saying?

Now, now. O'Reilly put his hand out into the air, on the spot where the three of them shared a vivid, mutual mirage the shape of Eastern Europe. *If the present does determine the future, we ought to be able to make the calculations in advance.*

Ronan, Ronan. No more time machines. I forbid it. They're evil. Just because civilization has had a nice long run toward the horizon, that doesn't mean we have to hit the vanishing point.

Where do you propose we stop, then?

Someplace realistic? Adie said. *Preferably with a nice café.*

Realistic? That's a sliding baseline. Every new machine—every line of code that we write—changes what we think of as realistic.

My God. You're really serious. You think that 350 million people in Eastern Europe are working out their destinies in some kind of Boolean pinball machine?

O'Reilly nodded. *Where else do you propose that destiny work itself out?*

I get it now. This is why you and the Armenian are always at each other's throat. You're really one another's evil twins.

Not at all. He wants to find the Taylor series that underwrites existence. I just want to anticipate the trajectories.

Look. This thing . . . She dismissed the Cavern with a wave. *It's just puppet theater. Everything we're making—just cartoon sets . . .*

My point, exactly. Theater captures the reality of human personality better than CAT scans can ever hope to.

Klarpol performed the four most widely recognized gestures for exasperation. *Spidey, I need your help here.*

Sorry, Adie. I think I'm with him. We're a symbol-making animal.

I know that, you geek. But that doesn't make our symbols real. We might get a leaf. We're never going to get politics.

Politics isn't irreducible, just because it's big.

Big? Big? Do you even begin to realize . . . ? You've all gone completely—

O'Reilly held out his open palm. *If we can date the universe, if we can come up with the theory of evolution, if we can shoot electrons through semiconductor channels, then surely we ought to be able to explain what makes groups of people do what they do.*

Explain, maybe. After the fact. But that's hardly the same thing as predicting—

Look, O'Reilly said. *Stand here. Right here. Head up. Keep your eye on twelve o'clock. When I say "now," press the left wand button.*

He took off his own glasses and went to the console. He coaxed the keys with his two index fingers, using a thumb for the spacebar. *OK,* he said. *Now.*

Adie found herself at the Earth's axis, the nations swinging generously around her. The planet's surface began to glisten like an oil-coated puddle. Detailed, scrimshaw stipplings came alive, modulating through cycles of incandescence. The whole globe scintillated, like central Tokyo from the night window of an aircraft. Countries sparkled like emeralds, their capitals amethysts. The embers of human activity invited her to come down out of the remote loneliness of empty space and warm herself by the fire.

Now and then, livid signals of hope and longing shot out in bolts across the continents, messages cascading across a telephone switchboard. Adie sucked in her breath. The glistening meant something, as sure as constellations in the sky once did. The lit net flashed denser than the circuitry inside a thinking mind. It was its own goal, the home that a displaced immigrant can only dream of one day reaching.

What . . . what is it supposed to be?

The cities of the world. Talking to each other.

Yes, but what are they saying?

Two things. "Give me more energy" and "Here's what you asked for."

Last month's trading in petrochemicals, Lim translated.

O'Reilly's eyes glinted like two more point cels in the mosaic. *Actually, they're next month's.*

Lim rocked back. *You're keeping a log? We'll be able to check how well you do?*

Of course.

Adie stared at the sumptuous pageant unfolding in the air around her. She paused, reluctant to step out of the diving bell. Then she walked through the projection. As she passed through the membrane, it played for a moment upon her own body.

It's lights, Ronan. Just lights.

He took a theatrical step toward her. *That's right.* He showed her his empty palms, then the backs of his hands. He stood against the north wall of the Cavern, a living silhouette, glowing with a luminous halo. *Just lights. But then, what isn't?*

It's my turn, Lim said. *Everyone out. Eleven until two. Says so on the sheet.*

Yes. Your rightful hour upon the stage. O'Reilly turned to Klarpol and offered his hand. She grabbed and inspected it, looking for the sleight.

Would you like to get a bite of something real to eat? he asked.

Something real?

Something other than a burrito, I mean.

Who's paying?

You are.

All right, then.

They drove down the hill to a twenty-four-hour falafel shack that catered to the TeraSys late-night set. *Ulterior motive,* he told her, once they were served.

That's a redundancy. Even our revealed motives have hidden ones.

He thought for a moment, in mid-chew. *Yes.* He laughed. *Yes, you're right.* And they both returned to eating.

After some mouthfuls, she prompted him. *You were saying?*

Hmm?

Your real reason for luring me into this tryst?

Oh. Right. Have a look at this, then, will you? If you don't mind? Had to sign for it at the P.O. this morning.

He handed an envelope across the table, blue onionskin, exotically stamped, and fringed with the airmail barber-pole striping around its edges. Adie opened it and removed a single, handwritten sheet.

Ronan, you shiftless bastard. You were supposed to come back here by now. Is this a contest of wills? Because if it is, I lose.

Adie lifted her eyes from the paper. *I can't read the signature.*

It says "Maura."

Wife?

Something like that. Housemate for the better part of a decade.

Adie returned to the page, the changed message. *Why are you showing me this? I mean, it's OK. I don't mind. I'm even flattered. But . . .*

I need a woman's read. Someone who can tell me what she's saying.

What she's saying? She's saying she wants you to come back.

Hmm. It's that easy?

Yes. It's that easy. You jerk.

O'Reilly bit off a mouthful and swallowed, in one continuous motion. *What do you suppose she means by "I lose"?*

Oh, for the love of . . . You can't mean this. Not even you. You need this spelled out?

I guess I do. First off, you ought to know that there was never any talk about my—

Look. She wants you. She loves you. She's surrendering. Work it out, or I'll cut your balls off for her.

Ms. Klarpol. You know I can't possibly go back.

Her head shot back. *I know nothing of the sort.*

You know what we're assembling here.

The Cavern? A glorified drive-in movie. Not worth screwing up a couple of lives over.

The Cavern is the race's next step. The consolidation. Nothing comparable has ever existed, except in our imaginations. And Maura wants me to walk away from it. How long has history been working at this device? Centuries. Millennia.

About a year, for me. And I'd trade the matter transporter in a second, and throw in the antiaging beam to boot, if someone wrote me a note like that.

They downed what remained of the fried chickpea meal in silence. They stood to go, each clinging to one side of the righteous impasse.

What I want to know, O'Reilly said, halfway out the door, *is whether "I lose" might mean that she's considering the possibility of coming out here to join me.*

Adie bit her lip in disgust. *Damned if I know, Ronan. Why don't you build yourself a little prediction machine and find out?*

26

They laid down the old floor over the newer one, wall to wall, an inch to the inch. The synthetic white composites reverted to knotty pine. Jackdaw, Adie, and Spiegel measured and cut each wood-grained symbol, planing the cured boards like the most careful of carpenters.

They tinkered and trued, pulling up the planks from the source room and shimming them into the target. It took some doing, for the original floor at Arles had traveled a good deal. The wood was old and warped, and often refused to behave at all. But plank by plank, the salvaged floorboards agreed to lie down in their new frame.

Adie insisted that they save the spotty varnish. She wanted the worn patches translated wholesale to their same coordinates in the rebuilt bedroom. That meant work, for origin and destination belonged to different ordinal realities.

Her goal was a floor that swam and sank just like the original, yet sat snugly on the joints of the Cavern floor it overlaid. She wanted an Arles you could walk on: a lumber bridge fitted across time and space, tongue in groove, the stains and nicks of its private history preserved intact.

Spiegel watched Adie walk across the translated boards. Where her feet trod on the illusion, Magritte-like, they occluded it. Jackdaw attended on her every hand-drawn desire. Spiegel put the postadolescent somewhere in his early twenties: two or three years older than Steve had been when he met the woman. Back at the beginning of creation, everyone was twenty.

Whatever made Adie choose the University of Wisconsin, Spiegel had long ago forgotten. He barely remembered his own reason for going to college in what *Life* magazine called "America's best place to live." What he remembered most about Madison was the cold. The town's average daily temperature hovered around 19 degrees. He'd followed a high-school sweetheart there, a woman whom he hoped to marry. They lost one another to multiple discoveries halfway through their first semester. So life always liked to run the little shill: the immortal cause vanishes, but the short-term effects last forever.

Stevie attended school on the Spiegel Memorial Scholarship, the family nest egg scraped together over two decades of middle-class scrimping. His parents meant the investment to give him a leg up in the practical world: fraternity membership, good connections, and a degree in civil engineering. Thirty credits into the process, little Stevie managed to sabotage all that, and more.

Madison was still reeling from its fatal bombing of the year before. The Army Math Research Center in Sterling Hall, "think tank of American militarism," had been gutted by campus radicals in the single most destructive act of sabotage in American history. The air on Lathrop Drive was still electric. A brilliant young low-temperature physicist lay dead, and a major national university stood teetering between revolution and revulsion, between *We can do anything* and *What have we done?*

Steve went back home to La Crosse that second Christmas, a semester's worth of dirty laundry in tow, and dropped his own bombshell on stunned parents. He'd found his real vocation. He couldn't, in good conscience, earn one more credit in engineering. He would study to become a poet. He stopped short of the phrase "true artificer," but it was in there, knocking around the back of his cerebellum.

This was the point in such stories when the father traditionally took the newly enlightened student prince out behind the woodshed and beat the living shit out of him. Maybe the Agèd P was too incredulous to deliver the beating, as he should have. Maybe, in the wake of the Army Math bombing, his father's own sickened convictions had simply dissolved. Maybe Stevie's raw exuberance carried him through. Whatever the cause, both parents simply went ashen and wished him well, writing him off to a career as a greeter at some terminal superstore up on the periphery of north suburban Kotzebue.

Some residual shred of sanity prevented Steve from telling his parents the reason for his conversion. It had come in Introduction to English Literature, a cakewalk survey course he took to satisfy his general education requirements. The teacher—in retrospect, probably only a hapless grad student caught up in the academic pyramiding scheme, awaiting his own superstore destiny—by way of lightening his class prep, had had each student recite and explicate a favorite poem.

And so in October of his twentieth year, Steve Spiegel sat in shock, listening to a shag-cut pug-faced girl across the room who had come to class tie-dyed on roller skates speak the words "Once out of nature I shall never take My bodily form from any natural thing."

The words, he supposed, were beautiful. The girl, he decided, was almost. But the way she said them: that was the warrant, the arrest, and the lifetime sentencing. Out of her mouth came a stream of discrete, miraculous gadgets—tiny but mobile creatures so intricately small that generations marveled and would go on marveling at how the inventor ever got the motors into them.

Once out of nature. The train of syllables struck the boy engineer as the most inconsolably bizarre thing that the universe had ever come up with. And this female mammal uttered the words as if they were so many fearsome, ornate Tinkertoys whose existence depended upon their having no discernible purpose under heaven. The words would not feed the speaker, nor clothe her, nor shelter her from the elements. They couldn't win her a mate, get her with child, defeat her enemies, or in any measurable way advance the cause of her survival here on earth. And yet they were among the most elaborate artifacts ever made. What was the point? How did evolution justify the colossal expenditure of energy? Once upon a time, rhythmic words might have cast some protecting spell. But that spell had broken long ago. And still the words issued from her mouth, mechanical birds mimicking living things. Sounds with meaning, but meaning to no end.

We'll put the door here, that girl's latest update said. *Start it flush up against the back of the left-hand wall.*

Spiegel and Jackdaw, her vaudeville apprentices, nodded in stereo.

We'll have to figure out what the floorboards actually look like, under the bed.

We can just reuse the piece we put in over there, Jackdaw said, all innocence.

No, no. That would be cheating. We have to follow the boards that he painted, and extend them. Work outward from the bits he could see.

Jackdaw groaned. *But it's all going to be invisible in the finished product anyway.*

Not to us, it isn't.

"But such a form as Grecian goldsmiths make." The girl's lips were a factory of ethereal phonemes. "Of hammered gold and gold enameling." Spiegel had never heard words pronounced that way—alloys of confusion and astonishment. Her mouth became the metal-worked machine its sounds described. Whole sentences of hammered gold tumbled out of it.

Stevie might have taken her for a drama student, except for the clotted paint under her nails. She finished reciting and launched into her explication, an associative ramble through the maze of images. She'd drawn a series of pen-and-watercolor sketches, visual aids to illustrate her points. Byzantium. A gyre. The mechanical bird, which looked to Stevie like an intricate, gold-leafed, cutaway, feathery Bulova.

This woman exuded a flavor he'd forgotten ever existed. She had the scent of immediacy, of planlessness. Existence was stranger than he'd ever realized. Every life held in its hands a bit of charcoal stick pressed from the ashes of the first campfire.

She must have felt his stare upon her as she gave her presentation. For when she brushed past him after the class let out, she asked, "That made absolutely no sense at all, did it?"

"You smell like something," he told her.

She laughed. "I'm sure you're right."

"No," he said. The breeze of association, the loose smell of free syllables played all around him. Pleasures too recently overlooked. Exercises out of the singing masters' book. "No. You smell like something my father used to keep in cans out in the garage. To clean paint brushes."

"That would be turpentine."

"Why are your fingers all green?"

She brought them up to her eyes. "It's not green. It's mostly chartreuse."

All he could do was nod.

"What do you do?" she quizzed him. Before any other data. Even before asking his name.

"Oh," he improvised, "I . . . write." He tipped his head to the side, toward the paperback *Collected Yeats* cradled in her chartreuse fingers. He tapped his own secondhand anthology, as if the volume were some hefty tab he'd run up at an all-night sidewalk café.

The bed should run from just inside that corner to right about here. The late-day Adie impersonator, her fingers now pristine, stood on an invisible X marking a spot on the Cavern floor that corresponded to points deep beneath the grid. She stood straight, arms at her side, turning her body into a surveyor's siting stick. Jackdaw, at the console, got a bead on her. He typed some words, and a reddish rectangular block sprang up along the wall's length, up to this woman's still-callow waist.

A *little higher*, she called out. *To figure in the blankets and headboards.*

Nothing in this voice still hinted at its precursor, the voice that had long ago told Spiegel, "Well, if you write, you ought to come to our Tuesday nights. In fact, I'm surprised I haven't seen you there before now."

"I mostly keep to myself. I work in a style that isn't really . . . fashionable these days."

Her eyes widened, bestowing on him their full prize. "In that case, you *have* to come."

Anything worth devoting a lifetime to, young Stevie figured, might require as many as three days to master. Since the next Tuesday soiree was five days away, he was still in reasonable shape. He hadn't written verse since a hit-and-run sonnet accident in senior year of high school. But as with all other problem sets, he did his best work under the gun.

He showed up at the girl's apartment—a funky, carved-up Victorian boardinghouse near Lake Mendota—on Tuesday night, nerves shattered by caffeine, folding and unfolding a spayed scrap of mongrel doggerel that was probably prosecutable under even the most generous interpretation of the Intellectual Property Protection Act. His spot of manic plagiarism was all the more alarming for being at least as incoherent as it was shameless, a "Sailing to Byzantium" in leg-weighted waltz time. And he dragged this little ditty into a room draped in more black than a Greek Orthodox Good Friday service.

What is it about black? he asked the woman, seventeen years later, as they waited for Jackdaw to dummy up the place holder that stood where the bedside chair soon would. *Black and the art scene? The fad that refuses to die. Why has every trendy crowd for the last two centuries embraced it?*

She smiled at him, preoccupied. *It's the perfect preemptive look, all-black. What you wear when you're not sure what the other guy is going to wear. Deeply conservative, passing as Rad. Why do you ask?* she asked.

He'd sat there, at twenty, dying a million Oxford button-down deaths while reincarnated greasers and beatniks took turns presenting their "work" and laying themselves open to the flagellation of their peers. Poetry, prose, sculpture, music, pictures: he'd underestimated the spread of the contagion. He'd stepped into the middle of an old blood feud, warring family factions contesting the last will and testament of this dead, penniless patriarch, Art.

The terms of the fight were obscure, even to those who had been at it for years before Spiegel blundered on the scene. But the war seemed to come down to whether that liberating anagram, now just five days old inside him, should be indulged freely or called to answer for those same abuses of privilege and power that had trashed the rest of the world. It opened Spiegel's eyes. Art was embroiled in the same conflict that had claimed the Army Math.

Aside from wanting to avoid his own all-expenses-paid trip to Southeast Asia, Spiegel had no real political agenda. He'd hoped this aesthetics thing would be relatively simple. Now the night was forcing him to take sides, to declare his allegiances on issues he couldn't even decode. All he knew was that he'd sooner stick his head in a gas oven than read aloud in front of this tribunal.

Forty minutes into the street-fighting, during an especially ugly exchange over the political irresponsibility of a bleary chalk abstraction, a short, stocky guy swaggered into the room wearing a Bucky Badger sweatshirt and toting a dirty gym bag. Talk broke off, and all eyes fixed on the infidel. The fellow reached slowly into his sack and withdrew a damp jock strap.

"This is my piece," he announced. "It's a conceptual work."

Protagonists of both stripes shouted the man down. He heckled back, creatively, in kind, and the session mercifully degenerated. Ted Zimmerman: the only name that stuck with Spiegel from that evening. The only person he cared to talk to afterward. A study in fearless delight. The man who saved Spiegel from having to read his first adult poem out loud in front of a room of hired aesthetic killers, there in war-torn Madison.

"My God, you vanquished them," Spiegel told Zimmerman, out on the chill front steps of the Victorian. "Three cheers."

"Vanquished?" Zimmerman asked.

For one uncertain second, Spiegel thought he'd misread everything. He gestured inside. "The war between art and ethics."

"Oh." Ted's nod went sardonic. "Mutual coercion versus mutual communion. Whose side are you on?"

"I wish I knew. So what do you do?" Nothing if not a quick study.

"I play handball. And I'm working on a damn octet on the side. Confessions of an apolitical man. You?"

"I do poetry." A lie he'd do penance for, by making it come true.

Ted proceeded to grill Stevie about everyone he'd ever read. "Yeats is fine. But man cannot live by fruitcake alone. Have you read Rilke?

Have you read George?" Spiegel shook his head knowingly, trying to memorize the names.

They graduated to novels, plays, essays. Zimmerman held forth on Habermas and Musil. He quoted from *Man and Superman*, delivered a brief history of the Successionist movement, and glossed over chitinous Frankfurt School tracts. To Steve, half the people the man mentioned were total ciphers. Talk graduated to concert music, Ted's real passion. Spiegel caught the names Schoenberg, Webern, and Berg, whom he gathered were a kind of upscale Tinker to Evers to Chance.

By the time they stood up from the cold steps, Spiegel had both a handball date and a considerable homework assignment.

"Time to go home," the composer announced. He breathed the night deeply into his lungs. "The two hours on either side of midnight. My favorite time in the day to nudge a piece forward."

"Mine too," Spiegel decided.

"Thanks for the words," Ted said. "We live our lives in hope of the company of women. But barring that, an amusing man."

Spiegel ran up against the line again a year later, still plowing through his friend's reading list. It jumped out at him, underlined, from Zimmerman's beaten-up copy of *Women in Love*.

Inside the house, the black-clad crowd still hashed out the morality of depiction, just as their affiliated revolutionary cells did, by the tens of thousands, in accredited institutions across the face of the divided country. Things showed no sign of reaching consensus anytime before daybreak. Spiegel found his hostess and thanked her for the entrée. The life-changing introduction.

"Make a friend?" Adie asked.

Spiegel shook his head, dazed. "The man's a genius."

Her eyebrows plunged. "Ted? Ted's a pleasure lover." The indictment sounded forgiving, as if the disease could infect even vigilant people. Spiegel felt himself deeply and beautifully at sea.

"You should give him a chance," he said. "Sit down and talk to him. It's amazing. Like trying to converse with a whole hive of social insects, crawling in all directions."

"Oh, Ted and I used to talk together pretty regularly." The girl held Spiegel in a wary stare. The look dismantled and reassembled him.

"Then what happened?"

"Then we started sleeping together."

His stomach pitched. He was at sea with the obvious. Everything good, everything transforming about this evening would be lost. Already, he loved both these strangers too much to choose between them. And he was still too young to know that choice was never an option.

Weeks passed before he caught painter and composer alone together. Neither would talk to him about the other. Spiegel wondered whether Adie was one of those muses to creative men who did all the actual creation herself. But there was something more to that relationship, something each gave the other that Spiegel couldn't quite name. Their mutual, gravitational pull passed through crowded rooms, without a single signal passing between them. Their closeness sailed forth, silent, invisible, painstaking—like the intimacy both of them struck with the things they made.

Artist and musician were joined at the hip. Their pact with their newly adopted poet excluded Stevie even as they tutored him. Spiegel doubted whether two people ought to be that close. Yet he drew closer to them, ready to swap places with either or take up any kind of triple orbit they asked, however unstable.

Ted dismantled Stevie in several dozen consecutive games of handball before luck and desperate caginess gave Spiegel his first two-point win. By then, between games, they'd worked their way through Schoenberg's *Pierrot* and Second String Quartet together, and Spiegel had begun to feel the air of another planet.

Zimmerman demanded reciprocal gifts of allegiance, scouting reports from lands he hadn't yet reached. Stevie obliged with pleasure, with memorized parcels of Eliot and Stevens, stray trinkets for the two of them to analyze that shared no common thread except the thrill of discovery and the whiff of bewilderment. But always Yeats: Spiegel returned to the man with such persistence that Zimmerman finally gave up trying to break him of the obsession.

Adie rode them both. "Do you two aesthetes ever read anyone who hasn't been dead for decades?"

A decade and a half had passed. Now they were all dead. The joints that had limbered in that brief spring had all ossified. Klarpol and

Spiegel, or their stiff adult puppets, straddled the amber planks of a Cavern that now resembled one of those rental storage sheds along the side of the interstate. No country for old men. Two adults, already fossil, stood with a youth completely unlike the one they'd both loved, a boy no more than the placeholder for a man whose life had peaked at twenty-three.

The Cavern filled with colored boxes, transparent shipping containers stacked against its walls. Spiegel, Adie, and Jackdaw milled about among the marker blocks, passing right through the spectral surfaces as they surveyed them.

Adie cast a cold eye over the consolidating bedroom. *The second chair looks too big. We need to scoot the washstand three inches to the left.*

The three of them hacked a path forward, advancing to the steady rhythm of prototype, tweak, prototype. Seattle and Arles differed so greatly that only the most desperate gaze could shoehorn the one into the other.

Just such desperate looking had set Spiegel loose, back in that free-range spring. He'd never thought to indulge in it before that May. Now no more beautiful a town on earth existed than their little bandit's roost. Across the campus, trees broke out in absurd petaled profusion. Life returned to life, sporting a spin, strangeness, and charm that Spiegel had never suspected.

All things merited writing home about, now that he had his own address. All things turned worth describing. Writing became what he did. He wrote about what passed for landscape, there in the Midwest. He wrote about secondhand clothes in a thrift shop. He wrote about liquor store parking lots. He stood in front of Sterling Hall, so recently bombed out, and made poetry out of the forgetting renovation.

He set up his easel in front of the canonical masterpieces, scribbling pale imitations of everything from Blake to Auden to Wilbur. The ratio of borrowed to earned fell in steady amortization. He loved the saintly, cassocked presumption of the process, loved the sense that, so long as he juggled the feet of his centipede lines, he did nothing to compound the world's misery and perhaps even, in some insignificant way, lifted it a little.

But as much as he loved writing, he loved even more having written. The work done, he'd call up the Victorian rooming house, reading his latest to the beatific woman over the phone. Or barring her, the amusing man. He courted them both, each through the other. Their threesome was itself a topic that he hoped to work into a sestina one day, somewhere down the metric line.

Adie and Ted told him they planned to live together in the fall. The news plunged him into a ravishing depression. Then they asked if he'd join them. A group of compatible souls was spinning off from the Tuesday night gatherings—a potter, a pianist, a writer of one-page fictions, and an actress, all, like Spiegel, in thrall around the companion-star system of those two core personalities. Stevie signed on without even asking about the rent.

The seven of them found the ideal venue, a three-story fixer-upper Carpenter Gothic, the top floor given over to a single finished attic they called the Grand Ballroom. The plan called for a continuous soiree, the Ballroom tricked up to serve as a twenty-four-hour group studio and concert hall. Adie coated the walls with art treasures, a revolving gallery of her own and other students' work that she constantly swapped for. The potter David fitted out the communal kitchen with a collection of incised celadon. Spiegel wrote and performed the inaugural toast, while Ted scored out a nightlong housewarming fantasia performed by Lydia, the pianist, and six amateur percussionists.

Among them, they planned to fix all that had been wrong with civilization since the very beginning. Shopping, cooking, and cleaning became happy common causes. The group pooled their nest eggs into a house kitty, the funds deposited in a joint checking account that Zimmerman, the unlegislated leader of the commune, took out in the name Mahler Haus. Their phone number, too, appeared in the book under the unsuspecting Austrian's moniker.

They commenced their standing banquet, the festivities interrupted only by the decision, now and then, to attend the occasional class. Tuesday nights revived, under new management. Whole ecosystems of outsiders drifted through the house, at various radii from the inner circle. The collective workshop cranked out existence's party favors, their manufacture driven only by mutual delight.

The tapestries that issued from this Gobelin factory all bore the millefleur border of sex. The housemates paired off in all available arrangements. On a semester-long tour of the vineyards, they savored one another's tastes without swallowing. Soirees devolved into soft-core Satyricons, seven, ten, or a whole baker's dozen bodies lying around the Grand Ballroom in a ring, their various parts affectionately threaded.

Throughout December, Lydia the pianist graced Spiegel's room, her chill extremities needing to be touched in four forbidden ways at once. By January, Lydia had drifted on to David, making way in Spiegel's bunk for a dancer named Diana, who wanted Hopkins in her ear as he held her corded thighs from behind, trying to fill her.

Sometimes at nights, when he sat working, Adie would come to his writing desk, sit on his lap, push back his hair, and appraise his face. But she never did more than laugh at his advances, plucking his hand from her breast like lint from a pullover.

Ted had women. Any number of them. Whenever new blood showed up at a house event, the composer had her feeling like Aphrodite's body double before the evening ended. He lived to prove that he could charm anything with two X chromosomes.

Zimmerman's perpetual act of seduction always resorted to the same time-honored weapons. He auditioned prospective partners on his best arsenal of quotes from *Women in Love*. "Let love be enough then. I'm bored with the rest." "There is a golden light inside you that I wish you would give me." And most-loved of all: "See what a flower I've found you." For those who still held out, he enlisted *Dives and Lazarus*. Women who resisted that tune were simply not worth further effort.

When that voluptuous folk melody trickled down from the Grand Ballroom, Ted's housemates knew to stay below. "I don't get it," Spiegel challenged him one morning, after the previous night's conquest had slunk off into daylight. "You slave over this jagged, atonal, mathematically rigorous stuff. How can you stand listening to that shmaltzy anachronism?"

Ted leaned across the toasted bagels and put one hand on each of Spiegel's shoulders. "You know the story about the woman who made Oscar Wilde listen to her daughter play a sonatina? 'How do you like the music, Mr. Wilde?' 'Oh, I don't like music. But I like *that*.'"

It stunned Spiegel: the success rate, the frequency and vigor, the beauty of the conquests, their utter willingness to disappear cleanly and completely afterward, when the mutual projections dissolved. Like nothing he'd ever thought possible. Stevie could not say what drove Ted's feats of appetite. Surely the man couldn't need any reassurance he didn't already possess. There seemed as little sport in the conquests as in the repetitive handball trouncings.

"Know what I like best about twelve-tone music?" Ted told Steve, as they looked over the reams of pencil annotations for his infinitesimally advancing octet. Pure Zimmerman: the annotations swelled while the notes stood still. "The appreciative female audiences who are so intent on distracting you from it."

Those appreciative audiences were sufficiently distracting to keep the music itself from ever materializing. Appetite against appetite, notes had little hope against skin tones. "Don't know about you and verse, buddy boy. But women are a great and mysterious motivator to me."

Adie had been right. The man was a fun lover. And all his endless, absorbent energies were but instruments to that manic end.

If it bothered Adie, she never showed it. If she retaliated with her own men, she did it so discreetly that Spiegel never knew. One night she came into Steve's room and lay on his bed, sketching into a tablet she held upon her knees while he sat in the bay window chair slogging through Derrida's *Of Grammatology*. He put the book down and moved to lie next to her. She draped her left hand on his head, still sketching with her right, a portrait that went futurist, once the subject abandoned it.

"Doesn't it bother you?" he asked her.

"Hmm?"

"All of Ted's . . . ?"

She sat up, tipping the sketchbook away. "All of Ted's colonial operations?" Still clear-faced. "It can't," she said.

He waited for explanation. None came. "What do you mean, 'can't'?"

She touched her thumb to the center of his forehead, stamping him forever. "It can't bother me. I can't let it. Life is long."

It struck Spiegel, in that moment, that he would never have a life mate. Never a real one, for any length of time.

By spring, Mahler Haus lay sacked and ruined. The winds of possibility blew utopia apart. The Madison bombing had spelled the end of world revolution. The Mahler Haus experiment in group living spelled, for each of them, the end of idealism. Each creator retreated to his private bedroom, and the Grand Ballroom closed its doors on group communion for good.

"Things fall apart," Ted told him. "The center cannot hold." But the man seemed untouched by the centripetal wipeout.

In Spiegel's memory, his parents' divorce the following year seemed a minor rehash by comparison. Now almost twice the boy poet's age, Spiegel couldn't recall the particulars of the smashup with any resolution. He felt only the shame of failed reciprocity, of free flights crashing back to ground level.

Things got recriminatory, fast. All soirees ground to a stop. Potter David's beautiful celadon dishes disappeared from the kitchen. The housemates liquidated the group bank account and settled all remaining bills through bitter back-and-forth. Ugly altercations ensued, about who'd lost the key to the cellar. About who forgot to shut off the oven. About who left the hair in the sink. Even when he knew it was his damn hair, Spiegel denied it.

Ted took the easy way out. Doors all over Madison opened up for him, the apartments of women who needed a new fix of *Dives and Lazarus.* "You son of a bitch," Spiegel laid into him, the night Ted came back to the house to move his belongings out. "You're going to abandon me in the ninth circle of hell, while you head off to fresh pastures."

"Think of it as an adventure." Ted smirked. "Besides. You're not alone."

"Who do you mean? Adie? What good is she? She's camped out over at her studio in the Education Building."

"You think I don't know that? She's not who I mean."

"Who, then? I'm left here to pick up the pieces. It makes me sick to my stomach, even to think about working. What the hell am I supposed to do?"

With a single, smooth motion, Zimmerman went to the shelves of the pillaged group library and found the red-spined paperback *Collected Yeats* that no one now wanted. He took down the book, slowly read, then scribbled something on the flyleaf. He chucked the volume at Spiegel, who caught it in mid-arc, as if they'd practiced the slant pattern for months. Zimmerman embraced his friend with the casual backslapping of joyous athletes. And left.

From his second-story window, Spiegel watched the figure jaunt down the leaf-exploding street. Only then did he open the ratty paperback and read the inscription:

> We have fed the heart on fantasies,
> The heart's grown brutal from the fare;
> More Substance in our enmities
> Than in our love; O honey-bees,
> Come build in the empty house of the stare.

The words came back now to fill this new emptied house, art's latest restored ruin. Adie squatted in front of the colored slab that would become the virtual Dutchman's bed. She held her hands out in front of her, in space, resting them on the pretend surface that would soon become blankets. Then she rested her head on those folded hands. *What's that cliché? The one attributed to every famous sculptor who ever lived? We just have to free the bed hidden in this block. Chip away everything that isn't it.*

They did, throughout that September and October. They chipped away, until the blocks became objects. Spiegel helped her with the caning on the chairs, the glaze of the water pitcher, the soft red nub of the bedspread. This time, the game did not stop with surfaces. Each furnishing graduated from flat illusion into volume and shading. More was at stake this time than mere similarity.

The bed stood out from the wall. It occupied its quarter of the room, so palpable that even Freese, on his first visit, gave in to the reflex impulse to smooth its covers. The room filled in. It materialized, up through the oils of half-finished underpainting, the penned cartoon here and there still showing through. On the Cavern's universal walls, they hung Arlesean wallpaper. One by one, the geometrical place-holders took on shape. And week by week, Jackdaw, the unlikeliest of Geppettos, labored away at the code that threatened to bring these woody constructs to life—to a life that life would accredit.

Spiegel carved, too, at the larger block of wood lodged inside the smaller puppet casing. And every image he embellished cracked open to reveal its batting.

After Mahler Haus self-destructed, Stevie had pressed on to get the worthless English degree, throwing good money after bad, unable to change courses or salvage the disaster. Of the whole circle of former idealists, the only ones he ever saw again were the two who had tricked him into utopia. The same couple who'd driven him out again.

Spiegel called Adie the month before she graduated. He roped her into a lunch date, where she ate nothing and smiled her way around all substantive shoals. Steve asked her for a copy of the sketch she'd made of him, that night they'd spoken of Ted.

"That? I've destroyed it."

The words hit Spiegel with a force out of all proportion to the loss. He stood looking down into the hole that awaited all creative effort.

"Destroyed? What do you mean, destroyed?"

"Crumpled up. Thrown away. Most of what I draw I end up pitching."

"You can't be serious. *Why?*"

"Because most of it makes me ill."

"God . . . *damn* it." The rage returned to him, the rage he'd felt when they torched their dream of shared existence. "Why the hell bother to draw it in the first place?"

"Good question." She thought for a long time. "I'd like to think that every mark gets stored. Somewhere."

He and Zimmerman continued to meet for occasional handball and Stravinsky. Ted still gave Spiegel his monthly homework assign-ment, readings to prepare and deliver. The soirees shrank to the two of them sitting in the corner of Gino's Pizzeria on State, the one where the New Year's Bomber had once worked. They'd hover over a large mushroom and pepper, struggling with scansion or polychords.

One night Ted visited the hole in the wall on East Mifflin that Steve had moved into. He brought a 1958 Georges de Latour Private Reserve Napa Cabernet—a monster wine well beyond undergraduate means—and decent red wineglasses as well. Ted chatted even more maniacally than usual. But he would not say what the celebration was until they opened the bottle and imbibed.

They talked modernism, the rind of archaism that had settled so rapidly on that radical aesthetic. "Have I made you read Joyce's *Portrait* yet?" Ted joked.

Spiegel sighed over the rim of his goblet. "Twice."

"Can I tell you something?" Zimmerman said, a slight change in cadence. "I seem to have MS. Just found out this afternoon."

It took Spiegel too long to decode, to figure out what the man had just announced. By the time he did, the moment for real comfort was lost.

In his memory of the event, Spiegel said nothing. Utterly, stupidly nothing. Nothing of use or condolence or aid, for the rest of the night. Ted, at least in memory, left shortly after dropping his bomb, still vaguely buzzing. "Oh. Hey. I've also finished my octet."

The topic sprung Spiegel from the spell that had fallen over him. "Really? That's fantastic. When do we get to hear it?"

"You tell me. As soon as I find eight players who'll sit still long enough to learn something that jagged."

That was his piece. That was the man's piece. Never performed, so far as Spiegel ever heard.

Chance threw them all clear of the wreck. Adie made her way to New York, the Butter-and-Eggs district, where she worked in the MoMA cafeteria and painted. Ted made his way out the year after, up to Washington Heights, where he waited on tables on a restaurant boat moored in the Hudson and studied graduate composition with Davidovsky, at Columbia. Spiegel graduated with a degree in English and four poems that he liked. He moved to San Francisco, as far from New York as he could get and still have crappy weather.

He floundered for a while, working dopey editing jobs, hanging around City Lights, more or less making a stock commedia dell'arte figure of himself. After about a year of shiftlessness, he got a card from the two of them. They'd hooked back up and were living together. Life was long. Three weeks later, Spiegel landed a bank teller's job and settled in for the duration.

From teller, he jumped to data processing, a vacancy in Operations that opened up after a junior operator went berserk and locked himself in the tape storage room with a bulk magnetic eraser gun. Fortunately the eraser, like the machines that had driven the operator to the breaking point, malfunctioned.

Spiegel discovered amazing digital aptitude. A surfeit of words and their ambiguity left him ready to love code's clean, definitive operands. Numbers were simple. They knew what they wanted. They rose and fell according to magnificent tabular design. The whir of the drive spindles, the chug of the card reader, the line printer's barrage all sounded a note of reason that, after the months of carping human clients—most of whom hadn't a clue what they wanted and conflated the Bay Savings Bank with their parents, tormentors, and lovers—struck Spiegel as heavenly.

A little judicious stretching of fact on his résumé landed him a software job with a financial planning outfit up the Valley. He claimed he programmed, when, in fact, he thought COBOL was a minor goblin and couldn't have picked Ada from Pascal out of a police lineup. Then he promptly taught himself the basics in the first three weeks of the job. There the mystery opened to him, the secret brotherhood between fact and its description.

You have to imagine it, he tried to tell the woman who'd first set him upon the path of living algorithm. He laid it out for her over a digitally fabricated face towel, crumpled as if its owner had been taken unaware. *My God! The Arabian Nights. The Arabian Nights.* The full strangeness descended on him again, as it had in the year when he first looked on it. Wonder renewed itself in his replay, as the natural world renewed itself in imitating code.

Think of it: you just spell out a few descriptions. OK: a lot of descriptions. But still, you type some words, the inner name of the thing. You describe how you want it. You build a topical outline of its behavior. Then you run the description, and there the idea is. Actual, working, in all its functional glory. Coming to life, on the terminal in front of you.

Adult Adie frowned at the thumbnail of the towel that they worked up on her screen.

No, Steve said. *You can't possibly understand. There are too many layers now, between you and the artifact. Assemblers, compilers, interpreters, code generators, reusable libraries, visual programming tools. It wasn't always like this. You have to imagine looking at this towel, this beautiful, woven, cotton towel, falling in natural folds, as good as cloth. Have to imagine looking at it and seeing the realization of your own words, your own perfect, workable essay about the way that cloth looks and feels and falls.*

Pygmalion?

He's in there somewhere. Orpheus might be closer. I'm telling you, writing my first subroutine was . . . like causing huge chunks of unravished bride to rise up, just by singing to her. A good, polished program was everything I thought poetry was supposed to be.

Stevie. You must have had a very peculiar idea of what poetry was supposed to be.

No different than any person who ever wrote it. I was going to get inside of reality and extract its essence, write down on paper the magic metrical words that, read aloud, would do their open sesame.

She looked at the screen, ready to deny everything. But she nodded. *The vital formula.* Sympathetic spells. Life's nail clippings. The impression of a body in bed.

He raced on, not hearing her. *There was this kid poet, and he wrote and wrote. He rubbed the magic lamp until the poetic self-abuse police threatened to come impound him. And still nothing happened. The incantation seemed to be defective. Then they put the kid in front of this terminal and initiated him into the secret syntax. A few simple rules, combined in a few elegant ways, and* blamm-o. *The thing works. It runs. The world does move. The rules churn. The descriptions step their way through their own internal logic. The lines of code set more switches, change more states. Commands produce results.*

The word made flesh.

Spiegel flinched. *Don't mock me.*

I'm not mocking.

Because that's exactly what it is. It doesn't matter if you're only talking about a formula for compound interest plugged into a general ledger program. Change any variable and the executing universe alters. Move it to the left, increment it by a quarter percent, and the new result gets spit out whole. It gives one a tremendous feeling of—

Power?

Perfectibility. Coding possessed a kind of reality check that sestinas never had. A program either worked or it didn't, and if it didn't work, it was wrong. Period. Something magnificent to that.

I made a lot of wrong paintings in my life. Believe me. And I didn't need any machine to tell me they were wrong.

But you never knew, completely, when you made a right one.

Adie wrapped her self-indicting silence around her like a shawl.

It's . . . funny, Spiegel went on. *Art made all this happen, you know. The whole digital age. Music did it. Hollerith got his idea for the punched data card from the player piano. From the Jacquard tapestry loom.*

Not guilty, Adie pled. *I've got an airtight alibi.*

That's what they all say. He nipped her chin between finger and thumb. *You have to imagine. Programming blew my thinking loose. Absolutely liberating. It freed me up in a way I hadn't been since . . .*

Since Yeats?

Since Yeats. The rules, the operators? They're completely open-ended. Extensible. Whatever you can imagine, they can build. Think of it: the universal behavior machine, able to build any gadget that crossed the human mind. Not a tool. The ultimate medium.

They dirtied the digital towel, enlarged it, opened it to the light, hung it back upon the sketched-in schematic of its hook, protruding from the left-hand wall.

You know, they say that a coder's whole concept of programming depends on his first language. Old FORTRAN dinosaurs are stuck in their own do-loops. COBOLers think the machine is only good for running accounts receivable. Kids raised on BASIC never break free of that GOTO. But you see, my first language . . .

Adie smiled, remembering, despite herself. *Was another code all together. You're telling me that you were fated to wind up programming golden mechanical birds?*

Well, we all end up working on whatever TeraSys lets us.

Jackdaw? Adie called to the one who was still a child. *What was your first programming language?*

The kid looked up from a screen filled with instructions. Somewhere in the sequenced lines, the tireless, interlinked description, a miraculous bedside drawer emerged, one that slid in and out of its wooden table. *Wah?* Eyebrows up, distracted. It took him a few processor cycles to parse the question. *First language? Assembler.*

But first languages never knew their last sentences. On that day when Spiegel left Bay Savings, he called his friends in New York to give them the change of address, never mind the fact that they'd never used the old one. Ted was out. Spiegel spoke with Adie, the same Adie who wouldn't remember the call when the time came to remember everything.

"He's starting to lose it," she reported. "Walking with a cane. He falls down a lot. Then he picks himself up as if nothing just happened."

It occurred to Steve that he could now probably beat the man at handball. "They say it can go into remission."

"Do they? What do they say about the chance of a doctor of music composition getting a job anywhere on the face of the planet?"

"Is he close to finishing?" Something to say, however feeble.

"Oh, any year now. Steve, it's unbelievable." Opposites mixed freely in her voice. "All the man wants to do anymore is compose."

"Does he still . . . ?" Spiegel began. But decency forced him to pull over before someone got hit.

"No. Nothing. Just sits there and writes music."

"Is any of it getting played?"

"Stevie, Stevie. What planet are you living on? Our apartment was broken into five months ago? The thieves took everything that wasn't nailed down. Except for the man's classical music collection."

"Is he at least . . . happy?"

"What a quaint question. Nice to know that at least one of us hasn't changed since college."

"You're still painting, aren't you?"

"Guilty. But at least I'm holding down a real job. Official table busser to the art elite." She admitted to still putting together a portfolio, however much she declared her readiness to cave in to the world's terms.

Her tone was too much for Spiegel. He wished he'd never called. "Let me know when you mount your show. And tell Thaddeus to give me a ring sometime."

She never did let him know. But Zimmerman did call, years too late, after Spiegel had signed on to work with TeraSys, surrendering to the century's terminal art form. Ted did call, after Steve could no longer imagine how far the man's body had decayed. He called from Lebanon, a flyspeck in the wastelands of southwestern Ohio. An old Shaker town, site of one of Mother Ann's visionary communities, waiting celibately up on a bluff for the world's redemption and wrap-up. A town whose chief industry had once been utopianism but was now the nearby close-security prison.

Ted was well. He was working. Oh: and he was also employed.

He had a job in that same prison, part of a four-year private college's outreach program, granting bachelor's degrees to convicted rapists, arsonists, and murderers. He had gone out on the market for a few years' running and had come close to landing a post in Utah. But the Mormons had not bought his cultural analysis of *Das Lied von der Erde*. So he ended up in the ruins of millenarian Warren County, teaching Rudiments of Theory and World Culture 1 and 2 to the incarcerated underclass of Dayton, Columbus, and Cincinnati.

What exactly was World Culture 1?

He wasn't entirely sure, but if Spiegel had any suggestions, he was willing to try anything once. He rather enjoyed it when 300-pound men with diagonal keloids across their faces could identify the start of a secondary theme group. And get this: the recidivism rate for the prison as a whole was 48 percent. For those who completed a degree, it dropped to 12.

Cause and effect?

More likely, those who could stomach World Culture for a couple of semesters were already those who had steeled themselves to the idea of life on the outside.

Job security?

Twenty to life. No reduction for good behavior.

How was he getting around?

Slowly. In a wheelchair.

Where was Adie?

Zimmerman was not quite sure. Still in New York, he thought. She'd had a show, while they were still living together, at a reputable SoHo gallery. The work had been written up, talked about in all the appropriate circles. It looked as though the art mafia were going to let her play.

Then she'd panicked. She took back the couple of works that had sold at the show, paying the gallery their commission plus a makeup fee to the buyers. She rejected the gallery's offer to think about a more casual, long-term relationship. Refused to keep the door open, even in the abstract. She held a bonfire. Ted wasn't sure how many works she burned, but the casualties were high and the ones that burned best were by far her most accomplished.

She'd started to freelance. Junk, Ted called it. Commercial design. Coffee-shop walls. Health-club logos. Ad circulars for fake New England mail-order houses.

At the time, Ted's own CV was coming back unopened from every academic job offering in the country. The MS was in remission, and he was pouring all temporary strength into a large-scale piece—a concerto for piano and orchestra. He was playing beat the clock, working away seven or eight hours a day on the concerto, and the hopeless effort was driving Adie up the wall. He should have been out doing something about his job odds, she said. When he asked her what that might entail, she grew even angrier.

She came to him with an ultimatum. Either he start looking for real work or they were history. He told her he'd always enjoyed history. So she split, leaving him only a P.O. box for a forwarding address.

Had he tried to contact her?

Had not and would not. Not good for either of them. She needed to be free of him. He made her feel guilty.

And she made him feel . . . ?

He'd never really stopped to consider.

He was still writing music?

This was the extraordinary compensation. Just as all hope was walking out the door, salvation blew in the window. Spiegel knew about computers? He made a living with them? Then he knew all about the first significant change in the production of music since Pan carved his pipes.

Zimmerman had no clue how any of it worked. Some digital necromancer, probably Asian, had taken the sound of a real clarinet, sliced each second of the waveform into forty-four thousand pieces, and pushed each of those pieces down into silicon. From there, the reed could be recalled at any pitch, duration, or intensity.

Not a perfect clarinet, mind you. Or rather, a tad too perfect. But Zimmerman wasn't about to quibble over sound quality. He had his Esterhazy in a box—every instrument of the orchestra at his beck and call, around the clock, each one capable of playing beyond the range of earthly instruments. He scored out music on the screen, just as he did on paper, and the miraculous music box performed every aural event he cared to specify.

The possibilities outstripped not only his wildest expectations but also his wildest ability to expect. For the first time in his life, Ted could hear the contour of his thoughts as he thought them. The tireless box played a presto stream of hemi-demi-semiquavers all day long without bobbling a note or pausing to breathe.

He set aside all concern for the possible and began to compose the music he most wanted to hear. The box realized anything that Zimmerman could describe to it. He wrote a piece for twelve piccolos in narrowest brilliant tessitura. He wrote a sonata for cello and piano that kept the piano in a perpetual pianissimo and never let the cello out of murderous thumb position. He wrote a frenetic solo for bass clarinet, thirty thousand high-speed notes leaping and crashing through all registers so jaggedly that no human could dream of bringing it off. He played the piece for Spiegel over the phone. Even through the tiny acoustical portal, the effect was dizzying.

Once Spiegel opened the channel, the phone became Ted's favorite obbligato instrument. If the thing rang in Seattle any time before eight in the morning or after midnight, odds were good that the voice at the other end would kick things off with a cheery "Lebanon, here!" A call might last the better part of an hour, Ted ecstatic with extended show-and-tell. "Wait," he'd say, his voice slurring in its great, decade-long rallentando. "Listen to that same passage played by a brass quintet." And he'd crash around making the changes, Spiegel hearing, in the struggle, just how bad things had become.

"Don't hurt yourself," Spiegel told him. "Send me a tape."

Not the same. Ted wanted the thrill of a live performance. And he could still manage all the controls, given time.

It worried Steve. "Are you OK out there by yourself? I mean, it sounds as if a lot of gear is hitting the floor with considerable frequency."

"And I most frequently of all. Never fear. There's a woman who comes by . . ."

Of course there was a woman. What had Spiegel been thinking? Two, in fact. A colleague who taught English at the prison. And Zimmerman's widowed landlady, who rented him three rooms in her antebellum house with its twenty-foot ceilings for $200 a month. From each according to her abilities.

In some lingering need for an audience, Ted called more often. For a while, they were in better touch than they'd been since that spring of their mutual discovery. But however often they spoke, that spongy, deteriorating voice on the other end shocked Spiegel. Not a gradual descent: a fall headlong down the staircase. Ted called to lecture, to hold forth, to assign belated homework, but mostly to play the world premiere of another fifteen measures. Now and then he remembered to ask Spiegel how things were going on the other end.

And then the bolt from the blue. The lottery: what anyone else but this crippled anachronism would have called his lifetime lucky break. An old virtuoso friend from Columbia days commissioned Zimmerman to write a piece for solo viola, for performance in the downtown New York avant-garde music demimonde.

You never knew about it? Steve asked the adult Adie. Years failed to erase his surprise.

Never.

It was performed a few times. Once in a space in TriBeCa, in fact.

The city's new music scene is pretty big, Stevie. Hundreds of concerts you never hear about, every day.

He was sure you knew about it. That you deliberately stayed away. It crushed him that you never showed up.

Crushed him? He said it crushed him?

Well, not in so many words.

The piece was as full of antinomian cheek as Zimmerman could manage. But for this audience bred on halting dissonance, he delivered lines as long and soaring as *Dives and Lazarus*. A theme and variations, no less, on the old fugueing tune "Idumea": beautiful, visceral, expansive, and, given the venue, hopelessly banal. The dedicatee almost refused to play the piece, so startlingly unshocking was it, so potentially damaging to an experimental reputation.

He did it to provoke the provocateurs. Said it was his Abschied *to the innovating world. You know: "It's not like I'm ever going to make it back to the city anyway."*

Idumea. I can't believe it. Idumea.

He also said that you . . . that you . . .

. . . used to walk around the apartment humming that tune.

Naked.

He told you that? How dare he?

How dare anyone? "Idumea" drew as many silent sneers as *Le Sacre* had once drawn catcalls. Shape-note Americana, second-rate WPA, half a century too late: the wry joke of a very select crowd, over the run of a very short season. But the gorgeous solo viola line lodged in the heart of at least one listener, a slumming double agent whose day job consisted of producing commercial musical scores. The fellow had been looking for someone who could do a thirty-second derivative Copland knockoff, and chance had led him to that someone.

Zimmerman never hesitated. It shocked Spiegel, and saddened him. But working for TeraSys by then, Spiegel had little moral leverage to preach against selling out. Ted worked up the piece in a little under three weeks. It was "Simple Gifts," returned to sender. Thirty seconds of hosanna from the world's first, radiant hoedown. Heavenly counterpoint, put to the service of a multinational consumer-products conglomerate intent upon wrapping its insidious agricultural chemistry in the patina of Shaker innocence.

He did that? That was Ted? Adie, incredulous, remembered the commercial spot. Remembered it in the back of her throat. The kind of manipulative, nostalgic sound track that you wept over in the solitary shame of your living room, with all the shades pulled down.

The delighted corporate sponsors paid Zimmerman well. Ted made a hundred times more for those three weeks of work than he'd made for all the other music he had composed in his life. The lump sum helped to cover what the prison college's group insurance refused to pay, when Ted at last had to move into Warren County's second-best assisted-care facility.

Life was truly long. Ted spent his days strapped in a bed in a nursing home in the Buckeye state, a forty-year-old avant-garde composer surrounded by the perfect audience: deaf nonagenarians. At least he had a private room—a cinder-block single compartment, the same dimensions as the one his old friends now redecorated.

Ted and Steve had spoken only twice since Adie's arrival out West. Spiegel stopped calling him. Ted could no longer hold the receiver. Even after one of Ted's nightingales bought him a speakerphone, Spiegel quit returning Ted's calls. It was not just cowardice. Ted's voice had gotten so faint and slurred that Steve had to ask him to repeat everything three times and still couldn't make out the half of each message. The brain was still intact, but it had begun to waver into places where Spiegel was not yet allowed. Silence seemed the more merciful ordeal.

Spiegel had not visited, nor had he seen pictures. And yet here was the place where the man now lived. Where else but this prototypical layout? Planks standing in for linoleum; cambered casements for molded plastic. The bed pressed up against the back right corner of the narrow box. No doubt the real bed was a tubular steel hospital apparatus wrapped in acrylic blankets. But in the invalid's mind, surely it resembled this rich red wood piled high in an eidolon of eiderdown.

And next to the bed, the rickety table: the perfect stand for Ted's MIDI sequencer, executing its archaic scores on a whole orchestral palette of digitally sampled instruments, playing them out through a pair of tinny speakers where Van Gogh's water pitcher stood. Perhaps a nurse came in and worked the mouse for him. Perhaps the machine,

unlike Spiegel, still understood Ted's voice well enough to take dictation. Perhaps the picture frames on the walls above his bed held snippets of laser-printed score, keepsakes of Ted's long, aural adventure.

This was the room that Spiegel helped to furnish, no matter what
chamber from the sunny South Adie thought she outfitted. The two of
them collaborated, carving down the cubes into the objects each hid.
Thousands of polygons hung suspended in space on the intersecting
beams of five projectors. The shaving mirror alone ran into the millions of bits, dozens just to fix the location and color of each hung
pixel. Behind its flinty blue reflection, voltage differences snaked
through an array of registers in a conga line so long that all that the
human eye ever saw was this massive epiphenomenon, this simple
looking glass that bore no earthly relationship to the worlds of oscillat-
ing semiconductance surging beneath its surface.

Over the weeks that Spiegel and Klarpol refinished their storeroom
of old furniture, Jackdaw assembled a library of interactive definitions—
reusable ball bearings that animated all the room's moving parts.
Through the staked pains of software's sieve—check lower bound X;
check lower bound Y; check lower bound Z; check upper . . . , set
StepRate . . . , fix ShadeOffset . . . ; for RotItem from –180 to 180, step
StepRate, if ShadeOffset <X then . . . else if . . .—Jackdaw began to
implement what the barest corner of any self-respecting efficiency apartment did glitchlessly a trillion times over, every unthinking second.

It no longer sufficed for each of the room's austere furnishings, their
continent-wide sheets of bits sliding along the moraines of video memory, merely to mimic solidity. Deeply nested C routines now invested
the smallest collection of boxels with real-world behaviors. The same
host electronics that sculpted these statues of colored air could also
sense and respond to the room's angelic visitors.

The visitors' solid hands still passed through everything they tried to
feel. But now a thumb and forefinger, pinched around the phantom
drawer knob, could pull it open. Even the designers felt the uncanny
effect, moving the wood-grained logic of an object they could not even
touch. However incorporeal, the towel ruffled when brushed. The windows cluttered shut at the first mime of force against them. And when
the transient user, suckered by half a billion years of evolution into

believing the visible, reached out by reflex to pat the bedcovers, those sheets miraculously turned their corners down as if waiting for the idea of a sleeper to curl up and inhabit them.

Water wanted to pour. Shirts wanted wearing; picture frames, straightening. An eerie hideout rose up around its makers. The ghostly placeholders began to stand in for their leaden referents. For finally, the brain conversed less with stuff than with appropriate response. It operated upon the working symbol, and for that, the less carrying weight, the better. Dimension, color, surface, motion—the full play of functional parts—implied a tenant who seemed eternally to have just stepped out for a moment. The visitor moved through a furnished efficiency where all the comforts and amenities performed as they should, with only the apartment's occupant eternally not at home.

The room solidified as the year dissolved. Expectation shot through Spiegel every time, standing on the floorboards, riffling through the Dutchman's evacuated things. Adie's belief, too, reached critical mass. Technology wanted something from them. The play of emulated, Arlesean light teetered on the verge of some announcement.

Whatever time passed outside the Cavern, the artist's bedroom hung in an eternal noon. The bedroom's blaze enveloped its makers, even as they worked at their midnight cubicles. The three of them settled into the silent routine of roommates, the new nuclear family sharing this close, sunny starter home. They worked alone, coming together at times to putter and refine. Perpetual nesting, permanent spring cleaning. The shared task of home improvement made talk unnecessary.

Ade? Spiegel said one night, violating that pact of silence. *Can I ask you something?*

The eyes said, "Do we need to?" The mouth said, *Sure.*

The celibacy thing?

Yes? She dragged out the initial letter in epic wariness. *And what exactly would you like to know about the celibacy thing, Stevie?*

He thumbed his nose at her, some avuncular nineteenth-century gesture new to him, its origins a total mystery. *Not celibacy per se. I've already assembled as much data about that particular subject as I care to, thank you. What I want to know is, don't you . . . don't you ever miss it?*

"It" being non-celibacy?

"It" being a partner. Companionship. A warm body in the house on a damp night.

Well, I have Pinkham, you know. She turned toward the creature, who lay curled up in his favorite spot on a rag rug inside a coil of coaxial cable at the Cavern mouth. She patted her thighs in invitation. Pinkham looked up, ascertained the absence of crisis, yawned, and curled down again. He refused to step near the simulated room. It bewildered him.

Don't you miss . . . surprising behavior? Something not reducible to axioms. A being as big and complicated as you are.

Oh. Pinkham is all that. And then some. He's a lot more complicated than I am, in fact.

All right. Call me anthropocentric. Don't you miss conversation? Talking in bed? A mind that isn't yours, to go over the day's mystery with. Someone to distract you, on those days when you feel like writing on the walls.

I never really trusted words all that much, she said.

Spiegel opened the shutters. Jackdaw's astonishing algorithm bathed the room in a crescendo of Provençal sun. Stevie fiddled with the casement, waving it back and forth without touching, like playing an etherophone. *Sex, Ade. You don't need it? You can go totally without?*

That depends. She looked away from him, not at all coy. *On what exactly you mean by "sex."*

He turned away too, hiding his blush. *You ever wonder why we two never slept with each other? I mean, every other possible permutation in that house went to town, at least once. Didn't matter . . .* He skipped a beat, but could not stop. *Whether they even liked each other.*

You didn't miss anything, Stevie. Believe me. She seemed to wonder, for a moment, just which way she meant to head. *Look. I don't know how it is for you. But as far as I'm concerned, solitude is not a hardship post. Being single is not some kind of jail sentence, Stevie. I like my aloneness. It's better than any other configuration I can imagine.*

Through the lab's partition walls came a group war whoop, the cheer of software engineers down the hall, delighting in some hard-won extension of their dominion deeper into the kingdom of comprehension.

For that matter . . . She pointed toward the hidden celebration. *None of us is anywhere near as alone as we ought to be.*

He caught her drift, without another word. Her worst fears about depiction were true. Evolution's most productive trick was to rig things so that the idea of need grew vastly more insatiable than the needs it represented. Feeling had nowhere near ample room in which to play itself out. Sex at best mocked what love wanted. The gut would explode before it could dent the smallest part of its bottomless hunger.

Another night came, one night nearer to the end of history. Spiegel and Klarpol busied themselves with fixing a chair that, when picked up and moved, tended to shed and leave behind a phantom right front limb.

You know what we need, Ade? Spiegel kept his eyes on a screen dump of the flawed data structure. He aired the idea as if he had just come up with it. *Sound.*

It took her a moment to register. But when she did, she clapped her hands. And again, louder. For every tatter in the mortal idea.

That's it. That's brilliant. Of course we need sound. It never occurred to me. This place is dead silent. That's why it seems like such a haunted house.

Well. One of the reasons.

You're telling me we could get the floorboards to creak whenever some-one takes a step on them?

That's what I'm telling you.

Unreal. The wood could thump when you touch it. The shutters could clack. Pinging glass. That's it. Every object will make its right noise. This will totally flip people out. Their ears will convince them of the thing they're touching.

Know what we really need? Music.

She cocked a head at the suggestion. Trying to figure out what he was after. Then she figured. *You know what, Stevie? We really don't. Music is not what we really need. It's the last thing in the world, in fact.*

He looked at her, already hearing. As if the room were already dosed in superfluous sonatas.

Realization took hold of her face. She fought back at the assault. *Oh fuck. Fuck it. You brought me all the way out here, after all these years . . . ? Just to get me to . . . just to try to fix me back up with . . . ?*

She crumbled at the prospect of losing the greatest Etch-A-Sketch a girl had ever been given. She hid her face in her hands, up to her ears.

No, his look said, too soft to hear. Not to fix *you* up. Not you per se. Zimmerman. To fix Ted. The one who really needed him. The one Spiegel loved, first of anyone.

27

The Therapy Room is a work in progress.

Its idea is as old as ideas themselves: to break the terror of existence by depicting it. Heights brought down to ground level, dried floods, cardboard invaders: a story of hurtful things that cannot hurt you any more than any story can.

Outside the Therapy Room, a white thirty-four-year-old neurasthenic female, Miss Muffet (not her real name), presents with acute, debilitating arachnophobia. After administering a history and physical, her doctors place Miss Muffet inside the palpable re-creation of a kitchen much like her own: a clean, well-lit Kenmore ensemble with lots of counter space. Just as M.M. grows comfortable in the surroundings, technicians bury her up to her midriff in spiders.

The patient's vitals spike off the charts. She screams and runs out of the representation, as if from the real evil. For the next two hours M.M. is a panting wreck, unable to go anywhere near the imaginary kitchen. This is a good sign. In order for the Therapy Room to work, the patient must credit it enough to dread it. Miss Muffet's gullibility makes her the ideal subject. She knows the nightmare of spiders is a fabrication. And still she believes.

As soon as the patient can calm down, they send her back in. This time, primed for the assault, telling herself that it's only an invention, she lasts a full thirty seconds. Miss Muffet laughs in cold terror after she reaches the exit. Her pulse returns to normal in half the time of her first exposure. She now knows she can escape the spiders anytime she wants. She can enter the kitchen, however horrible, and survive.

Real exposure can't teach her this, for real fear overwhelms all second tries. But the Therapy Room works at the limits of seeming. Belief gives way to evidence, spiders to spiderlike objects. Twelve exposures later, Miss Muffet takes to batting at her nemeses, frying them with the click of a joystick, racking up the kills like so many toy targets.

Out in the larger world, M.M. makes a miraculous parallel leap. For if the things she so lately took for threats turned out to be mere representations, how much more of a threat can the originals represent? Models reveal to her the model she has lived in. Symbols cure her of the fears those symbols stood for. Terror flattens into its empty sign.

The same cure promises help for all those disabled by the real. Burn victims will forget their pain, wrapped in a more vibrant light. Those paralyzed by fear of flying will make their connections. Post-traumatic stress sufferers, for whom no other therapy has worked, will skim the virtual canopies above firefights powerless to reach them.

When next M.M. sees a living spider, she rubs it out happily with her bare hands. The case history writes her final happy chapter: *Miss Muffet successfully desensitized.*

28

Every ten-minute chunk of May makes an eternity. But once the weeks are finally dead, you feel the month pass in memory in half a heartbeat. Time uses you; it lays you out. It advances glacially, gouging by inches your scarred inner continents. Then it vanishes, leaving behind no single landmark but white.

You kill the quarter-hours dune-ranging through the blankest Saharas, each kilometer of hard-won track wiped out by the wind as soon as you turn to look back. At huge intervals, oases punctuate the evacuated tracts. You head for whatever infrequent way stations you can scrape together.

Mother's Day, never marked by more than a week of low-level anxiety capped by an emergency call to FTD, swells to an international conference of sacred distraction. All day, the woman's face struggles to take shape. You fight for detail, work to recover the first sight your eyes ever recognized, the most familiar, most assumed, most beatific, nauseating, neglected, adored, abused. Hours pass trying to fix her features, to see past their gross lines, to zoom in beyond your usual myopia down to the local intricacies of cartilage, her smallest fleshy finials.

Her full-tipped nose swims into focus, your nose before its Anglo contamination. The pained laugh lines on the outskirts of her eyes deeping to plow cuts. Her chin's drumlins assume a detail that only enforced isolation could have given you. A haunted face, a hunted one. Framed in that copper coif of composure that it took you until the age of twelve to realize was not her natural color. Pahlevi copper. Before that, in pictures, Pahlevi blond. Westoxification at its finest. Hair color that would be hard to hide, even now, under the required head scarf. A face no longer welcome in the country of her birth, the same country that now bankrolls Sacred Conflict and their army of God's Partisans, the ones who have seized you, her baby, the flesh of her flesh.

All day long her muscles materialize, cling to the noble cheekbones, a grimace of pleasure peeking through the interdicting fear. Every brave smile apprises you of its bewilderment, the wild route of its arrival here. You make out the tuft of peach fur on her upper lip, there already in '51, the year that old Tavakoli and his family migrated to England in the wake of Mussadegh's nationalization of Anglo-Iranian Oil.

Three years later, in the returning Shah's wake, the freshly rechristened British Petroleum sought out her faithful father and reinstated him to his middle-management post. But by then your mother Shahnaz's lovely, peach-furred lip had captivated a handsome American serviceman loitering around London prior to his inevitable return to Iowa and a lifetime of agricultural extension lecturing. Veiled in white, in an incoherent Anglican ceremony where her whole displaced family did their best *ferangi* impersonations, your mother swore through that fleshy mouth to love, honor, and obey this American, to follow him into lifelong exile deep in a land that couldn't tell Iranian from Indonesian.

These features, this face: what could the domesticated prairie have looked like, through eyes so black and baffled? Not a question you've ever entertained, before Mother's Day inflicts you with time enough to entertain all questions. *Isfahan*, your mother's singsong once sang to you, *is half the world*. Growing up in Basra, Kuwait, and Doha could not have left too much room in her remaining half a world for a town like Des Moines.

And yet, the laughing, skittish voice tries again to tell you, *I never felt at home until I came to the United States*. The black eyes whose gaze you could never bear to meet dart away, caught in the compromise of something like truth. *People in the Midwest are so friendly. So ready to take you in*. By which she must have meant that Iowans, in their bounty, could not imagine how anyone would not want to be like them, given half a chance.

But she did, your hair-dyed mother. Did want to become that local and featureless thing. Did take on a rolling, open, Midwestern look, that history of no history. Did adopt the life that her cosmopolitan father, the emissary of empire, unwittingly trained her for, through her childhood spent shuttling among Oil's tap points. Did learn to sing, *We are from I-oway, I-oway!* Never at home until here.

The face that solidifies before you at morning grows old by nightfall. All those years, Shahnaz among the alien corn. Her ancient words, ways, and beliefs, hidden under a bushel. Her occasional Franco-Farsi, a mumbled *merzi* to checkout clerks or an accidental *khoda hafez* when leaving the rare party where she fully relaxed. Her annual covert Norooz celebrations, the third week of March, the flowers all hothouse imitations and the nougat candies all made with Jewel Tea Company bleached imperial equivalents.

Except for these lapses, she steeped her life in protective coloration, her olive skin aging, growing pale, each year refining its successive approximation of hearty farm stock until, by Mother's Day midnight, you can mistake her for white, the white of your father, your state, your upbringing. The apparition gazes on you, neither scolding nor imploring. With a simple look, she works her daily vigilance. This May exercise recalls you to the basic fact of her existence. Her life needed no further justification, so long as you and your brother still needed her to survive the world in which chance set you down.

Her two boys: all the light those eyes ever needed. Hers was the countenance of love, too circumspect for any photo to have captured. This is the mask of happy sacrifice. The face of the most maternal being that a child could conceive. Your icon for safety, for every comfort and care ever taken for granted. Your weight, your shame, your memory, your mother.

After sunset, her features dim. She disappears into the black of your enclosure. Nothing remains of her dislocated solicitude but that brow's accommodation, her motherly wiliness, the will to improvise. You cannot conjure her back. She morphs into the woman you never witnessed, the one who came into her own after you fled her faultless nest.

Your desertion must have changed those features, for eyes always betray the thing they look for. With you up in Chicago, teaching the global economy's privileged elites how to maximize their verbal throw weight, Kamran off building Peace Corps housing in Mali, and her hapless husband shrinking to nothing with each successive day of retirement, spinning down the tube into prime-time dramas of Texan millionaires, what could the daughter of Anglo-Iranian wandering, the born mother, still find, in the corn-rowed wastes of I-oway, to nurture? For whom could she go on living? What could absorb her surplus care?

She found a replacement, so fast it made you jealous. Force of habit, maternal instinct's inertia left her continuing to cook, cranking out sustenance as if there were still fledglings to eat it. Great, heaped mountain ranges of her family's favorites began to pile up in a home that no longer housed enough mouths to consume it all. At last a woman friend, a fellow volunteer at the 4-H, suggested a joint catering service, Shahnaz on the stove and native Rosemary handling the front office.

For two years, the women's experiment in grassroots capitalism coasted along on word of mouth. They served pork chops and mashed potatoes to confirmation parties and fried chicken and apple dumplings to golden anniversary reunions. All the while, your mother hid in her heart of hearts the conviction that people wouldn't really eat that way except out of ignorance. Once she'd secured a loyal clientele, the woman launched her calculated gamble. She introduced her offerings sparingly, slipping in a little *mast o esfinaj* or *khiar* alongside the glazed hams, and no one was any the wiser.

Emboldened, she graduated to saffron-flecked rice with bottom-of-the-pot and *zereshk pulow* at one party, an eggplant "Mullah-has-fainted" at another. Piecemeal, she deployed the full menu of raptures and revelations: *kabab koobideh, fesenjan, qormeh sabzi*. To these Persian mainstays she added a panoply of recipes reverse-engineered from a youth spent bouncing around all the capitals of the Middle East.

In that corn-fed desert, she built an oasis. Native xenophobia counted for nothing against a good rosewater rice pudding. Once the Iowans supped from her font, even lifelong steak-and-potato men came back for more. Culture had impaired no palate so severely that it could not recover on a few tastes of heaven.

Rosemary, the managing partner, drew up an exotic, Orientalized business card and christened the reborn business Iranian Delights. Des Moines never knew their likes. Nothing matched them for miles. They were a hit, producing a demand that they could not satisfy. They delivered the full, unknown flavor that life forever promised, for the same price as pork and beans.

After November 1979 they changed the name again, to Persian Delights, just as Anglo-Iranian had once changed discreetly into British Petroleum. But the greater Des Moines area still sounded the call to arms, patriotically renouncing all things spicy and suspect. Culinary multiculturalism surrendered its tenuous beachhead in the tall corn, beaten by geopolitics. Iowa renounced its ideal convert citizen, returned her to immigrant status in her adopted homeland.

Reconstructing her story is good for burning an hour, when you most need it. But the pain of imagining her is worse than the agony of time. Her details do you in. You'd call them vicious irony, if you still believed in so benign a thing. How she marched in the streets as a teen, beating her breasts, reciting slices of a Qur'an that she'd memorized in inscrutable Arabic, to the horror of her Westernized parents. How she sealed the lifelong pact with her American serviceman, whose greatest wartime experience had consisted of helping to move Patton's fictitious landing army around England, the thousands of cardboard and balloon tanks replete with recorded mechanical sounds meant to fool the Nazis into imagining that the Allies would land at Calais. How your parents embarked on eternal matrimony in an Anglican church, in a country that belonged to neither, yet held them both by the colonial lapels. How, Westernized, apostate, she all but lost her native Farsi. And now, from the street below, how the Arabic texts she once committed to memory percolate up nightly to serenade her monolingual son's window.

You spend a lifetime, another afternoon, trying to recall what it meant, growing up, to say you were half Persian. Never much more than the usual North American party game of Mongrel's Papers. Quarter Irish. Three-fifths Lapp. Nothing more than your run-of-the-mill experiment in high-school chemistry dilution. But you always felt a little pride at being more than the prevailing flavor, an offbeat breed, at least in this stretch of the prairie. Your sound-bite biography always made for good show-and-tell. It tied you to a country where you'd never been, one that you didn't know from Eden.

On into adulthood, you carried around this membership in a place forever closed to you. The year that you hoped finally to go visit, the door slammed permanently shut. The revolution would as soon jail the sons of the golden-haired Pahlevis as grant them visas. For months on the nightly broadcasts, you saw more of your homeland than you'd seen in the two preceding decades. Your mythic home-away-from-homeland turned, by an unholy alliance of mullahs and American television networks, into a demented parody, a nation of breast-beating crazies run by militant clerics with foot-long beards who captured innocent Americans and held them hostage.

That's not how it really is, your mother told anyone who would listen. Above all, her boys. *Believe me,* the crushed-olive lips begged. But her eyes studied the assaulting broadcasts, flecked with doubt at the distance between what she remembered and this latest round of electronic proof. *It's an old country,* she insisted, her fleshy face frightened. *Older than all this nonsense.* Persians were masters of the world back when the Greeks were still in preschool. This, too, will pass, and leave behind nothing but the astonished record.

Because you could not come to it, Iran has come to you. It happily exports Islamic revolution into the vacuum of this fractured country. Your kinsmen bankroll Ali, Walter, the Angry Parent. Your unknown half-ancestor strides out to meet you halfway, in the valley between you.

All through the summer, words come back to you. At meals, or during your half-hour sprints along your oval track, or in the middle of the morning bathroom ritual, now trimmed back to a frenzied seven minutes. Forgotten vocabulary, sometimes in your mother's voice, sometimes in the voice of those grandparents, fictional to you except for two short childhood trips Stateside when the Brits still pumped the oil and the Shah still issued the travel visas. Words return. The names of foods. The primary colors. The numbers from one to ten.

More than words: chunks of your mother's favorite stories, in translation. The one about the white-haired baby who grows up to be a mighty king. The one about a flock of birds who set out to find the fabulous *Simurgh*. They cross the seven valleys of Journey, Love, Knowing, Detachment, Unity, Bewilderment, and Annihilation, the thirty straggling survivors hanging on just long enough to discover, or rather to remember, that *Simurgh* means nothing more than "thirty birds."

Your cell is a nave. A ship, a dinghy adrift on the currents of wrecked empire. You lie back in the stern, shackled to your radiator, this room's rudder. Open seas leach you. You drift on the longest day of the year, bobbing near madness, the black overtaking you, infinite time, unfillable, longer even than those childhood nights when your own prison bedroom ran with a dread so palpable that sleep seemed certain death and death far better than this standing terror.

And then that frightened, fleshy face is there, next to yours, laughing in the dark.

What in all the world does a child have to be scared of? The old Persians, your people, called their walls daeza. *Pairi meant anything that surrounds. See? Pairi daeza. You have a wall running all the way around you. That, my little Tai-Jan, is the source of Paradise.*

29

At last, deep in winter, the RL team stood and watched the thing that that year had been building toward. It was as if arrival had waited on the cold and dark. Consequence held out for the vesper service, when light ducked below the horizon and inevitability tucked itself in for the evening. The Cavern workers stood by and saw a country unmake itself in one searchlit midnight, teeming with people.

Revelation carried the look of video. Late-night cameras combed the crowd, a mass milling to as many agendas as it had legs. Thick-coated people carried their hastily penned proclamations out into the night, along with their picks and flares and emergency champagne. A stamping winter herd steamed the air with raw breath. Deep in the Standing Now, lost between euphoria and panic, America watched Europe gather for its millennial bash, a decade too soon.

Sooner or later, everyone alive saw this happen, if not live, then on delayed broadcast, if not on archival tape, then in garbled pantomime. Once more the builders of the next world gathered together in the Cavern to witness the end of the previous one. But everything that each of them saw, he saw alone.

A woman who'd devoted her adult life to the religious avoidance of politics, who fled in revulsion from any system bigger than herself, stared in horror at the midnight party. She braced for the tanks again and could not look away. But this time, somehow, the tanks failed to come.

A man who'd landed in California as an orphaned child, who saw through the sham of identity by the age of seven and thus never bothered to build himself one, looked on the crowd smashing to bits the very stage they danced upon, and thought: My country is next. All boundaries will come down. There will be one Korea, as there was in the beginning. They will find my family, scattered in that chaos. My parents will want me back. I'll return to a home where I've never been.

By spontaneous signal across a medium thinner than air, two warring cities turned out on either half of their barricade. The happy violence gave off the feel of a sporting event—mass disaster tinged with religious awe. By instinct, they poured into the severed Platz, that forty-year-old scar on a continent's heart. A whole generation, raised to believe in this cement fiction, met at the Wall and passed right through it.

Those who couldn't squeeze in to ground zero spilled out along the split. As one, on a silent word, they smashed at the graffitied stone. Chunks flew off, each fossil splinter turning to instant history, shoveled into plastic bags for the overnight souvenir market. The imaginary barricade breached, half the success-stunned sappers foraged east, snapping photographs of a world about to vanish, while the other half streamed west into commercial fairylands, shocked to a standstill by how far shopping's fantasia had advanced in their absence.

The old, mass hallucination came apart at the seams. Cameras sallied out along the salients, soaking up this collective sabotage. A hundred happy souls labored in one residential neighborhood near the Versöhnungskirche, undoing the surgical cut that politics had sliced through its narrow-laned heart. Celebration held its breath, terrified with joy. Then it swung into communal destruction, a raucous town barn raising run on rewind.

Along one stretch, the razing snagged on a stuck slab. Worked from both sides, one fifteen-foot-tall block of concrete wobbled on its steel reinforcing rods, flipping lazily in the air like a sheet of damp cardboard.

At the far end of a long chord through the Earth's crust, an Armenian mathematician raged against this amateur demolition squad's ham-handedness. He shouted at the video transcription, already hours obsolete. *Ach! Wunderbar. Brilliant. These are the planet's legendary engineers? The sons of Krupp and Porsche? Would anyone who grasps the basic concept of leverage please step to the front of the mob?*

A man half the mathematician's age, nominally Italian, but belonging to no particular nationality except the International Benevolent Order of Programmers, stood by, gawking, as the membrane went permeable. Boyle's law, it seemed to him: the thermocouple yanked to allow free equilibration across that barrier. The aging boy nursed a childhood dream of urban renewal. Blocked-up subway spurs would now be cleared. Traffic could flow rationally, as designed, with all inefficient border checks swept away. Both sides would enjoy a windfall peace dividend, not to mention the beauty of simplification.

In a sorry excuse for a neighborhood local, a Belfast emigrant raised half a glass to the television above the bar, where an ecstatic battalion of barbed-wire cutters danced an allemande on top of their taken objective. *Best of luck to you, poor buggers. Reached the promised land, have you?*

He mimed a virtual glass-clink and sipped, a good-sport attempt to join in history's graduation party. He toasted the end of the life-long war, the end of status quo brinksmanship, the end of the market's last alternative, the end of mutually assured destruction, of gunpoint-guaranteed safety. He toasted the end of willed divisions. He toasted the New World Order, the beginning of nuclear proliferation, the steady slide into universal factionalism, the fragmentation past any ability of power politics to control . . . As he tipped his glass, the on-screen revelers waved their spilling magnums to toast the Irishman back.

An architect, half German, at least by family tradition, a man for whom the human race was a perpetual source of stress, whose Moses complex led him through a lifelong quest for peace that started with biofeedback and wended its way through est, yoga, crystals, acupressure, acupuncture, shiatzu, Rolfing, Alexander technique, antioxidants, herbal extracts, homeopathic medicines, and finally Prozac, sat paralyzed, reeling in the real-time feed issuing from his workstation screen. Now and then, condemned to participate, the architect cried out to no one in particular, *Oh God. This can't be happening. I can't process this. What in the hell is this all supposed to mean? What do these people think they're doing?*

This man's disheveled cellmate, an American who'd made it through the last twenty years on force of habit alone, a man whose Cold War existence came down to little more than the private contrition of forward motion, at last had to answer: *God only knows what they think they're doing. But they seem to be hitting that concrete wall with sledgehammers.*

And the wall, for its part, seemed to break.

30

The warm room is shelter against the surrounding cold.

Inside, you find a bed and a ready stock of blankets. Someone has seen to all needed provisions: sheets, candles, oil, towels. Cans in the pantry, wood in the cellar. Hooks and hangers, empty dresser drawers waiting to be filled by the stray refugee.

Outside, the wind hacks away with chill efficiency. Terminal winter settles in. Again, the world expels its baffled tenants. But the warm room takes all the roomless in.

The place seems almost to have known you were coming. Doors, stairs, windows all run exactly to your scale. The shelves carry all your best-loved books, and all those you have ever hoped to read. Your favorite nautical watercolors and cloud-teased landscapes line the front hall. All afternoon, each window's view outbids your eye's imagination.

You've stumbled upon this hotel, this makeshift hospital, by more than chance. Linen waits stacked up in the cabinets, dishes in the chest. Behind the bathroom mirror, soaps, brushes, and blades stand at sacrificial attention. Dry provender renews itself with each use. All these things have long existed, but never before like this. They seem to gather in this holding pen strictly for you to delight in them.

The warm room has no other reason but yours. As the mass displacement grows, its answer turns inward, its cure simple. But grace may be harder to bear than its brutal opposite. For the warm room exists only by virtue of a single, chill twist. Touch the wooden cup left out for you, pick it up, and turn it over. Run your finger along its smooth length. Put your lips to its waiting lip, and empty it: your mouth will find nothing more solid than idea.

The shower does not wet you, nor do the towels dry. You can flip through the pages of these loving books, but you cannot hold them. The vibrant clothes slip onto your body, but they give no feel. It dawns on you only piecemeal where you are. How you have dropped down through your own, scribbled rabbit hole into this thought museum and now sit gaping at the shape of your evacuated life from the far side of the mental mirror.

Maybe you lost your given life, searching for this escape. Or maybe you did yourself in, bitter revenge on life for failing you. Or maybe the world would have cut you up anyway, and only luck led you to this emergency windbreak just before succumbing. Something in your refugee heart never felt at home anywhere, except in this room of maybes.

Down the hillside from this mountain cabin, grim realism rounds up its latest deportees. Global affairs pursue their footrace, for not everyone has been sentenced yet. You've made it to this sheltered Switzerland just before the police dogs close their jaws on your ankle. Or: you've fallen, out there in the dark, along the frozen border, and the last thought that crosses your expiring mind is this fire-lit chalet.

In the warm room, you are the goal of all these stocked provisions. All things await the theater of your needs, here freed at last to work its changes. In the warm room, you are the doer of all acts, the receiver of all action, the glow that lights these sanctuary walls, the warmth these eager trappings radiate, the fading coal, the lone heat source in a world gone zero and random.

31

"You need something?"

The Shiite Cronkite asks so gently, it's almost possible to imagine that today he means it. You can't catch his eye. But perhaps a blindfolded head swing in his direction can still haunt him with the parody of a human glance.

"Walter," you say. Slower now, with all the gravity of a dying animal: "Walter. What's your real name?"

You hear him shrug. Currents of compressed air roll off his undulating shoulders and form in your ears, as clear as words. You put your hands out in front of you, on your wasting thighs, palms up.

"Tell me," you beg. "I know Ali's. Walter. Listen. I can't hurt you."

You hear him, this peasant driven off the desiccated land, here at the front only for that expedited ticket to heaven given to anyone who dies for the cause. You hear him put his head down. Astonishing. Impossible. Yet still, your attenuated ears hear it.

Softly, he confesses. Somewhere in your childhood's forgotten Qur'an, in the watered-down hadith that you ingested with your mother's milk, you recall a massive prohibition against lying. "Sayid," he says. Soft as his shoulders' shrug. Ashamed.

You hug him across this infinite gap between you. "Sayid what? What is your family name?"

"No, no," he says, on the edge of anger. Too much to ask. "Thank you. Do not worry."

"Sayid. Sayid, I need you to help me. I need some books."

The air around you lightens. He breathes out a wave of relief. Books: that's all. "Sure. I tell Chef. Tomorrow."

"Sayid. Listen to me. If I don't get books, I'll die. Do you understand?"

"Sure. I understand. You will die."

"Sayid. This is real. If I don't get books, I will go crazy."

"Sure. I know. No problem."

If you've learned nothing else in this nine-month gestation, you've learned that "No problem," in Sayidian Arabic, means "Big problem."

No books appear the next day. Or the day after that. But this game is long. Each day longer than you've dared to imagine.

You ride him. "Sayid. Yesterday is gone. Today is gone. Tomorrow is history. Still no books."

He snickers at your idiocy. "I understand. Chef say books coming."

"Tell Chef, madness coming. I will die, Sayid. I will die, and your men will get nothing from me. All your work will be a total waste. Worse than a waste. America will be very angry."

"Good." He snarls deep in his throat, the first step of spitting. The size of your error grows clear. "Good. We like America angry. America make us angry."

America, of course, won't be even vaguely put out. America won't even notice. America has done nothing for you, for three-quarters of a year: nine months that you've ticked off in seven-minute intervals. Your death would be one less distraction nagging at America's busy conscience. It has taken a solitary locked room—without resources, stripped of any touchstone but yourself—to commence your political education.

In the absence of books, you make your own. You resurrect your all-time favorites. The details come in gross, grainy chunks. The drill perfects itself. You lie back against the wall, as far from the radiator as the links of chain allow. Bone-cold all winter, the machinery now comes alive, eager to add its joules to the summer inferno.

You close your eyes and will yourself into another climate. The volume materializes in your hands, the weight, the heft, the binding's resistance. You turn the treasure over and over, resolving the details down to the publisher's insignia on the spine. Through your eyelids, you inspect the cover illustration. Your read the blurbs on the back, the synopsis, the ISBN, all the precious trail marks you once squandered so profligately when they were yours to waste.

Each page of front matter passes one by one under your sentry fingers. Hours may dissolve, just playing with the stiffness of the paper, before you get to the actual first sentence. *Lord Jim*, the forty-four-point Garamond Bold announces to your hushed house of one. And again, in thirty-six-point type, on the next wondrously superfluous page. Or *Great Expectations*. Every menu name becomes a whole banquet where you might dine out eternally, for free.

You reach the opening sentence, the fresh start of all things possible. Modestly boundless, it enters bowing, halfway down that first right-hand page. You lie back against your paradise wall, your pillow. You make yourself a passive instrument, a séance medium for these voices from beyond the grave. Politics has taught you how to read, how to wait motionless, without hope. To wait for some spirit that is not yours to come fill you.

My name being Phillip. No: my father's name being Pirrip, I called myself Pip. Something about a graveyard, five little stones as visible as the door of your cell, the markers of brothers who gave up on making a living exceedingly early in this universal struggle. Every turn, every further constriction in the plot—yours or the author's—makes it easier to keep to the general contour. Where you cannot recall a scene, you invent one.

You recognize that underclass orphan making his way in an indifferent world. He was the first present you ever gave her. A fake heritage hardback edition that actually sold for $12.95 in the Cut-out Classics bin at both of the mall bookstore chains. Gave it to her for her birthday, half a year after you started going out. Back in that year when you were still trying to feed her all your favorites, to hand over to her all your secret treasures. Love me, love my childhood. Love my books. Maybe you meant an element of remedy in the gift. It had shocked you when she told you she'd never read it.

She tore at the wrapping, excited. But she cried when she saw the contents. The price, you thought at first. Gwen knew prices, even of things she never bought. You must have come in a level or two below where she'd expected. Hurt, you bit back. Said that you'd make sure to get something more expensive next time.

But no. That wasn't it, she sobbed. A book was not a personal gift. People gave books to colleagues, to acquaintances, not to their intimate partners. You might have given this to *anyone*. It didn't say *you and me*. It didn't say, *You are the only person in the world I could have given this to*.

You tried to explain. It did say *you*. It did say *me*. This was a story that you'd read four times over the course of your life, one that had meant something different each time you'd read it. It did say *you and me*. It said you wanted her to know the things that you knew. You couldn't have given it to anyone else, you lied. She didn't need to know who else you'd once tried to give it to.

Appeased a little, she flipped through, smiling bravely at the opening pages for your benefit. She patted the book. Said, *Thank you so much. I'll let you know what I think*. Slid it carefully into the appropriate place on her shelves, then came and dragged you off to her bed, where she ravished you, abdomen slapping against abdomen in such fury that you lost yourself in her punishing metronome, feeling in that impact the force of the correction she needed from you.

Later you discovered, in Gwen's refrigerator, a fresh pot pipe carved out of a golden delicious apple lined with a little tinfoil. A little private birthday celebration, prior to your arrival, that she'd felt no need to tell you of. Her tears, forgiveness, ecstasy, and fury: all artificially enhanced, with you, as usual, the last person to dope things out.

The book stayed on her shelf for the next six years. To all evidence, she never touched it again except when she dusted. Never tried to read another word, straight, high, or otherwise.

The fruit bongs appeared and rotted, without fixed season, front-runners in a suite of little secrets, the extents of which you could only guess. She never much tried to hide them, but neither did she ever bother to announce their appearances. You offered to smoke with her, some weekend evening, when the two of you weren't doing anything the next day. *Tai-Jan!* Gwen said, in her favorite imitation of your mother, who exercised some fascination on her you never wholly understood. *My little pragmatic moralist wants to get stoned with me?*

It seemed worth not letting her get to you. Worth waiting her out. Worth trying to be the safety net, the model, the pillar of trust that she'd never before received. But you felt something forbidden, too, more than a little prurient, in the notion of getting lit with this woman, of tumbling into a web of shared sensation, all gatekeepers gone. Getting inside that cloud of private lust you sometimes glimpsed through the frosted-glass window of her skin.

What's your favorite book? you ask her, your brain pinging down a chain of associations, the night you do at last light up together. The melding that you'd hoped for comes off, at best, as a self-conscious swap of concessions.

She stares at you too long for it to mean confusion. It takes you about three lifetimes to realize she's mocking you. Her barricades and burning-oil look: What planet did you say you're from? Favorite trick to knock you back on your heels. Jockeying, even now, while the two of you share this brief vacation from yourselves.

Why do we always have to rank everything? Biggest? Best? Most? Boys: you'll really have to explain the concept to me one of these days.

You feel the flash of anger, the so familiar one, the rage that you can't voice without confirming her. *Don't need you to rank them. Just want to know the name of one that moved you. One that you loved.*

You asked me to tell you my favorite. My absolute fave rave. The one that vanquishes all the other comers. No secrets, now. Come on, name names.

Forget it. I'm sorry I brought it up.

Oh. My little Tai-Jan's feelings are hurt. Bad girlfriend. Her right hand administers a slap to her left. *Nasty, aggressive girlfriend. Does not work and play well with others.*

Yes, it so often crossed your mind to say. *Yes. What* you *just said.*

You don't say that. You say something different. This time, as always. *Look. It seemed legitimate to try to share in something that delighted you.*

Why can't you just let delight come up in its own good time? Why do you have to engineer everything all the time? Control the whole exchange?

And in the next breath, in her hemp-induced fog, she suggests that she straddle you while you sit on the reclining chair in the front window, lights out—her favorite position, a secret vantage from which she can look out on all the cars and pedestrians, none of whom can imagine what takes place inside the darkened warren that they pass by.

How desired and desolate she always made you feel—ever, ever—each of those gifts wrapped in the other's predicate. She stands, in your mind, like some Hindu statuette, one set of hands crooked and beckoning, the other set, palms out in front of her in the international body language for Stop.

The posture threw you off from the day you met her, in that florist on Highland, August of '78. You, ordering a dozen prosaic roses to throw into a stillborn cause, one already lost even as you tried to fix it with blooms. She, assembling a wild assortment of pastel exotics to send to someone she forever afterward refused to identify. The moment she looks up and sees you enter the shop, she smiles such a grin of vast recognition that you have to smile back, bluffing, wondering how you could possibly have forgotten so friendly and welcoming a face.

You fall to talking almost without thought, hoping her name will come to you after a couple of clues. But the clues all prove that you don't know this woman from Eve. Four traded sentences and you want to. She makes you want to. Open, uncomplicated invitation—like a neighborhood buddy knocking on the door of a Saturday morning, with a baseball and two mitts.

How do you like my creation? she coaxes, displaying it for you. *It wants to be a bouquet when it grows up.*

You make the sound of appreciation, out of the depths of your throat's greater helplessness. *What about* my *needs? Should I go with the red, the yellow, or the white?*

Depends. Is it a kiss-off or a suck-up?

Good question. You do a fair imitation of total paralysis. *I haven't figured that out yet*.

Definitely the ivory, then. Ivory is totally ambiguous. You can always claim misunderstanding later.

You can, and do. There follows the obligatory couple of dead heats of answering-machine tag. Would you? Love to. Say when. You, then.

The two of you cook a meal together, at her place. Vegetable lasagna, whose 3.5 grams of fat per serving would strike your mother as a disgrace to human dignity. You wash and slice and pulverize, feeling, despite yourself, as if you're preparing the buffet from which you'll sup the rest of your life. She looks on, smiling at your handiwork. The last time she ever lets you near the food prep.

Her running gag: Who said you could go near sharp implements? Does your mother know you're trying to drive a standard transmission? Someone has cruelly and senselessly led you to believe that joke is funny? Uh, friend: about this so-called wardrobe of yours . . . ? The feel of something invisible being forever contested in the flow of wit.

You share five or six more outings, for form's sake, moseying up to the inevitable test of desire. Bird-watching, stargazing: each an adventure, but never the same adventure twice. You feel some pleasure in the agonizing postponement, but she is more patient than you. Always she meets you under the gun, the taxi meter running, half a dozen plates up in the air, Post-it notes stuck all over her jumpsuit, appointments with strangers written in Bic on her palms that she has to consult before she can tell you when she'll be available next.

But always her eyes say *soon*. And when you part, with your ubiquitous and meaningless *See ya*, always she reins you in with a smiled "I believe you will."

Her random reinforcement schedule keeps you massively addicted. Her trick is to pick the moment, that precise evening when the concession seems real and all the wait leading up to it no more than a fluke she is keen to repudiate. She chooses the time and place, a sweet surrender of sovereignty for which she is careful to palm the claim stub.

There comes a moment in the night's right ascension when the lead-up tease, the slow, hinted rope tug disappears into the bin of all childish things. Then she spreads; then she solidifies. And all that night, your bodies exchange sightings, come within touching distance of a place that you will spend the next eight years trying to recover.

At the moment that she fixes her limbs to you, her commitment is unthinking: as utter as that between any two speechless animals. But she is absent as well, somewhere far away, deep in a formulating image. Who knows whose? Off in a place that is anything but yours.

Your two souths merge. You move your face to hers, sealing the ring. You will tell her that you love her, prematurely, helplessly, something she already knows, something she will snort dismissal at, glandular, clichéd, but the only thing that might help a little against all that life still has in store for the two of you. You lower your length, fulcrumed along hers, a shadow curling toward the foot of its wall as the sun wanders over day, your mouth seeking out her ear. But she speaks first.

You can do anything you want to me.

This is what you hear. Or at the most generous, the most rehabilitated, factoring in all faults of sound and audition, the tricks of the brain when showered in chemical joy at sight of the land it has succeeded in reaching. *You can do anything you want with me.*

For years, she will not remember. She will deny having said anything of the kind.

She rises from intimacy to wash off the drops of your body. Clean again, she wraps herself in flannel pajamas—yes, even in this heat—before she'll come back to bed. She accepts you against the ladle of her back. She permits you to commit, smiles at the stories you spin out into her ear, but does not return or extend them.

She's up before you, doing her sit-ups to progressive radio rock when you finally drag yourself out of her long-suffering bed. *Breakfast?* you ask, over the throb of the synth bass.

Not for me.

You commandeer a banana and wait for the routine to abate. It doesn't. Finally, you must get on with your life. The crucial skill here seems to be to ask for nothing, to wait with no expectations, to see what might settle on your sill of its own free accord. *See you soon?* you say, hoping that the hope in your voice feels in no way coercive.

Yes, she says, pausing in mid-step-aerobic long enough to kiss you goodbye. *I believe you probably will.*

Now you have only your own workout, your own daily routine to blunt the brutal memory working your gut. Only your daily thirty minutes off the chain, to tranquillize, to bring your eager grief low. Back on the leash, you match her sit-up for sit-up, exercise serving some awful, unshakable end, the stupid insistence on surviving. You fight against the steady atrophy of your muscles, work to crush the furtive hope that, should you by some accident ever be freed, and in the uproar of freedom come by chance across her, you will not look repulsive. You wonder how she likes beards, this wiry pelt that cups, petlike, into your hands. Groundless desire: the last thing we outlive, outlove.

You flip between following out this tale and fleeing from it. Ali's small sadisms—saying you will be released tomorrow; charging into the room at random intervals to catch you without blindfold; tossing a gorgeous orange just out of your reach—are nothing compared with recollection. You can deal with Ali, ignore his feeble invitations to believe. But against the torture of *expectation*, you have no defense.

Events seem blessedly bent on distracting you. This season produces some subtle shift in the front. One of the host of autonomous nations— the Druze, the Maronites, the Phalangists; the nomadic dreamers, daily harder to keep straight—some law unto itself is making a play to extend its jurisdiction. The tactics play out behind the gray screen of corrugated metal stapled across your window's gouged-out eye.

But you don't need to see these hidden developments to map their tactics. For days, rifled artillery lob their lazy cargoes in. You hear the distant puff of firing, count the intervening quarter-seconds, and feel the annihilating crush when it slams back to earth. Your brain does the ungodly calculus, the complex trig that locates in space the arc of each explosion. You mark the ebb and flow, the advance and retreat in your shaking abdomen, telling from the sound of impact the difference between a *suq* taken out, a playground, a parking lot, or the sheered face of an apartment high-rise.

Sayid spells out just who is on the move. *Afwaj al Muqawamah al Lubnanya*. The Lebanese Resistance Battalions, whose name forms the acronym Amal, the Arabic word for hope.

Hope is not the innocent you once mistook it for. It does not circulate. Yours cannot mean what another takes it to be. Even between you and the woman you loved, you failed to hold the thing in common. You went into the relationship generous and likable and easygoing, and came out shaken, the person she most feared, a pathological controller and manipulator. You could not speak to her without spinning out whole chapters of dialogue in your head—countering, wheedling, needing to destroy her belief that you were desperately needy.

In another life, on another infinite afternoon, when the shells abate enough to let you disappear again down the immaculate rabbit hole, she tells you. To your standing question, she answers simply, *The French Lieutenant's Woman.*

She looks up, vulnerable, appraising your reaction, a little frightened, a little shining. Relieved that you know it, glad for the pleasure she has afforded you, she asks back, *How about yours?* The easy reciprocity that you once thought could underscore all exchanges between people who cared for each other.

And you tell her all about *Great Expectations.* A simple, trusting swap of hostages. Surrender everything. We cannot hurt each other as much as life will. You tell her the whole sustaining story, from graveyard to cradle. *What larks!* you tell her. What larks.

Time in its endlessness brings you to a complete recitation. It takes two full afternoons with your eyes pinched closed to come up with the name "Miss Skiffins." But you have all the afternoons in the world. World, time, and focus, and you start to perform superhuman feats of synthetic memory. Desperate feats, deranged, like the reflex acts of mothers lifting two-ton beams off their pinned infants.

You've forgotten nothing. Whole scenes surface out of air. They pageant before you, responding to memory's every blush. And when they don't, you make them up again. *From scratch,* as the idiom goes. Week after week, and the complete architecture condenses under your aerial view. Why, here's a church. Why, here's Miss Skiffins. Let's have a wedding.

You take it then, this month's contraband reading, the blessed banality of your old existence, all the engaging, pointless complications that she smuggles in to you under the nose of your captors, your lost

Miss Skiffins, so unlike her real-life model, the one who lived in terror of being held accountable for ever having given anyone anything. How ludicrous the potboiler seems, how absurd and anemic, against the weeklong barrages that make up your day's only dispatches now.

But how banal the bigger text, the pointless serial novel of power, how static and tedious the scenes, how shopworn real life's theme, how lacking in invention and delivery and interest and basic narrative device, compared with the smallest mundanity of love, the chance at private denouement. You devise this simple test of lasting literary merit: which tale promises the best net present pleasure? Which will see you through the end of this hour?

All the Dickens that will ever return returns. Pip and his Estella go hand and hand out of their ruined place, and you are still here. Still here, after the story recedes, in the bombed-out rubble of your thoughts, a pile that you recognize only because it occupies the lot your house once did. Not even a blank, your mind. A nervous jitter. Twitching like some fourteen-year-old's desk-bound leg. You go for hours in the dark, not even knowing that you are shaking.

Someone brings you food. The stench no longer gags you, after this time. But something in this picked-over rubbish, not fit for hamsters, breaks you. You bang your chain against the radiator, no longer caring about the consequences. There are no consequences. You will die of blows or you will die of malnutrition. You lay into the pipes like a fire alarm. Someone rushes into the cell, intent on silencing you. The Angry Parent. He cracks you in the chest, knocking you back on the mattress.

It stuns you. He's always gotten one of the others to dole out the physical abuse. You sit back up, stalling to catch your breath, until your pulse lowers enough for you to speak. "Listen." You wait, curious, to see what you mean to say. "Listen. Tell me your name."

You hear him breathing through his mouth. You've frightened him. But he says nothing.

"Come on. We've known each other for a long time. Coming up on a year, before you know it. You've had me over. I've returned the invitation. We should know each other's name, don't you think?"

Without seeing his face, you could easily take the sound he makes for a titter. Or he could be tensing to release another blow.

"What difference does it make? 'Ali.' 'Sayid.' Who on earth would believe me? You're going to kill me anyway. Who are you afraid I'm going to tell? God?"

You're ready. Ready for the one quick, merciful bullet through the temple. So of course, he denies you. You hear him shuffle a little in embarrassment.

"Muhammad. Call me Muhammad."

"Muhammad," you repeat. "You are a Shiite?"

He coughs up a little fart of contempt in his throat. Not even contempt. Not even worth asking why you bother to ask.

"Muhammad. I once read somewhere . . . that Shiites believe food to be the holy gift of Allah. A mirror of the divine sustenance. Look at this." You grope about for the cold stench, put your hand in it as you hold it up toward him. "This is not sacred. This is not food."

He takes the platter from you. Leaves without a word. Sometime later, another meal appears. More than sacred. Edible. You'd say delicious, but for fear of gilding the lily.

The dish steams, a Lebanese knockoff of something your mother's exercise in capitalism once specialized in. A *bademjan*, the heart of the almond, the life of the heart.

A *halim bademjan*, with some angelic substance floating around in the stew, electrifying, a taste once deeply familiar to you that you now strain to recognize. But the harder you chase after the ingredient, the more it recedes. You take a bite; the word floats there, on the tip of your tongue. The memory struggles to the surface and dissipates.

You put down your spoon and wait. You try another mouthful. The familiarity fades with exposure. Every repetition reduces the miracle. You must name it in the last morsel or lose it forever. Then, before you get it to your mouth, restored by the bits you have already devoured, it comes to you. Meat. Chunks of sacrificial lamb.

You walk a tightrope between sassing your guards and falling at their feet. When Muhammad next visits, you thread your way dead down the middle.

"Are you the Chief? Are you the one that Ali and Sayid call the Chief?"

His silence settles out, indulgent. He sighs. It can only be a sigh. "Above every Chief, there is always one higher."

"But you can do things. You have some power. You got me that . . . meat."

"Allah is the doer. Allah alone is the getter of things. All power comes from Him and returns to Him."

"Fair enough. Where did you learn to speak such good English?"

"That's not important." Although, his tone admits, it would probably be of some interest to the U.S. State Department.

"Muhammad. You must listen to me. I am afraid I am cracking up. Not just boredom. Boredom is what I feel on the good days. My brain. It's coming apart. I can feel it. Like a damn zoo animal about to go off its nut. I'm this far away from the abyss. I'm going to start screaming soon, at which point you're going to have to kill me, and then you'll have nothing. Nothing. You'll be out a year of room and board and the cost of cremation, and nobody's going to trade you anything for me."

He makes some calculation, probably not mathematical. "What is it that you want?"

With your last shred of strength, you force down the fury exploding in you.

"I need books. I don't care what. Books in English. I'll take anything. I'll take the damn Lubbock, Texas, phone directory. I just. Need. Something to read."

"We will see," he says, after troubled consideration. "We will do a *fatwah* to see if you can have a book."

This sounds less than good.

Lessons follow in performing a *fatwah*. It's the old Iowa Fighting Fundy from Spiritus Mundi trick of throwing open the Holy Scripture to a passage, then interpreting the words as if they were a scrap of cosmic fortune cookie. Judgment by roll of the evangelical die.

You listen to them execute their oracular Three Stooges routine. You tilt your head back, stealthily, to catch the contour of your fate from under the lip of your blindfold. Ali flips the Qur'an open at random. Sayid flops his finger down. Muhammad, the intellectual, reads the selected Ouija utterance and interprets the augury. Decides what the chance passage means.

"I am sorry," he tells you, sounding genuinely chagrined. "We have consulted the book, and it says no."

You move toward them, trembling, to the full length of your chain. Your body starts to spasm so violently it scares even you.

"Then, bloody Christ. Consult it again. I'm not fucking kidding you, man. We need a yes, here. A *yes*, or there's going to be an incident."

In the scuffle, someone knocks you down. You slam the back of your head against the radiator in your fall. The Three Fates evacuate. You float facedown in the pool of your concussion.

You haven't even the will to remove your blindfold. You lie fetal, curled up in your own placenta. Survival is no longer a virtue, given where survival leaves you. On the far side of this nothingness lies more nothing, one continuous void extending to the ends of space, all the way to the vanishing point, where all lines fall into themselves.

But life has still worse whiplash in store. Years later, maybe even the next day, human noise penetrates your coma. Sayid, across an unfathomable gulf, tosses something on the floor near you. "We do another *fatwah*. We ask again. Everything OK. No problem." Getting nothing, he withdraws.

Another presence settles into your cell. The quaking in you starts up again in earnest. It takes you by your shoulders, determined to shake you back into sawdust. You cannot look for fear of reprisal. You saddle up near the new thing, crane back your neck, inspect it from under the safety of the blindfold. It's everything you fear it to be. Lying on the filthy planks, unswept since you came here, is that inconceivable device: a cunning, made world.

You kneel and pick it up. You freeze down there on the floor, crying. Afraid to so much as touch it, your fingers clapper spastically against the covers. You bounce the book in your hands, testing its weight for any sign of counterfeit. The mass of it swells up close to your eyes, in the slit of your vision. You hold it up close, trading off depth of field for detail and resolution. The weave of fibers in the paperback binding thickens into a jungle tangle.

Your sight scans up the book's length, seeking out the title that will sentence or deliver you. Terror is no less than desire with the chrome stripped away. In your atrophied eyes, the letters read like a line of alien hieroglyphs. Bizarre analphabetic randomness. English has no such series.

Then your pulse shoots into your ears. *Great*. Your word. Your title. You've done it, summoned up this book by the sheer force of weeks-long concentration. By some intricate, unsolvable plan, through the interplay of forces devised by that Engineer whom Creation but grossly caricatures, you have been looked after. The words you love have made their way back to you for awful safekeeping. Imagination survives its own cruelty. You've been set down in this hell for something more than mapping your abandonment.

For a long time, your eyes refuse the title's second word. Instead, they insist on the word that the word should be. But the surety of print survives your stare. You look again, and the title skids off into senseless-ness. You remove your blindfold and look dead on. *Expectations* some-how mutates into *Escapes*.

You drop the book, electrocuted. If no one saw you pick it up, they can't punish you for touching it. It lies there, upside down, innocent. Impossible to take in. As the immediate madness subsides, you tick off the possible explanations. A trap. A mistake. A senseless accident. A joke whose cruelty makes mainstream sadism seem like the Marquis of Queensberry.

It strikes you: maybe even Muhammad, with his clean syntax and accent, can't *read*. Maybe your guards' English extends no further than film and TV. They've bought this secondhand ream of paper scrap for pennies, down in the stalls of some bombed-out bazaar, left there by the last American with the good sense to get out of this suiciding coun-try while the getting was good. Not one of these men knows what he puts into your hands.

At this thought, something cracks in your throat. You can't place it at first, a shape so strange you can only wait in wonder for it to take shape. When at last you recognize the quick, dry convulsions, you can't stop them. Impossible to say how long you laugh, forcing the sniggers down, a secret from anyone beyond your walls.

The book they give you has been read many times. And recently, by all indications. You're not the first prisoner to have begged a *fatwah*, to have forced Scripture to deliver. Of course there are others, other Western bargaining chips, even housed with you in this very building. They are the muffled noises you hear at all hours, down this hall, half a dozen feet away, just on the other side of your own plaster. The movements to and from the latrine. The covered altercations. The others that you've read about, taken before your capture, or poor souls even stupider than you, snatched up since your own self-destruction.

You touch the cover that other escapees must have touched. Your hands turn the trembling pages, so recently turned by theirs. Title page. Other Books by the Author. Library of Congress information. Acknowledgments. Dedication. After each new leaf, you set the book down and look away. You wait for as many minutes as discipline permits. You try to pace yourself, to hang on, to savor this hurtful heightening, the point of your long deprivation.

You open to the first true page, the holder of possibility, the keeper of all things. Gorgeous human thoughts detonate in space all around you, extending their subordinate clauses, flinging their nouns around like burgeoning tracts of starter homes airlifted into arid wastes.

Grant all permits. Fill the available world with frantic marks. Cram the answers to the living exam into every legible cranny. Have each new version tear down the last, each manic utterance give way to further revision. Let people chatter forever. It doesn't even matter what we think we're really after. For there is no solace here, no win, no other end than this stream of urgent invention.

In real life, this book wouldn't hold your attention for five minutes. Now it bears the key to your continued existence. You cannot even say what *Great Escapes* is about. It may not be *about* anything. Every verb phrase puts on the full freedom of human movement. The slightest clichés, the worst throwaway inanities pitch you into whole preserves of wilderness whose existence you've forgotten. Even here: even into the dulled depths of your confinement, the hive extends its growing hum.

You vow to ration this opening chapter, to make it last at least through the end of summer. *Great Escapes* must be your daily introit and gradual. A single paragraph to serve as a matins service, another two sentences every other hour. The need to make astonishment last far exceeds your immediate urge to swallow it whole. The point is not to finish but to find yourself somewhere, forever starting.

You panic at the rapid slip of pages across the binding from the right width to the left. You scramble for a way to read without making reading's hated forward progress. But the whole book evaporates into fact before you know how you got to the end.

You close the back cover, sickened by what you've done. You seize up, you stand, you pace around on your chain. You close your eyes, guiltily savoring the cheap stories that you've just slammed down. You pick up the book and start again. It still holds some residual pleasure, but never again the launch into pure potential. Ten days from now, this dazed freedom still reverberating in you will have extinguished itself, starved out by repetition. *Great Escapes* is over. You will need another.

But for a moment, for a thin, narrow, clouded, already closing moment: this. When you come to bed that evening, you turn to tell her, *You'll never believe what I read today.*

32

The year that ended history came to its own end. The retaining Wall fell down, and all certainty came down with it. The Realization Lab's engineers entered 1990 adrift in a fluid landscape, stripped of all tether.

O'Reilly asked Klarpol, *How do you like living in a time without safe assumptions?*

Have you ever lived anywhere else? she answered.

A world without assumptions should have been a world without surprises. But every day brought new shocks to the invented landscape, shocks requiring perpetual invention to smooth them over.

Wiring the Cavern for sound made more difference than Adie could have imagined. More than it should have. The Arlesean Room designers brought in Rajasundaran, who'd done a stint down at NASA/ Ames in Mountain View, to give the sunny South a tongue. Every event in Jackdaw's cabinet of interactions now came into its audible inheritance. Chairs learned to creak, floorboards to pop. The wind outside the window began to hiss a stereo mistral.

The key is spatiality, Raj said. *We creatures evolved to believe in space, and that's about all you can say for certain about belief. We're binaural. Binocular. These are evolution's tricks for getting us to think in 3-D, and we can't help falling for them every time.*

3-D is a trick? Adie asked. She sounded hurt.

Sure. What isn't, finally?

They set to work voicing Arles, teaching the rented bed-sit to sing. To their arrays for texture and surface and dimension, they added sonority. The drawer coughed softly as it slid open. The pitcher pinged with the perfect pitch of porcelain. Off in the distance, past the edges of the casement, southward toward the invisible bay, gulls called.

Even the earliest results unnerved them. Six channels run through five speakers implanted in each wall face sufficed to raise the neck hairs on the most sophisticated visitor. They put Spider Lim, the human litmus, alone in the room. They flew a sonic pigeon through the rafters. He tracked the arc of the flapping bird, a fuller, more physiological belief than had he actually seen one. They broke a pane of glass in the center of the left-hand window. Spider jumped, a full-scale startle. He slammed his fist against his chest.

Don't ever do that to me again.

Sound is better than visual, Steve decided. *It's more immediate. More virtual to begin with. It hangs in space, getting sharper in memory.*

Adie ignored his invitation. She spoke to him now only when work required.

Raj sailed through the subaudible battlefield, unaware. *Every modality that you can add will square the level of believability. Every new affordance, every connection we can lay down between out here and in there increases the sense of immersion geometrically.*

Spiegel paced in place. *We need some haptic device. Some kind of force-feedback jumpsuit that'll resist when you try to walk into things. Pressure-hammers that'll bruise your legs when you scrape against the bed.*

Not necessary, Lim said. And showed them his shins.

Raj grinned. *At bottom, you know? At bottom, the mind wants to be taken in.*

Poor Jackdaw went back and affixed a new element to every data array, a variable pointer that would hold the clicks and pocks that Adie wanted to add to every plunkable object in the room. But he worked gladly. Rajasundaran's audio—the lowing and keening of it—had something of the innermost eeriness, something a visitor assimilated into her tissue before even noticing.

It knocked Adie out. *The sounds are so present! Better than the real thing. It's as if the noises are going off inside my brain.*

Oh, they are, Raj said. *They are! We do our real-time signal processing right inside those flaps of twisted cartilage of yours.* He wiggled his own flaps in question. *We put a microphone in a subject's ear canal, capture the chaos, and reverse-engineer the sampling. Waves crashing into waves, nodes and antinodes wiping themselves out all over the place.*

Sounds like the Lower East Side, Adie said.

You ought to try Jaffna.

That's where you lived?

Oh no no. Jaffna came to me.

Her hands dry-pointed the air in front of her, talking before her words could catch up. They scuttled, flustered, like the hands of library patrons at the five-minute warning, gathering together their materials and carrying their quarry up to the charge desk before it shut down for the night. *Explain.*

What is there to explain, really? Raj spoke in the subcontinental, singsong inflection of Imperial English, whose practitioners outnumbered all of England several times over. *My family and I were living our lives in Colombo. The Tigers made some high-profile power plays up in the peninsula. Our Sinhalese aunties and uncles decided that the Jaffna deaths required some symmetrical mischief to put them right. They voted to set fire to the hundred nearest Tamil houses, no matter that these belonged to their dear friends and neighbors. We beat a hasty retreat to Vancouver. A lovely city, by the way.*

What do your parents do for a living?

You mean before our move or after?

Both . . . Both.

A familiar story. You don't really want to know.

How . . . how did you end up living here?

Here? He cast a gaze back at the Cavern, where windows broke, floorboards popped, and pigeons flew about the eaves. *You mean Seattle?* The idea amused him. *I don't really live here. I'm just renting.*

Raj wanted to develop a high-level audio programming language to match the visual one that Jackdaw and Loque were assembling. He wanted fast filter transforms that would change a frog to a choirboy with a few typed commands. He wanted to spin the aural sources in space, make them wheel about with each turn of the head.

But as with images, acoustic precision exacted its price in responsiveness. Milliseconds loomed huge. Latency killed the sense of presence. Only the tightest virtuoso chorus of sounds would flush the ear into belief. Spatializing the noisy universe and synchronizing it with sight involved a bit of higher mathematical modeling called the Head-Related Transfer Function.

We should get the Armenian in on this, Rajan said.

Adie balked. *Is that really necessary?*

Nothing is really necessary. Not really.

He's so incredibly unpleasant. The man has raised ugliness to the level of haute art. He's ugliness's high priest.

They brought in Kaladjian. He started out on his best behavior, which consisted of not saying anything at all. He walked into the Van Gogh bedroom and shrugged. He tapped the shutters and rapped the porcelain with a hand-gripped Polhemus sensor, unhappy with the delayed pocks and pings. He stepped out of the room and removed the stereo glasses.

Why would anyone want to build something like this?

Why does anyone want to build anything? Spiegel answered.

Kaladjian shrugged, more concession than contest.

Over the space of days, the quartet of males slowly squeezed Klarpol out. Form and warmth, rapture and azure all collapsed into engineering problems. The tasks at hand were well defined, formalizable. Why did they need an artist any longer? They had Adie's careful, hand-drawn surfaces. Once the authorities got their composite sketch, the artist was just ballast.

Adie went to Sue Loque. *They're stealing my room.*

Your room? Didn't you steal it from some Dutch guy?

My idea. My eye. I took everything off the flat plane and laid it out in three-space. I repainted all the surfaces by hand. Every inch of it is detailed enough to look good at life size.

Now they won't let you play?

Well, they let me sit in. But they're turning the whole thing into this gigantic Rubik's Cube.

That's their thing. It's what they do, babe.

I know that's what they do. What am I supposed to do?

Sit in and listen, maybe? It's how I got into this racket.

Serious? What did you do before?

Before what?

Before learning to program?

Oh, I taught myself to program when I was twelve. I had to cover for my parents. They couldn't even handle their dimmer switches. But before I started listening in on the boys—before I learned how projects worked—I was . . . just a programmer.

Adie went back and listened. She followed the four males as they invented problems, then invented solutions to throw at their problems. She watched them communicate by grunts and silences. She studied Jackdaw, Steve, and Raj as they hacked at their huge triple concerto for QWERTY keyboards, lost to a runaway pruning algorithm, while Kaladjian etched away on complex functions with a number-two pencil into yellow legal pads.

She sketched them in turn, capturing their shared trances in her own media. Their facial muscles reminded her of her father's, snoring on the sofa in any of a dozen Quonset living rooms, sleeping off the latest controlled R-and-R drunk, twitching in a dream of final, anesthetized escape. But the goal of these four men differed from her father's on one essential account. Her father retreated into a place that he hoped would silence the outside world. These four men, on the other hand, worked to build a mutual mirage that would match its source, noise for noise.

There's some kind of major tension there, Adie told Loque. *I don't think any of them likes Kaladjian any more than I do.*

Bingo, babe.

He's a nasty man.

Deeply creepy. But he knows a shitload. So everyone manages to make allowances for him, on strictly practical grounds.

Well sure. That's easy for them. They come from the same world as he does. They speak his language.

Not really. Not with any specificity. Anyway, that's not the real issue. They put up with him. They use him. The social contract, hon. They're getting something from him they can't get for themselves.

I think he's masturbating over me.

He's what? You mean in private, right? Now how do you figure that? I'd really like to know.

Oh, I don't have any hard evidence. It's just this sixth sense. More like an eighth, if you're keeping count. I can always tell if there's somebody I'm working with who . . . ? It's like radio waves. You can't ordinarily perceive them, but if you have the right equipment . . .

Uh, Ade? Sweetheart? I don't know how to tell you this. But any one of us might be putting out that channel.

Rajasundaran alone enjoyed going head-to-head with the team's problem child. Indifferent to the drama of human personality, he savored each clash with the Armenian as if it were a good cricket test match.

We ought to make it, he said one day, *so that closing the shutters actually dampens all the ambient sounds coming from outside the bedroom windows.*

Kaladjian went for the easy kill. *A pointless exercise. A complete waste of processing power.*

No, it's interesting. What might damping do to create a sense of inside and out?

Don't ask vapid questions, Kaladjian said.

What is your algorithm for telling vapid questions from their opposites?

Jackdaw held up his hands in a T. *Please, guys. We can't afford to start with the philosophy stuff, again.*

Kaladjian ignored the chance for peace with honor. *A vapid question is one that any mature researcher recognizes as fruitless.*

You are willing to be ruled by consensus? You?

All right. Then it's one where the answer serves no end but itself.

Raj studied Kaladjian's face, as if he were his own portrait. *When you look at the Pythagorean theorem, when you draw it graphically . . . ? When you actually build little squares on each side, why should the two smaller squares be equal in area to the largest one? Is that a vapid question?*

Yes. Kaladjian smiled, even as the trap took shape.

But it is also a profound question as well?

Well. That depends.

Spiegel waved his arms, drawing fire. *There are no vapid questions. Only vapid questioners.*

May I ask you one? Adie asked Kaladjian. *Probably vapid? What exactly is your problem?*

Kaladjian blinked condescension. His smile easily absorbed the attack. *I suppose you find me largely contemptuous.*

Pretty much, Adie chirped.

The kind of mutual flaming that enlivened a good Multi-User Dimension turned Jackdaw's stomach when it occurred face-to-face. *Maybe we should put all this human stuff back in the box and get on with our work?*

The others humored him. Hours later, with the project scattered for the day, Adie cornered Kaladjian in his immaculate cubicle. *So tell me.*

Kaladjian looked up, waiting. *And what exactly would you like me to tell you?*

Why you're at war with the rest of creation.

The Armenian appraised her for the length of a short syllogism. *Is that what I am?*

Yes.

He thought for a minute. *You wouldn't understand.*

Adie swallowed the stream of ready profanity that welled up in her throat. *Try me with the dumbed-down version.*

Something in the challenge appealed to him. He gestured for her to sit, then turned his back on her and gazed out his window into the rain-dripped woods. *You know what I do for a living?*

Something to do with numbers.

His laugh condensed to a bitter nib. *I've told you already, young woman. Everything has something to do with numbers.*

Not young, she said.

The silence lasted long enough for Adie to think she'd been dismissed. Then he broke it, addressing the plate glass.

Say the thing that gives you more pleasure than anything in existence is to arrange a set of colored marbles according to strict and surprisingly sparse rules. God knows why, but the pastime fascinates you. So long as you're not hungry or cold or otherwise impaired, you want to devote yourself to it.

Painting, she said. *Something like painting.*

The hardest kind of painting. The most accountable. The more you push the marbles around, the harder it is to get them into interesting configurations. But you're not alone in the pursuit. A handful of other devotees have the same obsession. Everyone looks over one another's work, fixing and extending. You memorize all the beautiful moves of the grand masters. This goes on for a few thousand years. Every so often, someone stumbles onto a hidden wrinkle, one that puts the marbles into a surprise configuration, special, pleasing, something no one expected.

Each of them stared off at an altarpiece the other couldn't see.

Then, out of the blue, someone discovers that the marble game is a profound reformulation of an interlocking canister game, unknown to you, played by another circle of monks centuries ago on the other side of the world and shelved as a useless curiosity. These two unrelated, formally beautiful pursuits turn out to be, in a deep, singular, and unsought way, synonymous.

She nodded toward some analogy. The concealed and ubiquitous golden mean.

A truly shattering insight descends on some master practitioner. Colored marbles and interlocking canisters, taken together, form a perfect translation of phenomena in the physical world. The patterns of marbles and canisters compose a map of, say, the cycle of tides or the bends in a river. And this correspondence works, not only after the fact, but in advance of it. The game makes it possible to predict all kinds of otherwise unknown, otherwise unlooked-for, otherwise immeasurable events . . .

Her neck hairs rose up, obeying their own rules.

Every repeated time without exception, the harmless, artificial game advances in absolute lockstep with measurable event. The implications are inescapable. The marbles and the canisters—the simple but rigorous rules—somehow embody physical reality.

The veil fell, and she stood looking on this abandoned man. She did not know how he managed to remain behind, in such pain.

These inconsequential games mimic the most grandiose patterns we can identify. Gravity, time, light: name your fundament. Creation keeps to a few simple rules of interlocking shape and color, patterns replicating themselves across impossible distances. This is what the mathematician calls beauty. An ever more elaborate edifice spun out of the sparest symmetries. A perfection that outstrips all attempts to capture it.

She put up her palms in puzzlement. *This is a bad thing?*

He turned to her, his edge of aggression again sharpening. He stood and beckoned for her to follow, out the room and down the hall. They reached the Cavern, where Sybil Stance was taking her rightful slot on the sign-up sheet.

We have an emergency, Kaladjian said. *We need the machine.*

Ari! I'm right in the middle of—

Please. Ten minutes. You can have my hour tomorrow.

He booted up an environment Adie had never seen. A shape like a Cycladic figure mushroomed in front of them. Kaladjian put the wand through an unaccompanied partita. The figure metamorphosed, its planes sliding upon itself, turning inside out in a virtuoso conjuring act of knotted space.

All legitimate topological transformations of one another, he said.

Adie nodded, hooked. She saw a centaur. The torso of a naked Aphrodite. A wondrous stalactite. A nexus of ribbonlike tubes passing through their own surfaces. Proteus, unholdable.

We're going in, Kaladjian announced.

The figure swelled in the air around them, and they passed inside. When they steadied out again, they found themselves riding along the inside edge of a secret junction of knotted expressway lanes, the deeply entangled passages of a decadent queen conch.

Brace yourself.

Kaladjian hit a button on the wand. The waterslide surfaces fragmented into the mosaic of polygons that composed them. Shards flew in all directions, a shower of math-meteors. The community of screen phenomena—a capacious, fecund, and extraneous metaphor of the machine's internal states—revealed itself to be a bastard lingua franca where alien races could meet in compromise.

Adie's body grew large, galactic, her head wrapped in a cloud of stars. They zoomed out, pulling back to a distant vantage above what condensed into a spiral nebula. She looked out across a sweeping interstellar pinwheel, its slow spokes lapping around her midriff. Each wash of stars unfolded another billion years of cosmic evolution. She swelled to the size of God's recording angel, attending at the day of Creation.

It's . . . magnificent. I had no idea. She felt her eyes spilling over, and did not care. There was no foolishness, no vanity, no shame in anything a body felt, looking on this.

Yes. Now here is the math behind it. He pushed a button and the expanding universe fell away into a few polynomials, breathtaking in their slightness.

She tried to say his name: *Ari.* The tag soured inside her mouth. *I don't . . . I still don't . . .* The man's pettiness appalled her more than ever, after what he'd just let her see. *Where's the problem?*

The problem? The problem is that we still live here.

He spread his hands to indicate the projectors, the modular office furniture, all the ugly bundles of cable and molded-plastic printed circuits that filled the space around them. It dawned on her. His days of true research were over. He had done no useful math, no *beautiful* math, for years. He, too: banished to industry. Wherever the *there* that the colored marble game whispered of, this man could no longer reach it.

Words left Adie, to sound across inconceivable distances. *That is no country for old men?*

That is no country for old men. He measured the line, liked it. Perhaps he thought she'd made it up. *Clever of a young woman to see that.*

Not clever at all, in fact. Clever were those who had not seen, yet still perceived.

That was no country for refugees of any age. Some nights, when Spiegel knew Adie was home in her island hermitage, he would call, chatting away happily to her answering machine. He'd hold rambling conversations on her tape, knowing full well she was in the room screening and could hear every word.

Can I try something out on you? It's a Personals ad: "Carbon-based life-form seeking same to help fill the chilly immensity of existence." What do you think? I know, I know—the diction's a little off. How about this: "The universe is fifteen billion years old. I'm pushing forty. Looking for Solar System–based female in similar temporal predicament."

At first she listened in real time. After a while, she turned off the speaker, checking the backlog of messages only at long stretches. Finally, she pulled the machine's plug.

Early one morning in Arles, she at last hit upon the concealed hope that bound all these messy exiles to the same project. She stood in a room-sized cartoon among four men, each with his own agenda, each terrified that the breakneck pace of technology would prove too little, too late, each desperate to turn the Cavern into something more than a prohibitively expensive, slow, grainy, cold, monstrously cumbersome stereoscope. She looked through the windows of her provisional

Mediterranean summer cottage, down along the fabricated path to the coast, out to the invented sea, and the farther sea beyond that one. And she saw, at last, what these men had been for so long gazing at.

The Cavern was irrelevant. The Cavern was not even a flip-card deck compared to the Panovision it pointed at. The Cavern would shrink, year after rate-doubling year. Its carapace would wither away until all the pipes and projectors and reality engines fit into a gym bag. Steady improvement would knit belief-quality graphics into the living-room walls of every middle-class condo. Pin-sized lasers lashed to the stems of reading glasses would etch conviction directly onto living retinas.

The technology meant nothing. The technology would disappear, go transparent. In a generation or two, no one would even see it. Someone would discover how to implant billions of transistors directly into the temporal lobes, on two little squares of metal foil. If not in Klarpol's lifetime, then soon enough — just around the bend of this long, logarithmic curve. The clumsy mass of distracting machine would vanish into software, into the impulse that had invented it. Into pure conception.

Something gelled, and Adie saw this primitive gadget morph into the tool that humans have lusted after since the first hand-chipped adze. It seemed the prize at the end of a half-million years of provisional leapfrogging. It was not even a tool, really. More of a medium, the universal one. However much the Cavern had been built from nouns, it dreamed the dream of the unmediated, active verb. It lived where ideas stepped off the blackboard into real being. It represented humanity's final victory over the tyranny of matter. She'd mistaken this variable room for a high-tech novelty. Now Adie saw it as the thinnest first parchment, a thing that rivaled even speech in its ability to amplify thought. Time would turn it into the most significant jump in human communication since the bulking up of the cerebellum.

The mature Cavern would become the body's deep space telescope; the test bed for all guesses; a programmable, live-in film; the zoom lens of the spirit; the umbilical cord for remote robot control; a visualization lab as powerful as human fancy; a tape deck capable of playing back any camera angle in history; a networked web of matter transporters where dispersed families would meet and greet as holographic specters. It promised the wishing lamp that all children's stories described. It was the storybook that once expelled us and now offered to take us back in.

All this Adie Klarpol saw in a single, smooth glance. The men she worked with meant to assemble all these things, and then some.

Arles gleamed. The Mediterranean morning shone from out of the electronic scrap heap of the lab surrounding it. She watched the programmers test the latest audio algorithms. Video edge-detection routines tracked all movement in the room, punctuating any action that might generate sound. Jackdaw Acquerelli slipped off his shoes. He nudged them with a toe, under the lip of the bed. They scraped across the floor of the Cavern, a noise half actual, half synthetic. The elaborate basketball shoes sat like two hollowed-out white lab rabbits, visible through the illusion of the bed, but still beneath it.

Pretty soon, Jackdaw said, *any year now, this room will be good enough to live in.*

That, finally, was the hope. To live in the room that the painter's suicide vacated. The soul simply wanted better accommodations. Something more spacious to fasten to. Something more like itself than that dying animal.

It had taken Adie a year and a half to see what she was working on. The rest of the lay world made the same leap in the space of a single Memorial Day weekend. Overnight, an explosion of interest rocked the RL, as if the mountainside they hugged chose that moment to simulate St. Helens. Media latched wholesale upon this thing that it refused to call anything else but virtual reality. The public took so quickly to the fantasy that it must have recognized the contour from something it already knew.

The press launched a full-frontal assault. Journalists closed in on virtual reality as if on a celebrity murder. The luxury of monastic tinkering dissolved under the onslaught. Freese found himself devoting half his time to fielding reporters' questions. Disruption reigned supreme. The RL's mountain hideaway began to appear in speculative magazine accounts and TV news spots, reports that turned the lab's jerky, wire-frame predictions into gleaming, ray-traced chrome.

No one could say why, after thirty years of research in obscure labs across the Northern Hemisphere, VR overnight became 1990's cover girl. A couple of research outfits let the ghost out of the machine before it was time. Here and there, universities began to demo projects that suddenly had the whole world talking as if full-body dives into wrap-around LSD, robotic prostitution, and long-distance teledildonics would hit the toy store shelves by Christmas. Two or three start-up firms, eager to appease their serial venture capitalists, began to sell cheap telegloves, stripped-down head-mounted displays, and even body suits whose performance amounted to little more than faint holograms of their hinted potential.

In the Santa Barbara Sheraton, at March's research conference for virtual environment and telerobotics interfaces, Freese stood at the back of a packed grand ballroom. Just looking out on the sea of charged participants rearranged his viscera. His cobbled-up cottage craft had graduated beyond an esoteric discipline. Ready or not, reality engineering was about to become a full-fledged industry.

A world begging for deliverance cared nothing for a porcelain jug sitting on a rickety wooden bed stand. But the inexorable market machine that had, just the previous year, swallowed up the globe's last holdout nations already knew what it wanted from virtuality. It wanted holophonic videoconferencing. It wanted the Ferris wheel–cum–feature film. All-talking, all-singing, incarnate sex fantasies. Interplanetary mining from the comfort and safety of our own back yard. But the market craved something more significant as well. Something more fundamental.

Industry saw, in the Cavern and comparable virtual vistas, the race's next launchpad. The first commercial use of virtual space would be as a three-dimensional workbench for designing every physical trinket from saucepan to space station. In that lucid crucible, any conceivable device could be probed from all angles before incurring the expense of manufacture. Even the components for the next generation of Cavern itself could be taken for a 3-D test drive, revealing, in conceptual space, their optimal form before coming into the world. The amount of cash waiting to be thrown at the magic workbench, the sums waiting to be made could swallow the RL budget many times over, for generations upon generations. For the human project had many more goods to make, before its final triumph over goods.

It was here already: the Pong of Things to Come. Downtown, a dozen blocks from Pioneer Square, where Spiegel and Adie had strolled only months before, a technopalace opened up where, for ten bucks, University of Washington kids and frustrated Boeing execs could sit in networked cubicles and blast deep-animated representations of one another out of the infinite vacuum of space. And the month after that arcade opened, Hollywood released the first of several feature-length spawn—a heavily chromed rendition of the new Aladdin and his wonderful data glove. The grand future vision that the RL pioneered was rapidly being left in collective imagination's dust.

Must you Americans oversell everything? Rajasundaran asked.

Freese liked the aggressive ones. *Oversell? You can't oversell this. We're engineering the end of human existence as we know it.*

Not as I know it, White Man.

Still, Freese insisted: it *was* the end. The end of something. An end to the limits of symbolic knowledge. Beyond the hype, past the immediate feeding frenzy, the press had gotten at least that much right. But even in the thick of the current mania, no one had yet guessed how big this thing was going to get. No one.

The Cavern threatened the final disappearance of interface. Future operators would engage simulation in the same way that humanity's current version engaged material existence: using all the degrees of freedom built into their sovereign bodies. The right way to grasp the planet's mounting sandcastles of data was to step inside and poke around.

As the scramble for funds broke out everywhere, Freese took his ideas on the lecture circuit. The computer would go transparent, more invisible than all its crude, qualified precursors in representation. Talking to data would be like talking to a friend over the phone. Explorers would move through a literal forest of numbers, strolling through their woody representations and singling out by sight or sound or smell the significant trees, the hidden arbors.

Freese's techno-evangelizing carried a strong dose of private salesmanship. No other start-up in the fledgling reality industry had yet shown anything remotely in the league of the prototype Cavern. The Cavern, Freese teased, would make head-mounted displays and cumbersome gloves seem like Smell-O-Matic, SensaVision, or any other doomed evolutionary backwater. He always ended his speeches with the coy suggestion that everyone stay alive long enough to see the thing that their imaginations couldn't quite visualize yet.

But privately, back at the mountain, he fretted. He sent off an anxious e-mail to the brass at TeraSys. `The whole fad may quite simply fade before we get the real thing to market. In the current climate, potential clients for genuine immersion environments could well feel burned by their own expectations and sour on all subsequent demos, once the bubble bursts . . .`

As project administrator, Freese managed a delicate balancing act between come-on and kiss-off. He could say nothing of the project and risk being lost in a sea of false claims. Or he could promise the world and risk failing to satisfy. Already, knots of prospective cybernauts were queuing up in the RL's parking lot, cash in hand. But the Realization Lab was worlds away from showing anything that resembled a finished product. All they had was proof of concept.

Freese called a general meeting. Programmers, hardware jockeys, scientists, and designers assembled in the central atrium, the only nonvirtual auditorium large enough to contain them all.

This may be the first time I've seen some of you in the daytime, Freese said. *I'm surprised at how healthy you all look in natural light.*

Those are called monitor tans, Sue Loque called out from the gallery.

I figured it wasn't the diet. First off, I want to applaud every member of this group for the distance we've already come. When I think of our technical and aesthetic advances in the two years since we put together the Crayon World, it feels . . . He breathed in slowly and rolled his eyes. *It feels as if I'm watching a film about evolution on fast-forward. Those of you who spend night after night chained to the workstation may have started to take monthly or even weekly breakthroughs for granted. I don't, I assure you. If this project were to move any faster, I'd be unable to keep up.*

He's about to tell us that it's time to pick up the pace, Rajan stage-whispered. The room exploded in laughter.

Freese screwed up his mouth. *It's time to pick up the pace.* The room erupted again. *Well, not so much the pace. I doubt any one of you could work any harder or more . . . happily than you already do. What we need to accelerate, I suppose, is the release schedule.*

Vulgamott raised a hand. *Run that one by us again, Chief?*

More, quieter laughter.

Don't sweat the details, Michael. Here's the problem. We're all over ourselves, shattering yesterday's landmarks. We've gotten the polygon budget up from—what?—a couple of thousand per second? He looked at Spider Lim, who gave an infinitesimal nod. *To . . . what are we running now? I can't even keep track anymore.*

Spider cleared his throat. *Over a hundred thousand per wall.*

From ten to the third to ten to the fifth. In two dozen months. I'd call that impressive.

Lim, sensing the blow, stood up. *Actually, we'll have to step up just as many more orders of magnitude before we can start to deliver believability without a lag.*

I agree. Jackdaw addressed his calculator watch. *Reality demands something on the order of a hundred million. Reality . . . is ten to the eighth surface-filled polygons a second.*

Minimum, Spider agreed, and sat down.

Freese nodded. *You see? This is the problem.*

Reality is always a problem, Spiegel said.

The question is: when does the show stabilize and our act hit the road? At our current rate of change, the answer is never. The product would be forever obsolete before we got it out the door.

O'Reilly raised his hand. *It sounds like you're saying that Deep Pockets is wanting to see some more near-term return?*

I'm afraid they want a public press conference for the spring. By next year's SIGGRAPH convention, we're to do a grand rollout. The popular press between now and then will be whipping the public imagination into a frenzy. We'll need to show something, just to compete with the rumors.

Hardware, Software, and Design all took the floor to lodge their official reservations. But by the time the party broke up, the rules of the game had changed.

Freese saluted them as they left. *March of '91, then. Delivery Day.*

He wants us to be salesmen? Adie asked Ebesen, back in the cubicles. *This is all just about selling iron?*

The old guy hunched his flannel shoulders. *You knew it had to happen someday.*

No, I didn't, she said. *It never occurred to me.*

Know what you should make? Lim told her. He was gutting Rembrandt again, tossing the machine's outdated entrails into cardboard boxes full of priceless scrap. *A RAM room. You know: a huge blow-up representation of everything happening inside the real computer down at silicon level, right as it's running the simulation.*

She gave the notion three seconds. *Bad idea. Am I to take it, from this mound of scrap metal, that we are obsolete again?*

They say that the Great Wall was obsolete before it was halfway finished. Your average printed circuit board is obsolete before it's even begun.

Someone should go through all these junk piles, she said. *It's getting hard to walk in here.*

Lim looked up, horrified. *We can't throw any of that away. We might have to . . . refer to it.*

Why? Why? She picked up a shoebox-sized assembly, once a miracle of miniaturization, a whole interplanetary system. Now incompatible with everything. She dropped the chunk of parts. *Worthless.*

We can use some of those old motherboards as souped-up serial ports.

Spider, these things are all dead. Killed by bigger, faster, better. Cartons of milk past the stamped expiration date. Tickets for last night's concert.

TeraSys might be able to sell them to places that are still back at earlier machine levels.

You mean that Bulgaria might be interested in running its own experimental virtual reality program, now that it's joined the Free World?

I was thinking more like, you know, Arkansas?

She mentioned the elephants' graveyard to Jackdaw and Rajan. *This world digitization thing is the single most wasteful expenditure of effort in history.*

The kid bared his palms. *You think the hardware side is wasteful? At least you can make those things into doorstops and paperweights. At least you can pirate last year's million-dollar state-of-the-art research tool for its edge connectors.*

Rajan chuckled. *Right. Smelt them down to reclaim the two dollars and fifty cents' worth of gold plating on the pins.*

But software . . . ? Jackdaw said. *Nothing is more pitiful than Version 1. The biggest sinkhole of human genius in existence. The average lifetime of a given release is now shorter than the time it takes to learn its features. And as soon as Version 2 comes out, Version 1 turns into a time bomb in the operating system, just waiting to foul up any improvements in other software that postdates it.*

Let us put this in your terms, Rajan said. *Suppose all of world art came down to the last three months of images. Every time an artist painted a painting, it invalidated all previous paintings of the same subject.*

Sure. That's called commercial design. I did that for half a dozen years.

It's worse than that, Jackdaw cut in. *Most development has no coordination to speak of. The wheel gets reinvented a million times a day, even in the same company. Even at the same workstation. It took half a century of coding to come up with reusable objects. And even now, they're not all that reusable, because, you know, the APIs and the hardware standards are changing the ground underneath them by the nanosecond.*

Rajan's cranium went into sympathetic oscillations. *Truly demoralizing. Every basket of subroutines has to be invented dozens of times, each one doing the same thing in slightly different ways. Then all of these maddening, incompatible variants are thrown into public battle to determine which one will become the de facto standard, and everyone who puts money on the wrong flavor has to throw it out and start over again.*

Kaladjian came and stood nearby, cleaning off his glasses. *Fortunately for all of us, waste is this culture's greatest engine.*

The others looked up, snagged by some expansive departure from his usual tone.

Is that supposed to be ironic? Raj asked.

Kaladjian gave a victimized shrug. *Progress is destruction with a compass.*

Raj's nods accelerated a couple of hertz. *It does make one wonder what the finish line looks like.*

Adie dear, Spiegel said. *You've come to a world where truth is stamped with its own expiration date.*

Jackdaw grimaced. *Not to mention the obsolete media. We still have these ancient tapes from before we ported to the Cavern? They can't be read anymore. The machines that used them have all been upgraded beyond compatibility. And even when we rebuild an antique drive from scratch? The tape has decayed; it spits out check-sum errors every three records.*

The world is losing its memory. Raj toyed with a stack of printouts headed for the shredder. *Whole areas of the collective brain are being wiped out as its storage degrades. We've contracted a slow virus. Global Alzheimer's.*

Kaladjian lifted one shoulder. His tilted ear met it halfway. *Perhaps. But look how far we managed to get, from flint to silicon, before the enterprise shut down.*

The Cavern caved in for several days, while Lim and company finished debugging a new generation of graphics accelerators. Deprived of their magic testing chamber, imagination's prototypers hit a wall.

Maybe we should do a retreat or something, Vulgamott suggested to his fellow designers.

Adie snorted. *Maybe we should do a full-scale rout.*

Don't bail on me, please. I'm skidding out, here. Real deadlines. Real demos. No real place to test them. What's the imaginary world coming to?

Ebesen said nothing. He was ready to accommodate—always the path of least resistance.

Vulgamott got hold of a small cabin that TeraSys maintained up on the south fork of the Stillaguamish, near Mount Pilchuck. Art and Design booked the place for a forty-eight-hour stay. Ebesen's dirty flannel and corduroys, so squalid under fluorescent light, seemed almost indigenous, outdoors. Vulgamott, after two hours of the upland air, ceased twitching and began to breathe deeper. Adie went through a small sketch pad on the first afternoon. Thereafter she simply looked, with no more point than looking.

In wildness, description fell away into its parent density. The three of them walked out in the woods, into the network of living agents, rooted, burrowing, and airborne. They drifted their feet in the bone-mashing cold of the river current, the rushing fluid still imprinted with its past life as mountain snow. At night, the curl of their campfire smoke rose and obscured itself in the Milky Way's fainter smear. The haunt of owls on the hollow night turned the listening heart against all hope of representation.

They talked about what they had done, what they were doing, and what they would need to do before being anywhere near ready to release their work to the public. Months of mock-up had not yet even blocked out the floor plan of that furnished rec room of the cerebrum they pictured.

The vines of Rousseau's *Dream* had spread, lovely and profuse. Its creatures had scampered in modest For-Next loops through the coded undergrowth. But the forest had remained a thought without a deed, a look without a behavior, flat and planar, less a living thing than a cadaver's cross section. A visitor could walk into the jungle moonlight, but only along fixed paths, strolling past the successive cardboard props of a *tableau vivant*.

Out of this dream, they'd awakened to perspective. Their tools had all scaled up: frame rate, color depth, resolution, vertices per second. And the Arles bedroom exceeded the sum of these leaps. It zeroed in on that longed-for locale that no one had yet seen but everyone knew by sight. Its bed lay thick with invitation. The sun streamed through its casements, swelling and decaying in the length of a single visit. The wood floor bent to the weight of the current tenant. And yet even that humming space was no more than a single stereo slide. The bedroom filled out its frame, but no farther, refusing to venture beyond the grotto that housed it.

Now Design had to plan its next escape. Under the sap-heavy trees, the chilled antics of a Cascade stream between their toes, the digital artists turned over the problem, less through talk than with shared scribbles. The task was obvious. They needed a way to wed inimical worlds, to combine the dream of these two chambers.

Half a dozen months, Vulgamott repeated, past the point when either of his colleagues heard him any longer. *We're in a situation here, people. It's demo or die.*

Or both, Ebesen said. *"Both" remains a distinct possibility.*

In her mind, Adie wanded off down hinted-at ravines, lost in the extensions of sight, looking for the room they had to reach. The trick was how to find it without clues. How to resolve the place, without knowing what it looked like. In rapid succession, they torched each proposal put forward. All possible rooms either cloyed or curdled, too banal or too vaporous, too mundane or too incorporeal. Nothing both satisfied desire and yielded to available technique.

No more paintings, Adie said. *We tried that twice. We want something that will break out of the frame.*

All three knew the medium they would have to inhabit, already laid out for them. Vulgamott and Ebesen's architectural tool chest—now numbering in the hundreds of modular components, from the simple I beam to the ornate ogee molding—all but forced their hand. Their resizable image library had grown into an encyclopedia of smart architectural elements, one that made it possible for any reasonably patient person who could manage a pipe-cleaner sculpture or a box of Lincoln Logs to build her own pan-and-zoom Versailles.

With the suite of Palladian tools, prototyping a simple architectural fly-through shrank from months to weeks. The kit had never been meant as anything but its own demo, a proof of concept rather than a mission-critical development tool. Now it represented their only chance at hewing out a substantial show by press date. Even here, on the verge of the virtual, they were condemned by those absurd constraints, time and practicality.

They determined to build a dazzling building. But forty-eight hours in a remote, three-room cabin failed to produce a viable candidate. They were still tossing around possibilities as they packed to return to civilization.

Vulgamott tried to rally them. *We should do Vierzehnheiligen. An amazing space. Mysterious, sensual, organic.*

Adie jerked back, as if slugged. *Oh God. God, no. We'd all be insulin-dependent diabetics within a week. How about something clean, like . . . Fallingwater?*

A total bear. I mean, it's a staggering building and all. But how in the hell would we . . . ?

Too innovative, Ebesen agreed. *Too singular. The tool set wouldn't be much of a help.*

Well, Karl? Adie clasped her hands together in front of her face.

How about a time-lapse Troy?

Vulgamott howled. *Ebesen, you maniac. I divorce you, I divorce you, I divorce you.*

All right, all right. Nobody get excited. I vote for the Temple of Diana at Ephesus.

Oh terrific, Michael said. *Why bother doing an existing structure when we can do a building that has disappeared without a trace?*

Well, there is some basis for speculation . . .

How about the RL? Vulgamott proposed. *The perfect compromise. We have all the data at our fingertips.*

Kill me first, Adie said. *It's bad enough that we have to live in the place.*

Whatever we model, Ebesen insisted, *has to be well made.*

It has to be beautiful, Adie said.

Vulgamott let loose a bat-pitched scream. *It has to be doable. You people. I can't believe this. What a colossal waste, this whole hug-a-tree idea. Two days up here and we haven't figured out anything that we couldn't have come up with in fifteen minutes back in the gerbil-run. A beautiful, well-made building. For this we needed to eat Sterno-soaked vegetable kabobs and encourage chiggers in the joys of symbiosis?*

Adie took her leave of the two men and headed back up into the woods for a last look, before returning to made existence. She followed the streambed awhile, to a narrowing that she figured had to exist. When she found the place, or a reasonable facsimile, she looked around, listening for any sounds larger than a muskrat. Hearing none, she stripped. She slipped into the water and sat in the eddy of her own naked body. She spun about in the numbing current, her length a lodestone, until she faced upstream. Somewhere near this water's source lay the solution they needed.

She knifed in the water, a rose-brushed trout. She kept under for as long as she could bear. The liquid ran colder and denser than she'd thought. It contracted her arteries and hammered her head. She felt her ideas go soft, giving in to the snow-fed current. She worked back to the shore. It took her two tries to lift herself up on a boulder. As the glaze of water on her evaporated, her core temperature plunged still deeper. She huddled on the rock, hands around her knees, convulsing.

Adie? a voice twenty feet away called.

She screamed and splayed, grabbing the rock as she lost her balance. She fought to reach her stack of clothes, and she fell. She cowered, clasping her T-shirt against her nakedness. Down the path, through the skirt of trees, his back to her, his hands folded in a cowl over his head, stood Karl Ebesen. She closed her eyes, breathed out hard, and slugged herself in the chest, to restart her heart.

Ach, Ebesen moaned. *Jesus. Sorry, sorry, sorry.* Plaintive burlesque crept into his apology. She had to laugh. The most anguished she'd seen the man since meeting him.

Hang on. Give me two minutes.

Fright, at least, had killed the chill. Her clothes felt good going on, wicking the water off her skin.

She stepped out from behind the rock. *All hid.*

Ebesen lowered his hands and edged forward, shy caller in some overgrown game of tag. *Forgive me. I figured it would be worse for you to hear me slinking away through the branches.*

Not a big deal. My fault, really. She reached out to reassure his elbow, which withdrew from her touch as soon as politeness permitted.

That old spirit of noblouse oblige, he said. *Susanna and the Elders. A genre subject that for some reason has fallen into neglect in the last few years.*

She smiled. *They just don't paint them like they used to.*

His car had failed to start. He didn't discover the fact until Vulgamott was long gone. Adie was the only human within reach. *So I followed you up into the woods.*

Never for a moment suspecting that I'd be out splashing around buck naked.

Hedy Lamarr in that classic, Ecstasy.

Dumbo the elephant. In the feature animation of the same name.

They set a good clip back down to the cabin. Karl got in the car and tried it again. The thing made a hideous rasping sound. *It doesn't look like a machine that's bearing me a mortal grudge, does it?*

In fact, it looked to Adie liked a machine that had held on, capriciously, ten years past death by natural causes.

Have you checked the engine?

That's under the hood, right?

After an extended search, he found the hood release. The two of them stood above the open cavity and peered in. Finally Ebesen let out a harsh laugh. *Who are we kidding?*

She drove him to a service station on Mt. Loop Highway. A mechanic followed them back to the cabin in a tow truck. He pronounced the car beyond immediate resuscitation and proceeded to haul it in to the shop.

You go on home, Ebesen told her. *Drop me at the station. I'll wait there until they get it running again.*

Karl. Don't be an idiot. That could take days. And even that would be a miracle.

She forced him into her car, above his protests. He sat on the seat edge the whole way back. *Drop me off anywhere,* he told her. *Wherever it's convenient for you.*

Listen to me, Karl. I'm taking you to your doorstep. And when your car is ready, you're going to call me and I'll take you back out to the station.

He sighed and directed her to his neighborhood. As they drew near, she saw her mistake. The houses crumbled away to shacks while the yards blossomed into florid garage sales.

Right here would be fine.

Your doorstep, Karl.

His house turned out to have no doorstep. A rushed wrap of lattice-work around its base failed to disguise the fact that it had once been mobile.

He relaxed into the truth. *Would you like to come in for a minute?*

Sure, she lied. *I'd like that.*

Inside was even rattier than out. It consisted of a single, long room with a kitchen ell at one end and a sleeping area hidden behind a lacquer screen at the other. It would have fit into the Cavern whole, without too much scan and pan. But the Cavern could never have captured this room's most salient feature, its pungent desiccation, the acrid mushroom nosegay of the past. Smell would forever evade simulation.

Something to drink?

A glass of water would be great.

Tap water all right?

Hmm? Oh. Sure.

Every niche engendered clutter. Clothes, crumpled sheets of manila paper, battered anthologies, old newspapers, dishes and cups, packaging from bygone frozen dinners. But no sign of electronics anywhere. Nothing with a knob or a plug or a power light. Adie walked to the largest wall, drawn by a burst of images pasted on it. Several hundred photographs covered its surface in an unbroken collage.

Karl apologized from the kitchen. *I used to like to take pictures.*

Not a single one of the warped prints was younger than a decade. A swath through their middle showed where the arc of window light faded them each day. Most of the yellowing images were shots of a woman who, at the moment of exposure, had been about Adie's age.

Ebesen joined her in front of the shrine, a glass of tap water in each hand. *Wild, isn't it?*

What do you mean, wild?

He looked at her full on. *You don't see it, do you?*

She didn't even see what it was that she didn't see. Ebesen disappeared into what must have been the bathroom, returning with a Boy Scout shaving mirror much like the one hanging on the wall at Arles. He placed the silver square in her hands.

May I?

She nodded. This man could do nothing she might object to. She looked into the metal surface while he pulled her hair back until it disappeared. He rested both hands against her jaw, as if feeling for swollen glands. He lifted slowly, with delicate pressure, like a potter at the wheel. Her whole lower face rose up into her cheekbones. He molded her skin, consulting no references. He needed none.

Adie studied the result in the mirror. She turned and complied, holding the metal so she could look out on the wall of photos. And she became the cameo she was looking at. She shuddered, spun away from the photos, and dropped the mirror, freeing her face and hair.

Ebesen stepped back and raised his hands. *I'm sorry. Forgive me. Twice in one day.*

No, no. It was just . . . creepy, is all.

That is the polite word for it.

I'm not really . . . I don't really look much like her, you know.

No?

I mean, Karl. Really. You have to push my face all around. If you maul a person's musculature, you can make anyone look like anyone.

Really? Think we could do up Mr. Gates the Third as a good Baroque John the Baptist on a platter?

She laughed, against her will.

Ebesen sipped from his water. *Do you know her?*

Adie turned back to the photos. Did she know her? The possibility had never crossed her mind. She combed the mosaic again for some spark of recognition. None.

Should I?

He looked at the gallery, as at a police lineup. *Gail Frank?*

The name was common enough to sound familiar, but too common to place. One four-by-six exposure showed the woman in the middle of what looked like Washington Square, adjusting a mannequin into a fetal position on the pavement, surrounded by a few curious onlookers.

She liked to work outdoors, Ebesen said. *"Outstallations," she called them. Closed studio spaces made her claustrophobic.*

In the next shot, Ebesen's camera had caught Gail Frank in the act of binding the hands of the now-blindfolded mannequin behind its back. In adjacent Polaroids, she manipulated various other dolls, dummies, and human figures, stacking them up in shipping crates, loading them into mailers, packing them into constrained spaces in tight crystal lattices.

Gail . . . Frank. A performance artist? Something nagged at her. Some buried, peripheral thing.

Ebesen shook his head. *Remember performance art? Remember the seventies? God, we sure do slash and burn our genres these days, don't we?*

Something in the way he said these words opened the sluice of her memory. Adie's hand flew up to her mouth. *Gail Frank.* Of course. The story that had the whole of artistic New York bound and entranced. At least for a season. *The woman who . . . Mark Nyborg's . . . ?*

At the name of the fallen icon of minimalist sculpture, Ebesen's head jabbed forward.

Adie chose her words. *The woman he killed.*

Ebesen shrugged. *Maybe.*

Karl. What do you mean, maybe? The man pushed her out of a thirteenth-story window.

Fourteenth. But who's counting?

Convicted by a jury. Put away. As far as I've heard, he's still doing time somewhere.

Ebesen cleared a coating of papers off the stuffed chair and sat. He swirled his glass, then drained down to the white lees of plumbing scum. He stroked the empty tumbler like Beuys stroking his dead hare. *Wouldn't that be incredible, for all of us? I mean, if we could actually "do" time?*

You knew her? Adie shrank from the anemic formulation. The man had an altar of pictures erected to the woman. His home's sole decoration, aside from the piles of rubbish. *You were . . . close?*

His mouth tightened into irony's thin mail slot. *We were close. She . . . upgraded me for him.*

Her every possible response became impossible.

Strictly a matter of portfolio improvement. Gail needed to associate herself with heavy hitters. Reputation, standing, influence. That kind of thing. She was a creative vampire. Her own work fed off the attention that others were getting. After a couple of years, she outgrew whatever meager attention I was ever likely to receive in this life. And she grew into Mr. Nyborg, whose fame was expanding without limits.

Not fame, Adie snapped. *Notoriety.* Surprised by the anger massing in her. *A poseur. A salesman.*

Not without talent. She definitely traded up.

Adie looked at this man with whom she'd worked for two years in the closest of quarters. Even objection seemed shut down.

I can't say her departure left my life entirely impoverished. Gail was a . . . complex personality. It took me some time to realize that even grief brought its own kind of relief.

Adie turned back to the picture anthology. The woman displayed every available facial expression from hostility to helplessness—the same unbridgeable spread that any life indulged in. Gail Frank's face exerted an eerie magnetism, the pull of the scared expression that knows you want to look at it. The beauty of narcissism. Her face looked nothing like Adie's. Adie looked nothing like the woman.

She heard herself talking, from across an echoing hall. *And you don't think that man murdered her?*

Well, you know, Mark went off to a double lifetime prison sentence swearing that Gail . . . . helped herself over the sill.

Adie studied the woman, her public shows, her private non-disclosures. She shook her head. *Wasn't there something about repeated abuse?*

Another thing that I'd fail to give her.

And the neighbors in that building, testifying that they used to hear him, drugged, threatening at the top of his voice that he was going to kill her?

Adie swung around to face Ebesen. He was studying her with a quizzical expression. *You've retained a surprising number of details about the case.*

She shrugged. *I was a young artist, living in New York City.*

Ebesen stood up. *So were we all, once.*

He crossed the room without a word, walking away from her. The interview was over.

Karl. Please. I'm sorry.

He disappeared into his bedroom, behind the lacquer screen. She stood forever, wondering if she should let herself out.

Hang on, he called at last. *It's around here somewhere.*

When he returned, he was toting a cardstock portfolio like the one he carried around with him at the RL, only bigger and rattier. He laid it out on a plateau on top of the floor clutter. She came behind him as he flipped through the enclosed sheaves. With each riffled picture, she wanted to call out for him to stop and back up. But he was going somewhere, flipping so rapidly that every so often he tore one in his hurry. Every tear ripped into her.

At first glance, she took them for color photographs. *My God,* she said, after a handful went by. *What's the medium?*

These? They're just acrylics.

Holy shit. Did you use projection?

He dismissed her with a laugh. *If I'd used projection, these things might have been fashionable. As it is, freehand, they're just curios.*

She needed him to stop flipping, to stop talking, to give her eye a chance to correct the impression of perfection, see the blemishes, figure out how it was done. But Ebesen forged on faster. When he finally came to rest on the thing he sought, she wished he'd kept going.

The image jumped out at her, an obscene crime-journalism spread. Gail Frank lay clutching the sidewalk, with half the legs of a spider, but twice as disjointed. Karl turned the paper ninety degrees. *Odd, no? This way, she looks like she's scaling the north face of a sheer rock drop.*

Adie could only stare. Stare at the ungodly, omnipotent technique. Stare at the obscene subject matter, painted here as if it were the heart of tranquil eternity. A woman lay sprawled on the pavement, her mechanism smashed. Pressed up against the floor of the world, clutching it, as if sleeping at the bottom of a deep well. All she lacked was a chalk outline around her now-obsolete body.

You couldn't have seen this, Adie said. Adamant. Hoping.

He nodded in contradiction. *I did.*

In your imagination.

Oh, my imagination isn't that good.

She looked again, refusing the evidence. A hyper-real, lurid tabloid shot of the victim after impact. Adie's head tracked back and forth, a searchlight in denial. *This is . . . You must have painted this from a photograph?*

I painted everything from photographs. It's absurd, isn't it? I mean, what's the point? A photorealistic copy of a real photo. The camera can do everything the hand can do, a million times easier and more effectively. He picked up the sheet of paper, then let it fall. *Except be the hand.*

Karl. It's horrible. How could you . . . ? Where did you get the photo?

I took it.

She recoiled from him. Her hands pressed up to receive her face, taking disgust's mold. When they came away, her face was still there.

You don't understand, he said. *She's not dead.*

Those three words came from a place she couldn't look at. Her colleague, the bagman, a victim of the quietest mental illness imaginable.

I mean here. She's not dead yet, in the picture. In the photo I took of her.

She wanted to take him and hold him in his delusion, a greedy pietà, however much his body dwarfed her own. She reached out and took his elbow, cradling what she could.

He pulled away. *No. It's not what you think. I made this about ten months before her death.*

She shook her head. No: no.

It's from a favorite performance piece of hers. She used to find a nice stretch of public sidewalk down in the Financial District, get a demonstration permit, and then lie out on it for as long as she could get away with it. Used to scare the shit out of the Wall Street crowd.

Oh Jesus. Oh God. She watched the picture dissolve under her eyes, every detail changing to some identical other. *You're saying her death was a . . . piece?*

He looked again at the subpoenaed exhibit. *That's what her boyfriend told the jury.*

And you? What did you tell the jury?

I think it must have been a collaboration. A workshop effort. Ebesen shut the portfolio with brutal finality. *Mark, Gail, and me.*

You? Oh, Karl. How can you blame yourself for something that . . . She trickled off, losing her way out of the idea.

I shouldn't have been tempting fate. A person should never represent anything that they aren't willing to have come true.

Wait. No. That picture . . . had nothing to do with her death. You weren't even painting. You were just documenting the woman's . . . How were you supposed to know?

We know what we paint. And everything we paint comes into the world somehow. That's why God put the kibosh on graven images, you know. He didn't want the minor leagues fooling around with something they couldn't control.

She crossed the gap between them. She put her arms around him, to silence him. He made no move either to conform or to quit the sentence. Like embracing a six-foot burlap sack of rice. She pulled away, blunted, holding on to his flank.

Karl, you can't carry this around with you. Your picture had no bearing on . . . You're not responsible. You didn't do this.

Oh, but I did. Everyone does what they do, finally.

She let go of him. She stepped back, staring. He would not look at her. It fit together now, what the man was doing here, what he wasn't doing. All the things he'd never do again.

And you? he said, reading her thoughts. *How about you? What's your excuse?*

She shook her head. *I have no excuse.*

Why did you give it up?

She held her hair back with one hand and reddened raw. *Because. Because it was a racket. Because we might as well be in an honest business. Because art does nothing.*

He took her water glass from out of her fingers and vanished into the kitchen, leaving her the dignity of isolation.

You still love her? she called to him, for no reason. So there wouldn't be silence.

He called back, invisible, from the ell. *Still . . . ? What makes you say that?*

What makes you. She figured the reasons. Counted them up, syllogistically aloof. *The pictures.* Like some Central American grotto of *gracias* to the Virgin.

Oh, he called back. *That. Step back.*

It took her a moment to process. She stepped back. *Yes?*

Nothing? Step back again. Keep going.

She stepped back as far as she could, all the way to the opposite wall. She looked up again at memory's pastiche. Suddenly each individual picture — each discrete pattern of light and dark — diffused into the dithered dots of a newspaper halftone. Where there had been hundreds of images, there now was just one: a single, gaping composite of a female face. But exactly whose face, the composite lacked the resolution to disclose.

Something moved to the left of the illusion. She looked away. Karl had come back into room, watching her discovery. When he spoke, it was as if all life's ballots were already counted.

I had a box of photos lying around. Most of them were of her. And I had this idea. I don't get that many of them these days. It was just an experiment.

Art made nothing happen. Nothing but what had to.

By the way, he added, *she loved your show.*

33

"I need more to read," you tell Sayid.

He can't grasp the request. They've already brought you a book. What have you done with it? What is this *more*?

"I've read this one. Finished. Many, many times. I know every word in it. No surprises left."

He takes the book away. No new volumes come to replace it.

You must work on Muhammad. He is the only possibility, among the guards. Sayid has a soul capable of sympathy. But he is a simple man, a Bekáa peasant from a poor cotton-farming family, ending up with the Partisans more for the twenty-five dollars a month than out of any strong conviction. In his world, books are not even a luxury. They are an obscene irrelevance.

Ali is even less use. He has gotten bad again, these last two months. He'll come sit in your cell in the evenings, unrolling long campfire tales of who he is and where he came from. Practicing his English, like one of your innocent students. An eager, swaggering boy weaving a valiant epic out of his life.

"You know what my home is?" he says one night. "My home is Shatila." The massacred camp. Another night he claims, "You know Souq al Gharb? I live in Souq al Gharb. All Lebanese live in Souq al Gharb. Americans bomb shit from Souq al Gharb. Shit-scared, from a boat, out in the water! Because they know we will kill them dead if they come to us on the land."

"Souq al Gharb is not my fault," you tell him, behind the blindfold. But softly. You do not want to be beaten. You love your limbs. You may even use them again, in another life.

Ali unloads his story, in bits and pieces—embroidered, enlarged, but now and then, almost by accident, consistent.

"When I was a little boy, I love the Palestinians. Everyone hurts them. They are my hero. Then the Palestinians burn my village. Why do they do this? No reason. Then I am thinking: The Israelis are coming. They are finding these people who kill my father and my father's sister and my mother's brothers, and they are going to kill them. But what do the Israelis do? What do they *do*?"

He deals you a quick kick in the loins.

"I don't know."

"You don't know? They burn my village down again. Better than before. Why do they do that? *Why?*"

You tense yourself. "No reason?"

"Big reason!" he shrieks. Someone calls in Arabic outside the door. Ali reassures them.

You hear him advance on you. "They are not good people," you blurt, ready to scramble.

"They are bad people. Evil people." Agreement is as violent as argument. "Then the Syrian soldiers come in. I think, Now a real army will tell the Israelis a lesson. But he fails me, Syria. He stops before he reaches the south. He does nothing. He does shit."

You wade through this brief primer of recent history, trying to remember what really happened. The real chronology lies infinitely far away, political science, a dull, distant abstraction. You can never hope to understand what has happened here. But you must understand Ali.

"Then you Americans invade. You know something? It's OK. I am fine with America. Because maybe now someone is going to end things. Too many years of dying. Too many crazy people. But what does America do? Bomb shit from Souq al Gharb. From a boat, like a shit-scared girl."

A long silence, and you wonder if lessons are over again for the evening. But your teacher simply shifts from history to philosophy.

"No. No. The world wants us dead. Good; fine. The whole world is our Karbala. Too bad for the world. For every violence, we will give a violence. You kill, we kill. You play a trick on us, we bomb your embassy. You bomb our village, we kill your Marines. You think you are hurting us? You are doing good for us. You make us strong. You let Israel destroy Shatila? We kill you on that airplane. You bomb us at Tripoli? We kill three hostages just like you."

He falls silent, the spilled secret flapping in the air between you. One slip kills, in an instant, all your willed ignorance. Your tenacious denial in the teeth of the evidence.

Now you will pay for his error, his accidental confession. "Why me?" you rush out, to switch the game back to the abstract. Distract him with a new philosophical conundrum.

"Look," he says, his voice cold with whatever he imagines to be compassion, "America is not your fault." You've taught him a new word. "But you are America's fault."

You decide not to bring up the subject of more reading matter with Ali.

But Muhammad: he is this local cadre's thinking man. The neighborhood *Zuama*, the *Zaim*, the reigning brains. The Chef.

The request only annoys him. "We just gave you a book. You read too fast. You must make it last."

"Muhammad. I'm dying by seconds here. By tenths of a second. Milliseconds. Nanoseconds. My mind . . ."

He exhales, a single stale laugh. "What is it that you need to read so badly?"

You deliberately misinterpret. "Oh, a nice, fat novel would be fantastic. The fatter the better. Something meaty. Something nineteenth-century. *Moby Dick. War and Peace. Bleak House.* Whatever you can dig up. I'm not fussy. I'll read anything. *Canterbury Tales. Pilgrim's—*"

"Do not play the fool."

Something stiffens in you. Ready to go to war. You will not apologize for wrongs committed against you. This room is where your life will likely end. Safety means nothing anymore. You feel no need for a softer, later death.

"If you're only going to dribble out one title every time I break down and grovel, at least give me something I can read again and again. Something with some real estate to it."

"You do not know how most of the world lives."

"Muhammad, a book costs nothing. I'll pay you back with interest, after you release me."

He flashes at your taunt. "You want us to give you presents."

"Look. Look around you. See my luxury suite. See the presents you have given me." It makes you giddy, this flirting with destruction. This parading in front of the beast that will kill you without the slightest accounting.

His voice leans in to you, falling. "This is not your country. This is not a pretty hotel on the beach for rich, white foreigners. You are here for a reason."

You feel your hands fly up toward the sound and snap its neck. The speed of this rage, its easy closeness, scares you worse than the worst they have done to you. It comes out of you. You tear it off like a crust of bread. Press your thumbs into his Adam's apple until it crumples: all over for you, the eternal boredom, the annihilation, the endless, empty hell of self-loathing.

"I am here because I am a Westerner." A suicidal one, who thought the war could not touch him. Who walked into this massacre with open arms.

His silence flows outward, marvelous. "How many Westerners do we keep?"

"You tell me."

"You may count them on your hands and feet. Twenty, twenty-five, maybe. Not all belong to our group. For any one Westerner, a hundred Lebanese are in prison. Two hundred. Sunni, Shiite, Druze, Christian. Thousands of Lebanese hostages. How many of these prisoners get the books they ask for, do you think?"

"How are they held? Are they alone? Can they talk to each other? Can they tell each other stories?"

More silence. It can have only one source. He is thinking. Thinking about what you say. Hands that wanted to crush his esophagus now want to embrace his shoulders. The first conversation. The first real talk you've had for more months than you can remember how to say.

"What is it that you need from these books? What can you learn from them?"

How can you tell him? On every urgent page, in every book born of human need, however flaccid, puerile, slight, or wrong, there is at least one sentence, one where the author is bigger than the writer, one that sheds the weight of its dead fixations and throws off the lead of its prose, one sentence that remembers the prisoner in his cell, locked away nowhere, victim of the world's shared failure, begging for something to read.

"I . . . I can learn from them how not to be me. For an hour. For a day. You are crushing me, Muhammad. I need someplace to go. I need something to think about. Somebody else, somewhere else."

"Go here," he commands you, touching your sternum. "Think about what is inside you."

"I can only think about that . . . for so long."

"We have a saying. Everything in life is imagination. But in fact it is reality. Whoever knows this will need nothing else."

"I need . . . someone to talk to. I need . . . to hear someone else thinking."

"Mr. Martin, do you believe in God?"

The syllable is one of those auditory hallucinations manufactured from the faint puffs of artillery barrage in the air outside your crypt. A phantom, bizarre query, like the ones Gwen floats you sometimes, as you toss sleepless on your damp pallet.

Can he really be asking this? You will tell him anything he wants to hear. Tell him about your mother's youth, her feats of religious memorization in a foreign language, beating the Qur'an against her chest in public processions, that believer's life she led before landing in the Hawkeye state.

"That . . . that's not the shape that my . . . astonishment takes."

Silence stretches out between you. A small preparation, readying you for the coming moment when silence will be total.

The year makes its lurch toward spring. Your rear right molar begins to throb. The Chief, the big one, whoever he might be, ignores all requests for a dentist. There are no dentists. Dentists have ceased to exist. All dentists have fled this city, taken themselves off to the Anti-Lebanons, to airier altitudes—the mountains beyond the mountains.

You take to killing your roaches and assorted vermin, shipping their corpses out with your dirty dinner dishes. A ceiling leak wets the corner above the radiator. Over the months, the steady waterfall cultures a green-algae streak running down the length of wall. The slime necklace threatens to continue down the nape of your neck.

You point it out to the latest phantom on the far side of the blindfold who comes to feed you. "You see that green stain?" Hoping, behind your blindfold, that you point more or less in the general direction. "You must get rid of it. A man cannot live this way. It's unclean."

But this guard doesn't even bother to return the traditional *bukrah*, the annihilating *inshallah*. The rage of countless months courses up through the veins in your neck and spills over.

"OK. That's it. I've had it. I'm not paying you people a sou more in rent until you make a few improvements around here."

There is a silence as wide, as violent as history. You brace for the coming punishment. Then the voice of Muhammad says, "We are taking it out of your salary."

They come one day to make you submit to a haircut and shave. For the better part of a year, you have not looked on your own image. You don't need to. For the first time in your life, you can see your own hair and beard without benefit of a mirror. The effect must be something like a bad painting of Christ on velvet, only a little more Middle Eastern than he's usually depicted. It has been one of your lone comforts, to twist a five-inch hank around an idle fist for hours at a shot.

"No thank you," you tell them. The hair has become a source of strength, extruding daily out of your follicles. Your Samson fantasy: power proportionate to its untended length. The plaster behind the radiator has gone soft with heat and damp, and one well-timed, concentrated shove will one day push the soggy Philistine temple down on all of you. Your hermit hair, your curling strands of beard have become your private project, the sole vestiges of growth in a growthless place. Your visible badge of defiance, your rosary of focus. The measure of your captivity.

"Not to worry. I don't need a haircut just now."

They advance in a group, at least four of them. One of the voices you have never heard before. The others speak an Arabic in front of this stranger that denies even knowing you.

"Honest, gentlemen." You giggle. "I would prefer not to. I would prefer not to."

They unlock you and prod you to your feet. Their touch incenses you. They will *not*; they have no right. You push out blindly, shoving the hands off you. The knot of them falls back, startled by this madness. Then the zeal of retaliation, of method released. A knee jacks into your back, shattering your kidney and sending your spine into your stomach. One of them goes for the head, batting with the butt of a piece of metal that, even as you fall and ball up, you realize must be the electric shears.

It is over quickly. They drag you out in the hall, under a lamp. Crippled all the way down into your rearranged gut, you stop resisting. Three of them hold you pinned, while the fourth tears into you with the croaking shears. They prune your secret strength back to your skull, your scalp clipped repeatedly in the electric blades. Your face follows, beard more ripped off than severed.

They deposit you back on your mattress, continuing to vent their rite of group rage as they shackle you back up. Sobbing will not stop, nor your body quit convulsing. No food comes that night, or all the next day. No one comes to let you off the chain for exercise. When you reach up to feel your head, you feel only raw hide, patchy and diseased.

You lie dead for two days. You cannot open your left eye. Something in your abdomen has ruptured. Pain immobilizes you. Your pelvis has been smashed under a boulder. Even making a quarter-turn on the mattress ruptures you. Holding still is a duller agony, but lasts much longer.

You try to talk to Gwen, but you cannot raise her. Her image can't seem to hear you or tell that you're there. But then she can. She is crying. It seems to be for you. And then it isn't.

She is crying, because she is thirty-two and her life means nothing. *I'm a worthless, divorced waitress who's ten thousand dollars in debt. How can you stand being around me? You know what I should do? I should do something with my photography. I'm thinking about going back to school in the fall. Art school. You know what I've always wanted to get good at? Acting. You know: I can write pretty well. I've been thinking about doing some reviewing for* The Reader. *You know, they run these ads? Training to be a dominatrix? Men who just want to be disciplined a little? It's completely safe, they say. And it pays incredibly well. And it won't cost me a dime, except for the photo portfolio.*

Look, Gwen. I live in the real world. What you always told her, every time around. Horrified, you can't keep from repeating it. *I live. In the real world.*

She looks at you: This is the love that is supposed to improve my existence? You want me to believe *what*? You want me to live *where*?

She's right. This is no place to be caught out in.

Your hemorrhaging organs refuse to kill you. Nothing will put you out of your nausea. There is no misery strong enough to save you from consciousness. The world you live in demands that you eat again, that you recover, that your patchy, bloody fuzz grow back in.

The guards seal you off, except for your morning trip to the latrine. Even there, they rush you, cutting your allotment to six minutes, then five. They shove your meals through the cracked door in boats made of newsprint. No one bothers to come collect the leftover gristle.

Then, three weeks after your beating, when you can walk again and even do some light stretching, a present arrives. A forbidden transcript, dropped into your lap. Apology, chastisement, correction, discipline: you don't care what it means. Its thickness suffices, its mass, its heft, its length. A volume to be read no end of times. Words that can take you out of yourself. A book for those who believe in the unseen. The world-changer. The Reading. The holy Qur'an.

34

Loque sat entertaining Klarpol, in the safe haven of morning. *You know that our director used to fly military aircraft?*

Adie did not know. She knew nothing of importance.

Never in combat, as far as I know. He picked up the whole virtual environment bug from his exposure to it in the Air Force. One of the first generation of pilots to test out the Head's-Up gear. You know: where they project the instrument display as a graphic, right onto your visor? Man, I'd kill for a gig like that. The chrome, the leather . . .

The Air Force? The United States Air Force? They're into this stuff?

Loque cawed at her. *What planet core are you living in? The Air Force was building simulators a decade before you were born. Before digital. Whole film-wrapped rooms that pitched and yawed as you swung the stick around.*

The Air Force wants make-believe?

Everybody wants make-believe. It's the most powerful leverage over non-make-believe that you can get. By now, the Air Force must have toys that would blow our little Brownie box camera out of the skies.

But why on earth . . . ?

Come on. Use your circuits, girlie. It's a whole lot more cost-effective to let the little gunner boys kill themselves a few times in synthetic space than to have them all baptized under real fire. Hardware is cheap; wetware is what runs you.

Good God. Something issued from Adie that couldn't be called a laugh. *I'm working for Dr. Strangelove. Again.* She closed her eyes and shook her head. One palm flew up to supplicate, then gave up and fell back to her lap. *My dad was Air Force.*

Did he abuse you?

Ab—? No. No. Not . . . in so many words. Why do you ask?

You ought to try abuse sometime. I mean, on the receiving end.

Adie looked at Loque, the eyebrow studs, the chains and bangles, the new tattoo of barbed wire that had recently sprouted around her pale biceps. *Your father?*

Loque flicked back her grenadine hair. *It's what they do.*

No. Mine was too . . . too absent for anything like that. He got the dagger in in other ways. I went into art just to spite him.

Sue's head rocked back and forth. *Can't spite those guys. Can't fight the Air Force. Dad holds the patents on anything we might want to throw at him.*

How did he end up in industry?

Fearless Leader, you mean? Freese? You get too old to zap things, they turn you out to pasture.

God help us. Retired Air Force. What does he want from me?

Nothing much. Just wants you to design a world that will wow the press corps and excite the greater purchasing public at the same time.

I'm dead meat. Nothing we might possibly design can hope to . . . Compared to what the public already imagines, anything we make is going to seem like an inflatable jerk-off doll.

Hmm. Sounds like a killer app. Lot of folks are looking for just that.

Help me, Sue. You're my only hope.

Content's your department, babe. I'm just a tool guy, myself.

Oy, oy. Adie gripped her head in the vise of her two hands. *You're telling me that the boss was a fighter pilot, before he became himself?*

Sue nodded with vigor, her nose rings flapping happily.

Do you know about Karl Ebesen? Adie asked.

What about him?

About who he was, in his former life?

Sue shrugged. *We all want something from the machine.*

It messes us up, Adie decided. *It really screws us over, representation. You know that?*

Of course it does. Whatever hasn't been totally fucked up already.

The upgraded hardware was back up and running. The bit pipes that served each wall quadrupled again in throughput. The recompiled visual development software ratcheted up its efficiency, shoveling ever more data with fewer cycle clicks. It was the old Ben Hur galley-rowing trick with the tom-toms, only with semiconductors standing in for galley slaves.

Cavern time became that much harder to come by, now that real time became real. O'Reilly was first to get up and running with a new native-code version of his price-prediction model. He showed up on the shores of society one day with a startling announcement. *Within the next half a dozen months, oil is going to take a severe hit.*

Rajasundaran rose to the bait. *A hit? In price, you mean? Will that be up or down?*

Up. Significantly.

How do you know?

This is what the numbers indicate.

Yes, yes. Rajan gave his exasperated Tamil imitation of patience. *But for what reason do the numbers indicate this?*

Oh. The reason? That's not a question the model is capable of answering, just yet.

Nor did any model predict the hit that O'Reilly took first. It came in a letter from Belfast, surface mail, and insufficient postage at that. It had been a long time making the crossing and sat in his letter box for a few more days before he came home from the labs long enough to check. The envelope bore Maura's handwriting, but no return address.

He set the envelope on the kitchen counter while he poured himself something to drink. Liquid carrot: a delicacy peculiar to these United States. He looked at the thing, picked it up, held it to the light, set it back down, and took another swig of root juice. Maura always used a return address.

Unless she no longer had one. Perhaps she was already on her way over. Had given up the flat on impulse, had commenced shipping everything here. Such was the way she operated, that Maura. She had a gift for living with both feet, a zeal that came free with her high coloration.

O'Reilly set down the carrot juice and hunted around in his silverware drawer. He turned up a tiny paring knife that he'd earned as a lagniappe for sitting through an entire cutlery demonstration at a warehouse supermarket. He coaxed the blade under the envelope corner and sliced cleanly across the top lip. Pinching the corner open, he tweezered out the single sheet of note paper between his third and fourth fingers. He smoothed the message out on the kitchen counter and bent over it:

Ronan. I'm going to be married. You don't really care, do you? His name is Stephen Powys and he runs a bicycle shop in Hen's Lane. You make one crack and I'll wring your neck . . .

Stephen is probably no you, but then again, you're no you, either. At any rate, you're not here anymore, are you? We don't really need your blessing, but you'll give it to us anyway, if you aren't a total shit. Either way, I figured you'd want to hear . . .

He'd failed to predict the obvious: a new return address that he was not privileged to know.

O'Reilly refolded the note and slid it back into the perfect slit. He slashed the last slug of carrot juice with one clean backhand into the sink. He could not sit. He found himself outside, in front of his apartment building, heading west—the American bearing. His pulse rate set the clip, and he fell in with it. The real brilliance of this country lay in its square blocks. You could circle at random and still be exactly where you were.

She ought to have come out. Just once, just for a four-day, no-obligations, sample tour. If she had taken even a single look at what they were putting together, she would have seen. This work would overhaul the terms of human existence. It was his chance to partake in the discovery of fire. How could she think that he had any choice in the matter? Accuse him of selfishness or neglect? Everything he worked on here, he did for her.

They might have made a life out here, built a common house from the ground up. They might have laughed like idiots together, from their aerial perch above this magnificent, navigable panorama. She ought to have come help him map the infinite mystery of the subjunctive. But she chose instead to serve him with this, the indicative's last word.

Odds were good that he'd live to see at least the rough outline of embodied thought, the first human passage into living, active graphics. By the end of the day, he might even be able to travel to any spot of the hypothetical panorama he cared to visit. Only now, there was no one left he cared to travel with.

On the fourth swing past his apartment steps, O'Reilly ascended. He reentered his cavernous flat, the one he'd picked expressly because it was large enough to absorb the ridiculous proliferation of pointless stuff that Maura so loved to accumulate. There he pulled from his collection of a thousand years of Western music the one disc that was to have been their recessional music after their run down to the justice of the peace, whose address they'd have found in the Yellow Pages on the morning when they knew they wanted at last to do the silly deed together, for all time.

Mr. Big, of course. Because they wanted the best available blessing, and Maura could always have put on her beloved pennywhistles afterward. Cantata number 197, one of the wedding ones. A bass aria, for *nach der Trauung*, rolling in innocence, sung by a bass whose perfect, amused intonation declared that he had never lived anywhere but here, his vocal cords squarely at home in the bungled, compromised, roundly resonant place nearest to hand.

Ronan lay back against the folding card-table chair — he'd have pitched it instantly on her arrival — and let the text wash over him.

> *O du angenehmes Paar!*
> *Dir wird eitel Heil begegnen,*
> *Gott wird dich aus Zion segnen*
> *Und dich leiten immerdar.*

O you most delightful pair, he tried, padding out the words to preserve the meter. *May you every blessing find; may the Lord shine forth His Mind.* Not quite, but it scanned. *May all happiness caress you, and the Lord from Zion bless you.* Closer. May life all comforts bring you, and may God from Zion ping you. Wing you. Whatever.

In the rippling sequences, Ronan counted up all the partners he had ever had, every woman he'd ever slept with or sworn promises to, the ones he'd truly loved flush up against the ones he'd loved less. The ones he left without ever knowing. The ones who left him for a whole range of reasons, declared and undeclared. The ones who had cut him off from all wherewithal. The ones whom he drove stark frothing mad simply by being who he was.

He numbered them up in a dimensioned array. Then he counted Maura's. All the ghosts and goings-on she had ever told him about, and the ones he knew strictly through inference. The ones she replaced, and the ones she replaced them with. The lunatics and stalkers, the thugs he'd had to hustle out of the foyer, the dead little Michael Fureys he could never hope to compete with, the ones who stood under her memory's window in the dark rain, tossing pebbles at her pane.

Then he followed the list out to the second degree. All the partners that his ex-partners had partnered off with. And then Maura's, as far along as he knew them, inventing no one, leaving no one out. Couples split and divided and multiplied in front of him, pairing off and propagating in the well-lit room, a runaway chain reaction. He lost count, then took it up again.

He stopped at a hundred and forty-four, a heavily dividable number in anyone's book. Then he lined them all up, making a provisional seventy-two couples of them, leaving room at the altar for all the unknown permutations—a melee of brides and grooms, brides and brides, grooms and grooms—and married them off in one mass, cult American wedding while the bass rolled on through those pure, practical Bach sequences:

> Oh you sweet, delightful Pair,
> May this life its blessing send you,
> May the Lord always defend you
> And preserve you everywhere.
> O you sweet, delightful pair!

O'Reilly raised his ethereal stemware of now-imaginary ambrosia and toasted the pair in question, across a distance that no amount of technology would ever be able to close.

Somewhere near that night, Adie Klarpol ran aground on another song. The notes trickled out of the renovated Cavern like bats from an underground fissure at sunset. Plunked out, badly sight-read, the melody arose more honored in the breach than the observance. What only charity could call the arrangement consisted of a series of chuffed block chords, groping fingers having misplaced their fake book shortly after the last salsa-soaked hora. But no crime the interpreter inflicted on the notes could hide that tune from her.

The song seemed engineered by a dramaturge as clumsy as the musician who performed it. The tune itself meant nothing, an empty variable. Adie alone knew the width of its old reference, the trace that the intervals meant to untie.

Something in the amateur rendition stopped her, something beyond music. In mid-phrase, the choppy string orchestra gave way to a brass choir. The tune swelled and scudded off, elsewhere, down a farther spectral corridor. The notes spilled from some hammerklavier of speculation, the action of its keys so latent that each attack seemed to follow its own decay. No earthly instrument made these sounds. She needed to see the instrument that did.

The aural trail cracked and faded as fast as the bad performer manufactured it. Adie followed the tune down to the Cavern's mouth. She pushed open the Cavern door, as quietly as she could. There, as she expected, Spiegel labored over the shaky performance. But the concert instrument that he performed on shocked her out of all expectation. For there was no instrument.

Stevie stood swimming in a cascade of virtual menus. But his arms and fingers played upon nothing. Sound came out of the surrounding speakers, pitches that matched the movements of his hands upon the evacuated space in front of him. Spiegel looked down, studying his pantomime like the worst of beginning sight readers. He stared at the nonexistent keys as he flubbed at them, as if the added concentration of staring at the invisible might force it to behave. Ivory lever and felt hammer were but algorithms tripping upon empty air.

Adie stood in the doorway, fixed by this *danse macabre*. She swore out loud, and Steve turned. The spin of his shoulder set off an involuntary glissando. He whipped back to the anti-piano, taking a few dissonant pokes to find the pitches again from out of the cubic vacuum in front of him.

She crept closer, a chimp in front of its first mirror. Stevie fumbled through what remained of the tune, managing to cadence cleanly back on the tonic. In the silence, Adie applauded, stately stunned claps not for the keyboard technique but for the scary, technological bravura.

Spiegel bowed, a bobbing Prussian virtuoso, heels together, brusquely acknowledging the house. He beckoned her into the room and offered her the hidden toy to tinker on. He fit her each finger with a discrete position sensor and turned her loose. *Take it, Wanda.*

She felt out a D-minor chord in first inversion. She shook her head, admiring, repelled. *Too strange. Too freaking strange.*

You heard it here first, Stevie said, addressing an audience as invisible as the conceptual Steinway. With a few blinks through the floating menus, he patched her sound into a steel-drum band.

Aiy, aiy. Too spooky.

"Spooky," Spiegel repeated to the mock Carnegie Hall. *It's a technical term.*

But the familiar spacing of white and black keys fell into place under her fingers. She blasted through that two-finger exercise, the thing that even transfigured souls must noodle out at least once on eternity's Schnitger: chopsticks.

Care to deliver a road report to our home audience?

Something about the persistence of his shtick, his performing tone, alerted her. She turned toward the object of his chatter. Amid a golden age still life spilling a plenitude of worldly goods—null modem cables standing in for peeled lemons, flat panel displays for gutted shepherd's pies—a small black box sat watching them. A compact videotape recorder, about the size and weight of an ancient transistor radio.

She stared at him, a single, withering accusation. *Who are you taping this for?*

Spiegel's face contorted, caught. Who else? The same audience he'd been performing *Dives and Lazarus* for in the first place. He faced the lens and pointed at her. *What are we going to do with this woman?*

She stripped off the motion sensors and handed them to him. In the same smooth curve, she was back out the door of the Cavern lab. He didn't even bother to call to her. From the hall, she heard the words of his camera monologue falling away to silence.

The apology call came late that night, even later than his first recruiting call to New York, years before. She let the machine take it.

That wasn't an ambush, you know. I didn't ask you to . . . I didn't know you were going to walk in on the middle of taping. Look. What's the big drama? I erased it. Redid the whole thing from the beginning.

She picked up the receiver. For a long time she said nothing. *I hope you hit more notes the second time.*

He, too, slowed to largo. *Hopeless, aren't I? Well, he can use his imagination. It's more of a concept piece anyway.*

She snorted, and let it go. *So what's the story? Are you in regular touch again, or what?*

Depends. How regular is regular?

Are you telling him . . . everything we're doing out here? You tell him that I look old and spent and wasted?

And full of sleep, Spiegel echoed. *And nodding by the fire.*

That I've become a bloody-minded bitch?

You know how I am about the truth, Ade.

She blessed the telephone for not broadcasting facial gestures. *Stevie, tell me something. Whose life do you think you're writing, anyway?*

Oh, I'm not particular.

Just so long as the story has a happy ending?

Across the wires, there came only raw spacer.

Stevie?

Ted's . . . not good. He's had a bad falling off. He called a few nights ago, from the nursing home. I thought it was a crank call. Even after I figured it was him, I thought he was putting me on. Not his voice. Not his sentences. It took him two minutes to get through six words. And you don't want to know which six.

She closed her eyes. Kept them closed while she said, *Yes. I do.*

On the far end, a harsh exhale. *"Come out now. If you want."*

Adie clutched the line's silence to her ear. Soon she would need to make a sound, just to keep whoever it was, out there, tied to the other end. Every available word was a small death.

Spiegel spoke first, his voice veering. *I figured I'd make him, you know, a little piece? A little show, for light diversion? I don't even know if he'll be able to watch the fucking thing.*

Stevie? Are you going out?

Go? Out there? His voice caught at each consonant. He'd never considered the possibility. *To Ohio?* Vaguer, less reachable than any invented dimension.

I could go with you. She matched him, daze for daze. *I've been thinking. You're right. Whatever room we end up making here? It's going to need a score.*

The plane out to Cincinnati was almost empty. Having rushed to make the flight, they waited in the airport, waited on the runway, then waited in midair. Adie stared down through her smoky Plexiglas portal onto the crumpled sheets of the Rockies below. Stevie watched her staring.

All back projection, he told her. *You know. They put a few massive hydraulic jacks under the so-called plane, fake the dips and pressure changes, and treat us to the chroma-keyed Refreshing Landscapes tape out of the New Age catalogue. When the tape runs out, they fire up the fog machines.*

Her eyes stayed fixed on the panorama. But Spiegel needed to chatter. *People are way too mobile,* he said. *You know that? We run up the frequent-flyer tab like we're buying bagels. Look at us. Three thousand miles for a long weekend. On an impulse. My parents would be scandalized. They needed three weeks just to implement a two-hundred-mile bus trip.*

Not us. Adie addressed the back-projected Rockies. *We flew everywhere. Langley, Khorat, Chanute, Okinawa, Germany. Bounced around like pachinko balls, on an hour's notice. Half the planes I flew in as a kid didn't even have real seats.*

It's not right, you know. It's institutionalized schizophrenia. Close the door on Seattle, open it three hours later on Cincinnati? Guaranteed to make you nuts after a while. Something's wrong with full mobility. We need some obstacles. Places we can't get to from here.

At last she turned, her eyebrows mocking the peaks below. *My, my. Scratch a technocrat, find a Luddite. You're putting in seventeen-hour days trying to develop the matter transporter and you're saying we travel too much?*

His head sagged on its ball joint. *The whole point of machine imitation is to venerate the original. This . . .* He waved at the scandal of a cabin. *This turns the original into a cheap tart.*

Later, somewhere over a featureless jumble of felt-colored rectangles, she asked him, *How did you do that?*

An hour had passed since they'd last spoken. He squinted at her, unable to figure the antecedent. Adie stuck both hands out toward her drop-down tray and jiggled her fingers in the air. Pantomiming the pantomime.

Oh. The ghost organ? The looking-glass harmonica?

She waited, not even nodding.

All the parts were already in place. The position trackers. The waveform lookups and instrument definitions. The sound generators. The only new thing I had to write was the formal description of a musical keyboard. You know: if a finger passes through the plane of a key surface, x centimeters along the horizontal axis, go and get an F-sharp, and play it until the finger lifts or the envelope decays, whichever comes first.

Formal description? That's all?

That's a lot.

She put out her palms sunny-side up. *How complicated can it be?*

He reached out and touched a finger to her near earlobe. She did not recoil. *Tell me how to cook an egg.*

Cook . . . ? Well. Boil a quart of water —

Hang on.

What? Oh. Fill a medium pan with a quart —

Wait.

OK. Find a pan.

Ah! Now you've almost broken it down to the level of a complex subroutine. If pan exists and pan not in use and pan not dirty then for each cabinet of kitchen, search cabinet-sub-sink for pan, and so on, for another couple of hundred lines of code. Else if pan . . .

She nodded a fraction of a millimeter, forestalling elaboration. Then she coughed up a thought two years in assembling. *Software is the final victory of description over thing.*

He held her declaration in midair, turning it over. *With software, the thing and its description are one and the same. Any item that you can learn how to say, you can make, pretty much out of raw syntax.*

Saying and making . . .

. . . are one another's night jobs.

Wonder and disgust vied for control of her voice. *So that's why we want to do everything over again in software. Why we all want to move there.*

Well, it's no worse than words, really.

What are you talking about? It's a lot worse than words. It's words on steroids. Words are safe exactly because they're so fuzzy. Deniable near-misses. Give them teeth, and every teenaged thing that you ever regretted saying is out there drunk behind the wheel of the Chevy.

They went on speaking, trading their widest words since their old, disowned ones. But east of the Mississippi, Adie fell sullen with memory. Soon they began their descent, the return to all hurt and hostility.

They made their way from the airport on total improvisation. Adie drove; Spiegel navigated.

He knows we're coming in today? she asked, as they headed north along the state highway.

He did yesterday.

Rural Ohio rolled past the windows, lone farmhouses on their hillocks, each at the center of their few hundred acres. She fixed her eyes on the rushing cornstalks. Everyone's nerve cells were decomposing. Everyone alive. It was only a question of rate.

The nursing home stood a hundred yards from the site of the failed Shaker utopian community. Every original building had vanished. No plank of that old, spare ecstasy remained behind. Adie and Spiegel parked and walked up to the single-story brick building. Nothing distinguished this particular purgatory from the identical geriatric holding tanks that every town over ten thousand inhabitants tucked away somewhere, behind an eight-foot hedge. A waiting room for the abandoned: the last place any infirm would want to land.

Just past the foyer, a group of shattered bodies formed an enchanted circle around a TV set. On the screen, the National Little League Championship played out in silence, the sound track muted without the audience noticing. Heads bowed forward over their walkers in a silent prayer ring, their cracked-vellum faces poised for some sign.

Why is it, Adie asked, under her breath, *that the later in the day, the earlier a person falls asleep?* She blessed the enchanted circle as she and Spiegel pushed past.

They found their way down an ammonia-flavored corridor to the nurses' station. There they asked for Zimmerman. They found his room and knocked, but no invitation came from within. Stevie turned the handle and pushed. The door swung open upon their own invention. Bed to the right, bed stand to the left, unshuttered window in the middle. Only in this world, the artist was still at home.

Ted lay in bed, strapped to the raised headrest. His arms wavered in the air like dried seedpods on autumn's first breeze. The bewildered bulge of his face took them in, mouth sagging, eyes fleeing back into their wells of bone. Age and incapacitation had added thirty pounds. He'd grown a mane, like Beethoven's.

Ste-ven Spie-gel. The four syllables spread out over so long an astonishment that they lost themselves, like the word "Asia" on a good-sized globe.

Then Ted saw Adie. And her name took so long to come out that it never did.

Their embraces glanced against a body that could not manage them. Ted's limbs thrashed in grief and gladness. At last they settled, like stormed water seeking its level in the ocean's permanent bowl. Words were past considering. Then there was nothing but words.

They spoke of the flight out and of their luck in finding the home. *We knew this had to be the place,* Spiegel said. *The Welcome Wagon of catatonics up front gave it away.*

Zimmerman hauled back and sucked air. He seized up, a cracked ignition failing to turn over at thirty below. It flashed through Adie to call for a nurse. But Ted, in agonizing slow motion, was only laughing.

What . . . the hell. Am I doing . . . somewhere . . . like this? Can you . . . imagine?

Adie could. Could imagine. She wanted to tell him not to exhaust himself. Not to try to talk. Ever again.

On the bed stand where the washbasin should have been sat a portable computer. A wheelchair faced the lone window, looking out upon a bird feeder. Three drab sparrows flicked about in the seed. A day in this room would turn their bickering into top-drawer Verdi.

Against the left wall where the towel should have hung stood a hands-free reading podium. A book lay under its acrylic plate, pinned open like a museum butterfly. An automatic page-turning device beneath the acrylic waited with infinite patience for the thrash that commanded it to advance the story. The book gaped open at a chapter reading "Meditation Four: What God Can Properly Give."

Spiegel's eyes fell upon the deus ex machina. *No. Tell me it isn't true. Don Giovanni gets religion?*

Ted seized up again, the silent, sucking sound of freeze-frame mirth. He tried to grab Spiegel by the arm and address Adie at the same time. A little more myelin and he might have pulled it off.

This . . . man and I . . . have known each other . . . forever.

She held his eyes. *And you and I, a few days longer.*

The two males fell to remembering. The composer, his grasp on yesterday growing tenuous at best, reached back fifteen years and reconstructed all their old arias, note-perfect. Spiegel kept pace, as if this one-upsmanship of detail recovered from oblivion actually gave him pleasure.

Adie sat listening, eviscerated. When she couldn't make out Ted's words, she made them up rather than ask him to repeat a single vowel. The boys talked on, memories feeding on themselves, for in the end, there was nothing but reworking the one hope chest full of stories. For a while Adie walked around the room, groping every object she could reach. She looked over the small library of CDs, a medium invented since she and Ted had lived together. The tune that she searched for cowered there, among the others.

Do you listen much to your discs? A decade and a half of dodged questions, and this was the thing she chose to ask. She bit her tongue and hoped for a yes. At least some pit orchestra, to accompany the endless afternoons of sparrow-bickering.

Not . . . as often as you might think. They're hard to get to. Hard . . . to load.

She knew what "hard" stood for. "Hard" was the last euphemism that dignity left him.

Lunch came. A tuna salad for the resident, and a cube of Jell-O for his guests to share. Steve and the nurse, with orchestration from Zimmerman, moved him from bed to chair. Adie watched. TeraSys robots moved with more mobility and coordination. The body that had warmed her once, that she had warmed, now flopped toward its target like hardened rubber.

The nurse hovered. *You want some help with your food, Ted?*

He waved her off, the arm a brutal flail. *I will lunch alone with my friends. With whom I have not dined for some time.*

His fork performed a bravura, involuntary loop-the-loop. Steve, suppressing a laugh, started to choke on a bite of tuna. Ted flailed at him, and his fork hit the rug. This second fling sent celery chunks flying in all directions. The boys were both hysterical. And then they weren't. That long, wheezing suck of air that each previous time had turned into a laugh veered into another place.

Adie stepped into the breach before she even knew there was one. She pulled her chair flush against Ted's and took up his jettisoned fork. As if she had done it forever, each day of her adult life, she stabbed a chunk of tuna and steered it into this lunging little chick's mouth. Ted opened, received, and swallowed, also knowing the drill. Her free arm went out and encircled him, steadying the bull's-eye.

So how about that Little League World Series? she asked him. *Something else, huh?*

The corners of his chewing mouth pulled up in an almost controlled rictus.

Lunch decimated, the composer confided in them about his new project, just under way. A last-minute sprint to the finish, something midway between setting Scottish folk tunes and heaving up an Opus 111. The work lay hiding inside his portable computer. Spiegel fired the box up for a look. The full score appeared on the screen.

Spiegel cleared his throat in shock. *Chamber orchestra, Ted? Where are you going to find a chamber orchestra to play contemporary music these days? Or is this another soap-company commercial?*

Zimmerman howled. *Look at it. Read the notes, you Philist* . . .

Adie came up behind Spiegel. The two of them inspected the score, trying to turn the armada of formal symbols into a symphony for the inner ear.

How are you entering this? she asked.

It seemed one of the nurses, an amateur pianist, occasionally came and took dictation. It took Ted almost a full minute to say as much. *She's also . . . something of a . . . piece. It aids . . . the composition process . . . to have someone . . . to impress.*

The visitors traded disbelief. The man was dead up to the waist, with the tide rising. But something in him still pursued the conquest, long after conquest could be of any use.

I'll take some dictation if you like, Steve offered.

Ted's eyes went round and terrified: *Would you?*

Just don't try to cop a feel while I'm at it.

Adie stood to go. *I'm taking a walk. My bit to aid the creative process.*

She came back an hour later. Stevie swung around at her entrance, utterly panicked. His look accused her: Where have you been? It's hopeless. Hopeless. She came over to the screen. They'd added no more than four measures.

We're going on an expedition, she announced. *It's gorgeous out there.* She crossed over to Ted and draped herself around him. *You'd like that, wouldn't you?*

His eyes fled back into their place of wonder. *I . . . would . . . indeed.*

They dollied his wheelchair down the linoleum hall and through the rec room. The circle of charmed TV viewers now sat in communion over an extinguished set. No one objected to the fact that the screen had gone blank. At the sight, Ted sucked air in through the sides of his mouth—*eeegh . . . eeegh*—and Adie accelerated him out the front door.

His spectral wail only crescendoed, once out in the open air. Everything in this scared, small town that could possibly stare at him did. All Lebanon gawked at the man in a wheelchair, bellowing at this chance gift of freedom.

Adie leaned down to Ted's ear. *Sotto voce*, through the side of her mouth, she giggled, *Now, Grandpa, you fucking control yourself or we're taking you back to the can.* This only made Stevie pick up and propagate the horse laugh.

First time, Ted tried to say. *First time in six months.* Not fifty yards down the asphalt, he cried out, *My God!*

Adie slammed the wheelchair to a stop, bracing for crisis.

Look . . . at that . . . tree!

They turned toward the midsized maple that Ted's wavering arm stalk seemed to indicate. Steve and Adie looked up into the boughs, searching out a source large enough to rate the alarm. The branches drifted, a crowd of thousand-palmed arms waving callow-green, three-fingered salutes.

I've never . . . seen anything like it.

And then, looking, neither had any of them. Matte, shiny, then matte again as the wind flipped their surfaces, each leaf semaphored a single bit in a composite message too large to read. The trio stood until self-consciousness set in again, blinding them.

The cedars of Lebanon, Spiegel pronounced. Adie shoved him. *Good Christ, there's another one!*

They were, in fact, all over the place. Cheap and eager miracles, too common to look at twice. The wheelchair rolled slowly up the street, under that greening canopy.

It took some pushing to get to town. But town ended as soon as they entered it. Thirty-two places in the United States went by the same name, half of them having started existence as utopias. Texas alone boasted three of them. This particular Lebanon now existed, to the extent that it could be said to exist, as a theme park version of itself. The Glendower Shaker Museum. The junk-turned-antiques shops, the fleabag hotels upgraded to bed-and-breakfasts for weekenders escaping Cinci or Columbus.

Main Street ran its eight blocks before giving up the ghost. The expedition came to rest at Main and Broadway, awaiting the rapture, which, when it finally came, would surely be at least this quiet. Zimmerman swung his arm in a resounding upbeat, Adie's cue to cut up to Pleasant, circle around, and start the whole loop over again.

I can't believe it. It's all still here.

They never let you out? Spiegel asked. *Never take you for a spin?*

How could they? Too . . . label-intensive.

They ran the meager gauntlet of storefronts, Ted narrating the tour. *Good place to eat. Place I used to do my laundry. This . . . guy still fixes shoes. Can you imagine? A hobbler!*

Air spit out of Spiegel's pressed lips. *Cobbler, buddy.*

Unless he's a bad one, Adie offered.

Cobbler. That's what I said! Followed by the rasping inhale, the *eegh* of uncontainable glee at this, the black comedy of his existence.

Adie weighed the size of the two ratios: New York to this prop town; this prop town to the nursing home. Which was the farther fall? She was not good at math. Her private calculator tape rarely gave the same subtotal twice. But the answer to this long division was obvious. The second drop-off made the first seem level. The next drop would be no problem at all.

They rounded the loop again. On the third pass, revelation flagged. The thick, supernal gift past deserving now only fatigued them, at least the two doing the pushing. Spiegel broke first. *That so-called good place to eat. Want to give it a try?*

I do, indeed. And I hope that . . . woman we saw is still . . . sitting out front.

Spiegel and Adie traded glances. There was something supremely cruel to evolution. Desire survived the purpose of its burn.

In that public place, Adie again rose to save them. She ordered for Ted, spoon-fed him, and wiped his face without a trace of patronage. She helped the waitress clean up the glass that Zimmerman's lunging backhand managed to swipe from the table. And she ate her own meal as well, all the while holding up her end of the conversation.

Ted asked about her work out West. She described the magic lantern show, in detail.

I've told you about all that stuff, Steve kept interrupting. *Over the phone. You remember.*

Clearly he didn't. Also clear that Ted could make nothing of the sketch Adie now drew for him. But she carried on gamely, the only strategy ever available.

We're supposed to demo for the general public next spring, and I haven't a clue as to what we should be building.

Spiegel laughed. *She says that like she's saying, "I don't have a thing to wear."*

Ted just stared at his two lost friends, ecstatic with bafflement.

By the time they rolled back down the long hill to the home, darkness had settled in. The old folks were watching a video blooper outtake show, gales of hilarity pouring out of the set. The instant they got back to his room, Ted blurted, *Put me . . . on the bed.*

Neither healthy body knew what was happening. They worked the badly distributed sack, Steve under the shoulders and Adie at the knees. They floundered, slipped, and banged his deadened torso against the metal sides of the hospital bed, at last getting him more or less supine, face-up, and centered.

Pull down my pants.

Spiegel punched him. *Jesus, Zimmerman. Will you never change? Hurry!*

Thickened with emergency, Adie spent whole milliseconds wondering how they'd avoided this moment until now. She dove under the bed, the likely hiding spot, and surfaced with the bedpan.

Just put . . . just put me . . .

Between the two of them, they figured out the logistics. While Ted mewled in agony, the cause lost, Adie and Steve lifted his naked middle and slipped the pan underneath him.

I'm sorry. Humiliation bubbled up, broken, from Ted's throat. *You two. I'm so . . . sorry.*

About what? Adie rubbed his shoulder, looking away from his worthless, bared groin. *We got you.*

I'm in? His eyes retreated deep into their stunned corners. *I made it . . . ?*

She nodded.

Oh. His voice relaxed in a wave of wonder. *Oh! What a . . . good . . . day.*

How does he pay for the single room? she asked Spiegel, on the way to their own motel that night.

Steve had fallen away sharply from jovial to grim, the minute they left the home. *He made a fortune on those sell-out TV ads. The beatific Shaker rip-off. His thirty seconds of tonal recidivism.*

She closed her eyes, hearing the beautiful tune against her will. *That cash can't possibly last much longer.*

Neither can he, Steve said.

At the motel check-in, she surprised him. *One room,* she told the desk clerk. *With two single beds.* She turned to Steve. *Hope that's all right with you? I'm not sleeping in a strange room by myself tonight. Not after that.*

Nothing separated them but a bedside light. *My God,* Spiegel whispered into the dark. *The man can't go to the bathroom by himself. And he's still . . . he's still . . .*

Don't say it, she said.

Each faced the other's wall, silent for a while. *You know?* he said at last. *No lesson in life cripples me worse than "life goes on."* And he fell asleep.

She followed, mere hours later.

Adie dawdled the next morning, first in the shower and later over the complimentary continental breakfast. It crossed Spiegel's mind as well, just how many eternities they could knock off the tally simply by showing up a few minutes later.

When they arrived, Ted was waiting for them, agitated. *I woke up with this weird . . . idea. That you said something yesterday. About building a cave?*

Adie embraced him where he lay. *A Cavern.*

Technically speaking, Spiegel added.

Why would anyone . . . ?

Haven't you watched the tape I sent you?

Ted flailed in the direction of the TV room. *I don't go out there much.*

I spent weeks slaving over a hot workstation cooking that up for you, and this is the thanks I get?

Spiegel found the video on Ted's shelf. Grateful for the diversion, Adie collaborated in dragging Ted out and commandeering the set. And so the nodding, enchanted geriatric ring looked on at their first working demo of virtual reality, a new galaxy beyond their combined ken.

Steve appeared on the videotape, making a few off-color comments that no one, Ted included, seemed to decipher. Then he stepped into the Cavern and fired it up. He took a spin through the Crayon World, then the Weather Room, then the Jungle.

What is this? a blue-skinned, beaked woman asked. *A travel show or something?*

I seen one of them, explained a man attached to a tube of oxygen. *It's got to do with special effects.*

On the tape, Spiegel set the controls for Arles.

I did that, Adie said, holding Ted's flapping hand.

I . . . thought it was . . . Van Gogh.

Then the taped version of Steve booted up the invisible organ. His hands played upon air, and a deeper air issued from them. Ted sat forward, transfixed. Here at last was something one could learn from. They'd forgotten to attach his belt restraint. Adie had to reach over to keep him in the chair.

I need . . . one of those. But one . . . that doesn't need hands. Ted wanted to see the instrument again. He asked for a third look, but the rest of the audience shouted him down. He rocked his head all the way back to his room. *That's . . . the thing I'm going to be playing. Any month now.*

Somehow that day passed faster than the last. Time's aperture stopped down to match the stunted bandwidth. Steve took more dictation. *F . . . sharp. No. Make that a G . . . flat.* Even the simplest wholenote triads required endless revision.

Adie watched. Through the window, at the contested feeder, the sparrow industry worked out its continued survival, eating and excreting, twitching and chattering, inventing each minute from scratch.

They rolled Ted out to the terrace, hoping to store up the outdoors in the cells of his body. He asked for a windbreaker, despite the warmth. He seemed happy just to sit and look, without any walls to jam his focal length.

Spiegel, workless now for longer than he had been since college, paced in place. Already he wanted the airport waiting lounge and the flight back to Seattle. *So what do you do all day? How do you fill the damn vacuum?*

Ted's eyes opened wide. *For the last few weeks . . . I've been trying to remember . . . the name of every woman I've ever . . . enjoyed.*

Spiegel all but spit his teeth across the terrace. *How many of those that you enjoyed did you actually . . . enjoy?*

Not . . . many. Ted avoided looking at either of them. *I'm just trying . . . to put my story together. Where I was . . . when. I don't know.* Half a minute passed. *And why.*

Done, Adie laughed. *And it's taken me less than forty seconds.*

Ted stared at her, that look of myelin-stripped panic. *You knew . . . all of them?*

Not yours, you idiot. Mine.

Oh. Ted's grin worked against the width of the disease. *Oh. In that case . . . I wonder if you could help me with . . . the name of the cat woman?*

Spiegel tucked his face under his arm. Adie smiled sweetly. *You asshole.*

The . . . cat woman. You two . . . know the one I mean?

The three of them sat loosened by the breeze, looking over the accumulated wreckage of the past that still, somehow, seemed worth enumerating.

They didn't brave a restaurant again that evening. Instead, Adie ran out for candles and wine, a decent BV Napa cabernet that they drank out of paper cups. By dinner's end, there seemed nothing left to say.

Steve, as always, broke first under the silence. *Well. Shall we have a listen before we go?*

A . . . listen? Ted's face shrank in horror at the possible meanings.

To the chamber symphony, man. What did you think I meant?

The chamber . . . ? How?

Steve pointed at the computer and whirled his finger around in space—the obscure sign language for whirring electrons. *Through the magic of semiconductors. How else?*

Oh. It flooded Ted's voice, a bitterness so great that only an immobilized soul could survive it. *Oh. I thought you meant a real listen.*

But a fake listen would have to do, for the fake was all they had. Spiegel loaded the piece, set quarter note equal to sixty, clicked the cursor on the first measure, and released the synthetic music.

Notes spread over them in the dark, notes in a constellation that no one could have guessed came out of this man. The sound stunned Adie, even in the synthesized clarinets and trombones, even in the tinny approximation of inch-wide speakers. This music was not Ted, not any Ted either of them had ever known. It had no edge, no irony, no flamboyance, no demonstration of academic credentials. It was *tonal*. Standing waves of continuous, proscribed modulations outdid even *Dives* in luxurious archaism. Music meant nothing, except by convention. But this massive parallel data of pitches in time turned her viscera in a way unreachable by any paraphrase. There were things so complicated that only the ear could know them.

Sound snaked around itself, pointless and beautiful. The shaped sound counted for nothing. It demonstrated nothing. It proved nothing but its own raw need for a redemption that, finally, could only be denied. Something in this music had been lost in transcription. Some impediment to Zimmerman's conception brought about by the disease. Some inability to write what he meant, dictating through the ether while lying in bed.

But a look came across Ted's face as he listened. The music came as close to conception as the encumbered process was ever going to let him come. At last the piece trickled out, stumbling through the incomplete measure that Spiegel had transcribed that very evening. And when the chords decayed, the piece still abided in the night that scattered it.

Ted's eyes pleaded with the two of them. His mouth latched on to a sudden rush. *If I could just finish all four movements. It's music . . . that people might love. That people might think about and . . . feel. Not like that alien stuff we all used to make . . .*

You'll finish, Spiegel said. *And then you'll write something else. Because this one won't please you anymore.*

Yet, Ted corrected. *Won't . . . please me yet.*

Give us a minute, Adie ordered.

Spiegel's head jerked back. *I have been asked to evacuate,* he told Ted. *Goodbye. Farewell. Take care. Write if you get work.*

He walked without looking, out to the front room, where a ballroom of white-tied aristocrats swirled to the strains of a Strauss ländler. Near the door, a doubled-up woman, trembling against her rocker in time to the meter, hummed a descant to the ghost dance's tune.

Adie reappeared, pumice-faced. *OK. I'm done. Let's get out of here.*

Nothing outside could touch either of them. The rental car was their cocoon, a safe capsule heading north in the dark.

Were you aware, Stevie said to the Ohio night, *that a huge percentage of the population eventually gets sick and dies?*

Adie stared at the ribboning road. Finally, in a voice the color of that hypnotic pavement, she said, *Denise Girandel.*

Denise Girandel? Nothing. Then: *Denise Girandel! How in the name of hell did you dig up that one?*

She shrugged. *How many cat women are there in one person's life? Why didn't you tell him?*

I wasn't about to give the bastard the satisfaction. A mile went by. *Besides. Trying to remember gives him something to do all day.*

They pulled up at the motel. Spiegel sat still in the passenger seat, the motor dead. *You two should never have gotten divorced. You know that, don't you?*

Whatever you say, Stevie. Then, softer. *It's not that people shouldn't get divorced. It's that they can't.*

Hours into the night, she came into his bed. Looking for something— an explanation, a barricade, another mammal's pelt.

I'm not going to hurt you, she said. *I just need to lie here. I just need to hold someone.*

Holding lasted no longer than holding ever does. But when it came to the things she needed, hurt and hurting were not least among them. She kneaded into him, as if the thing she had to release lay on the far side of a wall, just out of her reach. She ground against him, less in pleasure than in desperation, in search of some permanence she meant to work on his body. She forced into him, desperate to press all shale to slate. He tried to say her name, but she put her fingers into his mouth, gagging him with desire.

Whatever release she wheedled out of the contact had nothing to do with him. He was just the nearest body, the closest living thing that would hold still. She fell off him finally, spent, holding him so that he could not turn to embrace her.

For the longest time she did nothing except to lie beside him on this single motel bed, returning to the unbearable baseline of sixty beats a minute. Then she reached over, her hand cupping around his face, a child playing guess who.

By the tips of her fingers, Stevie felt that his temples were wet. *Remind me,* he said.

She rustled up close to his ear. *Remind you what?*

Once out of nature. To look for something better than this body.

She stroked his temples, counterclockwise. Each trace around the circle undid one spent year. Then she placed his words—the past, the poem that he was quoting. Her fingers clenched. *Go on,* she commanded. Desperate. *Say it. Say the rest.*

He could not refuse her anything. He'd given her worse, more irreversible, already this night. His own voice rang strange to him, speaking into the black:

Once out of nature I shall never take
My bodily form from any natural thing,
But such a form as Grecian goldsmiths make
Of hammered gold and gold enamelling . . .

Her hand closed on the skin around his eyes. Her nails clenched, as she pressed back into him. He held still in pain, ready to be blinded.

That's it, she whispered into the gaping motel room. *That's the room we're supposed to build.* And set upon a golden bough to sing. *The place we're after. Byzantium.*

35

In time, whole days start to vanish. For a long while the orderly egg carton of the calendar has regulated your mind, kept it, if not productive, at least aligned. But now the carton starts to crumple, the eggs to break against one another in an angry omelet.

You carry on numbering the days, desperate for form, although the tally no longer correlates with anything. The week arrives when you can't make it from one Friday call to prayer to the next without disorientation. It pulls you up out of a night's sleep and runs you under the freezing fire hose—this drift into terror, into utter timelessness.

This room's day permits only the crudest clock. Sometimes it is dark; sometimes a little darker. The only reliable instrument here is your English Qur'an, that earthbound perjury of heaven's uncreated original. Its pages solidify into a discipline, the rigorous training for a track meet you must get ready for. Reading is your daily regimen, each session coming to a forced stop after ten verses, wherever that leaves you. Whole *surahs* dangle right before the end, or break off bluntly after just starting. Only the count counts.

You may reread the day's passage as often as you like, but not a word more. When the hours expand beyond their usual cruelty, you pore over the opening *fatihah* until it induces oblivion. But you keep to the day's installment. For tomorrow, after the forced march through the latrine and the return to the chain, this system will return you to the previous outing's exact stopping place, to start you up again in the slot where today has dropped you.

This ritual hammers out a few still moments to stand in. It steadies the swirl of eternity, for as long as the verses last. This time you ration yourself, sustain the escape. The Cow, the Bee, the Table: just the mystery woven into these chapter names diverts you from hovering madness. However reconfigured this Jonah, this Joseph, this Abraham, they make their way against the backdrop, under the Thunder, out from the Cave, along the Night Journey. *Say,* the words of the Prophet always start. *Say: were the sea ink for the words of God, the sea would fail before the words did.*

The verses themselves evade you. Their linked riddles will not crack. But the torrent of words, their sense-free cadences suffice to hold you, even in the absence of story. Their pageant of sounds drowns out your own incessant dunning. The throwaway phrase "and the water-bearer let down his bucket" expands in your eyes for hours, sounding in your ear for all the world like a soul-saving miracle, the most magnificent idea, the roundest image you have ever stumbled on.

But the secret side effect, the contraband payoff must never have occurred to your captors. They've already broken one divine prohibition in giving you this forbidden foreign translation in the first place. Surely they would confiscate the Scripture if they suspected the scope of its revelation. These measured-out passages keep you tethered in the flux of time. If you start at the *fatihah* and sum the verses you have read, then divide the total by ten, the quotient yields, by the miraculous dictate of numbers, the total number of days that have passed since you received the word. This is your new perfected calendar, dating not to any fixed year but resetting all dates to your own private *hegira*.

Most days, the balm of this word hoard outpaces the torment of its rationing. But sometimes balm and torment settle into a dead heat— starting and stopping, sentences and silence torturing one another to death. How have you been brought to this, staking yourself to the same book your mother once committed to memory without her understanding more than one in a dozen words? You reopen the wounds that that victim once inflicted on herself. *Did you think to enter paradise without suffering the violence of those who have come before you?*

They tame the abyss, these verses, better than any parade of orderly notches in the wall plaster could. But they cannot repair your own damaged mainspring, or synchronize it. When you return to the well of text, passages that you recall from adjacent days now stand split by several pages, while those separated by weeks in your memory run flush against each other. This evidence hits you, like a freshly discovered lump in your abdomen. You and lucidity have been parting company without your knowing. Mind has been resorting to the quietest drift, a protective hallucination finally gentler than the alternative.

All you can do is stay grappled to the book's planed planks, hoping that after each breaker, the timbers you've lashed to will bob back to the surface. The only recourse, when this morning slips loose, is to tie it to ten more verses. You listen in to the archangel Gabriel, dictating to the Prophet in his subterranean cave. This story extends itself only in hinted wisps, as if all readers already know the plot. But the more gloriously cryptic, the better. Each ten-verse maze holds you longer than the Sunday *Times* crossword ever did.

You search through the book, for a larger architecture, some forward motion that could pass for form. But the verses possess only the most astonishing organizing principle. The chapters proceed from longest to shortest, starting in prose and ending in prayer. Still, it swells, this staggering dialogue: God, His Prophet, and the cast of broken humanity, in a three-way game of telephone where only endless repetition forces the words to correspond with what they figure.

You lie in the Prophet's slime-laden cave, taking the complete dictation all over again. Say: *I seek refuge in the Lord of the daybreak, from the evil of what He has created; and from the evil of the night when it cometh on; and from the evil of the blowers upon knots. Say: I seek refuge in the Lord of men, from the evil of the whisperer, from jinns and men.*

You do. You say what it says to say. Out loud. You recite your *fatwahs* and divinations for a live audience of the word-starved. Chapter and verse. Forward and back. No one comes to tell you to break off. *Verily, man is in loss, save those who believe and do right, and bid each other be true, and bid each other be patient.*

For a long time, talking to the book is conversation enough. Then the book runs out. You restart the careful system of mental tick marks from the top. But this time through, you already know what the *surahs* hold. And all those repeated commands to *Say, Say* at last force you to take the ideas live, into the realm of surprise, of real listeners.

You target the simplest, most religious of your keepers, the next time he lingers over a delivery. "Sayid, doesn't the Prophet say that you must never steal?"

"Yes." His only available answer. For lying, too, is forbidden.

"The man thief and the woman thief. Cut off the hands of both of them, as punishment, for they have done very wrong. An example from Allah, for Allah is mighty and wise."

You grope for the book, hold it out, open to the Table. He takes it from you, but of course hands the tainted, unreadable translation back to you at once.

"Yes, Mr. Taimur." As grave as the world at issue.

"But you have stolen me. You have stolen me from my life, and from my mother, and from my . . . family. This is the worst theft of all. How can you do what the Prophet has told you never to do?"

You hear the man crumble in silence. The surf of faith crashes against the rocks of duty. You curse yourself. But you are ready to do worse.

"Mr. Taimur, I cannot know. I ask Chef. Tomorrow. *Inshallah.*"

As if you've asked for another haircut. He comes through two days later, to let you off the chain for your run. He says nothing. You wait until your half hour of exertion ends, and he replaces the iron ring on your ankle.

"Sayid, did you ask the Chief about . . . stealing?" You hold out your hands, the ones whose severing Allah specifies as punishment.

"Chef say not to talk to you. You think like a snake."

A snake and worse. A squid. A dung beetle. A human. A creature that would live at all costs.

"Sayid. Walter-jan. How much do your people pay you?"

He does not answer. However much he grasps the words, he does not understand you. You sense him fling his palms out, helpless.

"How much do you make? Twenty-five dollars a month? Thirty? You come work for me. I give you forty."

You cannot rouse him, even to anger. Getting him to kill you, for the moment, is past hope.

Deliverance almost comes, on the day you stop wishing for it. It begins one evening, during your thirty minutes of exertion off the chain. Gaunt legs work their oval until you find yourself logging a few hundred meters more than usual. You soak up a dozen bonus laps, exulting in this sudden increase in strength that leaves you able to shatter all previous speed records. But soon the laps so completely decimate your old personal best that something must be wrong.

You slow to a fast walk and take stock. Furtive reconnoitering near the door discloses nothing, no exceptional noises in the corridor beyond. The best explanation of this miracle is the most prosaic. Whoever was supposed to put you back on the leash tonight has forgotten his place in the rotation. The tick of the thirty-minute clock is finally silenced. Infinite freedom descends on you by accident, and leaves you no choice but to seize it.

You walk all night, a forced march through the checkpoints of crippling fatigue. You cannot squander this supreme windfall, not so long as life lays any claim to you. The epic trek leads off in the dark to parts foreign and unreachable. All those tucked-away peaks and archipelagos that you've never had the leisure to explore now stand naked. Liberty — a whole night in which to rub up against every degree of variegated plaster in the full three-sixty—unfolds with such grace that all bitterness at it having to end gives in to a larger awe.

All night long, wonder refuses to vanish. Unrestricted mobility. Crouching, cantering, contrapposto, tiptoe: all postures enter the available repertoire. North and South return, and East and West with them, dragging along every skew axis. Amazement, here in the pitch-black passages, is a tactile thing, feeling its way along the smooth-bore corridors into open defiles of feeling that you haven't allowed yourself since the earliest days of captivity.

With movement comes memory. A string of shuffle-ball-changes carries you back through a packed cocktail party of tongue-tied Japanese businessmen. Four hundred incredulous stutter-steps take you to the muddy crocus beds that your industrious girlfriend once caused to stud your lawn.

You lie down flat in the middle of this Grand Ballroom. You pry at the lip of your wall of sheet tin, searching for stretches that haven't been stapled down. You drop to the ground in front of the sliver under the door. Up close, through the slit of this science fair experiment, you can see the whole universe. The feet of your captors take turns on the watch, standing sentry over a suite of cells, cells that hold the lives of those taken along with you.

Hour by hour, the gift expands. You take possession of more room than you know what to do with. Free, at leisure, you pace back and forth across the gaping eight feet. You take up residence in the corner farthest from the radiator, pressing yourself against the far walls, sniffing their surface. Then disbelief shoves you on again, to more discovery. A strangeness spreads over you, one awful enough to seem the reason you were taken. Never again will you gainsay anything, or chafe against your allowed radius, or take a square inch for granted . . .

Daybreak's first covered strands are the cue to slip back to base camp. You lie waiting, acquiescent, on your bed of straw when breakfast arrives. They will see, in this harmless creature, how little need they have for the redundant lockdown.

But the sight of your freedom drives your guards insane. Bodies fly shouting through your room, enraged. Shadow puppets, through your blindfold, rush around in clumps, testing the lock, searching your clothes, slashing at your mattress with knives. How far do they think you could have gotten in your overnight excursion?

Voices lash at one another, spitting through their teeth like cornered rats. A feral, crazed face pulls yours up to it, its breath chamoising your cheeks. "How you do this? How you get out?"

"Please. I did nothing. The guard never came to lock me up again last night."

They haul you to your feet and slam you down again. A knee swings up, smashing your genitals against the back of your pelvis. One spongy testicle smears against this vise of bone. The wave of red shoots up through your spinal column and comes out through the seams of your skull.

Even unconsciousness cannot protect you. Each time you wake, the pain sucks you back under. You come to at last, your face in a pool of vomit, the half-digested dinner from your evening of liberation. The Qur'an can't tell you how long ago that was. Scores of verses pass before you can straighten up and stand.

By the book's count, they leave you on the chain for a full month. The day they take you off again, your atrophied flesh collapses after four slow drags around the oval. Two more weeks pass before you can lift your knees without puking.

Then, late one evening run, your laps closing in on their old target, it happens all over again. The half-hour trot widens into three-quarters. Once more, you feel the awful accident of freedom. The day's meals have all arrived. No one else is coming. Six mobile hours could easily build back half the muscle you've lost.

But there's something too casual this time, too obviously cat and mouse. A test of last term's lesson. A blatant taunt. A cheap trick to justify another beating. Anyone might barge in, at 2 a.m., to catch you *in flagrante*, flaunting your freedom. They are huddled, even now, over a hidden peephole in these walls, to catch you in the very instant of joy.

Sick and beaten, worse than an animal, you return to the padlock and submit. You close the loop tight around your own ankle. The metal clicks; your eyes swell with humiliation. The hate you bear yourself exceeds any that you can feel for your captors. They have their cause; you have nothing. All self, all dignity, sold. All night long, the pathetic dose of freedom that you deny yourself snickers at you from the darkness. Debasement complete, you bare all your openings to the rape.

36

They flew back to a Sound rearranged in their absence. Adie forced Spiegel to come home with her the night they landed. To her island cottage, her safe haven. Once might have passed itself off as an accident. Twice had to mean something. But still, she wouldn't tell him what. And he wouldn't ask, afraid she might tell him. Willful ignorance could still pass itself off as anything.

With nothing but touch, she unlocked a loft inside him, boarded up since college. He made love to a long-dead invention, she to the only person who loved her ex-husband more than she did. Sleeping together became a dare, a mutual suicide pact to cast off the last drag of ballast and lose what was left to lose. To raise loss to the level of high art. To scatter projection to the winds and push the past down into pure aesthetics.

They clung to each other as if it couldn't be obscene, so long as neither looked. Spiegel broke the pact of silence first. Less than two weeks after their return from Ohio, Adie logged in to her Cavern workspace. There, a missive in a bottle waited to ambush her. It launched itself from a niche in system memory that Adie thought had been empty. She scrambled to don a pair of stereo glasses. Beyond that, all she could do was stand and watch.

From out of nothing's well colors rose up. Specks of light off at various horizons rushed toward her from a slew of deep-space vanishing points. Space expanded along all axes at once. Her body succumbed to the pull of conflicting vertigos while the sky around her scattered with novas. Each star migrated to its own slot on the spectrum, only to split again into something fuller. The bursts bent closer over her, fireworks drooping back to awe their earthbound audience. Their flares passed a threshold of definition where she at last made them out: descendants of that first wire-frame leaf that Lim had made for her. Cut blooms from her abandoned jungle.

Petals rained down into the space around her. The full weight of the bouquet pressed against her eyes. She laughed at the trick, astonished. She flashed in anger. How dare Spiegel steal her tool set? The vector-drawn blossoms drew near, blowing away all pretense of ownership. These growths weren't hers to copyright. Even Rousseau had stolen them from too many sources to start counting now. Every human mark was mortgaged to the hilt.

She stood in this petal shower, someone's gift to her, someone from whom she had only taken. The day was coming, faster than these fireworks fell, a day when anyone could give shape to their innermost space and leave it on another's digital doorstep. All our private declarations of long love would come home for inhabiting.

The petals expanded until they had no more place to grow. Adie stood surrounded in a circle of stamens taller than she. The corsage grew bigger than the room that held it. The walls flashed pink, dragging her below the tissue surface. Still the view zoomed in. She passed through the cell wall and into a sea of cytoplasm, ever deeper down, punctuated by chaotic phase changes at each shift in gauge. Skeins of biochemical skeleton, pirated from Bergen's Molecule Room, rose up around her.

At last she found herself in another jungle, the flowers now huge colored spheres of amino acids, their entwined stems a dance of protein chains. The molecule bouquets bobbed on all sides of her, eager in space, whichever way she turned her head. And up flush against her, whispering binaurally close to her ear, the voice of the man who'd made her this living card said, *See what a flower I have found you!*

Darkness brought her back. When she again located the size of her own body, she used it to walk out of the Cavern and down the hall to the man's cubicle. Steve sat at his own workstation, toying with variable declarations.

It's beautiful, she told him.

She dropped herself into the scoop of plastic next to his desk that passed for a chair. The race that engineered the Cavern could not design a chair that comfortably fit the shape of a seated human being.

She shook her head at the colors she still saw. *So fast,* she said. *So quick.*

Adie! How long have I known you? How slow do you want to go?

Oh. No. Real blood shot up to crimson her face. *Not that! I mean, you built that . . . piece so fast. A few days.*

He leaned forward. He put his hand to her mouth, palm flat, as if he were blind and gazing on her for the first time. *I used one hundred percent existing parts.*

It felt by turns sacred and profane. A man lay between them in bed, dying between them in an unattended nowhere, having lost the last control over his body. They both made love to him.

I lived with you so long, he said to her, in the dark. *My whole adult life. Every year, you seemed more solid to me. And every year, I felt less real. I thought of you for so long, I felt myself becoming you.*

She let him talk.

She brought Pinkham, whenever she came to stay the night with him. *Love me, love my dog.*

Oh, I love your dog, all right. I haven't decided yet what to make of you.

And sometimes, stretched in bed, he'd watch her transported, tranced out, waiting on the edge of herself for the rapture to come, steering her whole body with telekinesis toward climax, moving herself the way she had once, as a girl, moved the shutters of that painted room.

Release would plunge her into a postcoital abyss so profound she would burst into tears, lost in the depths that such filling opened up. It was the greatest sadness that life offered, consummation.

It's nothing, she'd say, trying to keep her devastation from him. *It's not you. It's just physiology.*

Do you want . . . not to do this anymore?

You quit on me now and I'll kill you.

And sometimes, after they lost themselves to their bodies and lay slack, he'd look out to see her surreptitiously flexing her fists, balling and sloughing her thighs, as if to prove she still could. Recovering those moves for the one who had lost them.

Once, as they made slow, memory-stricken love, the phone rang. The obedient answering-machine speaker broadcast a message so thick and garbled it seemed a prank call. *De . . . nise . . . Giran . . . del!* Triumph blazed from the petrified voice.

Stevie tried to stop, all the sadness of existence pressing down on the small of his back. But pressing upward against him, Adie kept him inside her until their plosive end.

She held her own little memorial service in advance. It could not happen at home, now that another lived there. And the lab, of course, was out of the question. That left only the infinite outdoors.

She bought a battery-driven boom box, skulking through the purchase as if she were buying child pornography. She hid it in the backseat of the Volvo, and took it up into the strip of woods on her island's northwest coast. She parked off the road and, with a little judicious trespassing, made her way out of public earshot.

There under the canopy — *Look at that tree! Look at that . . . tree!* — she held her wordless service. She played it once through, the shameless bit of ravishing nostalgia Ted wished he could have written but would never be able to. Tribute, buyoff, plea bargain, indulgence: she could not say what the archaic song sounded like, except that it sounded like him.

Before *Dives and Lazarus* could exhaust itself once more, she heard a person coming through the undergrowth. Despite her precautions, someone had heard. There was no place left on earth far enough away to be inaudible.

She thought to hit the Stop button and scamper off before she could be caught. But the tune still had a few measures to go, and the sound of its cadence made her ready to suffer the consequences. A gnarled, bearded lumberjack in a red plaid shirt and jeans came through the thicket, glaring at her. He slowed his arrival to coincide with the music's end.

She launched into her apologies even before the last note died away. *I'm sorry. I'm on your property, aren't I? I was just . . . It won't happen —*

Thank you, the man interrupted her. *I'd completely forgotten that that piece existed.*

With one stray word, they had stumbled onto the Cavern room Adie was after. But they could get no farther than that word. Together, Spiegel and Klarpol brought their lone clue to Vulgamott.

Byzantium? As in the empire?

Adie nodded her head. Steve shook his.

Byzantium, as in the Yeats poem, Spiegel said.

Ask O'Reilly. He's the Irishman.

Well. Ronan eyed them. *It's not really my favorite of his poems, you see.*

Which is?

"*Meditations in Time of Civil War?*"

He pronounced the word to rhyme with "far." The Americans studied one another.

Buy you a pint if you recite?

You could have gotten it for free, woman. But it's too late now.

They went over to The Office, where the standing suite of TVs offered the full range of available data streams. O'Reilly parked them in a booth in front of the drive-through news headlines. Apparently history was still in the throes of ending. The largest, most heavily armed nation on earth was cracking apart, apparatchik by apparatchik, scattering its warheads into a host of makeshift republics. Western experts were fanning out through the Eastern Bloc, ministering to the total economic disintegration by doling out shock therapy.

The beers arrived. O'Reilly warmed to his. *You think the fourteenth century was a free-for-all? You think the Dark Ages were a major step backward? Amateur night, my friends. Small change. We're watching the show that those acts merely opened for.*

Spiegel laughed at the hyperbole. *Come on, Ronan. What are you talking about? The Cold War's over. The most destructive suck of resources in history.*

Well, that's your problem right there, friend.

What? You're going to get nostalgic for Mutually Assured Destruction, just because it was familiar?

It kept things in check, that particular madness. It kept those resources of yours from realizing their full capacities.

Ronan, Adie said, *I've never seen you like this.*

That's because I've never been like this.

The news cycled through its cavalcade. Europe's vacationland, Yugoslavia, prepared to repeat the unthinkable.

All right, we have a problem there, Steve conceded. *But doesn't that whole morass go back to the Ottomans?*

The Iraqis still occupied by force the world's most concentrated dome of oil, invited there by the United States, which now threatened Armageddon if they did not vacate.

Stevie fidgeted. *Well, you can't use the Middle East to prove anything. The Middle East has been self-destructing since the dawn of civilization.*

Now we know the reason for the oil price hike that my model predicted a few months ago. Too bad I couldn't predict the cause.

They'll have to back down, Adie said. *It's suicide otherwise, isn't it?*

O'Reilly pointed to her, then put the tip of his pointer to his own nose.

The news stories did not wait for explanation. They went on to describe an American prison population greater than Orlando, with a per capita cost that outstripped most Ivy League schools. Lockups, the cable said, had doubled in less than a decade, making no discernible dent in the crime rate. O'Reilly glanced over at the Americans and raised his eyebrows.

Spiegel shrugged. *We're a lawless people, Marshal. Always have been.*

Adie thumped the booth. *Hey! You promised us a recitation here. We're not picking up your tab if you don't deliver.*

"Meditations in Time of Civil War"?

Adie nodded. Stevie shook his head.

O'Reilly looked into the foam on his beer, reading the scraps of text there. *It's that bit toward the end*, he said. *The Stare's Nest at My Window.* The words, when he finally spoke them, came out in astonished starts, like a gift left on the table of an empty room, locked from the inside.

The bees build in the crevices
Of loosening masonry, and there
The mother birds bring grubs and flies.
My wall is loosening; honey-bees,
Come build in the empty house of the stare.

Each looked away from the others, into a lost place. O'Reilly on his country, Spiegel on his abandoned calling, and Klarpol on the bee-loud Crayon World.

We are closed in, and the key is turned
On our uncertainty; somewhere
A man is killed . . .

The bartender looked up at the word, that small shock in the midst of broadcast massacres.

. . . or a house burned.
Yet no clear fact to be discerned:
Come build in the empty house of the stare.

The Irishman's voice went small with exhaustion. *How does it go? Hang on. A barricade of stone or of wood . . .*

His chin jutted up to the television screen, where a barricade formed on command.

Some fourteen days of civil war . . . "Days," the man says. He sipped bitterly. *Last night . . .* he began, free-associating.

Last night they trundled down the road
That dead young soldier in his blood:
Come build in the empty house of the stare.

He stopped, unable to go on. He sat looking for something: the next lines. The next televised devastation. The next improvised technological fix. The next inadequate exegesis.

When the poem started up again, it wasn't O'Reilly. Adie jerked up at the sound of the foreign voice.

We have fed the heart on fantasies,
The heart's grown brutal from the fare,
More substance in our enmities
Than in our love; O honey-bees,
Come build in the empty house of the stare.

Spiegel sat in the bar's turbulence, lost to his private reading. The bursts of video clip pinned all three of them in the cross fire.

Ronan bent his head. *We could build anything. Anything we want.*

That's your trouble right there, Adie whispered.

Ronan looked at them, all smiles. *Whatever human ingenuity imagines that it's assembling, we must surely be getting close to the final upgrade. But you didn't come to hear my theory of history. You came to hear Billy Yeats's.*

Spiegel waved at Adie. *Our artist here has figured out that we're supposed to rebuild Byzantium. Trouble is, neither of us knows where exactly that is.*

You think the poet did? O'Reilly downed the two fingers at the bottom of his glass. Spiegel held it up in the air to get replenished. *First of all, you have to understand that the man was out of his fuckin' mind. Which is to say, Irish. The country doesn't leave you much choice. He more or less had to look for another place to live.*

Mad Ireland hurt Yeats into poetry? Spiegel mocked.

Yeah, actually. If you want to know the truth.

Adie fingered the syllogism. *If crazy countries made for poets, we'd all be drowning in verse instead of VCRs.*

The man never found a place where he could put down and live in good conscience. A place where heart and head could sit at the same table. That was his Byzantium fantasy. The zero point, the fulcrum for the whole insane machine of civilization. Sages standing in God's holy fire. The mechanical bird—tiny, gold-enameled gears and sprockets, singing perfectly, forever, of all things.

Beats the hell out of anything that Silicon Valley has come up with yet, Stevie said. *Or even the Japanese, for that matter.*

But you see, it's all the same project. That's what's so demoralizing. The thing that's best in people, the thing that wants to be pure and whole and permanent, the thing that won't rest until it builds its eternal bird . . .

O'Reilly pulled up short and hunched over. He gestured up at the broadcasting sets, the story of escalating ingenuity they spun out, a project now too monstrous for around-the-clock fiber-optic satellite coverage to catch up with even the smallest subplot. *We're all over it.*

3 3 5

O'Reilly's despair revealed itself in another collective shit-shoot at week's end. Freese called a meeting and laid out the revised timetable for the next half a year, leading up to the commercial Cavern rollout in the spring. Then he threw open the floor to the usual free-range futurism that any gathering of two or more of them always degenerated into.

Everyone agreed that the data transfer rates would continue to rise without foreseeable limit. Lim predicted they'd be able to move complex surfaces around at film quality without dropping a frame by the mid-nineties. When the curve of data compression and the curve of bandwidth crossed, people would be able to swap imaginative spaces as easily as they now traded roses or bottles of Chardonnay.

But who's going to make those spaces? Vulgamott wanted to know. *Doesn't matter how wide the pipes get, if all we're going to pump through them is shit.*

Aesthetic elitist, Rajasundaran said. *You don't think that content is also an engineering problem?*

Just you wait, Mikey. Once the Cavern develops an installed client base, things are really going to take off. Loque rolled the threat of fecundity around on her tongue tip, savoring it. *If we can get the kinks out of voice-activated, user-directed, high-level VR-CAD, virtual spaces are going to come pouring out as fast as users can dream them up.*

Vulgamott cocked his head. *And when exactly is this breakthrough slated to happen?*

By the end of the decade, Loque said.

Century, Jackdaw corrected.

Millennium, Rajan deadpanned.

Wait until the immersant starts to design pilot worlds on the fly. Clearly Loque couldn't wait. *Who knows what will come pissing out of the collective imagination.*

Kaladjian almost choked. *Who wants to live in a world pissed on by the collective imagination?*

We're approaching the point of full symbolic liberation. Free and infinite creation of imagery. Loque almost sang it, gospel-style.

What's the point? Ebesen asked. *Wasn't there enough imagery out there already?*

But reality had never been large enough, because the body had never been large enough for the thing it hosted. Where else but in the imagination could such a kludge live? The engineers carried on speculating. Human appetite would not stop short of the fully deformable universe. The walk-in hologram was right around the corner. Full-body force-feedback devices would extend illusion to the crucial sense of touch.

Electronic skin promised pleasures deeper than the real thing. Full six-direction telepresence would follow shortly thereafter, linking the mind to remote robotic agents anywhere in space, lifting human senses off the face of the planet.

Jackdaw opened up the latest hot topic—painting images directly onto the human retina. A couple of competing groups were busy honing micro-scanning lasers up to 10K by 10K scan lines, close enough to the resolving power of the retina to call an image continuous. *Now if you can get the bandwidth to flip these images at fusing rates, you can take direct control of the whole field of vision. The complete airspace . . .*

Belief, Adie said, *is not a question of bandwidth.*

Lim looked surprised. *What else can it be? That's the variable, isn't it? A question of how much symbol you can fit in the pipe at one go . . . ?*

I'm taking bets, Raj announced. *On the precise year that computer-generated worlds will first be mistaken for NSR.*

NSR? hapless Adie asked.

Non-simulated reality. You know. The secular world. All this opaque stuff.

They got together an ad hoc office pool. Everybody agreed to put up 1 percent of the pots of money they were all going to make, once their machine started selling. The one who came closest to guessing the year that simulation finally surpassed reality would win the kitty.

In the midst of the general hilarity, O'Reilly dropped his bomb. *It's all well and good for this business to have a long-term game plan. But if you're really interested in the future, you'll want to hear my latest projections.*

Having predicted, out of the blue, the current oil crisis, O'Reilly's models were enjoying a surge in market value. He invited a band of stragglers from the dispersing group into the Cavern. They stood inside his global interface, looking up on the planet's closed surface.

You're looking at the latest recursively updating map of world petrochemical production and consumption. He gave them a crash course in reading the data, the thermometer of colors from cold to hot. *We'll start in 1990.* The fractal smoke curls unfolded and refolded in such beauty that the band gasped in pleasure.

This looks just like one of our Weather Rooms, Sybil Stance said. *Like our ocean current work.*

You're manufacturing some very pretty singularities there, Freese added.

Bergen whistled. *We get these same cascade effects in the new biosim.*

The Red Spot of Jupiter, Spiegel decided.

O'Reilly ticked off the count. *OK: here's 2000.* The hots got hotter and the cools cooled off. *Here's 2010.*

He called out the mileposts without passion, having seen the sequence unfold countless times. The color zones began to break up and mix more richly. They spilled like ice crystals across a frozen pane. They swirled like paints on a child's easel. They fused like molten elements in the hearts of stars.

By 2020, all the earth's surfaces began tending toward the higher frequencies. Even the lagging continents started to heat up. The whole globe went beet red, blushing or holding its breath. At 2030, the color map staggered, stumbled, then plummeted. All tones free-fell toward blue.

After two or three attempts to stabilize, the remaining lit nations settled in around a handful of campfires. One by one, these too blinked out. Lim teetered on his feet and had to be walked around to keep from blacking out. The little band of virtual pilgrims stood in the dark, tittering.

Rajan broke the silence. *Amazing. I'd never have seen it if I hadn't believed it.*

Kaladjian gave in to outrage. *How can you presume to model that far out with any semblance of accuracy? Between faulty assumptions and compounding error, you're in fantasy land before you get two years down the road.*

You know the funny thing? O'Reilly replied. *I've run it a few hundred times, tweaking all sorts of parameters, sometimes quite dramatically. And I always get something like this.*

What about all the unknowns? Political upheavals. Crazy heads of state. Grassroots revolutions. Technological breakthroughs . . .

They're in the model.

How can they be in the model? You don't know them. That's the whole point. They're random events.

We don't know them, true. But the last thing they are is random. Those sorts of events aren't the cause of numerical discontinuity. They're the consequence.

Freese fought to look amused. *Well, Ronan. It's pretty clear what's happening. Around 2030, we develop the perfect alternative energy source.*

Then why that massive spike just before the crash?

We run out, Vulgamott asked. *Is that it? We just run out? Sustainable growth is a contradiction in terms?*

O'Reilly shrugged. *I'd expect a smoother tail-off, if that were the case.*

So it was with the groundhog race, cursed with the ability to cast its own mental shadow. No matter how dark the projection, someone always had heart left for another six weeks of the game.

At the moment, that someone was Jackdaw Acquerelli. *You know, 2030 is right around the time that we'll be achieving total human equivalence in silicon. In another forty years, we'll finally be out of here.*

Disappear into our own machine space? Spiegel asked.

Raj chuckled. *Why not? That's this five-thousand-year footrace's finish line, right?*

Maybe, O'Reilly said. *But even human-equivalent machines will need to consume some power.*

Sue Loque was first to remove her glasses and wander out of the Cavern. *To hell with it. Why should we worry about posterity? What has posterity done for us lately?*

The others trickled off after her. Kaladjian walked away clenched, calling back to his antagonist, *You realize this means nothing, don't you? Nothing at all.*

Absolutely nothing, O'Reilly agreed.

Whatever lay in wait forty years down the pike, other clients waited in line before it.

Who are they? Adie asked Stevie. *The people we're supposed to be pitching to. Who would possibly be interested in buying such a thing?*

Oh, the usual suspects. Academic researchers. The theme park people. The movie people. Whoever comes after theme parks and movies. You know: the ones who are always promising consciousness-altering, mind-meld video games in time for next Christmas.

But they'll be buying the box, right? The walls and the projector and the special accelerated graphics chips? Not . . . our rooms?

Bits sell iron. That's how it always goes. Nobody wants cables. They want what comes through them.

But still. They aren't . . . it's not like they . . . this won't exactly be a volume business, will it?

Spiegel stuck out his lip. *Never underestimate mankind's appetite for the next big escape.*

The next big escape came and sought them out. It landed on their out-stretched palms, a bird returning to its golden bough. Karl Ebesen led them to Byzantium. He told them what they were after, even before Adie and Steve could lay their meager evidence at the foot of his cubicle.

Byzantium? You mean the place where civilization wavered. The way that the world almost went.

Spiegel and Klarpol traded helplessness. *Sure, Karl. Whatever you say.*

The imperial capital. The one that kept Rome going for centuries after Rome died. The place where West almost traveled East. Or should that be the other way around?

Ebesen launched a search, knocking over his precarious stacks of sourcebooks and clipping files in the process. He located his discredited, yellowing anthology of world art, its pages halfway on the route back to ammonia.

Here's what you're after. He put his finger on a full-page black-and-white plate. *For close to a thousand years, the greatest church in Christendom. And for another five hundred years after that, the greatest mosque in Islam.*

Adie peered into the interior—hulking, mysterious, impossible to make out or take in. *This? But this . . . this is in Istanbul.*

Ebesen squinted at the picture. *Byzantium. Constantinople. Istanbul. A place like that can never have too many names.*

Or too many incarnations, apparently. Spiegel edged in for a better look. *Just church and mosque? Didn't they want to cover any other bases?*

Ebesen wagged his head at an elaboration more outrageous than the thing it explained. *Based on a pagan shrine. Built to outdo Solomon's temple. After a millennium and a half, still the fourth-largest church in the world. The Hagia Sophia. The Holy Wisdom.*

Adie stood staring, dazed by the space. *I . . . was there. Inside. As a child. When my father . . . was stationed in the eastern Mediterranean.*

And had sent a postcard to a girlhood friend of the inexplicable interior: "Make sure you see this once before you die."

They pumped Ebesen for all the details he had. They stole all his reference works. Then they went after every further source he could point them toward. Karl, for his part, had only been waiting for the call. The architectural building blocks that he and Vulgamott had for so long sculpted out of syntax and thin air now rose to the thing they were made for. The source from which those parts derived.

One thousand master craftsmen directing ten thousand conscripted laborers took half a dozen years to raise that model of paradise. The simulation team had between October and May.

Vulgamott took charge of the initial planning. *The first thing we need to decide, of course, is magnification.*

Adie stared at him, her face a blank.

Come on, he said. *Scale? How large we want the thing to be?*

I thought we'd just do it, you know: one to one?

Good Christ. Vulgamott struck himself on the forehead. *She wants it life-sized.*

Spiegel rushed to defend her. *At least we're not building in an earth-quake zone. Getting the vault to stay up shouldn't be hard.*

I don't know, Ebesen said. *The model has gravity figured in.* Thought, too, was an engineering problem. *If you want a thing to stand, it has to be able to fall.*

37

The room of holy wisdom spreads its tent beneath the dome of heaven.

Wood will not do, for its wooden parent burned. The building draws its stone from the farthest throws of empire. It cannibalizes for parts the world's great temples: columns from Ephesus and oracular Delphi, from Egyptian Heliopolis and Baalbek in the Levant.

It steals its palette of marble from the whole spectrum of imperial provinces: pink from Phrygia, Lydian gold, ivory Cappadocian, green from Thesselia, pure white quarries of sea-girt Proconnesus. Cut and dressed, the stone veins fan out to meet their mirror shapes at each facing's joint, picking up and echoing, like a stilled kaleidoscope, hints of heavenly device and earthly emblem, painted incantations, living creatures bolting through the symboled undergrowth.

The floor plan is a daring cross of conch and loggia. Basilica and hub—church architecture's two great streams—here flow together in a new confluence. And soaring above all, the dome rises to its awful altitude, climbing upward not to a point but cupped like the gentle firmament itself, a helmet resting on air, crowned in a crucifix, the world's protector.

The dome bends over a gaping hole wider than its engineers should know how to span. Nor is the day's faith great enough to make up the shortfall. The emperor himself, at the building's christening, stumbles dazed into the vast vacuum of the eastern apse, dispenses with the prepared *Deo Gratia,* and blurts out, *Solomon, I have outdone you!*

Mosaic saints man the walls at strategic points. Deep-color tile squares of hammered gold leaf dusted over a layer of glass tesserae and finished with a layer of glass paste become the world's first bitmaps. Up close, their resolutions pixilate into discrete rectangles. But from down below, at the eye's prescribed distance, the folds of a gown hang full, and faces escape the waste of history into some stilled, further conviction.

Under the monstrous dome, empire draws itself tight into a hardened chrysalis. This room will fall first to Christian invaders, absorbing into its galleries the crypts of those crusaders who pillaged it. Later, from the conquering infidels, it will adopt calligraphic Arabic disks and minarets, and a subdued mihrab slipped into the east end, tilted slightly on the axis to Mecca. Another faith will command those mosaic saints to be destroyed, but fear and awe will leave them merely plastered over, protected for blasphemous mass viewing, centuries on, in the age of global tourism.

The world's ongoing project will fling itself upward, amassing public works so huge that this one will shrink to nothing in their wake. But something in the race yet chooses to build this one, here at the world's turning point, at obscene expense, to lay out a crippling percentage of the gross domestic product—greater than the sums it sinks into any other item in its governance—to raise this fixed navigation beacon for sailors breaking apart in the Hellespont, this vast, cupped dome huddling over the destitute, this *omphalos,* the Earth's navel, its cut umbilical cord.

Ringing the dome run these words, cut there by the supreme calligraphers, this room's most recent owners:

God is the light
of Heaven and Earth.
His light is a niche in which there is a lamp,
the lamp enclosed in a globe of glass,
the globe of glass a shining star

lit from a blessed olive tree
neither of the East nor the West . . .

The room of holy wisdom is a ruin. The world's largest, as large as the ruinous world. And propped against the stripped arcades, amnesiac, disinherited, illiterate in the unreadable wreck, you pitch your home.

38

The Qur'an runs out. No more need for it; no schedule left to preserve. You find yourself sitting blanked, your brain playing teatime host to the virus that consumes it. You look down in wonder at your arms and legs, where they tremble out of control. Hours mold. Your eyes fail to latch anywhere. From far off, in this perpetual dusk, you watch yourself stare at nothing. A translucent globe of light materializes in front of you, suspended on nothing, a spirit on air. Only as it covers your face in a silk thread does it occur to you: a spider.

You curl up fetal, your chin tucked between your hands. This close to your ear, your nail, rubbing up against your cheap cotton collar with every inhalation, sounds like the bobbing of boats against their ropes at anchor. There is a creaking like the creaking of rope on wood. There is a creaking that needs gulls, that says waves, insists sea.

Shapes spawn from the room's shadows, then dissolve in the startle they produce. But livid aftertaste lingers in the spots where these phantoms flicker. You turn back into that child of eight, pulled from a deep night's sleep, three hours past the reach of reason. A boy swimming to half-consciousness in a room not his own, its lumps of furniture a forest too tangled to navigate, without measure, without bearing, where north could be anywhere and the walls are as wide as dread.

All your life, you've awakened in this placeless place. Always the same, in its alien layout. Even as an adult, you felt it come to nuzzle, this other man's interior decoration. As late as three years ago you cried out loud, a groan forced up through sleep's thick opiates, scaring the wits out of the woman sleeping next to you. Your bed, your room, your Gwen, asking, *What is it, sweetie? What is it?*

You couldn't tell her. You couldn't say. You did not yet know. Not the deep trace of infant trauma. A warning of the trauma that awaited you, a glimpse of your last, furnished efficiency, this northless one. One and the same: the room that forever troubled your sleep is this one that you finally wake up in.

The deed, the title to the place is yours now, and it's way past time to remodel. You go with a bookshelf in deep cherry, and next to it, a tawny leather sofa long enough to stretch out on. The sinister shadow that cowered for decades in the far right corner becomes a mission-style chair and footstool. A record player, neat on its cart, appears in what had once been fear's worst alcove. The swelling shelf of records crawls with your guilty favorites.

Nowhere can you find a phone. You don't seem to own one, or much miss it. Now and then there's a knock on the door. One that you can ignore or humor at your will. When it's not Ali or Sayid with your dinner, it's Gwen, come to see if you'd like to do anything.

It all feels a bit suspect, really. How nice she's being. She never had ten consecutive minutes for you, when minutes were real. Now she hangs around all the time, if only because her place is still a dump while you've done up yours to comfortable perfection.

You tell her yes, you wouldn't mind taking a walk. The two of you, outdoors, on this glorious day. And maybe you could talk, just a little, about what went wrong. Turns out your place is on the third floor. Turns out you're living in a decent neighborhood in Lincoln Park, eight blocks from the lake.

The light hurts your eyes. For a minute, you can see nothing. She understands your day blindness, and leads you by the hand. As if she has always loved you, and there is no fear between you. You walk west, along a street whose name you can't make out. Cars, bikes, and pedestrians swarm the thoroughfare. Every oak doorway, each bay window stupefies you.

She tells you about a new plan she has for making a living. She's decided to become practical. Live in the real world, like you. She's going to freelance, designing and creating business presentations. It will leave her more time. She won't be as stressed. She'll be happier, easier to get along with.

But in the same breath, she says that the stress was all your fault. You never accepted her. You never loved her as she was. She couldn't give you more than she was giving. You spooked the shit out of her. She could never satisfy you. You wanted out. You wanted to change her. You wanted an impossible synchrony. You wanted her bone marrow.

A shock rips through the afternoon air. The Howard El explodes into a blazing fireball. Then another blast, from the direction of Lake Shore Drive, the Corniche. Someone off beyond Grant Park is shelling the city. Gwen looks at you in animal panic. You grab her to you, and in an instant, you are back inside the apartment, huddled together behind the leather sofa.

Something in the scent of violence — the war, the sound of things detonating, about to be revealed — excites her. The clutch of fear turns into its other. She grips you, cowering behind the thin plaster skin that one stray caprice of geopolitics could turn into your crypt. The city is coming down around you, grinding itself to rubble, and she wants her last minutes of body. She's inside your ear, wetting it, withdrawing her tongue only long enough to repeat, *You can do anything you want with me.*

You debate the wisdom of bringing yourself off — in this, one of the rare opportunities you have to do it, the guards distracted by the greater chaos outside. Comfort versus cost, the fleeting injection of well-being versus the expense of energy in a place where dinner's pita crust and stale chickpeas barely cover the calories involved in lying still.

You decide in favor, as quietly as you can. You focus on estranging her, resolving her, posing her in the multiple welcoming and inflaming postures, the dress-ups that she never knew you wanted from her, positions she would have begrudged you had you ever suggested them. You feel the terms that desire condemns you to, the male life sentence, the need to possess the thing that refuses to know you. You need to escape tonight, more than you've ever needed any pleasure — escape not into this stranger fantasy, but out from under it. But where can the heart run to, finally, except the known? Your lust seeks out those mourning features, all her furtive Kodak poses that have for years absorbed your eyes, instructing you in her perfect confusion, drilling you in its inflections, all the familiar terrors of the native speaker . . .

At the moment that she joins her extremities to yours, her commitment is unthinking. Her grip is as utter, as unconscious as any between two needy animals. But vacant as well, absent, far away somewhere, deep in a formulating image. Who knows whose?

The mortar pounding falls off, its rounds expended. The two of you lie side by side, silent in the gulf that climax creates. Returned, you need to know. To ask her where she was just now, since she wasn't here with you.

Where was I? The question maddens her. She will not be bullied. *East Moline,* she tells you. *How's that? I was in East Moline.*

With?

With fifteen dollars. Burning a hole in my pocket.

To see?

To see a man about a dog.

Even her kindness is arch, deflecting. Nothing like a little more nuzzling to shut a man up. You have no choice but to honor her offer. You slide her toward you, prelude to your coming together again. But just as suddenly, she stiffens.

You ask her what's wrong. What you've done this time.

I don't like being moved. You're too much bigger than I am.

You throw your hands in the air. Affection is over for the evening. But your bodies stay close, flush, frayed, afraid to move away from each other into the wider chasm.

I would love to see you happy, you tell her. *I would do anything to see you at peace.*

You hear the false note, even as you make it. Love, that placating condescension. Aren't we past that yet, so late in this distance run?

Look. Gwen. Trying for softness. Trying for balance, for some good-faith connection. *I came into this relationship pretty easygoing. You wouldn't know it; I'm really very generous by nature. But you are slowly turning me into exactly the controlling, manipulative male that you're afraid I am.*

I don't think you're controlling, she states. *I don't think you're manipulative.* She dares you to call it a concession.

The world is all militias, you want to tell her. All power, factions, and revenge. There is no place else but the one place we can make.

Everything bloody and dead, except the two of us. But even that much would be begging.

I don't think I should have to second-guess myself every time I need . . . something from you.

I don't think you should have to, either.

You hear it again, her arms curling up in a defensive clinch. The bitter readiness to stay at war forever.

Truce, sweetie? White hankies? Halfway out between the trenches?

She detonates. *It's never enough for you, Tai. I am meeting you halfway. You don't want me halfway. You want me ten feet past you on the other side.*

Look. Pointless syllable, buying time until you stop shaking. *Look. Just tell me. Do you want to be with me? Make a life? Is it worth all this endless . . . ?*

A silence. Finally, she will be wide, will return, in kind, the surrender you want to give her. Finally she will leap free, meet you for that smallest mutual swap of sovereignty, the first exchange of trust you both so badly desire.

Well. Of course it's worth . . . But you make it sound like it's my—

Just say. Just say you love me. Once. Without countering.

Tai. What . . . ? How . . . ?

The rage courses through you again, as powerfully as when she spoke these words to you for real. *Oh to hell with you. Why don't you just pack your fucking antiseptic overnight bag and . . .* You swing your hand around to point at the window, or where the window would be, if it weren't sheet metal. This sealed aperture, twisted around in mental geography to align with your old southern exposure, the true-to-life direction of . . . *go home.*

Oh God. She falls away from you, cowering, as from the silenced mortar. Her voice goes spectral. Spooky. On the edge of an ocean you don't want to imagine. *You were going to hit me.*

All night long and into the following day, you redirect the scene. You adjust the mistaken angle of your backhand. You alter the words, change the pacing, fix the crooked gesture. Pay the penance of replay, summon up all the correction that editing can offer. Do everything in explanation's power to heal the misunderstanding. You reshoot everything for hours, trying to convince her, convince yourself, that the blow she ducked would never have been possible. That the anger you were feeling and the anger she saw were not the same.

Someone knocks on your door. You rise to open it, amazed to find her standing in the dingy, unguarded corridor. She has come back, in tears, wanting some better last word. You rush out to meet her. But the speed of your advance scares her, and she turns to run.

You rush after her, to prove that you can't hurt her. No guards stop you; it happens too quickly. She flees your attempted comfort, terrified. She stops, cowering, her arms above her head. You take her arms gently, to lower them from her face once and forever. She stiffens, and you pull harder.

In the flash of an instant, the tug escalates into the full contest. Now you could truly hurt her, slap her hard, to stop her struggle, to carry her back into the room's safety before the larger insanity finds you out here. And in that moment of violence, you are everything she has feared in you, everything she always knew was knocking around inside you, awaiting only this awfulness to be born.

She disappears. Throughout that dry season, she will not come back. But she leaves behind something more useful than remorse. For in that impulse chase, she has taught you how to spring from this prison down to the street below.

You pace yourself. You draw out the exercise in stages. You work up the block of Lincoln Park immediately outside your building. The goal is largesse, weight, a map on the scale of an inch to an inch. You stand still until every contiguous brick and block of concrete reconvenes. No gaps: you refuse to step down the street until every fuzzed foot fills out with casements and moldings.

Seventeen doors on your side of the street. Twelve, plus two shops and a parking garage on the other. Four stories of apartments, shoulder to shoulder, each one occupied with lives scavenging for scraps of love, scrambling to keep current, scrabbling to survive on the crust of the world's collapsing infrastructures. You move through this staggering set, a denser network than your eye ever made out when you actually lived there. Half a residential block lays out a universe so nauseatingly profuse that you need the safety of your cell even to consider it. Your Qur'an is right: the God of Creation is as close as your own jugular. And as far.

Your cell sits inside a similar hive, the hive in its own warren, the warren in a neighborhood as dense as the one you reconstruct. You try to walk abroad here, too, but every attempt fails. You can no longer resolve the school, or the faces of your students. For all the weeks that you lived there, your Beirut compound now stands locked to you. You can't even say what floor you now inhabit, let alone the size of this building. From the sound of traffic, the street lies no more than two flights below you. You try to fall quietly to this pavement, but can't. You open the door and take the stairs, but the city waiting at the bottom of the stairwell is never this one.

Lives swarm on all sides of you, through these walls, across the gully of street that the sun must surely warm and expand. Other lives live out their existences not a hundred feet from you: other Westerners, bargaining chips in a game the point of which even the principal players no longer remember. You hear their scrapings, their muffled back talk to the guards. You savor the evidence of their hurried ablutions as you rush through your own bathroom runs. But you can't see them, can't make them out.

A hundred meters farther out, two hundred, half a kilometer: your throw nets tear under the haul. Hundreds of thousands of Lebanese of all denominations live locked away in holes that bless yours by comparison, with no world superpower, however impotent, to demand accounting for their treatment. You put yourself in these streets, but they vanish beneath your feet. You've learned the ability to venture forth at will. Full-color, high-resolution. But always only Chicago. Always the near North Side, life before lifelessness found you out.

Through long practice, applied urban renewal, you fill in every surface of your former block. There you reprise your old existence, an invisible tourist, threading through the mass pageant. Incubus again, among the lives that you depended on for every particular, people that you fed off without even bothering to learn their names. What you liked to call a *private person*, a *solitary* one, all the dress-up terms for *parasite*. Now that you'd knock on their doors, enter their living rooms, give yourself wholeheartedly to your bit part in the improvised script, you can't. Your neighbors pass right through you on the street. You are the phantom you worked so hard to be.

They give you the keys to the city, abandon you to free excursions deeper downtown. You make a left on Clark and head down past the Historical Society. Jog over to Dearborn or La Salle, depending upon barometric pressure. The weather is always spring. When you stop, a Gilded Age mansion or pretty brownstone façade slides into focus. But you don't often stop, short of your destination.

The approach to the Loop, always on Michigan, picks up definition. The Hancock, the Water Tower. On the bridge, the full panorama comes back. The newspaper buildings, Marina Towers. But bit by bit, even the throwaway filler solidifies, the tumbleweed concrete thrown up in the alleys and interstices. You start to remember buildings you can't ever have registered in all your years living in this town.

But this is still not what you've come to see. You click off the last mile, down the superb stretch that the two of you took at most six times, in all your two and a half thousand opportunities to walk it together. The line of the lake opens. Buildings to the left of you fall away, leaving on your right a sheer cliff face of masonry and glass. When the explosions issue from the direction of Navy Pier, you hold them at bay. Nothing human can harm a single pane of this illusion.

Twin carved lions enlarge in front of you, proving your forward motion. The sensation is uncanny, like sitting on a stationary train while another backs up on the next track. If you can mount the stone steps, get past the coat check, the bookstore, the ticket booth, if you can climb up the grand central staircase without some street detonation or strip assault by sadistic guard, you are home free.

Once you reach that second floor, nothing can harm you. Time lies crumpled in a heap, back downstairs at the coat check. Always a footrace; you can't enter the museum except through that long walk in from the North Side. The slightest tracer can defeat you, any block along the way. But once you're here, the soul-pithing dullness of existence has no more say.

The day still advances at its old rate, but you no longer feel it. Your heartbeat races or freezes, turns on a pin, floats on a seascape, jumps through a circus hoop, does whatever you tell it to do. It trawls in the afternoon light, downstream from an old mill. It ascends into heaven with the Virgin. It dawdles, designless, at a café full of boaters. It floats in a porcelain footbath full of water.

Hours may pass in your absence. Sometimes you come back, and the gaping wasteland between lunch and dinner has vanished. Sometimes the day has not budged since you set off, and all you have to show for your weekend away is swollen feet. But so long as you are here, you are safe from both hope and its opposite. There is no long, no short, no tedium, no delay. Only the dimension-free now.

Time here is caught in the thinnest frozen section, sliced off and held to the light. At every inhabited moment, someone has needed to make these plays of line, these shorthands for *elsewhere*, for *ever*. You came here too rarely to fix in your mind more than a few dozen of these trapped eternities. But how many eternities does one person really need? Any one will fill all the space you give it.

Surviving to find your way here, you're free to range at will. You lie back in a manicured green park on what seems a riverbank. You stand on a platform in a glass-roofed railroad station, filling up with steam. Who would have thought you'd have such a memory for color? You cannot remember the color of Gwen's eyes, but you can make out the girl at the half door's, down to their nearest wavelength.

Here, in these galleries of hypothetical, your Qur'an turns its true face to you. You've failed to grasp it until now, the flash point of all faith, the law against depiction. The men who have taken you still adhere to the same ban that the West started out with — its second commandment, for God's sake. You stroll through the banned images, the forbidden fruit, heaven's stolen fire. This is the war that steals your life. Its front stretches out before you, farther than you can see. You've strayed into a factional flare-up, fluke regional politics. But even yours is just a tiny salient in the global sacred conflict, the millennia-long showdown between those who would fabricate God, forever sculpting and perfecting, and those who would suffer Him unseen.

Even being here indicts you. You're guilty, aligned. You are graven image's man, hostage for a reason. You can hope for no sentence less than the general bonfire. Imagination may be worse than the thing it would save you from. But what you will not abandon, you must live in. A place past hope. A place past place. A now indifferent to what happens next.

You press through the jumble of rooms, searching for that picture that you can't picture, the view that would make even death livable. On this upper floor, the two of you once stood looking. The simplest arrangement imaginable. Nothing: an open shutter, a few sticks of furniture. You turned to Gwen, to see what she saw. And she was weeping. Staring through wet lenses at that painted taunt, timeless and still, sadistically refusing her entry.

You should be able to summon it up in your sleep. But no; you must thread your way to where it hangs and look on it. No other way. Must have it there, in front of you, stroke for stroke.

The galleries are too many, the catalogue of old urgencies too wide. They maze you. The halls loop back inside their own folds. You have trouble steering your mental proxy. The puppet is willing but the strings are weak. Paint's apartments disappear down receding corridors, a nightmare rococo palace that lengthens with each step, its chambers filled with nativities, crucifixions, state-sanctioned agitprop, flattering bourgeois makeovers, pretty pastel picnics, nostalgic landscapes sprinkled with faked-up ruins.

Days unfurl when it feels as if you are closing in. All but there. A glow issues from down the hall, three archways away. You pick up the pace, forgetting, in your excitement, the original goal of killing time. She'll be standing, stilled and well, across this last threshold, waiting for you in the southern light, on the smooth-planked, scarred varnish floors.

Holy War always tears you back. For weeks it can leave you rotting, only to choose its moment of maximum intrusion. Ali, yearning for his school days in the States, bounds into your cell to chat about the Final Four. Some argument among your overseers, tuning their crippled TV to the latest Arabic-dubbed *Dallas* or *Knots Landing*, escalates to the brink of gunfire. Lesser sacred conflicts—a mutual suicide pact between trucks in the defile below, or the agonies of a soul in protracted illness—seep in through your insubstantial plaster. Each infliction returns you to a blank slate, to ground zero.

One night you walk clean to the goal. You come right up to it, and nothing breaks the spell. You stop in the archway, suffused by the Provençal sun pouring from the gallery beyond. You step across into this straw-colored guess, the one that made Gwen cry to look on. The peace that the two of you fought so hard to reach. Everything here has waited for you, the look of thought. Soap and water and towel, a spare shirt, a wall of tilted pictures: what more does a life need to live? The bed is a little narrow for two. But in such a room, she will want to sleep close. Here you can sit still until she finds you.

Days pass; weeks. No one can say how many, for here the hour never budges from its luminous noon. But something like time must pass, because your health returns and your reflection rallies each time you check the wall mirror. Words crawl back into your vocabulary: *safety, yellow, care.* One afternoon, a note materializes on the washstand: *Gone for a walk. Glorious outside! Come join me . . .*

Incomprehensible, then obvious. She has been here all along. Only, you've had to heal enough to see. You cross to the crooked shutters and throw them open. You lean all the way out into the light, as it has never before occurred to you to do. You turn to look for her in the sea-salt air at the precise instant that a rocket levels the building across the way. A shock wave rips through your room, bringing down the plaster ceiling and toppling the radiator, which just misses crushing your foot.

The azure walls atomize. Wood disintegrates. Plaster crashes against you. You turn to run, but falling stone blocks the way. You kick out like a horse in panic. The air clouds with debris. Shouted orders collide with each other in the mobilized chaos—all the city's muezzins crying at once. The explosion serves as a marker flare, the signal for the horizon's standing violence to hone in and go local. Beneath the blast, the screams of victims give way to a second assault wave.

The front advances to the street below you. You hear a squad work its way up the decimated street. Another squad pours from your building to mount a hopeless counter. You cower in what remains of the corner, your Qur'an tucked to your chest, the mildewed mattress pulled over you to dull your live burial.

The Marines have finally landed. The Navy Seals. The Airborne Rangers. The Joint Chiefs of Staff and hapless Central Intelligence have finally nailed the location of the Western hostages. At last they have come to stage your combined rescues, years after they should have freed you.

The assault fans out, slamming its canister rounds in all directions. The calls of makeshift chaos carry forward on the air. But the cries of the attackers take on an alien language. You listen, refusing, until refusal has no more toehold to give you. This is not the Navy Seals. This is nothing resembling your rescue.

Apocalypse settles in for a protracted firefight. Fist-sized bumblebees buzz the air, their trajectories vaporizing all objection. Death sounds like no imitation of it that you've ever heard. It is a duffel bag dropped on a laundry-room floor, the thud flat, clipped, stripped of drama. The abandoned shell of drama's spent surprise.

Above the chorus of ordnance, static shrieks. Automatic weapons punctuate the shouted monosyllables. Men yell plans to each other in the absence of all plan. Bullets thud into plaster, into concrete, metal, cloth, flesh. The squads thin out. Concussion's cadence slows to the blitting of a bug light.

A bullet tears a gap in your window's sheet metal, letting in more sun than you've seen in two years. The slit pulls at you, pornographic, until you stand and put your pupil into the torn tin corona. Through the peephole, an unfathomable universe. You've been too long without texture to make it out. It refuses to cohere beyond pure sensation—an ornate, deep-pile Persian rug tied by child fingers, thousands of knots to the inch. Smoky charcoal tones swirl into focus. A slab of concrete, sheered down its length, extrudes a tangle of steel reinforcement rods strewn with parti-colored scraps of rag. The most miraculous sculpture you have ever seen.

A guard comes screaming into the room. You step back from the hole, caught, staring at him full face, no blindfold. Your hands fly up in signs of innocence, but he ignores you. No sin you might commit can penetrate him.

His twisted lips spit out *Amal*. Arabic for "hope." Impossible. This assault force laying siege to the nest of Western hostages: Amal? Hope and God's Partisans are on the same side. You'd have sworn your sanity on it, if not your life.

The advance of this commando raid unhinges the guard, routs him. He scrambles for a place to hide. You check his hands; he is weaponless. Wilder still, you look down at where you stand. The blast that tore your radiator out of the floor by its roots has also shed your chain. Freedom goes unnoticed in such concerted dying.

In a heartbeat, you weigh him. He stands a full foot shorter than you, and though he has fed better for the last year and a half, the match is no contest. Beyond him lies an emptied corridor, a stairwell, a street full of men scrambling for their lives. No risk; no need for caution. You are worse than dead already. You lock eyes, trade an eternity of mutual knowledge. He gazes into you, sees a man with nothing more to lose. You shake your head, grinning, stupid with the richness, the ancient history. He slides two steps backward out the door and bolts it behind him.

The squad that tries to ambush your guards pulls back or falls in the rubble. Over several confused hours, all the Partisan guards surface, intact. You stay docile and bowed, in the fury of regrouping. But still your punishment proves severe. It comes with the noise that you'd hoped never to hear again so long as you lived: the snick of packing tape tearing off the roll. The sound of live burial.

They tape you without mercy. You fight to keep a gap around your nose and mouth. They seem vague about your continued breathing. Tape revolves around you, passed from hand to hand, binding you in a cocoon smaller than your body. They smash you down the stairwell that only yesterday stood wide open.

They insert you into the old death truck's recessed well. Your muscles refuse the memory. It can't happen again. You won't survive that exhaust-filled coffin. Your whole body begins to buck, but the tape holds you immobile. You scream from the base of your lungs, but your mouth won't open. The sound goes up through your head and stops, trapped against the layers of insulation.

They put you into the well wrong, wedged. The fumes suffuse your brain even before the truck starts up. The truck's broken shocks send each stone in the road through your kinked body. You pray. Pray for quick death, a willed heart attack, suicide by self-made embolism. Anything but this creeping suffocation. Fifteen minutes in the fume-filled secret compartment and no imaginable future is worth holding out for.

Deliverance comes as a drop into oblivion. A trapdoor in your coffin opens into an enormous gray staging area, empty and still. Then the warehouse gray refracts into all the colors of a furnished paradise. The room goes light, wondrous, spare, waiting for you. All here again: the shirt, the towel, the toiletries, those few crooked paintings on the wall. All human misery vanishes from the earth. You curl up under the moth-eaten red feather tick, intent on sleeping the sleep of the completed.

But someone's mouth tickles you awake. A set of lips on your lips, a pair of lungs pumping yours. Gwen's as you sleep, but a man's as you come to. A man's dark face, sobbing in a familiar foreign language. The shout of joy at your first movement just as quickly turns vicious. A circle of men take out their relief, kicking at your corpse, which, for a few moments longer, still evades feeling, immune to everything human. They slap your neck and punch your head. Every blow delivers you, and you grab at the rain of hands to kiss them.

Under your blindfold, you see night. Night out of doors, on the eastern Mediterranean, somewhere in Phoenicia, beneath the same stars that olive traders steered by, stencils of the world's first myths. They've moved you from the city, forestalling any new attempts to seize you, a living shell game inside the shell of a larger one, a coy three-card monte that will go on for as many millennia as empire continues to dream its dream of cleanness and faith continues to resist in its holdout pockets.

They prop you up and walk you through the bracing night. Who would have thought that life still had so much breeze in it? This same continuous wind once swept down out of the Caucasus, slipped over the Andoman, and scattered through the Great Rift Valley. You'd forgotten about wind.

They push you stumbling forward. This will be your last hundred yards out in the open for years, maybe for forever. Your cheek muscles inch the blindfold up a hairline. You scramble to take some hostage of your own back with you, into whatever new hole awaits. Some glimpse to ground you in the floating nowhere that lies ahead.

The greasy cloth rides up the bridge of your nose. You tilt your head back, raising the slit as high as you dare. The sight on the horizon stops you dead. Off at a distance too shadowy to calculate, thrown into relief against the night sky, stand the ruined columns of the temple of Jupiter. Baalbek—already a thousand-year-old backwater by the time the Romans set up their imperial tax stations and linked the town into their network of command and control.

You hoped to play tourist here once, long ago, in a world past reconstructing. Now you do, checking off the night-etched silhouette against the one filed away in your mental Baedecker. Six eerie Corinthian capitals, six stray verticals—all that's left of the belief they stood for. Jihad could not have built a more surreal set for your safekeeping. This glimpse of awful otherworldliness trips you up. You stumble, and someone cracks you across the crown of your skull. Then looking is over for this lifetime.

When the blindfold comes off, your new home opens onto blackness. But in the morning, real light streams through a million louvered slats. It pins you, blinded, to the bright, clean floor. What should have been another slime-covered cave is instead the opulent country villa of some wealthy sympathizer.

The room is a bare but blazing white. The floors are a handsome hardwood, and the ceiling's scalloped medallion surrounds a hollow socket that once fed a chandelier. French shutters stand clasped together. Most glorious of all, there is no radiator. No place at all to attach a leg chain.

You rise and walk. It's like one of those avant-garde plays, where the lead goes to heaven and doesn't realize he's dead until the fourth act. You edge sideways to the shutters, shielding your eyes against the concentrated blast. When your pupils at last attenuate—peeling back a year and a half of shadow—they refuse the evidence. Outside your window is a farm.

All morning, you trace tight, excited circles. You live here. You *live* here. Luck beyond rolling. At the first sound at the heavy oak door, you slip on your blindfold and wipe the stray canary feathers from the corners of your grin. But your guards arrive with drills, hammers, industrial staple guns.

You huddle against a wall, weeping. It no longer matters who sees you. The room goes dark, to the sound of sheet metal riveted over the French windows. Then worse: the sound of a brace being set into the floor. When the redecorating party leaves, you lift your blindfold. Your chain is back, attached to an iron staple large enough to moor a ship. Next to it on the floor lies a thin mattress whose stains trace a map as familiar as that of Iowa.

No prior breakdown can compare. No zero degree where the dead-drop bottoms out. The trench of depression rises up around you without limit. You grab hold of anything to slow the frictionless slip—the glimpse of silhouetted temple, the daylight farm. Drafts gust in through cracks in the wall. A brush of wind, the scent of grass, the rustle of a place that predates politics. But all of memory is not enough evidence to keep you here.

Days pass when the thought of what lies behind your sheet tin—all that has been taken away from you—plunges you into a place not worth surviving. Worse, this torment pays for nothing. Your whole sacrificed life does not right a single wrong committed against your holders. Half the world, held hostage, would be too little to fix history. And that thought cuts you loose to drop still deeper.

A clicking the size of a cricket keeps you from falling forever. It plays one day for the space of a few minutes. It sounds like the metronome a rat pianist might use when struggling to tame a rodent sonata. A tentative, regular ticking in the pipes of this rural château. The chirping of an artificial sparrow. A doll's clock. It dies out a measure and a half after it starts.

Then, two days later, it comes back.

Three shorts, three longs, three shorts. The international distress call of all ships at sea. It forces a whoop from you, then another, softer. A laugh, wet, spastic, soft enough to evade detection. Your east wall is another man's west. Just on the far side of those six inches, someone lives.

Just as suddenly, the broadcast breaks off once more. The dispatch quits, unanswered. Fifteen hours will have to pass before you're off the chain, before you can reach the wall to send back a reply. You pull on the metal staple in panic. The sender has given up on you, on your empty cell. You'll never hear from him again.

Then it occurs to you: this guy isn't going anywhere anytime soon.

The hours until your next exercise creep like a slug in a headwind. As the moment nears, thoughts vanish in an ecstatic buzz. Unleashed, you run an agonizing couple of diversionary laps until the guard disappears. Then you fall down convulsed in front of the altar wall, thrilled into silence.

It's as if the skies have finally cracked open with a message from beings a thousand light-years away. And now, after the thousand-year passage, Earth must send its one summary greeting that will take a millennium to return. Morse is not an option. Nor is any other compressed transmission. All you have is that ancient trick, the cumbersome, cuneiform stupidity: one tap equals A; two equals B . . .

You cannot waste time with anything so irrelevant as "hello." Just tapping M-A-R-T-I-N at a comprehensible pace with clear pauses between letters—making the inevitable fumbles and improvising a rapid-burst signal for "start over"—burns up a terrible fraction of your allotted thirty minutes off the chain.

Every letter risks detection. You tap softly, checking as you cycle through the alphabet for any hint of movement behind your door. Detection here would mean death or worse.

You come to the final N of your name and wait for a response. But the bottle-message drifts off into resounding silence. You repeat the whole word, although the act costs you more precious minutes. A second silence, even rounder than the first. Blackness comes on you at the inexplicable failure; the signal vanishes into the void.

But maybe he, too, can get free to tap only at certain intervals. The thought saves you long enough for another attempt. You struggle over what word should follow, the second most important disclosure after that meaningless first one. And raging against the inevitable choice, at the idiocy of having to say it, you tap A-M-E-R-I-C-A-N.

You quit while still safe, a full day's work. When the guard comes to lock you back up after your run, you're more winded than usual.

Some hours later comes a reply.

Junot. French. The answer dashes your vague fantasy of free and unhindered romps through English with a native speaker. You'd dreamed of a shorthand version of those rambling letters your brother Kamran would send each month, trapped in a Peace Corps–ravaged Mali: "Yours in appropriate technology." You'd hoped for the desperate consolations of shared diction. You'll have, at best, a hurried pidgin.

The next day, you telegraph him back: *bien.* A lie, by implication. The bulk of your French consists of your mother's Pahlevi-corrupted *pas vrais*s and *merzi*s, all the cosmopolitan affectations of the Shah's courtier class. But a harmless enough lie, to which you attach another: *courage.* At least any French he responds with will be slowed to a crawl. And you'll have a day to decode it.

Junot's next reply skirts the language issue altogether. *Jihad*, he tells you. *Hezbollah.*

You can think of nothing, in fifteen hours, to answer with but *oui.* Shorter, by a few precious clicks in your shared language, than its English foster brother. You add: *I know.* You look for some semaphore to compress all that you know, all that you've learned in this private school. *Eighteen months. You?*

You kick yourself for having said nothing. But on his next turn Junot picks up the English thread as if it signifies. *Thirty-six weeks. I know*, and as the words unfold in agonizing click-tedium, you wonder why he wastes such urgent time and risks such danger to say them.

Then he adds *your.* Then he adds *name.*

The word splits open and heaven air-drops manna. This man, this total stranger in the next cell, whose existence you were not even aware of until a few days ago, has heard of you. He recognizes the name you've told him. He has heard it, sometime in the year between your kidnap and his. The world has not lost track. You haven't disappeared. Your mother knows your fate. Your brother. Gwen.

Now time, your old torturer, changes color. There aren't enough hours in the day to digest what the Frenchman tells you and to think up replies. You hurry through your words, stumbling, losing count of your clicks, starting all over. You spin in torment as he types, willing him to hurry, fearing that each breathless pause means discovery.

You never dreamed that words took such numbing redundancy. You invent a code for "et cetera," faster and shorter than your original "do over," which Junot picks right up on. Improvements come piecemeal, improvised. You spend nights inventing whole new codes, drastically more efficient in their transmission. But their rules would take days to convey. And you can't stop saying things long enough to streamline their saying.

Tick by tick, teaspoon by teaspoon, talk returns you to its appalling density. You communicate daily, but never more than a handful of words at one go. Completing a simple dialogue takes a week. Sometimes you go a night without hearing from him, awful interludes in which you toss on your bed like a cheated lover.

Junot says that the English churchman sent to negotiate for the hostages' release has himself been taken, perhaps even killed. The news is at least half a year old, but it hits you with the force of a wire flash. He says the Syrians have occupied West Beirut, putting an end to the city's anarchy.

But not, you reply, a bitter day later, *to the war.*

You ache to cut through the waste of politics and ask him about the good stuff. What's new in music? Who won last year's Series? Any outrageousness at the Oscars? He can't know, and you don't ask. Nor can you give him the diversion he must crave.

You share all the insights of your protracted stay, the names of all the guards you have garnered, their assorted psychopathologies and soft spots. You learn of your awful luck.

Junot has begged for reading matter but has not yet gotten a single scrap. You tap out short *surahs* from the Qur'an for him, like singing in the dark after bedtime, delighting in written syntax all over again. All the while you live in danger of detection.

What you could not do for yourself you rise to do for him. Release can't be long in coming, you tell him. All the rational evidence is on your side. The two of you: each other's confidant, each other's clinical physician, each other's clown. You lie for hours at night, giggling at his ridiculous shaggy-dog jokes, the ones that take three days to get to their belated punch lines. The ones that open with the telegraphic formula: *Three. Tourists. Chinese. Indian. American.*

One day, the line goes dead. It seems at first a minor annoyance. You've suffered interruptions before. Some guard has almost caught him, and he must lie low for a cooling period. Or he is on some protracted punishment, restricted to his chain.

For a while you tap on into the darkness, hoping he can still hear you. But long silence wears away the sense of anything at all on the far side of the barrier. This Frenchman has let you down, has raised your hopes, then hung you out to dry. Your daily dispatches get shorter, more perfunctory. You want to save the good stuff for his return, when you can hear his live reaction.

The day comes when you admit Junot will not be back. You say *freedom*. You say *release*, although there are more frugal explanations. This abandonment makes last spring's hopelessness seem like a mercy killing. You hate the man, for reviving desire and all its gruesome reminders. For telling you that you persist in the world's memory.

His words are no better than those pieces of fruit that Ali sadistically tosses, just out of reach.

In your dreams these nights, you lean out through a bright, open window. But the window sash falls like a blade on the back of your neck, as crisp as that old French political expedient. *Joy looks out on all that it is not*, your book says. *But bitterness sees only itself.*

Sayid brings you your supper late one evening, some day in what must be late August. The air wears that oppressive stillness, but here it is not so stultifying as the city was, this time last year. Your country estate, the subtle shifts of its noise and breezes, has blessed you in a million ways, all powerless to make any difference. Sayid comes to bring you your usual plate of gristle, and you hear him weeping. It stuns your ear to learn of a grief that isn't yours. In its strange depths, his pool of sadness at once dissolves yours.

What in all the world can this bewildered, accepting soul have to weep about? His suffering twists the air around him. You cannot help yourself; some dead root in you, left over from years ago, twitches in this rain. You want to know what happened. So long as you live, it will hook you, the hint of word. You hear him set down the plate and back out to go. He, too, will leave you without disclosing the source of his bitterness. Then a discovery larger than your life: you can *just ask him*.

"Sayid." The movement stops, but not the muffled sorrow. "Sayid. What is it? What has happened to you?"

He searches for a way through his loss. "Hussein." Unsure how to go on. "Hussein is dead."

Some family member or close friend. Another victim of this eternal civil suicide.

"I'm . . . so sorry. When? When did it happen?"

The question baffles him. "When? At Karbala!" A thousand and a third years ago.

Pity, astonishment, and disgust—the whole grab bag given the human animal—pass through you in quick succession. But the flood of feeling recedes with Sayid, leaving behind only a single, sharp thrill. You know what day it is.

For the first time in months, you can locate yourself in time. Today is Ashura, the anniversary of the ancient sacrifice. The tenth day of Muharram, the month of mourning. Some quick thought and the application of your mother's formula produce the year: 1409.

But when *is* 10 Muharram? You spend the rest of the month—both months—worrying the problem. Like trying to derive the quadratic formula too many years after high-school algebra. The moon and the sun deny each other's cycles. By the time you conclude that mental conversion is impossible, you've lost count again, in any calendar.

You wake from a deep sleep, a creature gnawing at your face. You scream and spasm, sending some kind of beaked mammal flying across the floor. The guards ignore you, used to your nighttime apparitions.

But this beast is real. It glares at you from the corner where you've whacked it. You make it out: a mouse, feral and sniffing, no longer than your thumb, although a little fatter. Ounce for ounce, it looks at least as needy as a human. But infinitely more harmless.

The scared gray thing gives you a project to absorb another winter. It takes weeks to overcome your bad first impression and win her trust. You surrender the best scraps of each meal, always more than you can afford. In your moments off the chain, you leave stockpiles as far from human contamination as possible. When she comes out to examine the stash, helpless in the tug of its aroma, the human giant is there, lying still, just looking on, passive and given.

Each feeding station that she accepts gives way to another, imperceptibly closer to the giant's base camp. Desensitization takes forever, but it's precisely forever that you have on your hands. You've forgotten what it means to work steadily toward some goal. By the time she'll come within ten feet of you, she already forms your unwitting solace, your joy, your day's significance.

But she remains skittish as the day is long. Something about the disparity in your sizes. Something about being smacked across the room before formal introductions. There comes a day when she'll nibble just outside arm's distance. You're too ashamed to admit the name you've already given her, even to yourself, even at night when she wriggles her nose, inquiring, at your motionless body.

Conflicted for a reason. Conflicted for a reason, as the old televised talk-show public therapies liked to say. Pushing with the same hand that she used to pull you toward her.

Resenting any suggestion that you owed each other anything. But lashed together so tightly that even the vicious pulling away, even the cursing and eternal swearing off amounted to deepest intimacy.

In the days just after capture, your survival could spare no energy for any thought so trivial as love. Six months brought your radical education: happiness and desire were private distractions that allowed states to do their nightmare work unnoticed. A year embittered you to the fact that states had no more wherewithal than the most vicious of quarreling lovers. Eighteen months erased all human pretension past eating and sleeping, staying cool and dry, or calming your bowels until the next bathroom run.

Two years returns you to that first, unaffordable triviality.

More time passes. She comes almost right up to you. She'll take food out of your hand, if you hold it way out, palm open. She no longer turns and runs the second she's finished.

Late fall, the guards bring you a birthday cake. A single-layered, multicultural monstrosity of confectioner's sugar and identity politics, too freakish to assimilate. You don't want them to see you happy. To think that your stupid ecstasy has anything to do with this blundering kindness.

Joy snubs out when they bring the present. A Minicam, sitting on some bag-headed mercenary's shoulder like a handheld rocket launcher. You are to eat and enjoy this cake — just another well-catered day in the Beirut Hilton — while they videotape you for the pleasure of the home audience.

You eat to keep them from seeing you destroyed. You eat left-handed, a subversive signal to any National Security Agency official inspecting the video for clues. You eat bare-faced, no evidence of ever having had to scramble with a blindfold. You look at this man filming you, stare at him. Even with the lights and blocking camera, even through the makeshift hood, his features will stay with you longer than the tape will remember yours.

Muhammad stands off camera, out of vision, saying, "Talk to your family. Say hello to your friends." Throw yourself off a high place. Change stones into bread. You eat slowly, savoring the cake, despite yourself. You make your face a blank, a mask onto which the world can project whatever dream it is struggling to realize.

Who do these clumsy directors think they're fooling? What message can they hope to send? And yet your family will see this. Your friends. Impossible. Communication from beyond the grave. You see them seeing you. You look just happy enough for your mother to imagine that you're well.

They know your birthday. These martyrs know your birthday. And they can only have learned it from the American media. Someone at home has followed your story, this year or last, and wished you a televised happy birthday that your kidnappers intercept. Your birthday, somewhere within a week of where you sit. You'd forgotten you had one.

"Thank you," you tell the camera, in what comes out a mechanical drone. Who, on the many far ends of this transmission, will receive these words? "Thank you. I'm alive." You wait, like you wait for the mouse, for your voice to come back. "I am being treated well." Lied to and lying, using and used. The eternal compromise seems, at least for this instant, to favor you by the narrowest sliver. "Although the décor here could use a little work."

You gesture stage right, and the cameraman, by instinct, tracks you with a pan, before he realizes.

"Finish your cake," Muhammad orders.

He's caught you trying to palm a piece no bigger than a finger. "I thought . . . I thought I might be able to save a little for . . . later?"

"Let them see you eat the whole thing."

You eat the piece that might have given your only joy a little pleasure.

This pact with your manipulators seals your fate. The State Department will wash its hands of you for aiding and comforting the enemy. But it keeps you alive, for many nights running. Somewhere abroad, out on the globe's trade routes, repeatedly rewound and replayed, your phantom image converses with those who know you, those who hear your words.

You pass through an invented Halloween. A functional Thanksgiving. A genuine simulation of Christmas. You lift a fake glass to a new approximate New Year's.

Your pupils habituate to permanent, low-grade twilight until the crushing vacuum of a single day begins to play like high opera. Even this plotless, characterless, sceneless script reveals its unities. Its beginnings, middles, and inexorable, minimalist ends afford you a panorama, the sweep of a story unlike anything you could have followed when you were free. Surprise in the absence of uncertainty. You will live here for the rest of your life, a Galileo under house arrest, with no telescope to stick through the skylight. You will die here. You'll watch your own deathbed scene, breathless, attuned to the smallest detail, awaiting the only possible outcome.

Attunement teaches you. It is possible to love one person, and only one person, more than you love your own existence, and still not know that one. She made you needy, controlling. You made her willful and perverse. All a life-sized misunderstanding, put to rest in this larger place of enforced listening.

You had no cause to be so brutal, that last call she made you, just before your capture. No cause, the years of preemptive second-guessing, certain that you already heard her objections before she made them. Now that you both must live within perpetual eyeshot of the thing you missed—two humans, too late, making a space for one another—you can see past fear to the place fear never let you reach.

And yet, in the fogged celluloid of this focused dream, the story repeats. The home you both set fire to, again and again. The constant border incursions, the mutual banishment. *It's never enough for you. You're never satisfied. You want my fucking bone marrow.*

She didn't know you when there was a now. How could she know you in absentia? And the need you felt for her—the *love*—must become a crippling thing, so filled with self-inflicted misery that even redemption now would ring worse than hollow.

Perhaps, your only reading matter says, *perhaps God will place love between you and those that you are hostile toward. For God is powerful. And God is forgiving. And God is compassionate.*

The mouse comes out to gnaw on the pages of the book. On those words, *for those who can believe without seeing.* You let it nibble. Let the creature take from you everything it needs.

As belated thanks for helping them with the video, the keepers return your necklace. Gwen's good-luck charm, the one they confiscated from you on the first day of imprisonment. You sit gripping it, unable to quit sobbing. You press the sharp point of the charm into your cheek, trying to get your thoughts to stop. Guards come and wrestle you, pin you to the ground, and confiscate the charm again.

"Please. I am sorry. Please give it back. I won't hurt myself anymore."

A good deal later, after the gouge in your face has more or less healed, a hooded man comes in to snap your picture. Three days on, Ali brings you the print and tells you to sign your name across it.

It's some kind of bush-league trick. An amateur hoax you can't quite puzzle out. They force you to affix your signature to another man's picture, another Crusoe who only vaguely resembles you, gaunt and wasted from sockets to jowls, mizzled gray throughout the hair and beard, a fake-up that will fool no one. Ali harasses you into signing before you can figure out who exactly you're perjuring.

Maybe another month goes by. You almost forget about having taken part in the bizarre ritual. Ali bursts into your cell one day, aflame.

"See who is famous today? See who is in today's newspaper? American film star! Mel Gibson!"

"Gibson is Australian," you say. "Not our fault."

He waves a scrap of newsprint under your blindfold. Eternity's long-sought armistice. Page 6 of the *Herald Tribune,* and there is the old man's photo, identified as you. Someone has been duped, either you or the world at large. And you don't care anymore, just who.

"Please," you beg. "Let me just . . . hold it. For sixty seconds." Not to read the article about you. Just for the look, the longitudinal proof of things *happening.* The feel of it in your hands: your old breakfast table news.

He won't let you hold it, if only because you want to. But before he snatches it away from you forever, you catch a glimpse of the date. You take the number to bed with you, vowing on your life never to lose count again. You shelter the secret figure in your heart, protecting it from all human invention. You perform vast calculations on it, sums and differences, expansions and extractions.

The math's stubborn result rocks you. Simple subtraction slams you up against a figure too mythic for you to believe. You go head-to-head, putting it through the calendar's mill so many times your brain begins to bleed. And still it persists, staring at you in its perfection.

If you were in fact taken on that November day of '86 that has stayed lodged in you, and if the scrap of paper they waved at you was in fact today's, then tonight is precisely your thousandth night. And tomorrow will be your thousandth night, plus one.

39

The thing accreted like any cathedral, one stone on the other. Each wall's blocks were but ghosts, floating in array through a million dynamically refreshed video addresses a second. And yet, to the ones who hewed and tuck-pointed them, they passed for stones.

The designers fit their fly-through together in gross modules: first the ground floor, along with the narthex and exonarthex at the west entrance. Then, above the blending of aisle and apse, they placed the gallery. On top of that, they set spans of triforium arch to support the stunning trick of clerestory.

They worked for a month on the elevation alone. They studied the architectural analyses, the conjectures about what held the thing up. No two experts agreed, except in their astonishment. True to history, the group needed several tries to get the dome to stay in place. The window-ringed weight defied them. After the second time that it collapsed and crashed to the floor, Spiegel took to repeating, *Oh, the humanity!* But out of repeated disasters, radiance took shape.

That looming nave terrified Adie's dog. Pinkham had gotten used to the Arlesian Room, curling up in an empty corner, at most barking at the squeak of a floorboard. But those long, shrouded sight lines undid the creature. Something about the size of the undulating space, the smoke-colored arcades opening onto farther distances, spooked him. He would not set paw in it.

Vulgamott played module librarian, putting his finger on each new part and tweaking the object's properties as needed. Ebesen fussed over every spandrel and inset. This man, who had not cleaned his mobile home since purchase, insisted that every filigree and tracing be perfect. Their modular objects lay wrapped inside a larger code, bits as opportunistic as those pagan Venus-temple columns incorporated into Notre Dame.

Six weeks along, the mosaic team began to fuse. Their private differences got lost in the size of the undertaking. Lim and Jackdaw combined forces to solve the scale problem, getting the Cavern to house a grotto orders of magnitude larger than itself. Rajasundaran took on the challenge of that cavernous reverberation. Loque sculpted the shafts of changing light, those eerie threads spun out of the master source.

Adie took charge of the mosaic saints. Spiegel delighted daily in watching her assemble the stones. As she turned high-resolution photographic reproductions back into low-res squares of colored tile, the staircased edges of her own soul smeared and softened.

This must have been why you brought me out here, Stevie. Without even knowing it. I mean, I don't want to sound mystical or anything . . .

Why not? Go wild. Christ Pantocrator will roll with it.

It's just that . . . I'd forgotten what it feels like to be part of something bigger than I am. To have some work that I'm . . .

Destined to do? he asked. But the old irony hid itself under a bushel.

She shrugged. *Every person has something she's supposed to do. I knew this when I was little, but I forgot. It comes back to you, though. That's the beauty: you think you're lost. You stumble around forever without knowing which way is forward. But you turn a corner one day and your work is right there, smack in front of you. Tracking you like the moon.*

But you knew that, back when I met you. You already had your work.

She squeezed her eyes shut. *Knew. Met. You knew me when I was an ecstatic novice. When I first went to SoHo, all I could talk about was line and energy and light. Before I knew it, I was chatting away about bankability and impact and positive portfolio exposure. It's horrible. You can't imagine what an industry, what a . . .*

Factory?

She snorted. *You see? That's where we live.*

But Rubens was a factory. Ingres was an industry.

The Master of Flémalle wasn't.

Sure he was. The Church paid for those Annunciation panels by the metric ton.

Vermeer wasn't.

Lackey of the rising propertied class. Gimme a foot and a half of something in burnt umber that'll look good above the dining-room sideboard.

No, she said, almost violent. *Not the same. Those people were . . . looking. Pushing through appearance to the other side. You can see it in every mark they put down.*

Well, they're industries now, anyway. Whatever they started out as.

This is fact. The Scream T-shirts. The Klimt coffee mugs. The hyped exhibitions where gallery guards move the customers through in cattle cars . . .

So you liked it better when they turned away the great unwashed at the doors of the palazzo?

I liked it better when the human heart was more than a commodity.

And when was that, exactly?

God only knows. Never, probably. That's why I bailed. Why I ended up so completely lost, for all those years.

You ran to commerce to get away from commercialism?

In a funny way, yes. That's exactly what happened.

Adie, my Ade . . .

You have no idea how horrible it is. To give your life to a thing you think represents the best that humanity can do, only to discover that it's not about beauty at all. It's about coercion and manipulation and power politics and market share and the maintenance of class relations.

Then what . . . ? He teetered on the edge of making the obvious point. Maybe the obvious point was never worth making. *What's . . . different about what we're doing?*

She pieced her tiles together, in silence. Blue, rose, gold: sages standing in God's holy fire.

As a product? Maybe nothing. But as a process? It feels as if there's something we have to make. As if we're closing in on something that the world somehow . . . needs.

He laughed in astonishment. *I never thought I'd live to see you become the spokesperson for high technology.*

Not the technology. She grew shy, diffident. She did not say it. The sanctuary.

You see what you're making, don't you? His chin pointed at the paint-by-numbers coming to life on her screen. *Human portraiture. The thing you'd sworn off of.*

She blushed, a schoolgirl caught slipping a secret valentine into a mailbox. *Maybe so. But they're not my originals! And they're not especially realistic.*

When you work your way down to the damaged bits—the parts the Crusaders and the Turks destroyed? Are you going to finish them?

I haven't thought about it. You can't think too much about this thing. The one that tracks you like the moon. *I'll see when I get there.*

All the lab's orioles brought them scraps of colored rag to weave into the deepening nest. Nineteenth-century Orientalist engravings of the immense interior. Photographs shot from atop Sophia's descendant: Sinan's Sultanahmet, the Blue Mosque. Translations of the dazzling, calligraphic, verse maze that lined the inside of that stone firmament.

The whole felt fresh, like something from the days when making things was still young and not yet overcome by terminal success.

Freese suggested a treadmill, to speed the visitor through the enormous distances.

Adie vetoed. *No machines inside. It's a sacred space.*

They settled on a simpler propulsion. Lean in the direction of travel, and that compass point would drift toward you. Lean harder to run.

Why is the math so hard? she asked Kaladjian.

Which math?

Perspective. Proportion. Depth.

Perspective? Perspective is easy. Just the visual cone turned inside out. Once the Italians got wind of Arab optics, the whole globe was up for grabs.

Not that perspective, she said, harsh enough to surprise him. But he was alongside her in a flash. The most difficult man she knew was also among the smartest.

Oh. Perspective. Knowing where you are?

She nodded. He scribbled with a number-two pencil on a pad of blank canary legal paper. He drew her diagrams, space's irrefutable proof. *If being alive were a single problem in long division—how to divide infinity by threescore and ten—we'd have a reasonable chance of solving existence. But the solution for seventy years misses catastrophically for thirty, because the numerator is infinite. And those solutions, in turn, look nothing like the quotient for this year, this fiscal quarter, or today, let alone the next thirty minutes.*

We live between our next heartbeat and forever.

The mathematician shot her a look: How much do you know? *That's it. We are supposed to solve all the conflicting quotients at once. That is what makes . . . the math so hard.*

He lifted his eyebrows at her, as if he did not mind being of use, if only this once.

Revived by work, Adie returned to the play of her body. Limbered, she and Stevie tussled at each other, like fast-learning pups. Pinkham barked at the sounds of happy scuffling, and he would scrape his nails at the other side of the closed bedroom door to be let in.

Sex in middle age felt illicit, blunted, sad, curdled by knowledge, each of them aware how little a role the loved object actually played in the perpetuation of happiness. But neither of them could shrug off the forms of happiness. Joy grasped and dismissed them by turns, the only solace against its own affliction.

Adie opened. She tried on a whole wardrobe of abandoned clothes for Spiegel that she had never worn in front of anyone, even for the solitary mirror. She sported looks that weren't her, outfits that quickened her to inhabit.

She talked to Stevie widely, as she once had to her sister, in childhood. She talked to him of Ted, now without guilt or recrimination. She spoke of the things that had gone wrong. The ways in which their paired equations failed to balance.

She narrated the horrors of New York. The molestations in the subway. Rats the size of a healthy baby. The fashion of nihilism and runaway hipness. The serenade of all-night car alarms under her apartment window.

He smirked at her. *You miss it, don't you? Admit it.*

In your dreams.

She made him get out more. The trips stunned him. *Our ancestors spoke of this thing, the sun.*

She made him sit, dank and chilled, with a book in his lap, in her harvested garden. She took him to that hideout in the Cascades, her secret swimming hole. The water was too cold now to swim. They postponed full immersion until they got home.

There she lay waste to him, with a hunger that grew with each feeding. It surprised Stevie sometimes, the ferocity of it. Her sniffing him, tasting, holding him up to the light, inspecting. Searching his every part for some sensory testament she could never quite find.

You're not bad at this, she told him. His reward. *For an old guy.*

Yep. That's me. The Loin in Winter.

But each encounter fed the question in him, the one that would undo them, whether he asked it or held it under.

When you make love to me . . . ?

Yy-yess? she teased, touching him in a place, in a way to derail all words.

He took away her hand. *When you make love to me . . . who are you touching?*

She clamped. *Don't want to play this game, Stevie. Don't even want to visit.*

But she came back easily those days, even from his most willful disruptions. She wore an aura now that nothing could dissipate. A woman who had found, again, the work she was meant to give herself to.

Spiegel squinted, and called it love.

The word spread, a winter contagion. Jackdaw came to them and announced his engagement. *You're the first two people I've told. I haven't even told my parents yet.*

Jackie, Adie pouted. *I thought you loved me.*

Something in his stuttering objections said that the two facts weren't incompatible.

Spiegel clapped him on the back. *Fantastic, man. Who's the happy shackle-to-be?*

She's called Fatima.

Last name? Adie asked.

Morgan.

You make her change it, she threatened, *and I'll kill you.*

Spiegel waved for the floor. *Let me guess. Mother hails from Tunis and father from Piscataway.*

I . . . I don't really know.

Humor, Jackie. Adie wrapped her arm around the boy.

It's an analog thing, Spiegel said. *You wouldn't understand.*

So what's she like?

Oh, she's fantastic. All over the map. She's got something new going every ten minutes. And she doesn't take any shit from men, I'll tell you that much.

Have you set a date yet?

Date? Oh no. We're still working that one out. One of these years, anyway.

Get it in writing, Spiegel stage-whispered.

So when are you going to bring her around? We need to give her our stamp of approval.

Meet you people? Before we're legally married? You think I'm crazy?

Come on, Jackie. We have to see what you're getting into here.

Jackdaw grinned beatifically. *Use your imagination.*

What does she do? Adie heard herself, the parental interrogation she'd forsworn.

She's a docs writer. Real verbal chick. The mouth on her? Man.

You like that in a woman? Spiegel asked.

Acquerelli nodded vigorously.

What does she look like?

Stevie! Adie punished his upper arm.

Can't help it. I'm visually biased.

She's dark. Dark, and . . . uh, nice? About Adie's height.

Adie backpedaled. *Documentation writer for . . . ?*

Motorola.

Motorola? Steve dropped a beat. *Which facility?*

Chicago.

The penny dropped. *Where exactly did you meet this woman?*

In . . . in a Multi-User Dimension. On-line.

A MUD? And you haven't really . . . seen her yet?

Not. Really. Not yet.

Steve looked away. Adie examined the back of her fingers. The stunted gestures of liberal tolerance.

But of course we'll see each other, before we get . . . We're going to meet, FTF, pretty soon.

Face-to-face, Steve told Adie. To spare her the humiliation of asking.

They spoke about it alone, in bed, after lights-out. Spiegel spoke with real pain.

The kid. Falling in love with a character in a MUD. Because she's a fast-typing put-down artist.

Why not? Adie said. *That's his world. Who else is he going to fall in love with? The whole thing is always an exercise in mutual projection, anyway, isn't it?*

Is it? Some projections at least have a chance of surviving the light of day.

Then don't take it out into the light of day.

What are we going to do?

About what?

About keeping Jackdaw safe?

Adie put her hand out to feel this man's neck. *Stevie. Stevie. Who ever told you that safe is an option?*

The packet-switched courtship grew as rich as any love match. Router by router, chat room by chat room, the new couple negotiated their future space.

She hates TV as much as I do, Jackdaw told them. *She loves 'zines. I think I'll eat better once she's around.*

He started to dress more carefully. He even shed a couple of pounds of hacker's corn-chip flab. Adie caught him working out in the Cavern, waving the wand like a racket, hitting a projectile back and forth with a distant, animated stick figure a dozen feet beyond the Cavern's front wall.

Aiy. The age-old battle of man versus machine. It's not enough that they have to destroy us at chess? That they've started drawing better than we do? You have to teach them how to beat us at tennis, too?

Jackdaw stopped to look and lost the serve. *Oh. That's not a machine at the other end. That's Fatima.*

Fa—? Hang on. You mean there's another Cavern? In Chicago?

He swung the electronic racket and cackled at her dread. *No, no. She's sitting out there at a terminal, with a joystick. We converted the app interface and migrated it out to her client.*

Adie watched in horror: shadowy lives playing against living shadows. A sudden pupaphobia overtook her as she watched the boy volley, step out, recompile a few new lines of code, step back in and volley again. Like Buster Keaton's projectionist, slipping in and out of his own projection. She turned from the scene to bolt, but there was no way out of the frame.

Jackdaw came to them in mid-November, high on adrenaline. *She's traveling out here. Over Thanksgiving. For three days.*

Here? As in Seattle-here? That's great. Are we going to get to meet her?

You're joking. She's in town for three days. No way are we going to waste that on other people.

He returned to work after the holiday, destroyed.

Let me guess, Kaladjian said. *She's twelve years old.*

No, Freese said. *She's a hundred and twelve. But remarkably well preserved for her age.*

Rajan fell in with the cadence. *Don't tell us. You didn't realize from the name that she was part foreign.*

Her name's not really Fatima?

She's really a guy.

She's really two guys.

She's really a LISP routine.

Jackdaw's nose flared and his mouth caved under. One tight globe of salt water pinched out of the corner of his right eye. He turned on his heel and left, over the cries of group protest that only too late realized the truth.

Freese received a one-line e-mail the following day. Jack Acquerelli would not be returning to the project.

Jackie's departure plunged them all into a cloud of bad faith.

Not your fault, Steve told Adie. But she had long ago learned to discount forgiveness and work harder. And now there was more work for all of them, shorthanded, a man down with the match still in question.

Did not need this, Lim said. *Not with the finish line looming. The guy used to put in hundred-hour weeks.*

But eighty of them were just playing, Kaladjian said.

You're saying there's a difference?

Adie tried to absorb the bulk of those lost man-hours herself. She worked around the clock. She lived in Hagia Sophia now, and when she couldn't get into the cathedral itself, she pitched tent in the traces of its flat-screen shadow.

That's where Stevie found her, with the next intruding news.

What is it? she asked him. One look. *What's wrong?*

Doris Singlegate?

She shook her head, unable to place the name.

The Mole-Woman?

She snapped to attention, revelation already making its way up her neck hair. *What's happened?*

They let her out. After something like two years underground. They brought her back up to the surface. She passed a physical. A few small, strange things wrong with her body clock, but nothing critical.

Stevie. Just tell me. It's not like I know the woman.

She seems to have taken her own life. Back in her own home. In her own bed.

40

Your whole body rejects the evidence. Not possible. You can't have been here that long. Time lived and time retrieved don't match up. Those afternoons that took a year to pass shrink, in treacherous memory, to seconds. A month of them wouldn't fill an hour. You can't account for more than a few dozen weeks, let alone two-and-three-quarters years.

You clutch to that dead reckoning now, as if to life. Some desperately inventive internal storyteller has won you survival through your thousand-and-one nights. And now, by the terms of the old agreement, the sentence must be lifted.

But that, too, is only another fairy story: the thousand-and-second. It gives way to hundreds more, the fragmenting agonies of a world in the throes of universalizing, myths and fables that do not say why in the world they need you as protagonist . . .

At least America remembers you; that much you could not have invented. Your picture in the *Herald Tribune*, even now, after so long you have almost forgotten yourself. They will want a full account, should you live to tell. They will want a book, a story, even though there is no story. There is nothing but a pointlessness the size of eternal time.

Yet still, on days when the sun warps your corrugated tin cage like a cheap cookie sheet, in nights when the damp passes right through your one thin blanket and even thinner skin, seeping down into your bone, where it cracks your marrow, it calms you to write this book. Your head scribbles hundreds of pages at a go, and reads them all back to you, verbatim. For your memory has become prodigious, your story infinite . . .

You try passages out on the mouse. Practice oral recitations, triweekly checkups to test your trembling mind. On the day you left Chicago, you could not keep a new phone number in your head for fifteen minutes. Now you are a concert pianist of the verbal arts, performing huge narrative rhapsodies by heart. Who cares if the brilliant solos may be, in fact, the wildest crashing dissonance?

Deep in those prodigious mnemonic galleries, stores of letters to everyone you have ever cared for pile up in teetering stacks, awaiting postage. The gardens of memory grow so ornately, radioactively rococo that their topiary spills over in all directions and all paths return to lushest underbrush.

Things come down out of the attic that you couldn't possibly have left there. The more you retrieve, the faster the stockpiles of bric-a-brac heap up, fire hazards. The forms inside you beat for an outward shape. A way to tear free and be born.

Muhammad must understand the curse of literacy. "I need paper and pencil," you harass him, every chance you get. "Anything to scratch on. Anything, or the jinns are going to get me. Who is going to read it? What possible danger can it be? I'll hand it all over the day you let me leave."

He will not listen to reason. He treats you as if you are already mad.

"Look: you are Lebanese. The Lebanese *invented* the damn alphabet." The worst, culprit technology. The rod that dislodged the murderous boulder. "You practically created writing. Does that mean nothing to you?"

It does. Mean nothing.

The stories keep coming, flooding their banks, reverting. Your brain is a used bookstore that buys more than it sells. Its shelves will not hold. All things happen even to the shortest life. We all live forever. That simple discovery will break you.

You need to tell someone. You need someone to tell. You tell the rodent, until she, too, disappears. Even a mouse's life span makes more sense than yours.

She comes back, the phantom who will take the weight of these gifts from you. You sit on the foot of her bed, stroking her leg, starting in on the boundless backlog. "You'll never believe. I was walking down the street. Some men seemed to be struggling with a flat tire. I slowed down to see if I could help and they told me to get in."

But she is asleep already, before you even hint at the tales where that tale leads. How you always loved to look at her when she slept. Sleeping she did perfectly. Sleeping, she was unified. Out of her nighttime window, clouds roll past a bone moon, stratus stained the color of coral, scudded like sand in time's streambed.

She asks you to sleep in the other room, because your night movements wake her up. But this much she will abide—your holding her foot. And tonight, from this distance, you sum all the years invested, all the cost in equanimity and esteem, the flare-ups of self-righteousness, the scraps that you hoped for in return for holding back. The years that you waited, thinking that you'd be able to tell her about your day, one day, at day's end.

And this is the most she can give you, short of death and surrender: her foot, as she sleeps . . . And still, you would take it again, at the same expense. There is a whirring inside you that falls quiet only so long as you can touch some part of her.

You tell her anyway, as she sleeps. And half the stories that you tell her are just these: these moments of stolen peace, the rough fragments of your life together, coughed up on a shipwreck's beach, snapped beams worthless for sailing now, but still your only source of wood.

Sleeping, she seems an angel, although you know she will wake again. When she does, she rises up disconsolate. She presses her fists into her hips, to make sure she can still feel bone. She inspects her face morosely in the mirror. She asks you, *Do you like my nose?*

You love her nose. Every part of her: devastating, ephemeral.

Other men want me. Other men find me beautiful. Why don't you?

You scowl a little at her, a helpless spasm on your lips. You study her features in this light, light over which she has no control. I want you. I find you beautiful. Don't be stupid. The world cannot abide too many more games.

She asks you, *Do you think I should have it taken in? Just the tip. Just a touch. Maybe you'd find me more attractive if I had a nicer nose.*

You cannot find her any more attractive than you do at this moment. You tell her so.

Impatience crumples the flesh in question: *You're not being very supportive.*

You say you will support her in this and all things that she decides to do. That you find her heartrending as she is, and will love all changes that age adds to her. But if she feels the need to make some alterations, you'll find those beautiful, too.

You sit at the foot of another bed. She rises from post-op, mutilated. Both her eyes blackened, her cheeks a yellow bruise, a bandage across the swollen midline, she looks for all the world like a beating victim. Straight up from the ocean of anesthetic, she fixes you with the full accusation: *I hope you're happy now.*

You are not happy. Your misery has no bottom.

Misery, too, you might give to her. You might make a story of it, of your shared idiocies, one for her to laugh at from the safety of her next bed. Might remind her of all the follies that you two thought so urgent once, as best as you can remember them: your worst horrors, dissolved in worse sequels. All the desperate self-inflictions of an attempted life together, the little indulgences of privilege, called in by the wider war.

What did she say when she woke up next? That is the thread of plot from which you hang. Telling it becomes your last subversive act. The illicit pleasure of recounting, your one revenge on the things that really happened.

Then it is your mother's turn to tell, holding your childish foot and reminding you of things that haven't even happened in this life. You hear her ritual Arabian Nights read-alouds, spread for you and Kamran, well past the year when you should have been weaned from them. Her reading voice, flecked with what you knew even then to be a foreign accent, the keystone to the arched enigma of those days, smooths the total bafflement of childhood. How you used to slog through twelve harsh hours of brute-force realism, just to earn those thirty minutes of enchanted shadow, lying there bed-bound in oblivion's foyer, listening to her read.

Your mother the confirmed pragmatist, rigorous cooker and cleaner, the woman who once made the firemen wipe their muddy boots at the back door before letting them in to douse the burning basement, takes you for a spin in her fabulous Persian machine. She sets the levers, and out leap whole kingdoms, tangled harems, terrible wars. She turns the dials, and the three of you tear off, touring in every direction, past the speed of light.

She reads to you again from out of a book whose title, for all the years of your childhood, you thought was written in Arabic. But now, in photographic recall, you see it clearly enough to read off the stylized, flowing script: Saadi.

It was so; it was not so: there once was a slave who tried to alter his fate by running away from his master. But fate recaptured the runaway and sentenced him to a life of backbreaking work, building the master's mansion.

Many years later, a penitent appeared in the court of this master, knelt down, and pleaded. *I am that slave who ran away from you, all that time ago.*

The master listened to the news in horror. *If you are my escaped slave, then who is the man whom I have sentenced to a lifetime of hard labor?*

He sent for the innocent convict, a philosopher named Lukman. *How can you ever forgive me? I have stolen your whole life.*

But Lukman told the unhappy man, *Do not apologize. For you have your new mansion, and I have learned the only lesson worth learning about life, one that I would never have learned had you not imprisoned me.*

That is the message your mother sends you, from out of her bound volume, a quarter century ago. A fable she picked as preparation for the life that would one day take you hostage.

She tells you her favorite again, the story she always had to give you from memory, out of her best Farsi children's book, lost in the violence of repeated exiles. She improvises, embroiders by word of mouth, a deeper archaeology, the far-off lands even more suggestive in their state of ruin.

There was and there was not a great nature painter who painted a landscape so perfect it destroyed him. Each person who looked at the scene saw something different. But all saw envy, and all wanted what they saw. And those who wanted the painting most decided to kill the maker and steal the thing he made.

Each time she tells you, the story ends differently. Some trick of memory, either yours or hers. In one, the man's painted creatures warn him of the danger and foil the plot. In another, the painter's murder returns the beautiful landscape to overgrown weeds. In the ending that two small, stunned boys loved most, the painter evades his killers, who arrive at his house only to find the abandoned painting, now with a figure running through its farthest, faintest hills.

Death is not death, nor invention invention. Your single life replays all existence, the way your fetus quoted the fish it came from. All innocence, all mistakes, from your first frightened grunts to your late-night adult confusion, are yours again. All your moments condemn you to line them up and relive them, one by one. Your Enlightenment, your Dark Age, your puddled afternoons of Hundred Years' War. All times collapse into now, in the mind forced to a standstill.

She gave you a plant, once. Not your mother: the other one. A droopy, seductive, tropical thing. A peace offering she biked over and left on your stoop, after a bloody, five-day, knockdown standoff where neither of you would concede the other's terror. It thrived under your care for a good three months. After another patented spin-out, it began to wither. Its leaves burned back from their tips, as if torched by a butane lighter. Nothing you did helped. It limped along on critical. By chance it rallied, just before she started tentatively coming around again.

A couple more synchronized dips and recoveries convinced you: this plant marked the health of the relationship. A magic gift, a talisman out of a Persian book, it flourished so long as your love flourished, and would die, definitively, when love died. You and Gwen staggered to your battered finish, and the plant's leaves fell off completely, leaving just a few bald spikes to trim the afterthought of stem. You put the husk out in the garage and left it, refusing to recycle the soil or the pot.

A year later, closing up shop before your move, you discovered it. It sat in its banishment behind a scrap of chain-link fence, putting out new growth in the dark. You went inside and called her. She sounded glad to hear from you. There followed the best three weeks of your life together, unscathed because faked, sheltered by your certain departure.

Even this fiction ended viciously, in mutual recrimination, with your quick exit. As you left, you transplanted the hothouse vine to that strip of dirt that passed for a garden on the north side of your apartment. The thing could not have made it past that next Chicago Columbus Day.

Here in this dark room, in the one unrepentant slit of light your sheet tin permits, that plant proliferates. Its jungle rises up around you. How has it grown so profuse, with so little care? How could it have reached such a canopy without your tending it?

The world goes simple, finally. Air, water, light, heat. Recalling or forgetting. Liking or not liking. Finishing the evening's meal or leaving it. You have not been beaten much. Not suffered pliers or electric prod, burns or mutilations, and so, vastly better off than most of the world's full storehouse of politicals. Your mind, for a few more weeks, is still a model time machine—kingdoms, wars, harems—running at any speed, forward and back.

You've gotten out and seen the world, had a glimpse of the place that Chicago would forever have hidden from you. There are worse things than death by solitude. The silence of this infinite library hones you down to a single razor point. People, like those great sourdough pretzels that you'd personally martyr any number of the faithful to taste again, are individually twisted. The insight carries no horror, no bitterness, no recrimination. It is, finally, simple.

"The war is over," Muhammad tells you, on the twenty-third of October, 1989. Monday. *In Christian countries*, you remember from some long-forgotten text, *the day after the baseball game.*

He does not say how the war has ended, or who won. He seems neither pleased nor particularly stricken. He says only that you will be going home soon. For certain this time. That you must make yourself ready.

This does not involve all that many steps. They cut your hair and shave you, not as before, but with some attention and care. The prep still feels fake until the moment they bring you your old clothes, the things you were wearing on the day they grabbed you, cleaned and pressed, as if you'd only left them at the local laundromat, your claim ticket lost. They take your cheap cotton rags back, to pass on to the next tenant or sell on the international terrorist-supplies spot market.

And then you wait. For four days, then five. Waiting is what you're best at in the world, what you've had the most practice in. But this short sprint at the finish threatens to kill you. You sit a week with your prison-cell possessions in a neat bundle in your lap, ready to ship out at a moment's notice.

Muhammad arrives, a spark of rule-breaking excitement in him. He unlocks you. "Mr. Taimur. Come with us. We have a wonderful surprise for you."

You stand and flee in all directions at once.

"Leave your things. Just come."

You reach the stairwell, where they shove you not down but up. In the rush of novelty, this error does not trouble you. They take you up until there is no more up left. You feel yourself step outside, onto the roof of your prison. A guard at each elbow, you walk to the imagined edge. Only now does the fact grip you. Your whole life has been one misguided leap of trust, with no alternative.

"Sit down," Muhammad orders. His voice is pleasant, expansive. The command, completely insane. Those who climb up here with you line up behind you. To shoot you in the back. To torture you at last, after all these years. To push you off.

"Take off your blindfold." You do. "Do not turn around." You couldn't, even if everything in you tried.

You look up, into a huge black wall awash with stars. The night is silent and still. Larger than any night you can remember ever looking up into. You've forgotten how a night sky plays. It strikes you dumb, the frozen depth of it, the continuity. So many vertices, unnumbered connect-a-dots, the outlines of every picture imaginable. This world is not a story. This world is not an invention. Or there never could be so many of them, spread up there, circling.

You look up, and the night is clear. The mounted beacon moon pulls at this tide inside you. There is an awe, too large for the one we're engineered for. You look down, and the lights even of this maimed city match the ones that nature hangs out against its vacuum.

Why have you been allowed to see this? Your heart swells to receive the unanswerable gift of your captors.

Such a spectacle should have been enough. But up from below, a quick flare rises to rival the moon. A violet new light, the sole moving thing in this panorama, brighter, more beautiful than these mere fixed points, it fails to stay aloft. It falls on a mirror arc back to earth, shattering the point at the far end of its parabola.

If this war is truly over, then the next one has just started. Your guides have failed to anticipate this bonus light show. They bundle you back up and return you to the cell, before human ingenuity announces any new developments. You return to sitting, for days, awaiting further clarification, your real marching orders. After another week, you take your bundle off your lap and scatter it.

This time, you don't even stanch the bitterness. Too late in history. Too much already sacrificed. You ask each guard who comes to bother you. Was the whole sham just another setup, to pick off the last little bits of you they haven't yet managed to annihilate? Not one bothers to answer.

Whiplash sets in, its trough proportionate to the peak you let yourself feel. You pass into a blackness as narrow as that night sky was wide.

Food becomes an intrusion. Exercise. The daily defecation. Each time you move your bowels now, you smell yourself rotting. Your scat has become your father's. It gives off the pungency that filled your childhood, the stink of the disease that ate out the man's insides, the smell still haunting the family bathroom years after his death.

One morning, on your bathroom run, you take off your blindfold in the common sty to find yourself staring at freedom. Square on the shelf above the septic squathole, atop the months of uncleaned scum, the smears of shit both terrorist and hostage, sits a shiny black machine.

You can't even guess at the make or model. You know only that you can put your index finger down its throat without touching metal. You pick up the evil and cradle it, the first time you've held one in your life. You wait for the rush of power, but feel only heavy pain. All expectation has died in you, months ago. You've fallen away from all faith in the future. The façade is down and civilization's carpenter ants have come crawling out of the woodwork. God or some self-destructive guard has set this thing in your lap to use with impunity, to go out blazing, the last breakout, with no hope of anything except to retaliate.

Your hand hovers, paralyzed by obsolete decorum. Pointless beliefs that you cannot shake. The habit of morality cows you, even in the face of morality's full collapse. You set the black device back down on the shelf. Your last chance of escape disappears forever.

You come from the bathroom without your blindfold. Nothing matters any longer. The face of Sayid returns your look, first with shock, then fear. He puts on anger and charges you. One casual wave of the palm stays him.

"You left your gun in the toilet."

He blanches whiter than almond. He freezes and bows his head, as if your magnanimity in not blasting your way out obliges him to you. Forever, you stand and face one another. Then he sidles off, dashes for the bathroom to get there before the angel of the Lord. You head back to your cell, lock yourself in, and don your blindfold.

From that moment, you wear your blindfold at all times. If for an hour, then forever. No one can ever again punish you for having it off. And blindness strengthens you against the world's trick.

From down the corridor, you can hear the sounds of the others being forced in and out of their cells. Once or twice, in the shared cesspool, you detect what must be secret, wordless messages left behind by these other lives—parings on the floor tile, or wadded-up bits of shirt cloth. You live in the fear of direct contact. One day it comes. A new stream of taps against your wall forces you back. Thrill and despair fight inside you for the upper hand. Life will not relent.

Against your will, your mind organizes the incoming flow of bits into words. The new occupant spontaneously reinvents the same code you once used with the short-lived Frenchman, Junot. One tap equals A. The underground alphabet of first resort.

The taps say they come from an American journalist, grabbed before you. When you tap him back your name, he cuts you off: *We know*. He claims that others share the room with him, and names them for you. The announcement floats somewhere between joke and hallucination.

Your thoughts flit about you like bees. The thread of conversation grows impossible to hang on to. You lose count of letters or forget what word you were tapping out. The things the journalist types back don't make sense. He claims that the guards let him read an Arabic newspaper from time to time. He spins out bizarre, elaborate, journalist's delusions: the Berlin Wall has fallen. Apartheid has come to an end. The Soviet Union is holding free elections.

He tries to tell you that several Western hostages have already gone home. Clearly, his need to believe has led him over the edge. And you so badly need to believe these taps of your countryman that his hopeful madness threatens to take you with it. However cruel, you break off contact. You can't make him any better. But he has the power to make you much worse.

More time passes than you can comprehend. There is nowhere on earth it could have gone. You pull yourself inward and wait. Wait for nothing. Wait for the one possible release. Your soul smashes up its last human furnishing for firewood. When that is gone, the elements can take you.

You always thought that you loved your Gwen, that you might model a care that would wear down her suspicion, teach her the feel of gladness, that glimpse of how you might, together, steer your days to a harbored end. Only now you see it, in this bombed-out emptiness, how all along your love coerced her, manipulated, failed to credit her hurt, to legitimate her confusion, simply by demanding that she live the one scenario of shared happiness you were able to imagine . . .

Your love itself was the dictate she could not surrender to. All she had was sovereignty, her unilateral freedom to maneuver, to save herself from your demand for allegiance. You were her oppression, her tyranny, and whatever else she may have turned you into no longer matters. You always thought she pushed away, when, in fact, she only stood still against your pulling. All that your love could ever do for her was spare her.

So it is with your ruined life. All wars might end tomorrow and your capture would not. Kidnap is your keepers' only power, their lone proof that the future hasn't swallowed them alive. There is but one small difference: where love could not survive its cling, this hatred cannot let go and still live.

In the fall of 1990, your teeth begin to break off in your mouth. Something evil happens to them, some vast, advancing disintegration that chunks off bits of molar each time you chew anything harder than pita. You fight the throbbing, clamp down harder, grind the pain into a steady-state background of agony until, in one instant of delirium, you bite through an eighth-inch piece of the tip of your tongue.

You stand in blinding anguish. Grope your way to the length of your chain. You arch your back slowly, then spring forward, slamming your forehead into the wall.

Your head bounces off the concrete. Something issues from the impact. Your back arches and slams forward again, building your leverage. The drinking toy duck. Again and again. Your forehead slips against the viscous wet spot building up on the stone.

"Make it stop," you hear yourself scream. "Make it stop. Make it—"
And then it does.

For years, you've hung by your nails over this drop. Now your fingers straighten, their strength gone. All life has been a fight against this slide into chaos, and here at the end, you feel the slide win. You look down into the abyss, give up your grip, and drop.

41

This room is dark, and without dimension.

It has no door. Or any window where you might have entered.

42

Something doesn't want us doing this.

Antecedent? Spiegel asked his mate. If not his mate, then at least the woman who slept beside him. *What is this "this" of which you speak?*

Images. Look. A thousand years of mosaics. Every few hundred years they'd fill the place, floor to dome. And every couple of centuries they'd cover them over or rip them out again.

Persistent little suckers, them they. And more than a little conflicted.

Conflicted is not the half of it. Waves of iconoclasm. Waves of repainting. It's never-ending. Worse than the abortion debate. An all-out war for our eternal souls.

So who wins finally? I've a vested interest in knowing.

Depends on where you stop the clock. Check in one century, and the walls of the church are completely gutted. Check the next, and it's your worst billboard nightmare.

Wait. You're telling me that this figure you're working on was done in the thirteenth century and this other one in the ninth? There's no difference. Exactly the same style.

That's what the Byzantines would like you to believe.

But it's the Byzantines doing the ripping?

The Byzantines. The Roman Catholics. The Ottoman Turks. The modern secularists. Name your idol basher. And it's not just images. People die over this. Lots of people.

I don't see . . . I mean, what . . . what possible difference . . . ?

Spiegel's lover looked up from her expensive study plates, betrayed. He should know. He shouldn't have to ask. Form mangled the truth it housed. Every fixed image crucified the divinity it tried to copy.

Adie's tone grew chill. *Well. After all. God told us not to.* Burlesque skidded up against its own electric fences. *The second rule He ever gave us.*

Uh, right. And remind me. What was the first one again?

We're playing with the ultimate fire here. The one true prohibition. It's like God knew that if we ever got started drawing . . . She trailed off, conscience-stricken, in the face of the hi-res evidence.

That?

That we'd keep at it until the picture was done.

Something in him wanted her off the topic. Away. *So where does that leave us? I mean, we have a millennium and a half of possible interiors, ranging from figure-clogged to buck naked. Which moment are we supposed to re-create?*

She held her mouse up to her chest, a numbed virgin holding up her child victim for target practice again. *That's the only question.*

The container unfolded, as light bent in air. The eye, wandering through at ground level, slipped into so many slant archways, secret niches, and aisle forests, so many hints at further space that it could not make out the exact floor plan. All the action flew up—up into paradise's central dome and its flanking hemispheres.

Spiegel worked on the code that would move the pilgrim through so much sculpted emptiness. He turned the visiting body into its own joystick, accelerating down any arrow of the compass it leaned into. And he added a crowning stroke, so right it seemed a given. One raised index finger swept the visitor off the floor up into the soaring vaults.

No matter how often he tested the routine, Spiegel succumbed to the euphoria of flight. Here was the levitation all children dream of, the easy uplift of birds that the soul feels entitled to, brought weightlessly to life. He pointed his digit skyward. The ground fell away. The upper arcades drew close. He hovered in place, twenty meters above the church floor, drafting on the currentless air like one of those miraculous medieval monks who repeat the Ascension on faith alone.

The RL lined up to try. Even hardened hackers could not get enough of flying. Hagia Sophia was fast becoming the biggest thing since bull jumping. Neither Ebesen nor Vulgamott would take part. Lim did, and paid for his ride with a gushing nosebleed.

Adie insisted on including every flourish: the Theotokos, hovering in the eastern apse; the Deesis, harsh in its second-story south gallery. A single overarching volume arose from her anthology of parts. But her flight toward sanctuary played out as the most secular of footraces: her push for transcendent detail versus spring's public demo deadline.

She labored for longer than she could afford over each tile in the southwest narthex tympanum: Justinian and Constantine presenting the church and city to the seated Christ. Each mosaic emperor held up his gift of a scale mosaic model: tiny domed cosmos inside the tiny domed cosmos they decorated.

Stevie watched her work, excited by the stillness that consumed her. *So this is the dream of VR?* he asked. *Be of the world . . . ?*

She smiled and nodded. *But not in it.*

You know what we need?

Tell me what we need, Stevie.

Code that will crumble at the same rate mortar does. Stone that compresses. Joints that break. Bits of rubble that accumulate around the piers after the simulation has been running for a few hundred years. Rubble that no one actually programmed . . .

Oh, she said. *We already have that.*

They had the space sufficiently fleshed out in time to celebrate a simulated Christmas Mass. Klarpol and Spiegel spent the last few minutes of 1990 together, placing tiny stones into the vault of heaven.

Then came the New Year.

She could not say, later, that she hadn't seen. But she'd never once believed. For months she'd withstood the glut of informationless data issuing from the latest desert showdown, following without following. O'Reilly and Kaladjian had even placed angry bets on which side would blink first. But the age of blinks was past. The world's interface no longer responded to blinking.

Two weeks into the demo year, that electronic storm, so long in simulation, at last broke. Adie witnessed the opening shots by accident, on a television the size of a picture postcard that her Jordanian greengrocer stared at robotically as she tried to buy endive to bring home for dinner.

Two delirious American reporters trapped in a high-rise office babbled on, over satellite uplink, about the phantoms screaming across Baghdad's dome. She hurried back to her island, and Stevie. He knelt there on his haunches, on the bare living-room floor, three feet in front of the tube.

She set her plastic sacks of vegetable down in the doorway. *What is it?* she asked, knowing already. *What's happening?* As if that question ever had an answer.

"Baghdad was lit up like a Christmas tree," one pilot explained to the camera. "It was tremendous!"

"It looked like the Fourth of July down there," another boy said. "Just like in the movies."

"No," she said. Louder. Again. Hysterical. But no one paid her any attention.

The whole planet descended into the flicker of shared delirium. Scores of countries came onto the coaxial cable, just to get the twenty-four-hour feed. The Northern Hemisphere embarked on a winter of perpetual broadcast. On signal, by mass, silent agreement, an unbroken umbrella of full coverage stitched itself together.

No hiding place could escape continuous update. Wherever Adie went, she stood looking through the crosshairs. Her colleagues poured over every scrap they pulled off the cable feed. Downhill from the labs, gas stations and delis inundated her for free — aerial bombardment, like green stamps, supplied as a public service. Stevie, addicted from the start, would hit the Mute button and drag about the house, pretending not to look. A dozen times a day, Adie ingested the same Kabuki footage: slow-motion replays of sky-strewn annihilation, lit in the eerie palette of video infrared. She stopped eating. She began to throw up, at odd hours, behind the closed bathroom door.

Smart bombs beamed back video to even smarter bombers. Nose-cone shots documented their descents all the way up to the moment of deliverance. One missile steered itself down the midline of a twenty-foot-wide bridge. Another threaded the chimney of a suspected command-and-control center. Laser beams guided their cruise payloads for hundreds of miles over the wrinkled earth to land on a square smaller than the Cavern's front wall.

Pinpoint delivery turned evidence so intoxicating that no one who once looked at it could look away. The race had achieved the precision of its earliest dreams. Coverage worked to keep up with the apotheosis. But the more Adie watched, the less actually took place.

Event disappeared down the chute of choreographed news. She grasped at the accounts and came up empty-handed. People died without a sound, bloodless, thousands of feet below the all-seeing eye.

Overnight, yellow ribbons sprang up everywhere—tourniquets twisted around wounded trees—and no one could say exactly where they'd come from. Scores of mega-celebrities banded together to record a radio hit, their caring voices abstracting any hint of political stance into a general message of hope and ecumenical well-wishing.

At timed intervals, tuned to the perfect intermittent reinforcement schedule, the Joint Chiefs gave press conferences, explaining their multimedia clips in careful play-by-plays. A riveted Realization Lab tuned in to the course of the war's master narrative, its purposes as long and obscure as its means were swift and expedient. Violence seemed ready to expend even its viewers as collateral damage.

Babylon became a bitmap. Pilots took its sand grains apart, pixel by pixel, their soldier bodies tied to weapons systems by electronic umbilical, their every joystick twitch duplicating moves overlearned in years of now-consummated simulation. Nightscopes revealed minute movements, at impossible distances, in pitch-dark. Robot stalkers chased living targets. Formal edge-detecting algorithms told heat from cold, friend from enemy, camouflaged caches from empty countryside. Human intelligence migrated wholesale into its artifacts.

It was the perfect operation: the kind you carried out deep in enemy territory. It told no story, finally, aside from these abject images. Adie and Stevie stared nightly at a mute set, from under their bedcovers, forced to watch the upshot of everything they'd put their hand to.

We did this? she whispered to him. *It's us?*

He stared straight ahead, afraid to miss a scrap of acquitting evidence. *Of course not. Don't be nuts.*

The bombs with depth perception? The ones that can tell our vehicles' silhouettes from the Iraqis'? The cruise missiles with a whole digital map of the world inside them, so that they know exactly where to explode?

His shoulders dismissed her. Too defensive to mount a defense.

Stevie, I need to know. Her voice lay just this side of its own smart violence. *What have we been doing here? Are they using the same electronics as us? Are they taking our code?*

He smiled at the near-total naïveté. *The military? The Air Force invented virtual reality half a century ago. Mission trainers, flight*

*simulators. The Army made the first computer, back when the game was
still about beating the Nazis. They've been hip-deep into VR from the
beginning. ARPA built the Net. They ordered the first microprocessor.
You sow the Whirlwind, you reap SAGE.* He went on, numbly, dull. On
automatic pilot. *If you want to know the truth, we're stealing their code.
The whole runaway century, living off military spin-offs.*

She got out from under the covers and shut off the signal. *I'm sorry.
I can't watch anymore.*

No. Of course. You're right.

They curled up against each other for protection, warmth, sleep.
But each other wasn't enough. She could not lay still, but turned
every two minutes, on truth's spit. Of course the Joint Chiefs wanted
what art promised: to break the bonds of matter and make the mind
real.

You didn't know? he asked, in darkness, too small a voice to want a
real answer. *You really didn't know?*

She howled at the words, and he could not calm her.

She went to Jonathan Freese. *Who are we doing this for?*

Well, I've been doing this for myself. Who are you doing this for?

*Jonathan. Don't jack with me. Not now. Who's buying what we're
selling?*

He studied her, deciding whether to laugh or fire her. He showed
her the list of interested parties who'd already signed up for Cavern
demonstrations in the spring. He couldn't very well refuse to show her.
Disney, yes. Sony, yes. Half a dozen research universities, yes. But
among the rest of the roster were other agencies, groups whose upbeat
acronyms could not disguise their affiliation. Slaughter was a free rider,
a virus using them, using the RL, using the Cavern as a way of spreading its genome.

*You fucked me over, didn't you? Just like you wanted to, from the day I
signed on.*

*Sweetheart, I know we're all under a lot of stress here. I'm going to for-
get you said this.*

She did not even bother to give him the finger.

She sought out Karl Ebesen. She found him and Michael Vulgamott manning their cubicle, watching SCUDs and Patriots proxy-battle in the upper air. She put her finger to the screen they gazed at, where a trail of refugees streamed north. Her voice sounded almost level. *Did we do this?*

They looked at her, afraid to move.

This? Is this our fault?

Ebesen turned to look at her. *Everything . . . everything we ever do is our fault.*

She sat down by the side of his desk and broke down. He slid his chair toward her, baffled. For one brief moment, he seemed actually to touch her.

Since I was born? she said. *For as long as I can remember. All I ever wanted? All I wanted to do was make something beautiful. Something that wouldn't hurt anyone.*

He nodded. He knew already: to make something good of our work and days. That was the place all guilt came from. She couldn't want anything that hadn't already burned him.

She shook her head, enraged. Her sobbing sounded like a tearing veil. *Why didn't you tell me?*

He frowned. Scowled at her. Held up his helpless hands.

I know, she wept. *I know. I never asked.*

Her fault: her own doing, all along, from the very first crayon smear. She must have wanted it, somehow, to have gotten in this deep, without once seeing the size of the betrayal she so lovingly enabled. Death from the air would win out in the end. Remote and ingenious, all piloted by absent fathers, the warcraft were flying again, despite the gifts she'd drawn to distract them. Once before, the Air Force had thrown away her handmade bribes. Now, worse: they took all her pretty pictures and put them to use.

The Parasite Room had lodged inside her. The RL, the Cavern—all smart weaponry—were just first sketches for the next, larger assembly.

Her work here was just a rough draft for technology's wider plan. The world machine had used her, used them all to bring itself into existence. And its tool of choice — its lever and place to stand, the tech that would spring it at last into three dimensions — was that supreme, useless, self-indulgent escapism. The thing that made nothing happen. The mirror of nature. Art.

The war needed drawing, after all. The conflict had drafted Adie, made her its draftsman. She'd become death's seeing-eye dog, leading on into that place it could not navigate unaided. This she saw in full, even before the ground assault started. That girl's supreme paintbox had done its work. Everything that imagination had fashioned would now go real.

You're never here anymore, Spiegel chastised her. *Even when you're here. When I talk to you, when I touch you? It's like I pass right through you.*

I'm sorry, she faked, as calmly as she could. *I'll be better.*

Life outlasts this, he wanted to say. It outlives its portrait. *Look,* he said instead. *Are you trying to punish me for bringing you out here? Do you want to stop working at this? Do you want us to take off? Blow this peanut stand? I'm game, you know. I'll go anywhere. Just so long as we stay together.*

While they spoke, the road to Basra turned into a hundred-mile-long human ash. Helicopters filmed it in detailed pan, from a thousand attentive angles.

Can you give me root directory access? she asked, stroking him.

What do you . . . ? Can I ask what . . . ? But trust could ask nothing. *Is there anything I can help with?*

She smiled and kissed him, deep, past the lips. *Let me surprise you.*

He gave her all the system's passwords. He was love's dupe, its software engineer, ready to barter for any scrap of real-time connection he might get.

She destroyed the backup copies first. That much she'd learned, in her years of becoming digital. One by one, she mounted the archived volumes. And file by file, directory by directory, she erased her handiwork. It was not much, this retaliatory strike. It did not answer to what had been done. But in her own small way, Adie vowed to kill what she could.

Those projects to which she'd contributed nothing, she left intact. The Weather Room, the Large-Molecule Docking simulation: each maker would have to be responsible for his own designs. She passed over O'Reilly's Futures Room, the one that had predicted the Gulf War, the one that predicted the war beyond the Gulf. She left Kaladjian's wonderland of pure math unscathed.

Even in the worlds she'd helped to make, she picked around the others' contributions. She tore up her Arlesian floorboards but left behind Raj's ethereal creaking. She torched her dreamworld jungle, sparing those bits of vegetation that Karl had nurtured. Growth vanished into the void of zeroed data: the ebony flutist, the third monkey flushed from the undergrowth, the dreaming, almond woman that Spider Lim recognized . . .

She disposed of each redundant copy, as quickly as she could type the Kill command. Then she turned to the working master files, the living originals. How could delight have misled her so baldly? That illusion of purpose, the giddy sense of answering a call, of doing urgent work that only her hands could do . . . She could not send her portfolio back to randomness without a final peek. Fact had rendered her immune to the seduction. All she needed was five minutes, to see what that illusion looked like, stripped of belief.

She booted up the cathedral and stepped back in. She leaned into the nave's great hollow, feeling herself move despite her better sense. She pointed one finger straight up, hating herself even as she gave in to the soar. She let herself rise into the hemisphere apse, then farther up, all the way into the uppermost dome, now inscribed with its flowing *surah* from the Qur'an.

She spun her body in the invented volume, the largo ballet of an astronaut repairing failed equipment far off in the infinite vacuum. She twisted and looked down into the breach below. The God's-eye view: in the simulation, but not of it. And deep beneath her, where there should have been stillness, something moved.

She dropped her finger, shocked. The winch of code unthreaded. She fell like a startled fledgling, back into the world's snare. The mad thing swam into focus: a man, staring up at her fall, his face an awed bitmap no artist could have animated.

43

The room of the Cave is one continuous chasm.

Its chambers all connect. They run together, the way old Greek was written: no spaces, no commas, no periods, just one long flow without dams or rapids, a single subterranean stream that never changes its course. But never the same stream twice.

Here you have lived since childhood, facing the darkness, taking shadows for the things that cast them. On the walls of this room, a story unrolls. In it, someone just like you gets miraculously sprung. He turns to the light, which instantly blinds him. You cheer for him to run, but he turns back from the glare to the safety of this room.

Your eyes adjust to the light of this hypothetical. What you take to be the boundless world may be no more than just this underground spring. You make out the peep show to be just a peep show, but only through the clip projected in front of you. The clunkiest of puppets say *shadow*, say *story*. And in that tale—continuous, no spaces—the tale you've been chained to since birth, you make out the room you live in.

But even while trapped in that old scroll's closed O, the storytelling race has been busy. Millennia pass in the war against matter. Every invention bootstraps off the next. The tale advances; thought extends its grasp over things until it arrives at the final interface. The ultimate display, the one that closes the gap between sign and thing.

In this continuous room, images go real. You come to rest at last, in no more than the idea of a bed. The mere mention of love brings on the fact. The word "food" is enough to feed you. A carved-soap gun can kill your enemies. And a quick sketch of the Resurrection suffices to raise the dead.

The room of the cave is something more than allegory. But the room of the cave is something less than real. Its wall shadows ripple with an undercurrent of substance, more than representation, but not yet stuff. Notion springs to life from the same, deep source in which the outdoors is scripted—what the run-on Greek once called the Forms.

In this room, before this play of fire, you feel the deeper freeze just outside the cave's mouth. From here you can make out those more turbulent axioms, chill forces you couldn't feel until you touched your fingers to this coded pane.

You breathe in. You lean forward, and the images advance toward you. You look up and rise, or gaze down and sink. You materialize on a stony cliff, ruined streets cutting switchbacks through a grove of olives. You fly to the end of the cliff and lift off, careful to stay, this time, above the ocean but below the sun.

You learn to steer your fragile machine. You skim above the surface of a dark sea. You dive beneath these scattered reefs and float in your birthright air. The flight feels like reading, like skimming a thousand exhilarated pages, but without the brakes and ballast of an ending.

Everywhere you look on the horizon, there are more islands. You fly past them, but always more appear. Desire moves you through them, down toward their surfaces. You've found your way back to the cradle where this project started. Here and there, against the sun-bleached shores, an amphitheater emerges, or a temple to that same bleaching sun that trails you overhead. One minute the air is thick with autumn, the next, a sweet-sapped spring. The seasons track that kidnapped goddess through the year, wandering to and from her underground prison.

You fly too freely, or the land's geometry is wrong. Some titan fails to hold up his corner of the air's tent. Or you simply reach the edge of a story that, even at this final stage, remains eternally under construction. An embankment, pitch-white and blinding, looms up in front of you, too fast for you to take evasive action.

The scene crashes before you do. The room of the cave slams to a breakpoint and empties itself into error's buffer. There on the wall where the oceans and olives and temples were, where the marble crags ran from their spine down into their unbroken chasm, the machine seizes up, the faulty allegory crumbles, the debugger spits out a continuous scroll of words.

Only through this crack can you see where things lead. You step through the broken symbols, into something brighter.

44

In the room of shared experience, she disappears.

She vanishes just days before they are to give the demo for the first round of visitors from the secular world.

She's not the first to sign off and take up work elsewhere. The wizard Rajasundaran has already quit to join a team farther up the mountain, a loose confederation of technical visionaries backed by a serial venture capitalist who promises to underwrite wilder extensions of simulated space: direct electro-muscular stimulation tactors, ear monitor implants, digital-endorphin interfaces, 3-D scanners, force-feedback reality augmenters that slide whole data structures in and out of the visual cortex for direct parallel processing. Vishnu will assume all shapes before the world starts up again from scratch.

O'Reilly, too, decides to bail, just before curtain time. But he heads in the opposite direction, back to the body's home islands. The spur comes in the form of another handwritten note sent by archaic air mail. A shock to recall: the race is still dragging around sacks full of scribbled paper in the cargo holds of lumbering jumbo jets.

> *Ronan,*
>   *All right; so I lied. The wedding was just a literary device. Clearly it failed. And you know what's especially pathetic? The fellow I invented? This Stephen Powys character? He's even worse than you are . . .*

It is enough for him; more than enough. What was he thinking, after all? Midwife to the future: a man would have to be mad. He's seen what they're birthing—the runaway victory of the flat graph. The future does not need a midwife. The future needs an abortionist.

By Delphic estimate as shrouded as any, the species still had another forty years. Best to spend them locked up among the earth's most backward people, who won't get the news for centuries, in a place where even one afternoon can stretch out into an eternal *now*. He'll put himself up against this fantasy husband, projection for projection.

It will have to be a progressive arrangement, by Irish standards. But surely between O'Reilly, Maura, and this Powys invention, the three of them can reach some civilized understanding. He can return to the island of the damned. He can live in endless savagery, raise his children in savagery, await the savage future, and no one will ever be able to say just what may come of the life they'll make of it.

The rest of the team is in attendance. Lim, in his passion for assimilation, plays the emcee. He puts the clients at their ease, speaking to each in the common diction of equipment. He shows them the reality engines in the hardware room, thinking *Rembrandt, Claude, Hsieh Ho*, but identifying the Power Agate servers by their current model designations.

Here's where we started from, he tells the tour. Then he demos, for comic contrast, the first few primitive software rooms ever assembled for the Cavern. And something in those first childish endeavors—the nubby stray arc of crayon, after the distance they've come—jars loose an image in him. An aunt putting him on an airplane, telling him in a still-comprehensible foreign language that he must be big and brave. Handing him photos: this will be your country. This white woman with the funny, wedged head will be your mother. This woman, these features: yours.

Sue Loque shows off her prototype visual development environment, playing to the hilt her role as token crossover. Her boy's gee-whiz soul in a girl's pierced body keenly awaits all the possible worlds to come, when she will be no more than the tamest of fertile blurrings. The virtual world will leap past all birthmarks. No age, no sex, no race, no clans, no power politics . . .

The scientists trot out their visualization tools, environments that, even as they debut, have already become commonplace. Kaladjian treats the paying visitors with his standard contempt, for remaining stupidly human in the face of so much rigor. He and Stance draw the first applause for their climate theater. Bergen's biosimulator entertains the industry nametags for a full half hour.

Freese presides, smiling like a gracious head of state. But his heart is already elsewhere. Only two weeks earlier, he received his first look at civilization's next leap. He's been to a demo of his own, returning with a little piece of software that will turn the whole Net into a medium of universal exchange. He's come away with a glimpse of the thing the human yarn has been spinning itself toward, ever since its first campfire recitation: every soul in the world, serving as every other soul's twenty-four-hour server. Movable type was no more than a shadow puppet show.

The software he's seen is still text-only. But the breakout—pictures, clips, and, finally, the inevitable merge with VR—is just a few clock cycles away. The machinic phylum is on the move again, spinning itself out into another species. As always, there will be hell and turbulence to pay. But whatever the costs of this Next Big Thing, Freese means to be there.

The first wave of the Cavern's prospective purchasers stroll through a string of worlds of increasing visual interest. Spiegel runs flack, hinting to all parties that the best still waits in the wings. Hoping it still does. He hasn't a clue what it looks like, the country his mate has left them with. No one has had time to run the place through a final test.

He knows only that she is gone, that she was gone already, weeks before she left. In the last leg, just before the final tape, she'd become obsessed. Something had happened under the dome, some visitation invisible to everyone but the project's designer. She dug frantically at the structure, as if at the mouth of a collapsed mine shaft where people had been trapped.

She disappeared into the place she was making. Her immersion grew so total that he finally cornered her. *What is it?* he asked. *What's happening in there?*

Stevie, it's . . . I can't tell you. You'd never believe me.

Belief? When have I ever failed you with belief?

She looked at him, weighing the odds. Then she shook her head, dazed, denying, her own credulity spent. *There's . . . something in there. Something that wants out. Something we didn't make.*

404

I . . . don't understand. There? Where? Where exactly are you . . . ?

She turned to bolt, and he reached out to grab her—to force her now, this once, to stay. And in that reflex force, he lost her. She went passive, giving in to his stronger grip. He tried to turn her toward him, to lift her eyes up to his.

Ade. If . . . I didn't know better, I'd say you were cheating on me.

And the look she shot him then—caged, uncovered; *How much do you know?*—was worse than confirmation.

I believe you, he tried again, in the dark. *Wherever. Whatever you're . . . I . . . believe.*

But she was already off, lost in that emergency rescue mission her overworked imagination had devised. She worked alone, keeping some tryst, meeting some phantom assignation that Spiegel could not even begin to hang flesh upon. Her trips away into that private geometry were as terse and desperate as love.

Three weeks before the end, they received a cardboard box from a small town in Ohio specializing in Shaker museums and close-security prisons. It was filled with books, tapes, photos, and a handful of other archaic media, earmarked for the two of them, discovered by the orderlies who cleaned out the bedroom after its tenant's forced evacuation.

All Adie took from the inheritance was a floppy disk, Ted's last composition, the chamber symphony, in MIDI format. His bizarre, wilderness notion of a music that people might want to listen to.

That's your keepsake? Steve asked. *That's all you want, to remember him?*

Adie nodded once and made off with the file, a magpie thieving a shred of tinfoil for its growing nest.

She worked on Byzantium flat out until she collapsed in exhaustion. They sent her home, feverish. She came back the next day, over the group's collective objections.

Sweetheart. It's just a damn demo, Steve told her. *People are going to buy the thing, whatever rooms we show them. The machine is state-of-the-art. Someone will want one. Adie. Ade. It's not worth ruining your health over.*

She went back, feverish, to work as if health were no more than a guilty, survivor's privilege. A figment of the imagination.

She took her stolen shreds of code and quilted them into a landscape. She worked, deep in covert conversation with a life just out of earshot. The room might have gone on forever, a work in progress. But when her assemblage came provisionally together, Adie seemed to shake free, for the space of an evening, into a safe place. She came up for air and sat with Stevie once more, spent, silent, in the brief truce of accomplishment.

He read the fact in her face. *It's done?*

For now, she said.

For good, I hope.

Come on. Accredit me. I'm cutting-edge, for another few weeks at least. People are lusting for what I do. I can get a job anywhere I want.

So where might that be, exactly?

Search me. At least we know what we're looking for, now. At least we have a template. She hugged the loyal, uncomprehending Pinkham to her. *We'll recognize it when we see it, huh, pup?*

I'm going with you, Spiegel said.

She put her palm on his chest, the gentlest refusal. He grabbed her wrist, and she drew back.

Ade, listen to me. Nothing I can make . . . makes much sense. Without someone to make it for.

She smiled a sfumato smile, the grin of one already sacrificed to canvas. Her finger came forward again, to trace his ribbed flesh, connecting the freckled dots she knew now by heart.

How long have we all been cooped up here? she asked. *My God, it's been forever. Like death. I've got to get out of this place. Head south. Do some sightseeing. You know: I don't know the first thing about what it looks like, out there?*

We can see it together. Better. Stereo.

Stevie. I need . . . to reinvent myself. Alone. In situ.

He said nothing.

She worked her mouth again, struggling. *Just . . . give us a headstart. Six months. Then come find us.*

Where?

If I knew, I'd tell you. She laughed and swept her arms. *No, I wouldn't. That would be cheating.*

No clue? Anywhere?

Sure. Scavenger hunt. How big can the place be?

Big, Adie. Big enough for us all to get lost in.

Small enough to fit in a shoebox, buddy. And shrinking by the nanosecond.

She disappears just days before the audience arrives. Drafts an escape hatch and slips down it, off through color's interface, into the negative space, between the single brushstroke, the vanishing point that the hand invents to fool the eye.

What's left of the design team stands in front of the Cavern mouth, waiting for their cue. Vulgamott paces, cursing under his breath. *Damn artist. Bugging out at the eleventh hour. Leaving us to run the thing alone.*

Ebesen stands by him, wearing his first new shirt in years. His trousers, too, can only be a goodbye gift, if for no other reason than that they fit. *Of course we have to run it alone. That's the whole beauty of fake reality.*

Vulgamott pretends not to hear him. News is something a civilized person shouldn't have to do more than watch. *What if it doesn't work?*

Nothing ever works, Ebesen reminds him. *That's why we keep fixing it.*

But in this room, the room of shared experience, the group show comes off without a hitch.

45

The room that holds you falls away. Space opens out in every direction, too big to see across, the biggest single opening that has ever surrounded you. Your eyes need time to adjust to the size of it, the glare. A single dome rises so high above you, its shell might as well be the thing it stands for. It hovers over a nimbus of forty windows, suspended on a crown of light.

In the mystery of sealed volumes, the space is larger than its container. At ground level, under the angeled pendentives, beneath the lofty clerestory hung on its massive piers, your body shrinks to a single bit, the smallest switch in paradise's registers. Here is the oblivion life has always wanted—the chance to fade back into the scale that birthed it.

Your eyes start ignorant, but slowly get knowledge. Pillars from the earth's four corners, stolen or permanently borrowed, display all stone's available hues. The walls are enameled with living pictures. The floor plan is too richly scalloped to decode. All you can do is wander, deeper in.

Only movement reveals the room's full size. You drift forward, setting in motion free currents of air. The eddies cascade, accumulating into trade winds that whip through the open nave. The winds collect in pressure zones and fronts. They rise and cool; their moisture condenses in tiny thunderheads that soon, off in the bays beyond the north arcade, break out in a time-lapse storm. Rain falls and evaporates again, before it can moisten the dark floor tiles.

Somewhere above your head, the carved stone capitals seethe. Spandrels unfurl their runner of vines. Out of those tangles of carved leaves, there coil denser strands. Surprised, you point. And pointing, you rise. You draw near the carvings, through more space than you'd gauged. The vines sharpen and swell. Up close, they turn into knotted hanks of macromolecule, twinning and twining in the air's interstices.

Hovering in a nimbus to the east—the needle's Jerusalem, the map's Mecca—a mother cowers, holding her infant in front of her like a shield. On the child's face, a plan already hatches: all-out subversion of the omnipotent State, the bafflement of vested interests, the last defeat of matter. The mother's face is pure fear. She's lost her baby already. She looks out to the west, on the chasm in front of her, on her boy's future, his fate as a political, his inevitable death at the hands of the authorities whose only goal is ever to preserve the domestic peace.

Around the doomed nuclear family, huge black medallions proclaim the name of God and his servants: Allah, Mohammed, Ali . . . Perched below these in the apse, a ghostly sphere spins: the world's nations, their parti-colored surfaces swirling like oil streaks on a stirred puddle. Their colors flare and go dark and, after an endless pause, blaze through their cycle again.

The space seeps music. Its score breathes in time with your breath, a chamber symphony beginning in your inner ear and traveling outward. The pitches take on the line of your thoughts and give you others.

You stumble upon a safe haven, just off the sacristy. A corner outfitted just for you, with provisions, clothes, a place to clean up and rest. You can stay here for good, all human needs met. You sit on a cane chair and crane your neck out the window, looking out onto the sea, the Bosphorus, the Golden Horn.

A shattering barrage drives you from this paradise. You run back into the violated nave, where phantom crusaders and holy warriors now close for battle up and down the columned aisles. The great church goes pure theater. Grainy, mosaic footage plays against the paint-stripped tympana, digital clips from the earth's flaming islands: human chains, laser-guided night shots of bunkers erupting, walls shorn up and hammered back down again.

You try to flee. But now the bombardment rips right through you. This violence is harmless, as innocent as any projected image. You rise up and watch in awful fascination. It plays out in every corner: the first war, the war over pictures, the showdown that imprisons you. The blasts explode in the name of a project too large to figure out, a game whose ends care nothing about your own.

Across the invented gulf of space, shells detonate. Fresh explosions rip through the giant hall, each one touching off others. Stone by stone, St. Sophia collapses into a cavernous ruin.

Up from the cracks around you lick tiny tongues of green. A jungle springs up, and in the jungle, a naked, couched Eve, pointing with wonder at the fires all around her.

Then you hear what can only be the buzzing of insects. They mass you, a sudden swarm of flat, paper bees, no bigger than your thumb, the work of a child with a new paint box. They form a fireman's bucket brigade, flying up into the gallery, each carrying between its legs a colored square. One by one, they add their point of color to the damaged portraits: a wasted Christ, a ravaged Baptist, a Madonna who cannot for the life of her figure out why she's been drawn into this hopeless endeavor.

Paper bees patch at the mosaic, stone by stone. They race the spread of the vegetation. They buzz in insect single file, relentless, returning empty to the hive, to your hands, for refilling. With a child's labored realism, they rebuild the length of the damaged stone bodies. They reach the feet, freeing the captives. The images step from their wall down into the jungled nave, rejoin you where you lie, stricken with insight, in the undergrowth.

The inner church goes dark; fluorescents blaze back on. Transcendence collapses again to the width of a walk-in closet. The future's clients—the demo buyers, the Joint Chiefs of Staff—remove their shuttered glasses. They look upon the alien world that drags them back. They wince in the flush of light, squinting to make things out.

Inside this room, the world re-forms itself. Outside, there is no saying. Against the real, *perhaps* must plead no contest. But from the demonstration room, no one walks out the way he came.

46

The morning that Muhammad comes for you, you already expect him. Your ears have attuned to subaudible frequencies. You hear a message in his step, from miles down the locked corridor. You hear upheaval in his voice, even before he speaks.

He thinks he wakes you. "We Arabs have a saying. Rise before the sun, because the earth steals the hours before dawn from Paradise."

He makes you pack your ridiculous sack of belongings, as you have packed so many times before. An old game, this terrorism. They have it down. But gone already, you've become immune, free of hope, safe from all belief. You do as he says, obeying with nothing more than the pointless shell of your body.

His voice hides a note of relief, a sympathy for you, so far as anyone can feel sympathy for another. The care cuts into you. It riddles you with chances, each one more terrible than the last.

He takes you off the chain. Panic descends when he leads you, blindfolded, into the hall. Men call out to you in Arabic, touch you on the back, applauding your shoulders. They take you to certain death, or worse. Now, before dawn, in the hours stolen from paradise. The single fact of your existence, the one that ought to be purely private, beyond history, past politics, even your death will be played out on any number of stages, not one of them your own.

This time, they do not tape you, a minor mercy worse than any harshness. They place you loose into the coffin, one last training in asphyxiation before the final run. You pray for a merciful death, as you have prayed before, racked on this transmission as the truck slams against the cratered streets. You pray, knowing your prayers do nothing. This is part of what has broken in your brain: to keep asking, knowing there are no answers but chance.

The truck draws close to the cursed city, passing through several checkpoints. It makes no sense. They could have put a bullet in the base of your brain, back in the countryside, unseen. They could have fed what flesh you still possess to the farmyard dogs.

Faithful to the core of human cruelty, they pull you from death and revive you. You cannot stand without aid. They force you inside, and the return to enclosed space calms you. Some rendezvous transacts itself, some tense handoff. Your captors leave you in the hands of an unknown third party. The earth starts to shake violently. Not the earth, but something closer. As close as the veins in your neck. Your own meat and blood.

A man is speaking softly to you in accented English. "Please remove your blindfold. You are among friends."

You refuse. You stall for time. "Perhaps in a little bit."

He offers you food, drink, clean clothes, a shower. "You are free," he says.

You laugh: a short, hard monosyllable of phlegm.

"You are on the way home," he says.

You tear off your blindfold in a flash of last rage. The game, the torture must end here. You have no more life for it.

You find yourself sitting in a dingy office, across the metal desk from a slight, gray man in burgundy tie and short-sleeve white shirt. He offers you his hand. You shake it, although your hand is shaking already. The feel of another's skin rasps against yours. His voice shrieks in your ear. You touch his desk, the papers on it, the pen, the photos. You cannot stop touching these slight impossibilities. Your arms and legs quiver beyond controlling. Distress must finish you. You start to break. You replace your blindfold over your eyes.

He says you will go first to Damascus. You recognize the name, from some ancient myth. From there they will fly you to Turkey, transfer you to a military plane bound for Wiesbaden, and a full debriefing. "It will be difficult at first. You must go as slowly as you need."

He tells you that the world has changed since your capture. You hold up your hand to stop him. It quakes as if you are waving. "Maybe later." Perhaps next week. Perhaps never.

You sit in a hotel room in Damascus with all the shades pulled tight. One of your caretakers is there with you, to make sure you don't harm yourself. He asks if you'd like to see a newspaper. The *International Herald Tribune*. "Last week's," he apologizes.

"That's all right," you tell him. "I'm a little behind."

You peek, and a vision of civilization spins away underneath your fingers. The permanent war, the balance of horror, the only reality you've ever known: all have vanished, replaced by the next, more dangerous morass. The world has wired itself up in your absence. You can recognize nothing. Someone's thumb rides the Fast-forward button as you look on from light-years above, a view of the earth from a distant star, the planet's burning fossil already whiffed out even as its glow just reaches you.

You work to control the newsprint sheets. You see yourself staring out from page 3: the forced prison picture, the one that bears no living resemblance to you. Every other fact is wrong. The piece says you are about to be released. It misstates your age. It says your mother is dead. It claims you're married to a hospice worker and have a five-year-old daughter. Just beneath it, a second article describes the thousand archaeologies uncovered in this year's local firefight. An ancient forum brought back above ground, from under the mortared-down Banco di Roma . . .

You fold the paper back up and slip it under your hotel closet door, where it can harm no one.

The first official American comes to greet you. He talks a wall of spectacular gibberish. The country is proud of you. You have done a patriotic service that will not soon be forgotten. Your brother is on his way from Chicago to Germany to meet you.

"And may I just add, personally?" He smiles. "If we never hear the name Gwen Devins again, it will be too soon." He shakes his head in admiration. "The woman is relentless. Without mercy. She has absolutely worn out her welcome in all diplomatic circles."

At the first interrogation, they go easy. But already they ask you: How? How is it you can still be here, after the years of where you've been?

You do not tell them now, though in time you'll have to. They won't be able to make out what you have to say. How you gave in to the final abyss, how you dropped into the darkness beneath your permanent blindfold. How in the moment that you broke and fell, you never hit. How you saw, projected in a flash upon that dropping darkness, a scene lasting no longer than one held breath. A vision that endured a year and longer. One that made no sense. That kept you sane. A glimpse of the transfer-house of hostage. Of the peace that the world cannot give.

You'll have to say, someday: how the walls of your cell dissolved. How you soft-landed in a measureless room, one so detailed that you must have visited it once. But just as clearly a hallucination, the dementia of four years in solitary. A mosque more mongrel than your own split life, where all your memorized Qur'an and Bible verses ran jumbled together. A temple on the mind's Green Line, its decoration seeping up from awful subterranean streams inside you, too detailed to be wholly yours.

You couldn't say what style or era. It might have been anywhere on earth: a deserted hangar, big enough to house the rest mass of salvation.

Massive bars of light eroded the stones. You shrank to nothing in the size of it. But you did not disappear.

The walls bore the wounds of a protracted battle. Something had been decided here, or deferred for centuries. You stretched your swollen legs and walked, and the exercise kept you going. Strange flickers led you deeper into the light, until you stood dead center, under the stone crown. Then you heard it, above your head: a noise that passed all understanding. You looked up at the sound, and saw the thing that would save you. A hundred feet above, in the awful dome, an angel dropped out of the air. An angel whose face filled not with good news but with all the horror of her coming impact. A creature dropping from out of the sky, its bewilderment outstripping your own. That angel terror lay beyond decoding. It left you no choice but to live long enough to learn what it needed from you.

Someday you will have to tell them. At some future news conference, when your sanity seems more certain. For now, you sit on the plane to Istanbul, blinking and flinching.

You find that you walk with a limp. You find that you cannot tolerate sun, or movement, or noises, or too many people within ten feet of you.

There is a truth only solitude reveals. An insight that action destroys, one scattered by the slightest worldly affair: the fact of our abandonment here, in a far corner of sketched space. This is the truth that enterprise would deny. How many years have you fought to hold at bay this hideous aloneness, only now discovering that it shelters the one fact of any value?

You turn in the entranceway of illusion, gaping down the airplane aisle, and you make it out. For God's sake, call it God. That's what we've called it forever, and it's so cheap, so self-promoting, to invent new vocabulary for every goddamned thing, at this late a date. The place where you've been unfolds inside you. A space in your heart so large it will surely kill you, by never giving you the chance to earn it.

But you have the chance. Here. Now, for nowhere else exists. You pull your fading solitude around you, the last way left to see yourself in this glare. And how you will survive another's company again becomes the only real problem.

For a little while, you are that angel. Ephemeral saintliness hangs on you. It will not last. Already, irritations seep into your fingertips. You feel yourself slipping back to the conditions of living. But for a time, briefer than your captivity, and only because of it, you are burned pure, by everything you look upon.

You step from the plane and see them, as in the world newspaper photo they instantly become: two forms racing to meet you across the tarmac of Istanbul. The woman who has saved you, and some smaller other. Your eyes search for an empty prison to hide in. There will be talk; there will be touching. There is no earthly way that you can bear it.

Your love rushes toward you but stops short, sobbing at the thought of real contact, of what happens next. Her small shadow steps forward from her. You look down and see your girl, this Scheherazade, whose name plays everywhere across her face, clutching a picture she has drawn for her foreign father. She clings to you as if she's known you all her short life. Grasps at long last the fable she's grown up on.

"Look," she says, shoving her drawing into your shaking hands. A crayon man, returning to a crayon home. "Look! I made this for you."

Freeing hostages is like putting up a stage set, which you do with the captors, agreeing on each piece as you slowly put it together. Then you leave an exit through which both the captor and the captive can walk with sincerity and dignity.

—*Terry Waite*, *ABC TV, November 3 1986, shortly before his capture*

ACKNOWLEDGMENTS

In telling the story of Taimur Martin, I have drawn on the many memoirs of the Westerners held hostage in Lebanon. I am indebted to these extraordinary accounts.